MW01242203

The Mark of the Damned

BOOK TWO
THE VORELIAN SAGA

C.D. MCKENNA

THE MARK OF THE DAMNED

The Vorelian Saga

Copyright © 2022 C.D. McKenna

Published by C.D. McKenna

First Edition: March 2023

Printed in the United States of America

eISBN: 979-8-9855460-8-8

979-8-9855460-7-1 (paperback)

979-8-9855460-9-5 (hardcover)

Library of Congress Control Number: 2022922637

All rights reserved. No part of this book may be reproduced, distributed, or transmitted in any form or by any means, electronic or mechanical, including photocopying, recording, or by any information storage and retrieval system, without permission in writing from the author or publisher, except for the use of brief quotations in a book review or article.

www.thevoreliansaga.com

Cover Design by Cherie Foxley

Map Illustrations by Eve's Worldbuilding

Interior Design and Formatting by Dragan Bilic

This is a work of fiction. Names, characters, businesses, places, events and incidents are either the products of the author's imagination or used in a fictitious manner. Any resemblance to actual persons, living or dead, or actual events is purely coincidental.

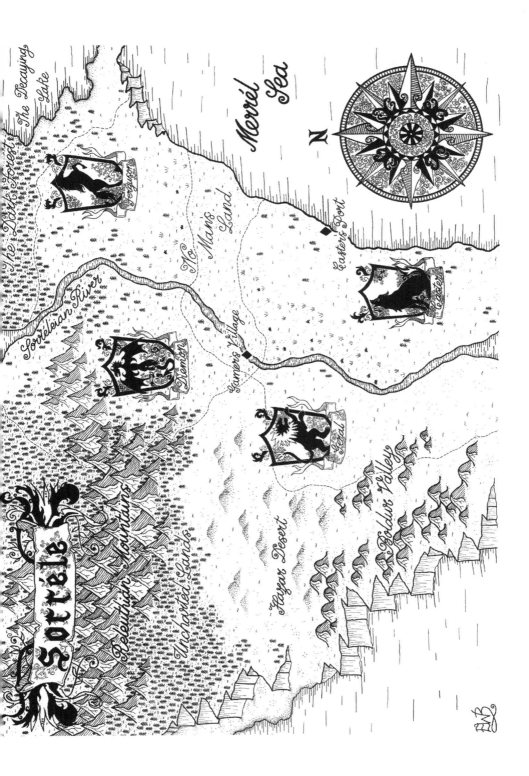

CONTENTS

To all the memories of yesterday.

One day, we will make an Empire with those.

PART 1

"Destiny, my dear, are we ever prepared?"

~ Vorelian Scrolls

VISIONS

Five Days Ago

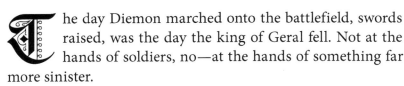he day Diemon marched onto the battlefield, swords raised, was the day the king of Geral fell. Not at the hands of soldiers, no—at the hands of something far more sinister.

Dark Energy.

In the five days since, the moon had since risen full, and the desert rains had cleansed the ground of the blood. Fires had been erected to burn the bodies of the fallen men, tended by Gerallian soldiers. But as the dead burned, a new, malicious force had arisen.

A plague. Cu'cel.

The disease was quick, unforgiving, and cruel. Victims started complaining of black spots that sprouted along their arms, but no amount of herbs could treat such evil, and soon, the black spots deepened. They began to rot, and the skin died. The sores oozed blood, and without proper intervention, they became infected. Bandaging did little to reverse the ailment.

Within a day, victims began to see them—the visions. Dark, chaotic, destructive. Every victim spoke of the same images. All claimed to see him, the man. The one who whispered to them. He was cloaked, and a sword sat on his hips, a blade of prestigious design with pearl-white metal. The man walked among slain bodies and through fire. His voice was soft, captivating to some and terrifying for others. But when asked what this man spoke of, nobody could answer. Some claimed it to be Sekar, the God of Darkness himself.

But that whisper had quickly been suffocated by a new and far more chilling rumor, one closer to home and carrying with it irreparable damage. That these visions were of the king himself—Morei Geral.

For the day Diemon's queen fell was the day the king of Geral harvested fire. His act had been quick, the results instantaneous. Over forty men surrounding Morei had burst into flames, both Geral and Diemon soldiers alike. Every single one of them had burned alive. Their screams tarnished the air and soaked the soil, forever engraining in it.

The turn of events was so sudden that nearly every man on that field stopped, paralyzed by the horrific view. In the complete silence that followed, Ezra ordered the Gerallians to attack. And attack they did, catching Diemon soldiers off guard and slaying them where they stood. It was the push Geral needed to win the battle and reclaim lost ground.

The queen had been impaled by a spear, her body slouched forward when it was found. Blood stained the wood of the spear and dried at the corners of her lips, for she had hemorrhaged. Her death was a victory, but it was nothing compared to such an ominous power.

There was no feast that night, no drinks, and no victorious cheers. For once Diemon had fallen, the attention turned upon the king. He was unconscious, surrounded by a sea of dead, all charred. Yet he had been left unscathed, protected by some unseen force.

It had not, however, protected his mind.

Power like Dark Energy was untamed Chaos, unstructured and volatile. And now it ravaged the king. The body was a result of structure—a tamed force, Light Energy. Submitting the body to unstable energy would undoubtedly fracture the barrier separating the mind's order from Chaos. Order defines man, but without it, the mind is victim to unnatural forces.

That day, Morei fell unconscious, and he had yet to wake. A fever ravaged his body, and his skin remained pale and slick with sweat. The curse of his ailment stretched further up his arms and decorated his hands. From the outside, the king appeared grotesquely ill. The staff followed orders by Emerald and Peter to care for him, but they whispered many dark things among one another about the state the king was in.

Those rumors reached the city.

People blamed the king for the plague.

Nobody stopped to question that perhaps the king was victim to the same visions, the ones that consumed the sick.

They tormented him and mocked his slumber. Morei became restless as the visions grew unbearable. Staff could hear him from down the hall, screaming, but it never lasted long. For the vision would change, and the king would find himself in yet another reality, each one far crueler than the last.

He was shackled to monsters that wanted to consume his soul, victim to a power that would inevitably become his downfall.

In an act of submission, the king allowed these monsters to have him. It had been because of them and them alone that he had harvested fire with such intensity on the battlefield. Morei had given himself up to protect the city, to protect the people.

The consequences were irreversible. He had won the battle, but the war had just begun.

THE PRICE
OF FREEDOM

Present

Cyrus slid the silver coins across the market table.
The young girl grabbed them without looking up and studied the Krye closely. "Whoa, I haven't seen these in a long time. We use Cyan currency here, sir. See?" She pulled a coin out from the pouch strapped to her waist and flashed it. The metal was tinged blue and imprinted with a giant crown.

Panic flared in Cyrus's chest, followed by irritation at the sight of the ancient currency. He was starving, and he wanted the sweet bread. "Will you take the payment?" He kept the cloak's hood pulled well over his head, shadowing his features so that no one could see his silver eyes. They would give him away as a Dragon Rider.

She quickly nodded and dropped the coins in her pouch, the silver menacingly bright against the blue metal. "Oh of course! We take Krye as well, since it's the standard Vore currency, but we don't see it much anymore unless someone is traveling. Are you traveling, sir?" As she asked, she handed over the loosely wrapped half loaf of sweet bread. The buttery, sticky glaze glistened under the sweltering sun.

Cyrus took the bread, careful to avoid touching the glaze, and nodded.

"Where from?" Her question was as innocent as her big brown eyes, but Cyrus still felt on the defense, and he didn't want to share too much. After the last season, his wariness was well justified.

"From the south. You have yourself a good day, young lady." Cyrus turned and walked before she could ask anything more. All he wanted to do was keep as low a profile as possible. It was safer that way when one was in a foreign country like Eiyrăl.

More specifically, he was in East Razan. The ground was packed beneath his boots from the countless feet that had traveled it. All around him, people in rich-colored shawls and jewels walked by, their laughter bright. Children with braids ran past him, the boys' hair as long as the girls. Old cathedral architecture made up most of the buildings, the stone off-white, some with red sigils painted on the oak doors with intentional, pristine craft. The smells of various spices and deep-fried goods wafted through the air. To the left, an Energy Harvester made a rose bloom wide in front of a dozen women, who awed in response. To his right, market stands with various assortments were packed with people who spoke passionately, sharing their stories. The city flourished with more life than Cyrus had ever been exposed too.

He tore into the sweet bread, finding it soft. It was freshly baked and still warm. Cyrus ate as he walked, not wanting to wait until he reached the outskirts of East Razan, where Sozar would land for him. Right now, the dragon soared high above the city, looking like nothing but a large bird.

The Rider's Sword bounced off his leg underneath the gray cloak as he stepped to avoid a young boy who ran by, shrieking with joy. Cyrus smirked between bites. Children were the most innocent and purest creations, only tarnished by the world they were raised in. Just like he was. Raised in an orphanage, he'd been taught at a young age his parents had abandoned him—forced to find self-acceptance in the mines of Diemon. He had always dreamed his parents were out there. It had been that dream that kept him going well into manhood. That he had a family, waiting for him.

And Kyllian Razan, the king, would hopefully give him that answer.

After discovering Sozar's egg in the mines and fleeing the city he had called home for twenty-three summers, Cyrus had found himself in the presence of a madman who still held on to the family he had murdered. The events that had unraveled in Evander's home had hollowed out a piece of Cyrus's heart and filled it with poison. Guilt and regret seeped deep into his bones, wilting his courage and bending his morals. Cyrus was a man, but he was a man with blood on his hands. It could have been avoided.

That was only ten days prior, yet Cyrus still thought of Evander every day. He had already had a half dozen dreams reliving the horrific event, and in each dream, it felt like Cyrus was more and more the villain. Sozar had tried to reassure him that what had happened was a necessary evil—a small price for freedom, as the dragon had told him—but if this was the cost to walk a free man, he wasn't sure he wanted to pay. The events in Geral seemed crueler, more real, than before. He had run from that dungeon after taking the life of a soldier, but that too now seemed avoidable. The mere memory of these men made his breaths shallow and his heartrate quicken. Honor had died in those mountains.

Cyrus swallowed another mouthful of the sweet bread. As he did, he hoped to swallow the bile that had risen in the back of his throat. It worked somewhat, and Cyrus turned his thoughts outward, paying attention to the surrounding people.

There was a woman standing next to the Energy Harvester, but she wasn't watching the entertainer as he manipulated roses for the ladies. She was watching Cyrus. Thick, ashy blond hair hung straight down her back, shimmering in the rays of the sun. Her skin was porcelain and her eyes dark. Dressed in a blue halter-neck dress, she had her arms crossed and a resolved look on her face.

Cyrus averted his eyes, cursing. He didn't want the attention. Whoever she was though, she was stunning—a gem cut with the steadiest hand and polished to a shine. Without even realizing it, he had been staring back, momentarily captivated.

He needed to focus. Crumbling up the paper that had wrapped the bread, Cyrus dropped it in a small fire pit as he passed, which looked to be used for trash—something he had not seen in Diemon, where burning pits were reserved for the higher class. The flames took hold of the paper and cracked with delight, devouring it in a matter of seconds. The man in charge of the burning pit poked at the fire with his metal prong, and the flames hissed in response.

Cyrus would need to somehow get into the palace and to Kyllian Razan, although how he would do that was a mystery. He couldn't walk up to the steps and barge through the doors—he would be killed in an instant—but he also didn't want to request an appointment. That would likely take a full moon cycle, given he was not a citizen of the city.

A devious thought unfolded itself in his mind, making his lips curl upward. Nobody ever said he had to walk into the palace. Sozar could fly him low once the sun dipped behind the horizon, and Cyrus could hop onto one of the balconies and then get to the king that way. It was a glorious plan. It might get him killed, of course, but it was a risk he was willing to take. If it worked, he'd be face-to-face with the king and could get his answers.

But what if he doesn't have the answers you seek? Sozar asked, intruding on Cyrus's thoughts like thunder breaking the silence of a serene day. The dragon's concern was sincere and had been shared already, but that didn't make it any easier to hear that Sozar was pessimistic. Sozar didn't believe the king would have answers—by Greve's grace, he halfway believed their trip to East Razan was wasteful, and had not been shy to let Cyrus know that. But when the young man challenged the dragon about where they should have gone, Sozar grumbled and couldn't give an outright answer. Simply put, they didn't have a purpose, and the dragon was exhausted.

What Cyrus needed was an advocate, now more than ever. They were all each other had, and Cyrus sometimes felt like Sozar didn't consider that maybe he didn't want to hear the bad. They had been running for practically an entire season, even crossing the Ashen Sea for this chance. It was all Cyrus had left—to figure out who his parents were and if they were still out there, if a family wanted him to return or not. His silver eyes were proof that his parents had been Dragon Riders. But where they were and why they had left him in Diemon was a mystery, one that Cyrus held with bitterness and betrayal. They had abandoned him to that city and never looked back.

He will have answers, Cyrus replied, keeping his voice steady in their mental link. He didn't want Sozar to know how much that question got under skin, not now. It would do no good to get in argument while they were so far away from each other and Cyrus was surrounded by strangers. But when he peeked behind him, he found the familiar blue-dressed woman close.

We're being followed. She was close, too close.

The dragon stirred, uncomfortable. *Are you sure?*

Cyrus grunted in agreement under his breath, as if Sozar were standing right next to him. *Let's find out.*

Cutting right, Cyrus broke from the crowd and down a side street. It was quieter here, but he stopped twenty paces in and looked at the stone walls that made up the buildings to his left and right.

He had taken the wrong turn intentionally. If this woman was following him, he wanted to know what she wanted, and how she had picked up on the scent—there were plenty of people with cloaks and gloves on. The last thing he intended to do was walk her right to Sozar.

The next side street up was where he needed to go. Cyrus waited until he was certain she would be behind him. Then, with a sigh, he turned. As expected, the lady was right there, only ten paces away. She bore no weapon, but Cyrus instinctively dropped his hand on the hilt of the Rider's Sword under his cloak.

"Don't," she ordered. Her voice was sweet like honey, but he still didn't trust her. "I just want to talk."

"Cornering me isn't really grounds to talk," he retorted. Sozar's anxiety seeped into his veins, making Cyrus's heart flutter. *It's alright*, he assured the dragon.

If you die, I will burn this whole city to the ground, Sozar snapped.

"I didn't really corner you," she replied with a shrug. "You're the one who took the wrong turn. It's a dead end, but you knew that, didn't you?"

She was clever. "You have me," Cyrus told her, and raised his hand from the hilt of the sword. "What do you want?"

She took several slow paces forward, her rich, dark eyes never leaving him. "I want to know why a Dragon Rider is in my city."

Cyrus felt his heart quicken and his breath catch. "I'm not—"

"Don't lie to me, Rider." A smirk touched her lips. It was obvious she was proud of herself.

She knows who I am. But Cyrus couldn't say he was surprised. This was one of the oldest cities in the Vorelian world. North of here, if the maps were accurate, lay the Rider Federation—the home of the Dragon Riders when they had reigned. It had been a brief lapse of concentration that had cost him their cover. He was solely responsible for this.

A growl emanated in their bond. Sozar was pissed and rightfully so.

"You don't have to be afraid," she added as she took another step. "But I am going to ask that you accompany me."

Cyrus raised an eyebrow. "You really think I'm going to listen just like that? I've spent countless moon cycles fighting for my life. You're no different than the rest of them."

"And will your dragon protect you when I expose your identity right here and demand your head?" She crossed her arms and gave him a challenging look. "Listen, I'm not here to harm you or your dragon. I'm here to help."

Cyrus let out a cold laugh and glared at her. "Sure doesn't seem that way, does it?"

"Right now, nobody knows you're here. If you follow me and keep your head down, we can keep it like that, and I can promise you food, water, and a bath, which I'm sure you'd appreciate after your travels. The choice is yours."

Don't do it, Sozar advised. *Last time we accepted help from a stranger, you nearly died.*

Yeah. Cyrus dug his boot into the ground and sighed heavily. *We don't have much of a choice here, though. She strikes me like someone who doesn't bluff.*

If something happens . . . Sozar warned.

There were several options ahead of him. Oblige and accompany the woman, who could potentially be luring him into a trap, or bolt and hope he could reach the outer edge of the city in time before the Razan soldiers caught up to him. The streets were packed, which would make it difficult to navigate, and he risked the chance of being outsmarted by citizens who had spent their entire life mastering this city. Escaping Geral had been nothing but Eazon's luck—not a day went by that Cyrus didn't remember how bizarre it was that he'd been able to escape with his head. But here, right now, he didn't think that the God would assist, and he wasn't willing to make a bet on it either. Already, Cyrus could tell that the dragon was circling closer to the city, waiting for the chance to dive if needed. The thought made him anxious. What if Sozar got himself in trouble and couldn't fight everyone off? Would Cyrus be able to live with himself?

No.

Don't, Cyrus stated firmly. *Nothing will happen. The city is massive. If something doesn't feel right, you'll know. Other than that, keep a low profile. It's you they probably want anyways, not me. Stay out of sight.*

Meeting the woman's gaze, he nodded. "Fine, but if I feel just the slightest bit threatened, I'm gutting the closest person to me." Cyrus motioned at her. "That'd be you, so best be wise with what happens next."

The woman pursed her lips, and they held each other's gaze for a moment too long. It left Cyrus wondering about all the things he'd do to her if the situation were different and he could treat her like a proper woman rather than a potential enemy. Finally, she lifted her chin higher. "I understand. Best be off then, shall we?"

Cyrus approached her as she turned back to the main street, and he soon fell into step next to her. This close, she smelled like a bouquet of roses and stood a head shorter than him, but she carried herself as if she were the taller of the two. Cyrus respected it, and he didn't argue when she cut straight through the crowd. A handful of people stepped out of their way, but Cyrus kept his head lowered, not wanting to attract anyone.

They continued to walk at a brisk pace, and when they broke free of the majority of the crowd, Cyrus took the opportunity to speak to her. "What's your name?"

"Zorya," she replied, glancing his way. Those dark eyes enthralled him. "And you?"

"Cyrus. You hold no weapon. I've seen a lot of people here without weapons. Is that common?"

A coy smile touched her pink lips. "You are a true traveler, Cyrus. Razan, both the West and East cities, are safe places. We are a prosperous and generous people with no crime, save for the occasional child who steals a loaf of bread in a bet with his friends. We pride ourselves on it, and because of that, most of us who have been raised here don't walk openly with weapons. It shows our mutual trust."

Cyrus contemplated this. "So, let's say the man we just passed pulled a knife and attacked the crowd. With nobody having weapons, who would stop him?"

"The people would as a group," Zorya explained. "Just because we are weaponless doesn't mean we are ignorant to violence."

"No, but you're ignorant in your trust of others," Cyrus said. At her stunned look, he added, "I'm only pointing out the obvious here. You can't incriminate me for being cautious."

"No," she said, dragging the word out, still eyeing him. "But it would do you good to find some trust in others."

"Last couple of time I did that, I almost died," Cyrus commented, his tone dripping in dark sarcasm. The corner of Zorya's lips twitched up, but she didn't reply. Instead, she turned her eyes forward and they continued to trek down the street.

You would benefit from more socializing, Sozar commented dryly. No need to reply to the dragon's baited remark. Rude or not, Cyrus was not here to make friends.

It wasn't long before he noted the architecture change to a more pristine and gaudy appearance, where windows were framed in gold and the steps to the solid oak doors were polished stone. He looked around, taken aback by the extravagant builds. The ground gave way to smooth cobblestone, and along the sides of the street, long gardens stretched, full of exotic flowers.

Looking ahead, he felt his jaw go slack.

The palace was before them, and it was massive. A city within a city, by the looks of it, protected by a wall of stone and iron. Tall windows faced outward on both the first and second story, all framed in the same gold. The stone was white and polished, reflecting the light of the sun in a blinding fashion. A thick iron gate with two roaring dragons on either side was guarded by a group of soldiers dressed in dark forest green and gold armor. The Razan crest stood in the center of their gold tunics, two crescents overlapping with a line curling downward. At their hip, swords lay sheathed.

Unable to help himself, Cyrus nudged Zorya in the shoulder and whispered, "Trust, huh?"

She looked up at him and raised an eyebrow. "It's not every day I get to bring a stranger home." Zorya flashed him a smile and kept walking straight for the palace gate.

The statement rocked Cyrus, and he nearly lost his footing. "I'm sorry, what?"

Zorya didn't break her pace, forcing him to keep up. "What? Getting nervous now?"

"No," he responded with far more force than intended. She glanced at him as he continued to speak. "I mean, who are you? Why are we coming here? I thought we were going to some cottage next to the river, not to the palace!"

They were too close to the guards now for him to turn back, and he knew that she knew that. Ahead, just past the gates, rich green grass and more exotic flowers continued to run the length of the cobblestone path, which appeared to lead right to the entrance. Cyrus's heart was pounding, making his ears ring.

"Princess," the guards greeted warmly. "You've returned with a guest. Does he have an appointment?" The left one clasped his gloved hands together and smiled as the right one began to open one of the doors to the gate.

Cyrus gawked at Zorya, seeing her entirely in her light. He had threatened a royal family member—the princess of the king he wished to meet. For a moment, he thought he might lose the sweet bread, but he swallowed the vomit back down. Threatening royalty might as well come with a first-row seat at the execution table. The confidence and air she held made complete sense. The way the crowd had parted for them, as if there had been some unseen force nudging them away—she was a princess, the daughter of Razan, and the entire city had known it except him.

Cyrus studied the princess as she smiled and gave the guards a soft nod. "He is the Dragon Rider, men. The times are changing, and the Gods favor us."

To blatantly share that information drove Cyrus mad. He had spent countless moon cycles trying to hide himself, and suddenly, three people knew of him. Every part of his skin crawled at the wrongness, screaming of danger, and he wanted to run. He held his ground, though, not ready to look like a coward in front of her. Cyrus had to keep his word.

"A Rider . . ." The left guard trailed off as Cyrus met his amber gaze, removing the hood of his cloak. Cyrus took a deep breath, hoping to show the same confidence as Zorya.

"By the Gods," the one on the right said, turning from the gate and pulling out silver beads from a pouch on his belt. Cyrus recognized them as Hyle's Beads. "I never thought I'd meet you." He kissed the beads then, the scruff of his beard scraping against them. "It is an honor, Rider."

The left one followed a similar greeting, but Cyrus hardly heard them. He nodded and acknowledged them, but he felt weak. Cyrus was a man, nothing more, and it felt strange to be treated as something above the rest of them. It made him squirm underneath his own skin.

"We must get him to my father," Zorya announced. "He will be thrilled."

"Oh! Of course." The guards scrambled to get the gate open for them, and once it was, Zorya stepped through. Cyrus had no choice but to follow, feeling dazed.

The two soldiers bid them farewell, but Cyrus barely registered what they said. He watched the cobblestone pass underneath him as he walked. The sun's heat felt cool against his skin, and his mouth was dry as they crossed onto the palace's property and the gate closed behind them with the boom of finality.

Zorya Razan, daughter of Kyllian. The man he was desperate to meet, but he hadn't wanted it this way. This way was risky, political—it could get Cyrus in trouble. If he had just kept his head down and not gawked at Zorya, Sozar would have been dropping him on one of the countless patios of the palace tonight. It would have been dangerous, but with far less consequences if he could escape and run.

Cyrus had always been good at running, but he wasn't good at confrontation. And he certainly wasn't good with politics.

It seemed, after all he'd done to chase freedom, he was right in the den of the lions, chained. Swallowing, Cyrus said, "I suppose you won't take what I said earlier seriously?"

The last thing he wanted was to have his first impression with Kyllian be that Cyrus had threatened his daughter. That felt like a real nasty way to start things off.

Zorya laughed, her voice bright and dancing ahead. "I won't tell if you won't. Given your situation, I would have done the same." When they met eyes, she winked. "Now, do you still not trust me?"

"A loaded question when you didn't tell me you were Kyllian's daughter," Cyrus retorted.

She smiled. "Fair enough."

Cyrus let a pent-up breath out and checked in with Sozar. The dragon soared over the palace, as close as he could without being identified as anything but a bird. Cyrus could feel the beast tense, ready to tear the entire city to shreds given the slightest justification. It did nothing but make his anxiety rise. *Easy*, Cyrus told Sozar, trying to reassure him that all would be well. Not that he believed it himself, but saying it sure helped.

The dragon didn't reply, his unhappiness broadcast in his silence, so Cyrus retracted his thoughts and focused on his surroundings instead. There was nothing he could do to put the dragon at ease, and right now, he needed to focus on staying alive.

They continued to walk in silence. Ahead, the palace grew closer, its archways becoming taller. It felt like the castle was preparing to engulf him, never to let him go again. Cyrus wasn't sure what to say to fill the void of silence between them. He was a ball of emotions and confusion. In an instant, everything he had worked for had been tossed out the window. His path had changed—or had it always been that he would stumble on Zorya like this? That was a question he would never know the answer to.

Destiny was a finicky creature, one that Cyrus would never dare to understand. He still had yet to understand whether the Gods controlled destiny or if it was an entirely different force. Perhaps not even the Gods could control it, and they too were susceptible to such games of life.

All he could hope was that whatever lay ahead would contain the answers he needed.

BITTER AND BROKEN

"We can rest here a few days."

Syra stared at her hot duck stew, the flavor turning bitter in her mouth at the sound of those words. She swallowed, but it was forced. Her stomach twisted in knots. To remain still in one place was to dance with Death herself.

It was ignorant to assume they were safe. They weren't. They hadn't been safe, and it seemed they never would be. After the disaster at the Nighthunter Federation, the Raveer ship she had boarded with the help of Zane had turned into a living nightmare. Only a few had survived the pirate invasion, mostly the prisoners that she and Zane had released, including Roman, Vic's father.

Vic Resanson. The man she had been ordered to find in Dryl's final wish, in a letter she still had tucked away in the pouch of the belt that held Death's Sword around her hips.

They had manned that ship the rest of the journey, unable to rest for longer than a handful of hours at a time without the help of a full crew. It had been grueling, exhausting work, and her muscles still ached. By the end, her eyes and skin were dry, and her clothes were tattered.

Finally, they'd arrived at Roman's home, stationed in the heart of Jasper Village, down a street with five other beautifully built stone homes. This one was no different—vaulted ceilings with an upstairs and downstairs, along with a spiral staircase that was wide and tall enough to drive a steed through.

The galley they sat in now was used by maids, but upon their arrival, Roman had ordered all staff to retire. He was a man of many secrets, and even after ten days out at sea, it seemed she knew less about him than she initially believed.

Zane scarfed down the last of his stew, then put a hand to his chest and belched. "That's the best damn stew I've had in days. What lovely lady cooked this?" Zane reached over and tore a massive piece of bread off the loaf in the center of the island. Without saying more, he started dragging it through the remnants of stew in the bowl.

Roman lifted an eyebrow. "His name is Jyle. He cooks everything."

Zane halted midchew and slowly nodded.

Even though Syra knew practically nothing about Roman, the three of them had built a strange trust out at sea, something unbreakable. It was a trust built off survival. But as much as Syra wanted to embrace this newfound alliance, she couldn't, because she'd felt that same level of trust with Kar and Dryl.

Then Kar had betrayed all of them, and had no doubt been behind Dryl's murder.

The memories crashed in around her in an instant. Placing a hand on the butcher block counter, she took a deep breath. Anxiety and anguish unlike anything she had ever known smothered her.

Syra tried to take a deep breath, but it caught in the back of her throat. It had been Kar who stood over her aboard that ship, stuck between the realm of the living and dead. She had not needed to see his face to know it was him, to understand that he was watching her. Kar was powerful, far more so than she had been prepared for, and he had wanted her to know that.

Roman and Zane knew. It wasn't like she had a choice. When the Guardian had released her from his hold, she had awoken on the floor with the two men over her. The Onye, the beast that had wreaked havoc on the ship, sat just outside the door, watching her as she sat up.

She'd let that beast out; she'd been the reason all those lives had been lost. Her idea, and hers alone. Passengers and crew members had been slaughtered because of her selfish need to stay alive. Pirates had been murdered without mercy, and she had been left with nothing but their bloody, mutilated bodies. She could still hear the crunch from the Onye feasting upon the slain.

Syra had hardly slept since that night. Sure, she had closed her eyes and drifted off into slumber when the exhaustion had been too great, but she could not relax. Not when she knew she was being watched. And when she did succumb to dreams, they were not ordinary—they were cruel, monstrous, and haunting. In the nightmares, she was stalked by a hooded man, who always managed to stay just out of reach. Kar. Memories contorted into a heinous visual of the man she once trusted, hunting her.

Venomous shame coursed through her veins. The men at this table were in danger because of her. Wherever she went, Death followed. A Soul Speaker had once told her that, and at the time, she had shoved the warning aside. But now, it was too real to be ignored. Her father, Dryl, innocent people . . . and now Roman and Zane sat across from her. If they hung around long enough, they would be next.

"Syra?"

She jolted from her thoughts and stared up. Roman was leaning on the counter, giving her a hard stare. Zane had stopped eating and was also looking at her. She knew he was uneasy about the thought of Kar watching them. He had been raised to believe that Death Seekers only showed themselves when something terrible was going to happen. To him, Kar was not just a threat, but also a bad omen.

Syra cleared her throat. "Yeah?" She tried to keep her voice steady, but it still shook a bit.

Roman's blue eyes didn't blink. "You okay?"

She bit her tongue, guilt turning her breaths shallow. "I'm fine. Just exhausted."

"Aye, it's been a long journey," the older man agreed, and rolled his shoulders as if for emphasis. "We can rest tonight, though. King Matthieu doesn't know I'm here, and this small town doesn't pass much attention."

The reference to the king of Raveer only made her more unsettled. "You really think with a bounty on all our heads, we're safe?" The question came out almost hysterical, and she dropped the spoon into the stew, where it clanged against the ceramic bowl. "We just snuck off one of the king's ships. The port will be alerted, and soldiers will be sent to find out who left a ship abandoned with no record of docking or a count for the crew members. And don't forget the Onye onboard. Let alone the blood smeared all over the place. No," Syra spat. "We're not safe. We can't rest. We can hardly sleep soundly with that kind of mess we left behind. We'll have the whole kingdom after us before dawn."

Zane held up a hand. "Let's keep a little bit of optimism in this."

Syra scoffed. "Dryl was optimistic too, and now he's dead."

The men stared at her, likely wondering if she had lost her mind, but it didn't matter. No matter how hard she wanted to believe they had the upper hand, that they could outsmart a Guardian of Death, she knew they couldn't.

Zane pushed his bowl ahead of him. "Maybe one of us can keep an eye out? Take shifts through the night."

"And when the staff members ask why we're stalking the halls at night?" Syra pointed out. "They will surely be up throughout the night, checking on things and performing various duties."

Roman waved them both off. "They will speak of nothing. They are trustworthy. Trust me on that. Many of my staff have been around for countless summers and have been involved with several of my more . . . illegal business trades. They are good."

Syra didn't reply, but she still didn't trust them. Frankly, it was difficult to trust anyone at this point given the betrayals she'd faced. Zane was a good man, she told herself, but there was a wall between her and everyone else, built out of the broken fellowship of Kar and Dryl and the brutality of watching her one remaining family member die.

"So, that's what we'll do," Zane announced, obviously trying to keep the conversation going. "I'll take the first watch, Roman second, and then you can take the watch closer to dawn. It'll give you some time to rest."

Syra didn't acknowledge the plan, only shoving her bowl out of the way. No longer hungry, she folded her arms and met Roman's gaze directly. "You've been quiet this long, but it ends tonight. We are at your mercy in a home that is yours, surrounded by staff you swear will keep their mouths shut. It's time you talked, Roman—if that's even your real name."

Zane lifted an eyebrow and turned his attention to the other man. "She's charming, I know," he commented dryly. "But she has a point. It would be nice to know where we go from here."

Roman took a deep breath and dipped his head. He didn't speak, and the silence that followed was marked by the faint footsteps of one of the staff members upstairs.

When the man finally did talk, he spoke with resolve. Even in his own tattered clothes, he gave off the air of authority. "Vic didn't just go to Mourale Mountains, he went to the Infernol." He paused and laid a hand over his right wrist. "The Infernol is our only hope against what's to come."

"Let's back this up," Zane cut in before Roman could say more. "Against what?"

The man cleared his throat. "The Infernol isn't some old organization waiting to bring back a dead empire. It was made to protect the future of our world against Henry Junok."

"Henry Junok is dead," Syra blurted out.

"That's what he wants us to believe," Roman responded, his voice soft. "Public records show that he died, but there is evidence showing that who we thought died and who actually died are two different people. Henry is alive. The Infernol has no doubt of this, and we've spent the last five decades trying to find a force strong enough to defeat him. We believe he's tucked up in the City of Liral. It was the heart of the Lirallian Empire in its day."

This information came as a blow, ripping the air out of Syra's lungs. The concerns of Kar and the Raveerian kingdom suddenly felt petty next to this revelation. Henry Junok had been killed with the fall of the Lirallian Empire over four centuries ago. It was impossible for him to still be alive. "How can you be so sure?" she asked.

"It was no lie that Henry was and still is the most powerful Energy Harvester, having mastered an element of Dark Energy. The Demon Killer was just a small reflection of what he is capable of." Roman shook his head and leaned back in the stool, crossing his arms. "It's believed that he's been protected with the help of Sekar."

Zane busted out laughing and almost fell out of his chair. Syra stared, unsure of how to reply or what to even say. "Excuse me," Zane wheezed between chuckles, "I'm going to need that run by me again. You're saying that not only is Henry alive, but that he's partnered up with the God of Darkness himself?" He got lost in a fit of laughter again and wiped at his eyes. "That's outrageous."

"And so is the idea that living men are ripped from their homes as children and raised as warriors for the underworld.

Yet"—Roman motioned at Syra—"she has proof, and knew them personally."

"Yeah, but—" Zane stopped short and cleared his throat. "Okay, fair enough." He looked over at Syra and gave a nod of acknowledgment. She smiled, but it was small. As small as she felt right now.

"Gods," she mumbled, drawing their eyes back to her. "The same Gods that weren't there when my father was killed or when Dryl was attacked." The words were hostile. "Those are the same Gods that are letting this happen. How can you be so certain they are real, Roman? What you're telling us is that a man—no, a monster—has befriended a God."

Syra hated to admit how she felt, but it was obvious. She hadn't asked for any of this, and prior to the disaster that her life had become, Syra had been a strong follower of Drügalism. She had spoken her prayers and given her thanks, and for what? To be tossed around like a sack of flour in the hands of fate while the wicked grew stronger?

No. It simply wasn't fair.

Syra swallowed down the growing, all-encompassing repulsion. "Does everyone in the Infernol believe that? That Henry is alive and has been aided by Sekar?" she asked before anyone could reply to her previous statement.

"Yes," Roman stated without hesitation. "The Lirallians are amassing in significant numbers throughout their city. They've doubled in size since last season. It is unlike anything I've ever seen."

Syra nodded, but it was to herself. To believe that Henry Junok, the man who had nearly destroyed the country of Diyră, was alive and well made her skin crawl. If he was alive, so was the Lirallian Empire. Kar felt minuscule against that thought. Her bounty, the Demon Killer, being on the run—it all suddenly felt worthless.

The Lirallians were gaining in number, but that meant nothing if there was no proof. "What evidence do you have?" she asked. "How can anyone be so certain Henry is alive if no one has seen him since his execution?"

The older man shook his head. "Insiders, spies—the Infernol has our ways of gathering information when needed." He brought the copper mug to his lips and drank.

That was not the answer she wanted to hear. If anything, it created more questions. Even with Roman's certainty, she refused to believe a man like Henry Junok was alive.

Zane inhaled and shook his head. "Man, I got to tell you. This is not where I thought I'd be. A bounty on my head, hunted by the same soldiers I used to lead, and now talking about some dead guy and Gods. I'm going to need something stronger if we're going to keep this up."

That got Roman to chuckle, and Syra followed suit, but it came out more as a snort of disbelief. Zane was right. This was outrageous. "So," she said, "we go to the Infernol?" It felt like their only reasonable option, regardless of what they believed. If they could secure her safety, she could figure out her next steps.

Roman pursed his lips. "That wasn't entirely my intention . . ."

"Then what?" Syra asked. "Stick around and wait for an army to corner us? We aren't safe in the open. If the Infernol is in the Mourale Mountains, then we go there, where there are numbers to protect us." What she really wanted was to avoid another run-in with Kar.

"She's got a point."

The voice came from outside the galley. Zane and Syra stood immediately, unclipping their sheaths to draw their swords. Chairs screeched against the marble floor with their sudden movement. Body tense, Syra stared at the doorway, waiting for the man who had spoken to show himself. Roman pulled a steak knife from behind him.

"Easy there," the voice called, and stepped to the doorway, holding his large, pale blue hands up. "I am not your enemy."

He was a Guardian of Death, but his strong jaw and crimson eyes reminded her of Dryl. They were almost identical. The Guardian's hood was drawn down, displaying his black hair styled to the side, the tips brushing over his brow. The smallest hint of a Marking licked at his neck. Even his smile was similar to that of the Guardian she once knew. It was undeniable.

"Who are you?" Syra asked, needing to know what she already believed.

"How'd you get in here?" Roman demanded.

The Guardian dropped his hands and took several steps into the galley, but he halted out of reach of any of the weapons. When he spoke, he looked directly at her, his eyes telling a thousand words. "I'm Zarek. Dryl's brother. And your staff"—he looked at Roman—"they didn't stop me."

Syra swallowed, then took a deep breath. "He never spoke of a brother."

"We didn't necessarily see eye to eye for a while," Zarek said.

"Well, you're a little late for reconciliation." Venom filled her words. "He's dead."

The man didn't flinch. "I know."

His coolness enraged her, and she took a threatening step forward. "Did you do it? Did you kill him?"

That elicited a response. Zarek's eyes gouged into her with fury. "You really think I would kill my own brother?"

She scoffed. "Try me."

Zarek looked over at Zane and Roman, then back at her. His nostrils flared, but when he spoke, his voice was steady. "You seem tense. Want to talk about it?" He was toying with her. Syra kept her ground, refusing to play this game. Leave it to a Guardian of Death to crack a joke in the middle of a threat. Before she could say more, Zarek added, "This might be a story you want to sit down for, Syra."

"How do you know my name?" she insisted.

A smirk touched his lips. "Ah, now you're interested." Zarek took a step toward a chair, and she let him, unsure of how to react. Curiosity had her by the throat. She followed and sat back down, making sure to keep her sheath unclipped. Zane was staring at her with the look of someone who had just seen a ghost. Roman remained passive, the steak knife lying next to his right hand.

Syra raised an eyebrow at Zane, who now sat across from the Guardian. The man inhaled and looked at Roman. "Got anything *really* strong?"

Without replying, Roman got up and walked over to a tall pantry. He opened the wooden door and stepped in. Clinking sounds followed, and after a moment, he stepped back out with four short copper mugs and a decanter of milky liquid. "Kendell's Milk," he announced, and set everything on the counter before them. Then he poured even amounts in every glass and passed them out. As he handed one to Zarek, he commented, "For the warm welcome."

The Guardian didn't reply, but he did take the mug.

As everyone settled back and looked at each other, Syra felt like she was at Zarek's mercy. Answers. All Syra wanted was answers. What would the Guardian say to the last book of the Soul Realm being taken, or the fact that she no longer had the Demon Killer? By the damn Gods, Zarek knew her name, and that alone was enough to break her defenses and make her beg to know what he knew.

Slowly, she lifted the mug to her lips and took a sip. The creamy liquor burned in the back of her throat, tasting strangely of blackberries. When she set the mug down, Syra saw Zane reach for the decanter to refill his drink already.

When he was done, he slid back into his chair with a deep sigh. "Okay, I'm ready."

That provoked a quiet chuckle around the table, and no one said anything more.

Then the Guardian came to life, his eyes trailing over everyone at the island. But when they settled on Syra, it was as if he were only here for her, and when he spoke, she was certain the words were meant that way. The world went silent; even the noises on the street outside from villagers fooling around ceased.

"Let me tell you a story."

A BED OF THORNS

The sleeves restrained Morei. The red-embroidered fabric was too hot in the sweltering desert sun. Sweat prickled his nape and down his back. The boots stifled his feet, the woolly socks unbearable.

But he was dressed as a king should be.

Morei's gaze was locked on the horizon. The Hazar Desert had never been welcoming to strangers—stories of men being devoured by strange beasts kept curious minds away—but today, it looked particularly ominous.

To the south, ahead, stood Boldur Valley, with its massive rocks that held stories as bizarre as their origins, stories about the whispering dead that captivated their victims with enchanted songs. To the west, the Uncharted Lands sprawled outward—never explored because no man could cross the Hazar Desert and return. North and back stood the treacherous Releuthian Mountains. Their peaks, even at such a great distance, were visible and clear. The home of the Dark Lord himself, or so the stories told.

Stories. All of it was stories. Tall tales Morei had grown up hearing from citizens and his parents alike. Stories that now felt more real than ever before.

The king rubbed the back of his neck. His fingers came away with a layer of sweat, and he laid his hand back on the hot stone railing. The patio felt like the safest place for him regardless of the heat.

For behind him was a reality Morei loathed.

The king had awoken only yesterday from the endless torment some might have called sleep. But he hadn't been given accolades, no. He had instead been ordered to present himself before the council the following morning—today.

For while he had been unconscious, Geral had fallen apart.

The plague now known as Cu'cel, an Old Tongue word for "ungodly" or "evil," had claimed nearly 250 citizens in less than eight days. The people were terrified, and they had every right to be.

But they had begun to blame the king for this. All of it.

It was comical, really, in some vicious way, that the people would turn against Morei when he had nearly died for them. His actions on that field had kept the city standing. It was he and he alone who had saved Geral. Nobody else.

But nobody would ever see it that way. The people wanted a scapegoat, and Morei had become just that.

His eyes shifted along the curse that decorated his hand. Black veins snaked their way over the skin, visible to all eyes, unavoidable. Morei had weighed wearing gloves for the occasion with the council but thought better of it. If the citizens believed him to be responsible for Cu'cel, then the council was no different, and hiding his curse would only make him appear guilty.

The king could not hide from this reality any longer.

Morei inhaled the hot, humid air. The late-morning sun was high, and not a cloud painted the sky. The stench of burnt flesh clung to his senses—just outside the city, the dead were on fire. Bodies collected every afternoon were brought to three pits just outside the city to the west. And when night fell and the heat was at its lowest, Geral soldiers lit the firepits and let the victims of Cu'cel burn. It had been decided as the safest disposal method, but some citizens clung to their dead relatives, desperate to give them a proper burial.

The act of withholding bodies was now punishable by death.

Violence had increased. Citizens lashed out at soldiers and each other in fits of uncontrollable rage. People were afraid. They wanted answers, and Morei couldn't blame them.

He exhaled and gathered the courage to turn. They were waiting on him—Geral soldiers to escort him, as if he would run. But his chancellor, Peter, was here, along with Emerald and her commander, Kiren.

He turned. Within the king's chambers stood the party of waiting individuals. Soldiers rested their gloved hands on the pommels of their swords while Peter stood with his arms crossed. Kiren kept close to Emerald, even though he was not necessarily needed there. Drew had been voted as the new commander of Geral only two days after the battle of Diemon. The man would be at the hearing, the first time Morei would meet him.

Not necessarily the most ideal circumstance, but there was no choice in the matter.

Emerald's commander was unnecessary, but Kiren was making it clear that he did not trust Morei completely. They may have fought together, but it ended there. Kiren had fought to keep his queen alive, and Morei had fought to keep the city standing. They respected each other for that, but no more.

Emerald looked at Morei. Her rich green eyes held him in his place. Gold bangles along both arms accented her blue summer dress. It was held up by a gold collar that snapped around her neck and then cut deviously low between her breasts. Her skin was touched with a hint of color that told of a rich heritage. When the king had awoken, he had not only learned of the twisted reality his city was living, but that Emerald had revealed her title. She had faced the council only a day after the battle and bared her intentions out for them all to judge.

But she had withheld the dreadful night she had drugged the wine. An act such as that against royalty was punishable by death. Although, Morei was certain by now that the council would not have punished her for such an act, but rather encouraged her. They wanted him out of this city—and preferably dead.

Nobody could convince him otherwise.

As far as he had learned, the council had been accepting of the queen of Junok in Geral's halls, but they had not necessarily had a choice. Emerald had proven herself honorably and taken the lead in guiding decisions and offering advice where she could give. The people needed a leader, and Emerald had offered just that.

A stranger had been given more respect than the king. It twisted the dagger that was embedded in his heart, the one that had been shoved into his chest the day he stumbled on his dead parents and was blamed for their murders. He could not remove it, no matter how hard he tried.

Peter, dressed in his white satin attire, dipped his head toward the king. "Your Majesty," he acknowledged. The soldiers mumbled their respects, and Emerald nodded, but Kiren remained still. His hazelnut eyes drilled into Morei. Kiren had questions, ones that the king could not likely answer.

Morei stepped toward the entrance, leaving the safety of the patio behind. He bore no weapon, only the clothes on his back. The council had requested the king not bare his serrated sword. It lay to his right now, on the cherrywood table in its black sheath. But Morei had not complained, because he did not need a weapon to make his point.

He met everyone's gazes, but Kiren's especially. The city might be in shambles, but he was still king. He would make sure that everyone knew that.

The commander held his stare, and heartbeats passed. In this moment, Morei could have overwhelmed Kiren and taken control of his mind—it was always easiest when the victim held eye contact—but he didn't. Forcing his authority on the commander would have done nothing, even if it would have satisfied the king. So he waited until Kiren squirmed under his gaze and looked away.

A smile tugged at his lips. Nobody could ever outmatch Morei. He had nothing left to lose, nothing to give.

The commander shuffled his feet and cleared his throat. Emerald raised a scrutinizing eyebrow. "Are we ready?" Her voice dripped with nectar. Even in the heat of the circumstances, the queen had a way of singing a song that only he could hear, a song that he could listen to for eternity, regardless of if she was cruel. She was a queen, and she could not risk failing her people or lineage. That meant she had to be ruthless, just as he did.

Emerald had stayed, but it did nothing except dig a hole of distrust in his chest. The queen could have left. After all, she had gotten what she wanted, or so Morei believed. Maybe she wanted more—perhaps she'd wanted Geral for herself all along, and he had just been foolish enough to believe that her games had ended the night before the battle with Diemon.

The thought pissed him off, and he looked away from her. The king needed a word with Emerald, but it would have to wait. "Let us be off," he told them all. His voice sounded foreign on his tongue.

A tendril of dread snaked its way through his mind. The king was being watched. The soldiers had hardly moved, their eyes never leaving him, and rightfully so. His skin had paled, and to the untrained eye, he would have looked ill. Yet the black veins that covered his hands and arms would alert anyone that the king was cursed—that he was soul bonded with demons.

That made people wary. He was a monster to these people. A tragic one, but a monster nonetheless.

A few more seconds passed, and nobody had moved yet. Whether they were terrified he'd burn them all alive or wondering if he was a ghost, the king did not ask. Instead, he pushed his way through the crowd and toward the door. Once he laid his hand on the cool metal of the lion tail handle, movement erupted behind him.

Perhaps he was only a king by name.

"Let us take the lead," one soldier announced, and then added, "Your Majesty."

"Hm." Morei stepped out into the large hall. It was stifling, likely because no one had opened the windows. He glanced around but didn't see any staff. "Have the windows been opened?"

A younger soldier stepped out of the room and answered, "No, Your Majesty. The smells from the . . . ah, fires are at their worse in the mornings." As Peter, Kiren, and Emerald exited, the soldier closed the door behind them all. "Apologies for that. Would you like the windows to be opened?"

Morei waved his hand. "Not necessary, but thank you." The idea of smelling the dead along the halls of his own home repulsed him. And the in-palace staff and soldiers did not need to deal with that when there was already so much going on.

The soldiers took the lead, and everyone fell into step. The song of their steps filled the hall with a deafening tune. It was outrageous to be guided from his own chambers to go anywhere. Yesterday had been no different, but it would end today in the council hearing. The king would not be treated like a traitor. These people were alive because of him, and if they didn't see that now, they would soon enough.

He took a deep breath of the hot air. Peter walked to his left, while Emerald and Kiren followed behind. If the queen wanted to prove her loyalty, now was the time, but she did nothing.

If she was here for entertainment, she would surely get it.

The chancellor nudged Morei, and he looked down at the redhead. Peter's blue eyes twinkled. "It's good to see you up," he said, his tone warm. It sounded abnormal in this group.

Morei returned the smallest of smiles. Peter was always one to remain positive. "Perhaps I should have stayed unconscious, Chancellor. This reality doesn't appear to be more welcoming than the one I was in."

He pursed his lips. "Nobody could wake you, and there were nights we could hear your screams from down this hall." Peter shook his pudgy head. "We thought you would never wake."

"And I'm sure some hoped I never would," Morei remarked coldly. Several soldiers glanced back his way, but he ignored them. The visions he had succumbed to washed over his thoughts. Fire, destruction—and the woman. The redhead. She had borne the ancient Demon Killer, the blade responsible for the Diyrãllian Massacre at the hands of its maker, Henry Junok. Every time the king had reached for her, the visions would shatter and be replaced by the screams of victims. His victims. Morei would glance down and find blood dripping from his hands, the crimson bright in the light of fire.

Over and over, he had seen her and been unable to reach her. But in these visions, these nightmares, the king was distinctly aware that he had to find a way to her. If she was the end to all this, then he needed her, though he didn't know how or why yet, or even who she was.

Morei had an idea, though. Nearly a season ago, word had reached his ears of a woman on the run—one who had been in Caster and fled. The reward for her capture had been extraordinary, enough money to set up a family for generations. The king had learned that she was dangerous, a redhead named Syra Castello. That was all he knew.

But if this was her, then dangerous she was.

"Your Majesty." The voice interrupted his thoughts, and Morei glanced over to see the chancellor staring at him. "Are you ready?"

They were at the doors. The Geral crest glared at the king. If this was his reminder of the promises he had taken from what felt like lifetimes ago as king, then Morei heard. It did little to change his outlook, which was growing bleaker. He was a king not because the people wanted him, but because of the blood that ran through his veins. Nothing more than a placeholder.

He let out a long breath. Behind him, the party awaited his lead. Soldiers rested a hand on the doors, ready to open them once he gave the word. The king wasn't ready yet. He turned to face the one person he had the most questions about—Emerald.

"Is this what you wanted?" he asked, not caring who heard.

The queen's eyes widened. "After what I've done for you, this is how you thank me?"

"The only thing I should thank you for is destroying what little respect I had from the council." The king looked over at the nearest soldier, the young one with brown eyes. "She stays out here. This will not be for entertainment." Morei glanced at Kiren. "Him too."

The soldier nodded. "As you wish, Your Majesty."

Emerald fumed, her eyes glaring into him, and he smiled in return. "I wouldn't want you to waste your time, Your Majesty. Politics can be so *futile*." He waved her off before she could say more, turning back to the doors. "Let's get this over with, gentlemen. I'd like to visit the city before the heat is at its worse."

Peter touched his arm then. "But the risk—"

"I'm already ill," the king remarked. He laughed at his own comment, even as the others remained still. Then he met the chancellor's eyes as the laughter died from his lips. "Surely if the gods were real and wanted me dead, they'd have come for me and not the city, no?"

Before Peter could say more, Morei gestured at the soldiers. The doors gave way to the push and glided smoothly open.

It was time to face the council.

47

THE TALE OF TWO BROTHERS

arek inhaled, his expression dancing between anguish and cheer, as he took a drink of Kendell's Milk. When he set the mug down, he spoke quietly, but in the silence of the galley, his voice filled the entire room.

"Dryl and I were several summers apart. He was older, but we were tied at the hip. Best friends, and always getting into trouble together. Our age difference didn't show in our actions—we could have passed as twins, and on occasion, we told people that we were."

He smiled, lost in thought, but it quickly turned sour.

"Then our home was attacked and raided by pirates—the White Horn pirates. We were in a small village on the northern coast of Creitón, Tyrik Village. It's so separated from the rest of the country that no one could have tried to protect us. The pirates came and destroyed everything, killing dozens of villagers who tried to protect themselves. Our parents shoved us underneath our floorboards in our galley. We were ordered to stay quiet and hold on to each other, so we did."

Zarek lowered his gaze. "Our parents were slaughtered right above us. I can still remember the blood dripping through the boards and onto Dryl and me. But we followed their orders and kept quiet, too terrified to question anything further, knowing damn well that the bodies that lay above us were theirs."

Syra blinked back a wave of grief and took a drink. The burning sensation brought on by Kendell's Milk felt small compared to the sorrow that filled her. Glancing around, she saw that Zane and Roman were as still as statues.

"We waited for a long time," Zarek continued. "Until we were certain it had to be safe for us to leave the confined space. Dryl told me to wait—being the big brother he was—while he investigated through the home. It didn't take long to realize we were alone and that the wails of the remaining villagers were those mourning their loved ones."

The Guardian of Death shook his head. "It was the first time we had witnessed death, and our parents' no less. They died protecting us. We cried long into that night, sitting with our backs to the galley, staring at their bodies, as if somehow that would make a difference." Zarek scoffed to himself before settling his eyes back onto Syra.

"When dawn came, we were awoken by the creaks of floorboards, having drifted off at some point. Three Guardians stood before us. Back then, Guardians were openly welcomed in Creitón and even invited on occasion for festivals." Zarek shrugged at his own statement, eyes twinkling. "We were once revered."

The corner of his lip twitched upward. "Fyne was the Guardian who first spoke to us, who showed us a new world. He told us that we were selected by the Gods to do greater things, and that if we allowed it, we could seek purpose in the Gods' work. At that time, it was spoken as an honor to be selected for such a thing, so we agreed and were brought back to the Soul Realm."

Zarek paused briefly, but no one spoke up. The two other men stared at the Guardian, and from somewhere in the home, Syra heard a maid laugh. She leaned forward and grabbed the copper mug, wrapping both hands around it to steady herself. She had so many questions, but she kept quiet. Zarek wasn't done yet.

The man dropped his eyes toward the liquor in the mug as he continued. "It's safe to say we excelled in our training. It gave us an outlet and a purpose. But it came at a cost—our friendship, our brotherhood. I blame myself, but at the time, I was ignorant."

He looked over at Syra again, staring right into her soul. "Laz, the previous ruler of the Soul Realm, grew ill, and his daughter, Shevana, replaced him. But with her rise in power came the destruction of a realm we once protected." Anguish filled Zarek's eyes, and they became glassy. He blinked quickly and averted his gaze. "The Soul Realm was once beautiful, but it has long since fallen into the hands of the very beasts we swore to protect the dead from."

A chill ran down Syra's back.

"Shevana ceased the creation of new Guardians and allowed these monsters—creatures unlike anything you've ever seen— to rise. Demons are the least of your worries." He snorted and shook his head. "Pass the decanter, please."

For a moment, nobody moved. Syra was paralyzed in her seat, eyes locked on the Guardian. She had come to accept demons—mindless beasts that ravaged the Soul Realm like starved animals—but monsters? Zarek spoke of them with finality, and it made her uneasy. The Guardians of Death were supposed to be the best of the best. They were protectors of the realms, warriors for the dead; they weren't supposed to be outmatched.

Finally, Roman reached over and slid the half-empty glass container to Zarek, who filled his mug to the brim. When he was done, he set it down but didn't return the decanter to the center. Instead, he lifted the mug to his lips and took a large drink. Once he had swallowed, he let a hiss escape his lips. "That is some fine Kendell's Milk."

"I know." It was Zane, his voice distant, though his eyes were still locked on the Guardian. Everyone was waiting for him to continue.

Zarek pursed his lips. "Dryl approached me one last time before he abandoned the order—we had all but stopped communicating. We existed together only because we had pledged ourselves to the Soul Realm, nothing more." He ran a hand through his hair, obviously tormented by the memory. It reeked off him like food gone bad. "Dryl told me that the times were changing and that the Demon Killer had been spotted in possession of a girl—you. Under Shevana's rule, nobody actually had any clue what was going on with the living. Our attention was focused on the crumbling Guardian Order."

He took a deep, unsteady breath. "Dryl told me that he was leaving and that he wouldn't hate me if I set the whole damn order on him because he knew I was doing my job. We had already been on Kar's heels, but it had been unsuccessful." Zarek set the decanter down with a loud thud, a muscle in his jaw ticking in frustration. "And then I heard that he was killed. That was when I knew I had waited too long, so I left—abandoned everything."

He ended so abruptly that for half a minute, no one stirred or spoke.

Syra watched the anguish rage behind Zarek's eyes while he took another drink. He was hiding more, she knew. His eyes gave it away, at least to her. Lifetimes of untold stories were packed away with delicate care, and while she may not know everything, she knew one thing: the Guardian felt responsible for the murder of his brother. Reaching out, she laid her hand on the wood near him. "It's not your fault."

"Maybe it's not, maybe it is," Zarek whispered, both hands wrapped firmly around the copper mug now. "But I could have been there to protect him, and I wasn't."

She retracted her hand, unsure of what to say. Grief was an ugly monster, and she was in no way equipped to fight against such a vile creature. Instead, she grabbed her drink and sipped, numb to the burn.

"I lost a brother once." It was Zane.

The table came to life and looked at him. Fleetingly, Zane's glacier-blue eyes darted between them, as if he regretted speaking, but then he pursed his lips and continued. "Lost him to a scuffle outside of the main city walls in Raveer. Dumbest thing ever." He shook his head. "A bunch of villagers got angry over some petty income tax, decided to march to the main city, and when my men and I tried to deal with it civilly, the villagers lashed out. My brother was caught in the crossfire—a spear went right through his neck, and he died instantly."

"That's terrible," Zarek acknowledged in a soft voice. "I'm sorry."

Zane waved him off. "Just know that I understand."

The Guardian gave a curt nod and looked over at Syra. "I tell you that story as an act of trust, Syra."

With his gaze on her, she blinked. Several options lay before her, and after a moment of thought, she chose the least hostile route. "What do you want, Zarek?"

The Guardian looked around. "Where's Kar?"

Agitation bubbled up in her, followed by the blackest shade of shame. "Kar betrayed us," Syra mumbled, eyes down. "Cornered Dryl and me in the Nighthunter palace before taking the Demon Killer. I have no doubts that he is responsible for Dryl's death."

"You've got to be fucking kidding me," Zarek exhaled. The surprise in his voice dragged her eyes back up to his red seas. "I don't understand. Kar was one of the most loyal warriors I knew, and his passion for keeping the Soul Realm alive was over the top. He obsessed over it."

Syra swallowed. "Yeah. I think it's safe to say we didn't see it coming."

"Where would he have gone, though?" Zarek pressed.

She thought back on the memory of that dreaded day. Syra could recall as clearly as her own hands the cold thrill in his eyes once he had come clean about his intentions. It was so obvious to her now. "Then he was lying to you just like he lied to Dryl and me. Kar has something big planned, but I have no idea what." She wanted to mention the remaining book of the Soul Realm being taken, but she kept her mouth shut. That was not information Zane or Roman needed to hear.

"We go to the Infernol," Zarek stated firmly. "I see no other way."

Zane lifted an eyebrow. "Why?"

"There is information there that will change your perception of the world." Zarek's voice was quiet. "You are all in this"—he motioned at Roman—"and you are far deeper into the Infernol than you've let on, I take it?"

The statement forced Syra's eyes back on the older man. "What does he mean?"

"You're already siding with the Guardian?" Roman teased, trying to keep the air light. "I can't say I'm surprised."

"Your wrist," Zarek stated flatly. "You're branded. You've touched your right wrist four or five different times since I've sat down." Roman raised a surprised brow. "Don't think four centuries of being alive hasn't taught me to be observant. Dryl did the same thing constantly. Go ahead, show me."

Syra watched, waiting. Never had she seen Dryl do anything out of the ordinary, but she hadn't necessarily been looking, either. Roman sighed and extended his right arm out, sliding the sleeve of his shirt up. He bared the inside of his wrist, and as promised, there was a brand. The skin was white, scarred, and raised in a rose. It was the length of her thumb, small but undeniable.

Zarek eyed the brand. "He had the same. Dryl told me only members of the Infernol Circle were branded. Is that true?"

Roman nodded and withdrew his wrist. "Aye."

The Guardian inhaled. "Then you can guarantee our safety upon arrival at the Infernol." It was not a question.

Roman moved to speak, but then stopped. He rubbed his wrist a few times before nodding. "Aye," he said again. "I can do that."

Syra let out a pent-up breath that she hadn't realized she was holding. "Why didn't you say anything?" she whispered. If he held this secret, then he might be withholding more.

Roman shrugged. "Openly speaking about the Infernol is grounds for immediate execution, no matter where you are, Syra. I didn't speak about it because I didn't know if I could completely trust you."

An eye for an eye. She gave him a slow nod as she drew the drink back up to her lips. "I see." The men at this table did not know her entire role in this mess, and she didn't intend to speak about it—although Zarek likely knew more than he was letting on.

"Alright," Zane mumbled, eyes locked on Roman. "So, we leave for the Infernol as soon as possible."

Syra wanted to ask a thousand questions about the Infernol, but she held her tongue. Now was not the time. What was important was that they had a plan, because they couldn't stay here in Jasper Village.

"We will have to cut around Raveer," Roman said through a sigh. "We simply can't risk cutting straight through. It would be suicide."

"I don't want the risk of being recognized," Zane added. "A commander going rogue and fugitives on the run from both the Nighthunter Federation and Raveer? Come now, it would be a recipe for disaster." He finished the sentence with a grin and lifted his glass. "Cheers."

Syra snickered and shook her head. Zane had an uncanny ability to crack a joke at the worst of times.

"It'll double our time," Roman explained, leaning forward. "We can stay close to Raveer, but we need to avoid the main roads. I'm sure men will be tasked with hunting us and sketches will be made up."

"Bounties on my head are typical," Syra commented, raising an eyebrow. "So we avoid the main road, and what—bribe the inns on the outskirts of Raveer to house us? Seems risky."

"But it's all we've got," Roman pointed out. "The people in Raveer aren't as loyal as you might think. A lot of hardship and bad luck will do that."

"Until you put a million Krye in their face," she remarked, taking another drink.

"Optimistic," Zane murmured.

"And what of you?" She directed the question to Zarek. "What are your plans?"

The Guardian looked surprised. "To protect and accompany you three to the Infernol. It's the least I can do to finish what my brother wanted."

Syra pursed her lips and looked away. When the time came, she and Zarek would have a long conversation.

Roman slapped a hand on the wood counter. "Then we leave tomorrow afternoon when the sun is low. I have steeds and plenty of supplies we can use for our travels."

They all sat there in silence, letting the conversation die between them.

Syra's thoughts traveled. She wanted to know more about Zarek and his sudden interest in the group, and why he was truly here—she didn't entirely believe that his primary goal was to protect her. Yes, he held guilt for Dryl's death—that was obvious—but as a stranger, it felt extremely risky to have him here. Yet they couldn't turn him away. Zarek would be a massive asset in protecting them, and if he was here to betray them, then it was already too late.

Having another member added risks of being identified and betrayed. Those were the biggest concerns Syra had, but it wouldn't matter. They would make it to the Infernol before the world caught up with them. Before destiny laid a hand on their lives once more. They had to.

TEA WITH THE KING

The tea burned his tongue, but Cyrus hardly felt it. In fact, he could barely think straight. The nerves wracked his body and made his hand tremble just the slightest, spilling a splash of scalding liquid onto his hand, yet he didn't feel it. The gloves he had worn now mocked him from inside his cloak where they were snuggly tucked—but he had felt it inappropriate to wear his grungy gloves inside this exquisite palace. It felt like a pitiful attempt next to his dirty clothes, but he shrugged that thought off, too anxious to care. His breaths came in short bursts. It felt like he was going to explode from the inside out.

He was both cold and hot, nauseous and starved. The tea was flavorless against the bitter nerves that coated his tastebuds. The chair squeaked as he adjusted himself a bit, moving his left foot out to steady himself better as his head spun. Grasping the hot cup with both hands in fear of dropping it, Cyrus waited. Each heartbeat passed like a season, dragging out far too long.

Cyrus was in Kyllian's large study, sitting in the plush chair across from where the man would be seated at any moment— the king of Razan, Zorya's father. The thought poured into his growing anxiety. He had traveled for so long to get to here, yet he was not at all prepared for what might happen. Words were useless on his tongue, his mind blank from nerves.

The silence in the study was deafening, but Cyrus took the opportunity to glance around. The ceiling was decorated with crown molding and painted dark green. The gold walls were covered in framed paintings of what he assumed to be different family members, because he recognized Zorya to his right in a red gown, her smile candid and perfectly caught by the artist's brush stroke. She was younger in the painting, perhaps only sixteen. The desk in front of him was grand, a slab of some kind of silver wood that Cyrus had never seen before, with dark grains throughout. A bookcase to his left was stuffed with books, some stacked in front of others as there was no more room to properly store the material. It was an odd sight, given the vast size of the palace and this study. On the desk, parchment, ink, quills, and a small dragon statue stood rearing, and an hourglass, which still had half the sand spilling into the bottom, marked half an hour had passed since Cyrus had sat down in here. He had been the one to flip it.

Cyrus wasn't sure if the time dragging on made his nerves worse or more manageable. He made sure the cloak covered the sword sheathed to his hip. The soldiers had not instructed him to remove his weapon, and he had not offered. Nothing would keep him from parting from the strange and striking Rider's Sword. It felt like it rightfully belonged to him and no one else, despite how he had come to possess it.

The door behind him opened out of nowhere, and Cyrus almost dropped the tea from surprise, but he managed to keep his hands gripped firmly on the ceramic. He moved to place the cup down on the desk and stand, but a warm voice spoke quickly.

"Please, do not rise," the man said. "I hate that rule with royalty. Makes me feel like I should hand out bribes or demand everyone to kneel, although I can't figure out which one is worse. Nasty world these days, hm?"

As Cyrus turned his head to take in Kyllian, he inhaled deeply, trying to keep his head clear enough to form a single sentence. The man was tall, both in spirit and physicality, standing easily a head taller than Cyrus, and he didn't even need to stand himself to know that. The man was lean, but he carried himself like a warrior. As he sat down across from Cyrus with a graceful motion, holding his own cup of tea, he smiled and revealed porcelain teeth. He had salt-and-pepper hair, a short beard that framed his jaw, and brown eyes. "My apologies for keeping you waiting. Your arrival, well"—he tilted his head side to side and chuckled—"it required me to make some immediate accommodations to the staff and security."

Cyrus immediately thought back on what Zorya had said about trusting each other, but he didn't bring it up. "I don't want to be a hassle," he confessed. "I didn't even intend on running into Zorya—er, the princess—as I did. It just kind of happened." He had no idea how he should refer to her when talking to the king.

"So she tells me," Kyllian replied, and took a sip of his tea. He was dressed casually for a king, Cyrus realized, his blue silk button-up giving no trace of his title. Kyllian didn't need clothing to show his royalty, though. It was all in the way he carried himself, much like Zorya. It was not something he was used to. At least in Diemon and Geral, King Morei and Queen Reaza dressed the part in their public appearances. Perhaps the culture here didn't call for it.

Cyrus suddenly wished he'd paid more attention to his studies.

As he set his cup down on the desk, Kyllian clasped his hands together, and a gold band decorated with emeralds flashing from the light of the room caught Cyrus's eye. It was on the pointer finger of his left hand, indicating he was married by traditional Vore practice. "How long have you been in East Razan, Cyrus?"

He used the cup as a means to channel all his nerves, holding it between his legs where the king could not see if his hand trembled. "I arrived yesterday, so not very long."

"And you, I assume, traveled by your dragon?"

"Yes."

Kyllian nodded. "I want you to understand that you are safe here. We are an old people, and much of what Razan is today is thanks to the Dragon Riders. Our respect is the highest for you and your dragon. May I ask, is your dragon a male or female?"

Cyrus swallowed, trying to keep his voice from shaking as he spoke. "Male. His name is Sozar."

"Ah!" A twinkle lit Kyllian's eye. "Named after the first miner who stumbled on gemstones in the Releuthian Mountains, am I wrong?"

"You are correct," Cyrus affirmed. "It felt fitting since I found him in the mines there."

"Fascinating!" Kyllian reached forward and picked his tea up, taking a long drink. Cyrus followed, taking his own, then lowering it back between his legs as Kyllian set his cup down. The king's eyes were soft as he extended a hand forward. "May I?"

Cyrus did not need to ask what the man meant. Kyllian wanted to see the abnormal scar, the unique mark of each Dragon Rider, that rested at the base of his thumb on his left hand. Its reddish hue contrasted sharply against his tan skin—skin that had seen the harsh weather of the sea and the brute force of the sun.

Cautiously, he handed his hand to the king, who took it in a firm grasp. Kyllian examined the scar. Silver eyes could be a bizarre and random characteristic, but coupled with the raised scar, he could not be denied as a Rider. The king dragged a thumb over the mark, the touch calloused. Heartbeats passed, and he was afraid to speak. It was as if Kyllian had been caught up in his own trance, leagues away and lost in thought.

"Tell me," he finally said, releasing his grip on Cyrus's hand, who gratefully took it back into his lap. "Have you had troubles on your travels?"

Cyrus pursed his lips, unsure of where to begin or what to say entirely. For a long while, he sat there, collecting his thoughts and deciding what to say and how much to share. He thought of Morei Geral, that blasted Demon King. Then of Queen Reaza Diemon, the challenges of keeping Sozar safe and out of the public eye, and finally Evander. Cyrus thought of the bizarre book that he had taken and the letters between Evander and Kyllian—how they had referenced each other as brothers. From outside the study, footsteps echoed as a group of people traveled past, their voices muffled by the protective walls.

When he finally spoke, he told Kyllian most of everything, but left out the fact that he had killed Evander and anything about the discovered letters. He was careful about how much he shared, noting that anything he spoke of could be held against him. The king did not flinch or bat an eye at the mention of Evander, the man in the Releuthian Mountains, but Cyrus didn't want the king to see him as a murderer by telling the truth—a heartless one at that, who may have killed a royal brother. Perhaps killing Evander had been his only option, but he still felt like a monster for taking the life of a simple man.

Kyllian asked several questions, but for the most part, he remained quiet and listened. As Cyrus spoke, he felt a weight lifted off his heart. It had been the burden of his life, finally released. When he was done, Cyrus no longer felt nervous, but at peace.

Sozar stirred. *Well done, hatchling.* Warmth flooded their link, filling Cyrus with satisfaction. The dragon supported what was shared, and that made him feel good.

The hourglass was long done, but no one reached to reset it.

Kyllian slumped back in his chair and sighed. "I have heard rumors of King Morei, but hearing it from you clarifies what I have recently heard." His expression darkened. "It is truly a sign of the times, I fear."

Cyrus hadn't heard about Morei since he had fled into the Releuthian Mountains, and even in the days leading up to that, he had been too busy planning his escape to listen to the soldiers' gossip. "What have you heard?"

"Terrible things," Kyllian answered solemnly. "King Morei is rumored to have harvested Dark Energy in the form of fire in a battle against Diemon. Unfortunately, the dragon-crested city lost—" The king tilted his head respectfully in Cyrus's direction. "I had previously heard he was ill, and had had my questions, reasonably so, but you confirm my worries." Kyllian shook his head. "Bloody times lay ahead, and I am relieved to know you escaped such a sinister force."

The air had shifted. No longer did Kyllian seem cheerful, rather tormented by some unspoken thought. Cyrus shifted in his seat. Dark Energy was a force not even the Gods would touch, or so the stories were told. A power so twisted and raw that the soul of any man who toyed with the untampered energy was destined to go mad or die from being consumed by the power. If the king of Geral has mastered this, then that would make him one of the most dangerous people in the world.

"Can I ask how you know this?" Cyrus asked, thinking of the city he had grown up in laid to waste by Geral. He didn't want to believe any of it. The idea that his home was outmatched by the blacksmith capital made him disappointed. Diemon was better than that.

But the disappointment was quickly followed by the sour taste of betrayal. Diemon had taken away everything from him. He wasn't sure how to feel. So much had happened since he had fled.

Kyllian inhaled, suddenly coming to life again. He winked. "I have special ears, Cyrus. I can't give my secrets away so soon, but in time, you may come to understand how I know and see all."

Cyrus nodded. *In time . . .* He had no intentions of staying that long. Based on Sozar's grunt between their mental link, he knew the dragon felt the same.

The door opened again, and Cyrus saw Kyllian smile wide, looking summers younger. "Oh, my love, I didn't expect you to come given the project you were working on."

"Don't be silly," someone replied. Cyrus turned in time to see a beautiful woman approach, her gown a royal green with gold threading down the sleeves and body. Her blond hair was braided behind her with several loose strands framing her face, sprinkled with a bit of gray. This was the perfect picture of royalty. She carried herself with dignity as she approached Cyrus. "Nothing would keep me from meeting a Dragon Rider," she added with amusement.

Cyrus stood, all nerves gone as tradition took hold of his motions. He reached out and grabbed her hand delicately, giving just the slightest bow. Kyllian may not have wanted the traditional greeting, but Cyrus would be damned if he let a woman such as her be treated anything less than royalty. "My lady," he acknowledged. "The honor is mine." Cyrus raised his head then, and smiled. "I understand now where Zorya gets her beauty from."

The queen beamed. "Well, what flattery! A Dragon Rider who knows his manners. I like you." As Cyrus let her go and sat back down, she walked over and stood behind Kyllian, laying her hands on the back of the chair. "Have I missed anything?"

Kyllian reached up and lovingly touched her hand, which bore the same ring he wore. "Cyrus was just telling me about his travels. I will fill you in it later, Lorelei. What I want to talk about is your living situation," the king said, and brought his eyes back down.

"Living situation?" Cyrus asked, his voice dropping. "I don't need any housing." He'd come for answers, not for a roof over his head.

"Oh don't worry," Lorelei chimed in. "I would not be able to sleep with myself if I let a Dragon Rider go sleep anywhere but the nicest room. It is the least we can do."

Traditional rule was to never turn down the offer of a king or queen. Cyrus swallowed, looking between the two of them. "I can't—"

"You will," Kyllian added more firmly. "Given your travels and situation, I would find it unacceptable to see you out of these palace walls knowing you had nowhere to stay."

"Has Kyllian told you just how important you are to us?" Her blue eyes paralyzed him in his spot. Cyrus wanted to ask what he'd come here to ask, but he wasn't sure now was a good time.

"I didn't go into detail," the king commented, and grabbed the cup of his tea. They spoke as if they were having a leisurely conversation, not in the presence of a Dragon Rider. It struck Cyrus as almost odd, as if they should be discussing dinner plans, not his life. He was beginning to feel increasingly cornered by the two.

"Well." Lorelei exhaled and smiled at Cyrus. "Dragon Riders are the reason Razan stands today. Kera's Port was named after the first ever Dragon Rider. Nobody knows her exact heritage. There is no document or history about her, except that Kera was the first Rider to have ever existed. It was her hard work and loyalty that helped ships cross the Ashen and Merrél Seas and land here—she guided them. Those ships held our ancestors. Without the help of Kera, I fear we would not be the city we are today."

"Or country," Kyllian pointed out.

Cyrus nodded once more. Perhaps Diemon was selective with what they had offered in history—he had never heard of this before, but he didn't say anything. Regardless of what was true or not, he was in no place to challenge their claim of Kera being the first Dragon Rider or that the country stood because of her.

"Is Sozar nearby?" Kyllian asked, leaning forward now. "Our palace was built to accommodate the dragons when the Rider Federation still stood, so we have plenty of space for him to walk freely. Food is no issue. Our livestock is his to choose from."

Even though Sozar had been quiet for the entire conversation, the dragon's mind flared with eagerness. *A free dinner, they say?* It was coy, playful, and the dragon that Cyrus knew so well.

Sozar, Cyrus spoke. *What are your thoughts?*

Do we have much of a choice in this matter?

Cyrus sighed, not realizing he had done it out loud where Lorelei and Kyllian could see. *We could turn away now. Forget it all and fly.*

To where, Cyrus? Sozar's tone was sharper now, more challenging. *My muscles ache, my throat is dry from the salt of the sea, and I must rest. If they offer a sanctuary for nothing more than being kind, then we owe it to take it.*

Yeah, but what's the catch? Cyrus countered. They already had nearly an entire country against them. Adding another city to that list felt unnecessary.

No law will bind me. If they dare to enforce a pledge, we fly.

Cyrus considered the matter. Sozar was right. They held no obligation to pledge fealty. They had already abandoned their country. What was the difference if they fled this one too? The idea panged him. He had never been a man to break laws and royal agreements so freely. It felt so wrong, but it freed him of all moral obligation.

When he realized that, Cyrus felt at peace. Regardless of what happened, he was in control. If this city failed him as Diemon had, then he and Sozar would fly. But for now, they would take advantage of the resources and rest.

He looked up and realized the two had been watching him closely. Cyrus felt his cheeks warm, having zoned out to speak to Sozar and not even catching himself doing it. After traveling alone for so long, he couldn't say he was surprised by his own actions, but he made a promise to himself to be more aware of his surroundings and actions moving forward. Especially if he was going to be surrounded by people, like Zorya.

Taking a deep breath, he pursed his lips before he spoke. "Alright, Sozar and I accept, but on the condition that there is no obligation to pledge myself to you." The words came out far more abrasive than he intended, but Cyrus didn't apologize. It had been a long ten days.

Kyllian was quick to reply. "That was never our intent, Cyrus." He stood then. Cyrus quickly reaching across the desk to meet the king's outreached hand. As they shook, Kyllian added, "You are safe here. Now, please, instruct Sozar that he can safely land in the courtyard. We will meet him there."

"Thank you for this. All of it," Cyrus replied, feeling both relieved to have a bed and cautious about what he'd just agreed to. But he was desperate, tired, and in need of a bath, and his curiosity toward Zorya tugged at his mind. He wanted to speak to her more, catch a glimpse of her dainty figure, and start off on a better foot than they had. Not that she struck him as someone who needed to be apologized to, given her quick comebacks and clever attitude, but Cyrus wouldn't be able to live with himself knowing her first impression of him—a Dragon Rider—was him threatening to kill her if she crossed him.

I will wait to land until I see you, Sozar informed Cyrus before he could speak to the dragon directly.

As they all walked toward the door, he felt Kyllian clasp him on the shoulder like a father would a son. "Whatever you need, you tell us, and we will make it happen if it is in our abilities. Do you understand?" He leaned in closer then and dropped his voice. "And tomorrow, when you're settled, we'll talk."

Cyrus eyed him. The king's words dripped with pride. Kyllian was a man of his word, that much was clear. "Yes, Your Majesty."

"Please," the king firmly responded. "Call Lorelei and me by our first names. You are under no obligation to consider us above you. We are your equal."

The events of the day had been more than he was anticipating. Just over an hour ago, Cyrus had been eating sweet bread in the street and wondering how to get into the palace so that he might speak with Kyllian. Now, he was being escorted by the king and queen of Razan to meet Sozar in the courtyard. It felt like the Gods were finally on his side.

"Fair enough," Cyrus said, proud to have come this far. "Then Lorelei and Kyllian it is."

A DANCE WITH JESTERS

ady Rose was dead, a victim of Cu'cel. And that left only Lord Polis, Lady Steral, Lord Fredrick, Lady Ferrel, and Lord Jire. The once-packed mahogany table looked vacant and far too large for the few members who remained.

Morei made himself comfortable at the end of the table. Peter sat to his left and the new commander, Drew, to his right, dressed in a white satin tunic. The commander was younger than the king expected, likely shy of twenty-eight summers, and wide shouldered. His brown hair was cut short, and his eyes were dark. They were the eyes of a man who had seen far too much death, and they gazed upon Morei thoughtfully.

The king nodded at Drew. "Welcome, Commander."

The commander gave him a slow nod in return. "Not the circumstances I was hoping to be elected in to, Your Majesty."

That comment tugged a smile from the king, but he did not reply. Drew was right. These were not the best times to be elected into. If the commander was listening, then he had already heard the rumors about Morei and his ailment. In a different reality, the king would have sat down with Drew and spoken to him directly about the responsibility of his new role and answered questions he might have—usually with drinks in hand. But this reality was unforgiving.

Kaleb sat on the other end of the table, the quill in his hand ready. Only fourteen summers, and this child had seen so much already. It was a shame.

The council was silent for a moment, either because they weren't sure who would speak first or because they didn't know what to say. The last time Morei had been in these walls, Lady Dail and Lord Rodrick had been brutally murdered at the king's hands. He knew why he was here, and if they wouldn't say it out loud, he would.

They had wanted this meeting, and they would have it.

The king looked at them all. The sapphire ring flashed as Lord Polis messed with it anxiously. He was beginning to become annoyed by that ring. "Council," Morei breathed. The word tasted bitter on his lips, and they tensed in response. "Do not think I am foolish as to why I am here." He waved at them. "Spit it."

Lady Steral snorted and brushed a lock of hair from her overdone face. "Well, if no one will say it, I will. Your Majesty— if that is what you still are—we are afraid. This is no ordinary illness. And after what happened on that field, are we really in the wrong for assuming you are the reason this is all happening?" The remaining councilmembers nodded in agreement and flashed the king wary looks.

They were afraid of him.

Drew leaned back and rubbed his jaw with one hand. If the commander knew what was good for him, he would stay out of this conversation.

Morei laid his hands out bare on the table. Eyes darted downward to see the black veins for themselves before returning to his ice-blue gaze. The king waited to ensure he had everyone's full attention before he spoke, keeping his voice soft. "I will not waste my time with pathetic rumors. I nearly died on that battlefield for you all." He took a deep breath and noted the stench of sweat mixing with the fragrant oil the ladies wore. "What has become of me was not my choice, and what has become of my city was not my choice either. And yet, you all still believe that this—everything—was what I wanted. Have you forgotten your places?"

Lord Jire answered. "You are the only one who is working with such evil magic." He squirmed under the king's scrutinizing gaze. "If this is the Gods' way of punishing you, then stop. We cannot die for your actions."

Morei took the bait, unable to help himself. "What did I do to the Gods to deserve the murder of the only family I ever knew?" He waved his hand to silence anyone who dared to speak over him. Now was not the time. The king didn't need to hear their words—he had heard enough before this meeting had even started.

"I'm not here to prove my worth to any of you." As Morei spoke, he looked around the table. Kaleb wrote quickly, his hand splayed on the parchment to keep it from moving as he dipped his quill back and forth from the small jar of ink. The sound of the quill against the parchment annoyed the king, just like Lord Polis's incessant return to that ostentatious ring. "I am the king of Geral and will remain so. Whatever you want to call me, do so, but do it to my face and not behind closed doors. Do you understand?"

Silently, the table nodded at him. Drew followed, his brown eyes sharp. "Good. And if any of you have a problem, then speak to me directly. We don't have time to point fingers. We need to find a resolution to the bigger problem—Cu'cel."

Lady Ferrel, with her hand fan clutched tightly between her fingers, cleared her throat. "And what if we believe the origin of this sickness is from a malevolence, Your Majesty? Is there a solution for that?" Her breasts, as always, were damn well close to spilling over the edges of her dress.

The eyes of the council weighed heavily on him. Morei searched through his mind, desperate to find some old piece of information that could explain the origin of an illness such as this one. But none came to mind, and certainly no solutions. "We need to do our research," he finally admitted. "I've read the report—we've tried our traditional medicines with no luck. We can't risk this spreading to the other cities if it hasn't yet." The very idea made the king's breaths go shallow. The damage of that would be irreversible. And if it happened to leave the country of Sorréle and spread to other countries? The era of the Vorelians would become nothing more than a memory.

Lord Fredrick spoke up next. His small frame made him look closer to Kaleb's age. "How can you expect us to trust you?" He gestured at the sparsely surrounded table and continued, voice shaking, "Lady Dail and Lord Rodrick died by you. You murdered them, and need I remind you that such an act is treasonous, even for a king." Fredrick raised his hand to halt Peter. "Do not educate me in my area of specialty." He leaned forward and narrowed his eyes on Morei. "You threaten us for our loyalty, but you will have no such thing from me."

The lord stood then, his blue robes billowing around him in a frenzy. The chair screamed against the marble, but no one flinched. Fredrick approached the king and jabbed a thumb into his own chest. "Kill me!" he yelled. "That's what you want, right? To kill anyone who questions you?"

Morei stared, temporarily lost for words. The urge was there. The urge to rip Lord Fredrick's tongue right from his pitiful mouth and watch him scream. It was so tantalizing that he could practically taste the sweet metallic delicacy of the blood against his own tongue. Here a man stood, offering himself up like cattle ready to be slaughtered. To question his authority and disrespect him in this very room was disgraceful. Morei was no king if this was how his council felt.

But he knew better. This was a ploy to expose the beast that lurked just underneath Morei's skin. He leaned forward and let a small smile creep across his lips. "I like my victims with a little more fight in them," the king hissed, then sat back in his chair. It had been the wrong thing to say, but he no longer cared. Cu'cel was the last straw. The council officially believed Morei to be the monster they had all sought for him to be.

Lord Fredrick fumed. His skin molted into a rich red tone, and his nostrils flared. "I will not serve such a thing as *you*. I am done." He marched forward, his boots shattering the heavy silence that gripped the air. The doors slammed open behind them, and Fredrick continued down the hall, his steps fading. The movement of the soldiers caught the king's attention.

"Close the doors!" Morei ordered without turning in his seat. The shuffling of metal and boots saturated the room as the soldiers closed them. After a moment, nothing but silence remained. Morei rubbed his pointer finger and thumb together methodically, but with enough pressure that the skin turned white.

"Let him leave," the king commented, more to himself. He looked at the remaining members. "Is there more?"

"Your Majesty," Peter whispered. Morei met his blue eyes. "There is more."

At that, the king noted the other councilmembers tense. Whatever the chancellor knew, they knew it already. Once more, Lord Polis touched that ring. "What is it?" Morei asked, refusing to look at anyone else. It felt like it was only them in the room until he heard Drew shift in his seat.

The chancellor cleared his throat and produced a scroll from beneath the table. It was tied with a simple leather string. Peter slid the parchment over until it reached Morei's fingers. Slowly, the king untied the string, noting how smooth the leather felt. It was new. Once the string was off, Morei unrolled the scroll, placing the parchment flush against the table. The black ink glared at him from its place on the document, and the king recognized the wax crest stamped into the bottom.

Caster.

"What is this?" Morei whispered, even as his eyes grazed over the document. He read them, but not in order. His eyes jumped from sentence to sentence in a mad dash to decipher the meaning. It was all too clear what the king of Caster was saying, but it still didn't make it easier to read.

They were halting all imports and exports to Geral because of him. Because of Morei.

"We have thirteen days," Peter explained. "If we do not reply that we are removing you from the throne in that time, Drexis will cease supplies." He fell quiet and dropped his eyes to the parchment. "What happened on that field is spreading like wildfire, Your Majesty. They are calling you the Demon King."

The term glared at him from the letter, but Morei could hardly read it. He swallowed the bile that had risen in his throat, but he couldn't tear his eyes away. Not yet. The king read the letter again, noting now the tone of disdain seeped through each word. It was a letter meant to entice war. Clever.

If Geral took arms against Caster, King Drexis could use that to his advantage when seeking more resources. As this letter indicated, Geral was ruled by a tyrant, a king with false promises, by evil. "Does Drexis know?" Morei mumbled so low that only the chancellor could hear.

Peter shook his head. "No," he answered. "Cu'cel seems to be only concentrated in Geral based on my reports."

That did not sit well with the king. Perhaps this sickness was because of him—perhaps he was a conduit for something sinister. "He wants me to resign, but there is no one to take my place." The words tasted sour on his tongue. Lifetimes of the Geral bloodline lived in him. This was his place, his purpose. To not be the king his family and ancestors raised him to be meant he was nothing. And if he was nothing ... then he had failed to be anything at all.

"We can vote on such matters," the chancellor whispered. His tone was gentle, paternal even, and it pissed Morei off. If this was his way—the council's way—of seducing him into giving up his title, they were wrong.

"There has to be another way," the king stated, looking around the table. He slid the parchment forward. "I will not bow to empty threats."

"Caster is our only hope of receiving supplies!" Lady Ferrel remarked. "Your ego will not feed this city, Your Majesty. Food will."

"Our livestock continues to deplete from Cu'cel," Lord Jire pointed out, his tone soft but firm. "Crops are dying at a drastic rate. We will die without the supplies of our imports."

Agitation burned under Morei's skin, and he forced a deep breath in. "Then we lie." The council stared at him, unblinking. "We tell him what he wants to hear but continue as we are."

Drew shifted in his seat. "All due respect, Your Majesty, but he may require proof of a new king or queen. Word alone will not suffice."

"He is right," Peter said, and reached for the document. He rolled it up, careful not to damage the letter as he tied the leather string. "Drexis will demand proper documentation of the title transition, and that is something we cannot forge." He stared at the king. "Do not ask for such a thing, Morei. You know as well as I do that such an act would be blasphemous for the family name."

The chancellor knew Morei well. The idea of forging a title transfer had crossed his mind, even if it had been fleeting. But Peter was right—it would be a disgrace to forge that document and stamp the Geral name on it. Morei knew better, but he was desperate, and he would not allow just anyone to determine who took his title from him.

He looked around the room, everyone awaiting his response. Maybe they trusted him to take the lead on this, or maybe they were just afraid to say otherwise. Morei glanced at his own hands—the hands that had murdered dozens. The people at this table no longer saw the boy who once ran through these halls, or the boy who had constantly found himself in the throne room in the late-night hours, staring at the stars. No. What they saw was a man who hungered for blood, who was unforgiving and could not decipher the line between good and evil.

The king met Peter's inquisitive gaze. The chancellor would never admit it, but he too saw Morei as such. If he believed otherwise, the chancellor would have tried harder to prove the king's ability to rule.

"Then let me choose." The words escaped between his lips at barely above a whisper. An audible shift met his ears. They were relieved. This was what they wanted. "Give me the day, council. I will decide on who I believe is worthy to take the throne and who can carry the Geral name." Before anyone could reply, he raised a finger for emphasis. "The documentation of the title transfer will be authentic, but I will still have a place at this table. My word will be final. Is that understood?"

Morei would not let someone else make decisions on the direction of Geral. He couldn't. To be a king took countless summers of training and preparation. This was not a duty that could simply be handed over—one had to be groomed for such responsibilities. "In title, they will be ruler of Geral, but behind closed doors, I make the decisions," he whispered. "Is that understood?"

It was the only way he could do this. Morei could not let the people starve for his own ego. He had been raised a king, and that meant the citizens of Geral came first. Everything he did was for them. It always was and always would be. To abandon their needs would be to abandon his purpose.

The air was growing thin. Morei could no longer get a full breath as he inhaled. Perspiration coated the back of his neck, and the room was becoming unbearably hot. The beat of his heart quickened; the clothes felt unforgiving, suffocating. He needed to get out of here.

"I assume we are done here," Morei said, and stood. The chair screeched against the marble, and he cringed at the sound. Kaleb stared at him across the table, his large brown eyes unblinking. He was but a boy, the king reminded himself. A boy with no future if he could not relinquish his title. "Continue your matters without me. I need some fresh air."

As he turned toward the door, Lord Jire spoke up. "And what of the lady, Your Majesty? The queen?"

The question halted his steps, but before he could say anything, Lord Polis added, "Did you know?"

This was not a matter he would discuss with the council. They had already taken his pride, his purpose. They would not take his privacy too and exploit his life for their entertainment. They had already done enough.

Morei turned his head slightly, his back still facing them. "Let me deal with Emerald," he said. With that, he fell back into step and shoved the doors open. The wood was smooth against his hands, cool to the touch, but he hardly noticed.

"Do not follow," the king ordered. The soldiers halted in their steps behind him, but he kept his pace. If they had questions, they could speak to the council. What mattered now was putting as much space between himself and that dreaded room as he possibly could.

The weight of the conversation made his knees weak and his shoulders ache. How had he fared? He didn't know where to begin, how to digest those words, and how to proceed. The people of Geral wanted him gone. That was the only reasonable conclusion Morei could grasp. And it infuriated him.

If they couldn't see what he had done for them, then he would prove it. Morei would prove himself to them. It was the only chance he had at reclaiming the respect he deserved.

He would find a cure for Cu'cel.

DRUNK AND WISE

he air was cooler than Syra had anticipated. The breeze tickled her skin and ruffled her hair, and she pulled the wool blanket tighter around herself.

She was outside on the back porch of Roman's home, staring out onto his property. It wasn't much—the jaw-dropping architecture and massive home made up for the less-than-impressive territory. Stone walls taller than she was loomed on all sides to keep prying eyes from looking, while a wide wooden and iron gate provided access to her left. To the right stood the barn. It took up the majority of the space, and a wagon sat next to its entrance.

The smell of hay and manure wafted through the air, but it didn't bother her. Syra was used to the odor from her summers in Caster. Roman had goats—she hadn't gone and checked in the barn, but she had heard them cry several times now.

Next to her, a single lantern glowed, casting an orange light across the stone porch. The village was asleep, with most of the lanterns snuffed out for the evening. It gave the stars an opportunity to burn bright in the sky. She stared, letting her thoughts wander.

Zarek was Dryl's brother. He had arrived with no invitation and with a life story that felt incomplete to her. The Guardian left a bad taste in her mouth, there was no other way to put it.

Yet she couldn't entirely blame him for that. Her experience with the proclaimed Death Seekers had not been positive thus far. Certain cultures, such as Raveer and even a majority of the Sorréle country, believed Guardians to be poor omens—bringers of bad luck, death, and other terrible things. Syra never considered herself superstitious, but given recent events, she was beginning to think there was some weight to the beliefs.

Sighing, she gripped the blanket tighter. She was being ridiculous. That wasn't why she was suspicious of him. No. It was because he was another risk, another opportunity to be hurt, and she was pretty tired of being lied to and taken advantage of. Zane and Roman might not be perfect, but they hadn't shown a bad bone yet. Well, besides Roman withholding information about his place in the Infernol.

That wasn't sitting right with her either. But at this point, she was prioritizing what mattered and what could wait, and right now, Roman's reluctance to share his place in the organization felt petty next to their life-threatening situation. It wasn't right, but his reasoning also made sense. In time, she would ask, but not now. Her primary concern was figuring out Zarek's true intention. If it was just to help them reach the secret organization, then so be it, but she needed to be sure of it and not let her guard down.

"This seat taken?"

The question ripped Syra from her thoughts, and she glanced up. Zane stood there, drink in hand, with a lopsided grin. His hair was a mess, and he looked disheveled in general. He was already making to sit when she nodded and scooted over just enough to give him space on the steps. His body heat cascaded over her and penetrated through the blanket, but he smelled thickly of Kendell's Milk.

"How much have you had to drink?" she inquired, keeping her voice low. In the silence of the evening, it felt appropriate to speak quietly.

Zane eyed the copper mug. "Ey, I think a lot?" He took a swig.

Syra snorted and shook her head. "You're going to feel like cow dung in the morning."

"Oh, I've had far worse," he muttered into the night.

"Where are Zarek and Roman?"

"In the study," Zane answered, and wrapped his other hand around the mug. "They're rambling on about politics, and I just simply don't care." He cracked a wide smile at her. "I'm more curious about you."

She nodded, already on defense. "Yeah?"

"Yeah." He nudged her through the blanket with his elbow. "What's this Light Bringy or—what did he call you? The Death Seeker? Don't answer." Zane stopped and scrunched his face into a dramatic scow. Then he lit up. "Light Bringer! It *was* that. Yeah, what's that about?"

Syra had dreaded this. She had known instantly when the Guardian had said that earlier that Zane had latched on to it. He had been trying to get information about her since the night with Kar. He knew she was hiding information—that much had been obvious to her—but she wasn't sure how pushy he was willing to become to get the answers he wanted. She just hoped he'd get the hint that she didn't want to share, even if he was currently compromised.

"It's nothing," she remarked with a shrug.

In the low light of the lantern, Zane's warm, tawny skin reflected ashy. "I think you're lying to me." He drew the sentence out almost as if preparing to sing. Then leaned in real close. "Do you think I'm an idiot?"

In his drunken state, the question was borderline playful, but it made her stomach drop nonetheless. Syra swallowed. "No, I just don't think you need to know."

"Does Roman know?" he pushed.

She shook her head. "No, and don't think I'm spilling anything when you're drunk like this." The breeze ruffled her hair again and sent a shiver down her back, even with the blanket.

Zane eyed her and then took a long swig. When he lowered the mug, he belched. "Excuse me," he muttered. "Kendell's Milk does terrible things to my body, even if it's the best damn thing there is."

She chuckled, happy to move on from the topic. "No apologies needed."

They sat there in silence for a bit, an unspoken conversation passing between them. She was happy to have company, and Zane's of all people. He had proven to be a breath of fresh air in the disaster known as her life. Even if he was nosy, he didn't mean any harm, and for the most part, he remained fairly respectful of her privacy.

The goats cried again. From somewhere within the village, Syra heard a woman laugh in delight, and she smirked to herself. Someone was having a good night.

"I had a shitty childhood," Zane said abruptly. Syra looked over at him and saw him staring outward, his eyes locked on nothing particular. "But for anyone who meets me, they would never know, and I keep it that way."

She raised an eyebrow.

"My brother and I were constantly in competition for our father's approval," he continued. We'd sabotage each other whenever we could, exceed in our studies, and do just about anything to get his attention." He shrugged and looked at her, somber now. "Our father nearly destroyed our relationship."

"I'm sorry," she whispered.

"It's whatever now. Son of a bitch is dead, and you know who did it?" Zane stared at her, waiting for an answer.

"I don't know," Syra confessed. "Tell me."

"Our mother," he said. "Imagine the look on my brother's and my face when we found out our mother committed a crime that could get her killed and our family name banished from Raveerian lips. At the time, we were both succeeding in the ranks, and I was quickly climbing my way to be the next commander."

Syra stared at him. The chill of the night, the cry of the goats, all of it disappeared as she took in the man before her. He had admitted to committing crimes as the commander, but she hadn't anticipated to hear that his criminal history spanned back summers. "What did you do?"

He gave her a wry smile. "Nothing. That was our mother. We staged a murder and got her set up for an entire summer's worth of compensation." He gulped down the rest of his drink, leaning back to catch the last few drops. He almost fell over, but caught himself at the last moment on the edge of the stairs. "Oh, close one, ey?" he laughed.

She chuckled. "I think you should hold off on more drinks, Zane. Get some rest or something, but for the love of the Gods, please don't have another drink."

The man was making to stand, but he wobbled and leaned against the stone pillar. "Yeah, yeah. I think you're right. Say, you going to bed soon? You look exhausted."

Raising her brow, she scoffed. "I think you should be concerned about how you're going to do your watch in this state. Sober up."

"You break my heart, fierce warrior." Zane turned and started to walk, but slowly.

"Hey, Zane?" Syra called. "You think Zarek is trustworthy?" The question came out before she had time to consider it. She peeked over her shoulder at the man. His empty mug was swinging loosely from his grip.

He tilted his head at her and squinted. "Don't you think if he wanted us dead, he'd have done it by now?" Zane waved her off before she could say anything. "You got trust issues." The statement came out mumbled, but it was loud and clear to her ears as he made his way inside and closed the door behind him.

She looked ahead once more and found her eyes locked on the step below her. Zane was right—she had trust issues, but it wasn't without cause.

Syra took a deep breath. The man was drunk, and she wasn't even sure if he'd remember anything he told her in the morning. She'd have to poke at him about it, see if he recalled the conversation. Part of her hoped he didn't, because if he did, then he'd remember asking her about herself, and she didn't want that.

Frankly, she didn't want any part of this disaster. She wanted to march right into the study, tell everyone she didn't need them, then walk out of this home and never look back. A life in hiding sounded far more enchanting than a life being hunted. Alone, she could sneak away to some country like Eiyrǎl and start an entirely new life, leave this old one behind. Right now, it felt like no matter what path she chose, the outcome would be the same.

Kar would reach her. And she didn't want to find out what he wanted with her.

Instead of marching into the study or walking out of her own life, Syra remained stationed on the stone porch, her eyes locked on the stone beneath her. The blanket pacified her emotions, and she let her thoughts die as the crickets sang into the night.

THE DEAD'S SHADOW

The sun caressed the back of Cyrus's neck as he halted in the wide courtyard with a handful of others. He kept the cloak tight to protect the Rider's Sword from any unwanted eyes. At some point, he might have to reveal the weapon, but until then, Cyrus would keep the sword's origins a secret. Kyllian, Lorelei, and Zorya stood next to him, while to his right, several Razan soldiers halted.

Sand-colored walls hugged the courtyard. Etchings of various sigils decorated the stone, some faded and others new. It was Old Tongue, but what they meant, Cyrus did not know, and he hardly cared. All around them, blossomed flowers stood proud, colors vivid and unlike anything he had ever seen before. Vines devoured the stone, branching in and out of fractures. Speckled gray cobblestone was polished to an unusual shine beneath Cyrus's boots and massive fountains stood in all four corners. The sound of the running water broke up the deafening silence of the courtyard as everyone waited for the dragon's arrival.

Large archways housed deep rooms that appeared to be caves gouged out of marble. Dragon holds. Cyrus knew without asking that the half dozen gigantic rooms were what Kyllian had referred to earlier when he had explained how the palace was built. Inside, where not even the sun could reach, Cyrus glimpsed broken stone in the one closest to him—stone bigger than any man. Despite the height of the walls, the palace loomed to his right. Standing here now, it truly felt like he was in the middle of a massive city—the palace was overwhelming. Diemon's was pristine, and even Geral's was worth noting due to its size, but nothing could compare to this.

As Cyrus drew his eyes back to the people around him, he noticed them all looking up. Everyone's gaze was trained on the sky above as Sozar took his time descending from the air. One did not rush a dragon, Cyrus had concluded, and it seemed everyone here understood, for no one spoke about the length of time that passed.

Cyrus should have felt relief for being so warmly accepted and knowing that Sozar was safe here. But he didn't. An uneasiness blossomed in his chest as he stood here. This was the first time since Sozar had hatched that Cyrus was presenting him to people openly—by consent. There was no preparation for the way it made him feel standing here now. They had run from everyone, and now Cyrus felt like he was walking Sozar right into a trap. All his protection and risk had come to this moment. It felt unnatural.

Relax, Sozar said, breaking through the nerves. The dragon's voice was soft and peaceful. *I am not worried, so you shouldn't be either.*

Cyrus rolled on his heels in response and looked up. *You don't have to do this if you don't want.*

The remark went unacknowledged by the dragon. To his left, he saw Zorya glance over to him, but it was fleeting, and he didn't have time to return her gaze.

Shadows fell over them just as Sozar flared his wings wider in preparation to land. The low thump of his wings beating against the air filled Cyrus's ears, and he swallowed down the nerves. There was no turning back now.

Gasps of awe followed as the dragon settled himself down on the cobblestone as gently as he could without damaging the stone from his talons and weight. Cyrus met Sozar's fiery yellow eye as the slitted pupil dilated. Nobody moved, and Cyrus understood why. He was stunning.

Under the sun, his black scales glistened, reflecting various shades of gray that danced over the stone as he moved. The dragon stood nearly twice as tall with his head raised, crested with horns along his jaw and down his spine. They trailed to the end of his tail, where a final one sat, spear-headed—a perfect weapon for sweeping enemies away. The dragon's white talons clicked off the stone as he turned to take in every single person there before he folded in his leathery wings.

Massive incisors peeked through from his mouth as Sozar dropped his head. The dragon exhaled long, hot breaths, ruffling the hair of the women as he perused the crowd. When he came to Zorya, he stopped and stared with one of his eyes. Cyrus watched, unsure of what was transpiring, but it was quick. Sozar raised his head and took several steps back. *I don't feel any threat. Now get this leather off me.*

A sack was tied to the horn just above the base of his shoulders, and without much thought, Cyrus walked over and untied it. It held crumbs of his remaining food and the *Book of Liral*, which he felt protective of. The tome possessed a strange energy, and it had both unsettled and invigorated Cyrus. In all his attempted and failed trainings with harvesting energy, this book had been a powerful beacon to train with—he could identify its energy in the noise of the world. Not that he had harvested from the book's energy—no, something inside him had kept him from doing that. A gut feeling. Cyrus didn't entirely understand the energy or why the book possessed it, so he had refrained from doing anything. In the travels over the sea, he had also refused to take it out of the sack for fear he'd drop it and it to the sea. The sword had remained strapped to his hip, while the book had remained in the sack for protection.

Now that he was here, he would take advantage of the stable ground.

When he was done with that, he untied the several leather straps that kept the makeshift saddle on and slid it off. The leather hit the stone, and Cyrus heard a commotion behind him. He had completely forgotten about the onlookers.

Cyrus sighed and laid a hand on Sozar's scales. He was more exhausted than he wanted to admit, and it was impacting his awareness. If he weren't being watched, he would have curled up on the stone right here and slept under the dragon's wing. Muscles aching, Cyrus was acutely aware of just how dirty he was. It has been nearly half a moon cycle since he'd bathed properly. He wasn't about to count his plunges into the warm waters of the Ashen Sea as proper bathing, although they had been fun.

It is alright. Sozar moved his snout above Cyrus and let a large puff of hot air out, ruffling his blond hair, which was now bleached by the sun.

Turning, he hoisted the sack up higher and looked at the gathering crowd. More staff members stood, eyes wide, while countless pulled out Hyle's Beads and kissed the ceramic. When he looked at a handful, he found tears coating their cheeks, including Zorya's. Kyllian wrapped an arm around Lorelei and hugged her tight. A hushed murmur swept the crowd of onlookers, but Cyrus caught a man say, "The dead's shadow, he is," and cringed at the comment. That was not how he viewed the dragon, nor would it ever be. Uncomfortable, he was ready to disappear from the public eye.

This was what they had all been waiting for. This meant more to them than Cyrus would ever dare to try and understand. To them, he was their beacon of hope, a new beginning, a chance. But he wanted nothing to do with any of it. Cyrus was a man, nothing more, and Sozar did not deserve a life driven by the needs of others.

Kyllian broke from the crowd, taking several steps forward before halting. He looked between Cyrus and Sozar and then swallowed. "I have heard stories about dragons, but never have I been able to look upon one as I do now." The king lifted his hand, palm facing upward, toward Sozar. "Nothing has prepared me for this moment."

The dragon turned his head and dipped his snout so that it brushed against the king's hand. Cyrus watched as Kyllian's breath caught and he took another cautious step forward before running a hand over the hard scales. To see others react as they did now was bizarre, given that Cyrus had spent an uncountable number of days in the presence of the dragon. But he kept his mouth shut. So long as Sozar was comfortable, he would remain quiet and respectful. Still, he could not shake the urge to fly away from it all. After being alone for so long, this was too many people.

When the king was done, he looked over at Cyrus. "Is it alright for Lorelei and Zorya to greet him too?"

He is afraid to speak to me, Sozar pointed out. *Let him know his family is welcomed.*

Cyrus nodded. "Yes."

Kyllian smiled wide and reached back for the queen and his daughter, who stepped forward carefully, as if the dragon's mind might change. Cyrus felt a wiggle of pride in his chest as the princess looked upon Sozar and then at him, her dark eyes now bright with delight. Sozar snorted softly in response to Cyrus's feelings, but he didn't say anything.

"I don't know what to say," Lorelei whispered, laying a hand on the dragon's shoulder.

"There's nothing to be said," Cyrus said respectfully. "No praise or compliments are needed. Just enjoy."

The queen smiled, and Zorya stepped between her parents, letting a hand graze Sozar's snout. With her other, she wiped her eyes and laughed. The sound was odd in the hushed awe of the growing crowd.

"What are you laughing about?" Kyllian asked.

Her cheeks flooded with warmth, and she shook her head. "Just this entire thing. I didn't wake up thinking I was going to meet a Rider and dragon today, but here we are."

"Here we are," the queen agreed.

Cyrus gave a sideways glance at Sozar. *Are you speaking to the princess?*

She is kind, he replied.

With that, Cyrus dropped the topic, not wanting to admit the jealousy he felt, sharing his link with the dragon. Never had he doubted Sozar's ability to speak with anyone or anything, given his ancient life force—Evander had shared a conversation with the dragon when he had become compromised—but Cyrus had not been prepared for his connection to be shared so freely with someone else. He had no idea how Zorya had remained so stoic about it either, but that would be a conversation for later.

As the sun fell lower in the sky, the crowd shifted. Staff members and soldiers alike took their turn greeting Sozar, who was far more patient than Cyrus could ever have been. His feet hurt, his back ached, and his eyes were dry; his stomach rumbled at one point, and he was certain the entire crowd heard, but no one paid attention. The sack remained over his shoulder the entire time, for he refused to set it down and risk losing the book.

Laughter soon filled the air. The soldiers stood, entranced, as the remaining people filed through. Cyrus had no idea what time it was when they were finally done. The only thing he was aware of was Lorelei guiding his arm and saying, "Let me walk you to your room."

Sozar remained where he was. *I am to be fed. I will be here when you are taken care of.*

"Taken . . ." Cyrus trailed off as exhaustion unlike anything he had felt before dragged at his limbs. He was so tired that he could have slept for days without stirring. All his remaining energy had drained as he stood there under the sun.

The queen looped an arm around his and walked with him, patting him affectionately. "I think you will like the arrangements." As she spoke, Cyrus blinked, trying to keep his head clear enough to nod and listen.

She spoke of clothes, bath soaps, silky sheets, and grand windows, but Cyrus hardly followed. He was weary from the travels and acutely aware of how much he was leaning on the queen, who was shorter than him. Cyrus tried to straighten, but Lorelei quickly waved him off, saying she didn't mind. "After everything you've been through, a shoulder to lean on must be wonderful," she told him.

And it was.

THE ASHES OF FLOWERS

If Death had a home, Geral was it.

Morei had heard the wails first. Out of tune, sporadic, and loud. They increased the closer he'd gotten to the city's main street. He didn't need to ask to know they were coming from the mourning citizens, nor to know that the wretched smell permeating the air was that of the dying.

The odor made his stomach turn. It was rotten, and mixed with the unkempt scents of the unbathed. The unbearable heat of the day stifled the air—a thin layer of sweat coated his brow, which he routinely wiped away with his sleeve. Coupled with the lingering aroma of fire and burnt flesh, the king wanted to gag.

He adjusted his glove and gripped Sunny's reins tighter as he entered the main street. Morei had dressed himself in a simple tunic and a cloak, keeping the hood up and over his face. The king had finished it off with a pair of gloves to hide the black veins snaking over his hands. Even Sunny was dressed in nothing more than a simple saddle and bridle. He would be seen as a passing citizen, nothing more.

Nobody had come for him when he left the council chamber. But the king wasn't so sure that was what he wanted. Morei wanted to know he was adding value, not being treated like a servant of the Dark Lord. As he dressed Sunny, a hole had ruptured in his chest. Perhaps he was as evil as the world wanted him to be. Maybe he was the only one who didn't see it.

A child clothed in dirty rags ran by. Morei watched as the young boy reached a wagon and grabbed a piece of bread that had been left exposed. The boy didn't look twice before he bolted from the wagon, just before an older man stepped out from around the corner of a store. The man pulled at his sleeves to conceal a black spot on his arm, then looked up. Morei averted his attention and continued to ride forward, toward the city center.

The scene unraveling around him left the king speechless. Wagons had been set up every forty paces with horses harnessed to them. To his right, a couple of men carried the body of a naked woman and tossed her into one. She landed with a thump against another body.

They were wagons for the dead. Morei should have looked away, but he couldn't.

Her skin was ghostly white. Patches of black, rotten flesh decorated her body, some still oozing blood. A laceration spread from her upper lip to her right eye, where all that remained was a gaping, bloody hole. But what startled Morei the most were the spidery black veins that stretched over the woman's collarbone. Veins that looked just like his.

His breaths went shallow, but he continued forward. A little girl screamed from behind him, and he glanced back to see her being dragged away from another wagon by a man who had to be her father. As she fought him off to reach the wagon, Morei spied a black spot on her neck.

Cu'cel spared no one.

Ash coated everything. It was the ash of the fires from the night before. The ash of the fallen, of the dead. It was what he breathed in, what surrounded him. Each breath he took, he was breathing in the victims.

Morei looked up. Toward the horizon, a cloud had sprouted. If Geral was lucky enough, it would rain and cleanse the city. But rain would not heal those dying from this ailment.

If luck had any say, Cu'cel would pay Morei himself a visit.

The thought was morbid, but it still had crept its way into the forefront of the king's mind. It would surely give him a better reason to hand over his title. More importantly, it would prove to these citizens that he was not the one responsible for such an atrocious sickness. But it wouldn't, he knew. Morei was sick already, and with a far more malevolent ailment. To contract Cu'cel would be a blessing.

The city center was ahead. Wooden posts had been erected, with letters nailed to the tops, a practice that was used to pray to Greve, the God of Strength. A crowd of people stood and knelt in the city center. Some carried decanters of wine in their ritual for Helyna, the Goddess of Love, murmuring the prayer "love is endless." Just in front of the posts lay a pile of coin pouches. A practice for the God of Luck himself, Eazon. To steal the Krye would be grounds for bad luck. The more that was placed, the more people believed that Eazon heard their prayers for him. They were bribing a God for his affection—a God that didn't exist and would never hear them.

A woman passed by, deep in prayer. Her hands clutched the iconic silver beads that Morei had once burned. Hyle's Beads. The carved wooden sun was hanging free from her clutched fingers, swinging with each step she took down the street. The woman wore a maid's dress, the bottom half covered in dirt, the braid of her hair unkempt. She looked as if she hadn't slept in days.

The desperation was sour on his tongue. Morei swallowed his repulsion and halted Sunny. The shire flicked his ears and obeyed. The king swung his foot over and slid to the ground. His boots hit the packed ground hard, jarring his legs. To his left, Morei could see the healing wound of where the arrow had struck Sunny. The scab looked to be a few days from flicking off. Black fur had already sprouted underneath, shoving its way through the scab where the skin had completely healed. It was good to see his shire fine. If anything had happened to Sunny, the king would have lost it.

He gave the horse a firm pat on the neck. "Stay here, buddy," Morei mumbled. He didn't tie Sunny up because he didn't have to—a trust that had taken summers to build. Instead, he laid the reins over the shire's neck.

Satisfied, he turned and walked toward the center. Morei kept his head tilted to prevent prying eyes from potentially recognizing him. His serrated sword was strapped to his hip, underneath the cloak. As the king approached, the sound of the prayers grew louder. They were calling upon all the Gods; prayers overlapped with each other, tunes shifting dependent on what was being said. The sounds of the wailing citizens were suffocated out by the song of these people.

It was a song the king loathed to hear.

A little girl ran up to him just as he neared the outer edge of the posts. She had a piece of parchment in her hand, and her long blond hair hung halfway down her back. She had to be no more than eight, but deep lines decorated the skin underneath her big blue eyes.

"Are you here to say a prayer?" she asked. The question was so innocent, so pure.

The king knelt to her size and smiled. "Perhaps," he answered. "How long have these people been here?"

She blinked and looked at the crowd before looking back at him. "Some have been here since Cu'cel started. Others, like her"—she pointed at a woman dressed in rags—"just came this morning." The little girl swayed on her feet, and her expression grew serious. "Are you sick, sir?"

The smile faded from Morei's lips. "No," he answered, his voice soft. "Are you?"

She shook her head and sent her blond hair every which way. "No, but Father is." The girl pointed behind Morei, but he kept his eyes on her. "We bring the sick there when they are close to crossing over," she explained. "Father is over there."

Morei nodded slowly. "And your mother?"

"Keeping Father company," she explained, and then offered the parchment to him. "Will you say a prayer for him?"

That was a request the king could not deny a child. He took the parchment from her hands and was careful not to crumble it, even if he had no intention of writing on it. Morei had not come here to say prayers, he'd come out of curiosity. To see the horrors for himself. But he could not tell the girl that, and he surely couldn't tell her that he was the one the people blamed Cu'cel on. He was the monster she was hearing about.

"I will write for him," Morei lied, and smiled. "Thank you for the parchment." He made to stand, but the little girl reached out and grabbed his hand with a hold far too firm for a child. The king halted and stared at her.

The little girl's blue eyes became glassy. "Do you think we're going to die, sir?"

Morei swallowed. The question left a chill on his skin, even in the heat of this day, and all he could do was gawk. What he wanted to do was wrap her in his arms and hug her tight. He wanted to take her from this reality, to shield her from the horrors, but he couldn't. Instead, the king wrapped his gloved hands around her small one and gave just the slightest squeeze.

"No," he whispered. "We won't." At that, he let go and stood. Morei towered over her, and he looked down just as she looked up at him. "I'm going to go write now," he said, lying again. Without waiting for her response, he walked past her. He could feel her eyes boring into him from behind, but he didn't turn.

Morei kept the parchment in his right hand as he approached the posts. Countless letters surrounded him, nailed to the posts. They piled over each other, some torn and others dirty. Some letters had been shoved over the nail, splitting the parchment and leaving a gaping hole in the center.

Behind him, chants and prayers continued, but they sounded leagues away as curiosity overcame him and he began to sift through the letters and their contents. Some wished for the return of their loved one, while others begged for an end. Several letters even asked for supplies. He made quick work, not wanting to draw too much attention, although it was apparent no one cared. The king was surrounded by people, but he had never felt so far away from them as he did now. Everyone was caught up in their own reality, withdrawn and disconnected.

He couldn't blame them.

A raven landed ahead on one of the wagons. It looked about and dipped its head toward the bodies. Then it cawed loudly before taking flight again. A vulture took its place moments later, three times the size. The beast struggled to grip the edge of the wagon, flapping its wings for balance. Its bald head disappeared into the wagon's depths.

A man yelled and ran over. The vulture lifted its head, blood now dripping from the beak, and screeched in anger before launching itself into the air. The bird barely missed the man's assault. Morei watched, caught in a spell, but as the man slammed his hands down on the wagon in a fit of uncontrolled rage, the spell shattered. Several individuals nearby glanced over nervously before returning to whatever it was they were doing. The man looked around and stormed off, cursing.

The king opened the letter he had laid a hand on. Childlike writing stared back at him, hardly legible.

What he could decipher made his blood run cold.

It was a letter asking for forgiveness, begging that the Gods take away the king. Morei swallowed as he shifted his attention to the next letter. This one called him the Demon King and blamed him for Cu'cel. Swallowing, he opened another one. Again, he was accused, and the writer begged that the Gods stop punishing the citizens for the king's crimes. It suddenly felt like the eyes of everyone were on him—that this had all been a ploy to bring the king out into the open. To make him vulnerable.

Anger surged. The people didn't understand anything. They didn't know what he had done for them so that they could keep their freedom. Morei had a duty, and that duty was to keep them safe. He had delivered on that the day Queen Reaza fell.

Morei had heard the rumors that the citizens were accusing him of Cu'cel, but up until this moment, it hadn't felt real. Here, now, he couldn't avoid the bitter truth.

His grip tightened on the last letter until the parchment crinkled under his fingers. It released a small cry from the stress before silencing. Morei stared at the letter for another moment, tempted to tear it off. If the people truly wanted a monster, then he would become one.

A sudden urge to look up struck him. A woman was staring at him, eyes hardened. She was older, likely with grandchildren, and her arms were crossed. Her grayed hair was still speckled with copper, and it was braided to the side. She wore a simple, soft, indigo maid's dress with sleeves. The bottom was dirty, but based on the way she carried herself, she didn't care.

It was obvious she recognized him. The king returned her inquiring gaze with his own, both curious and wary. She stood far enough away that countless people swarmed between the two of them, but none took note of the silent conversation they shared.

She wanted him to come over. That much became evident to Morei's intuition, but how she had recognized him was a mystery. With others dressed in cloaks, it wasn't like he stood out, and yet this woman had found him in the crowd.

Morei had a decision to make. Part of him wanted to turn and walk away. Sunny was waiting where the king had left him. He would save himself the hassle of having to deal with her. That also meant he would have to return to the palace, though, and if he was honest with himself, he didn't want to. It felt like the palace had progressively become a giant dungeon—one that imprisoned only him.

That king had a duty to the people still. It gnawed on him like an incessant fly. He couldn't just walk away. If she recognized him and he didn't fulfill his responsibility to her, then what kind of king did that make him? Rumors or not about his place in all this, he still had morals.

Swallowing, he tucked the parchment the little girl had given him into the inside pocket of his cloak. He knew what he wanted to do.

THE MIDNIGHT BLADE

loorboards creaked.

Syra lay there, listening. Someone was up in the home, walking about. She assumed it was one of the maids at this awful hour in the morning, but she couldn't be sure. Roman would be up right now, as he had agreed on the second watch of the night. She had already heard them exchange words in the hall several hours ago, which meant her time was coming for the third and final watch.

She should have slept, but she couldn't. It was a foreign bed in a stranger's home, and as soft as the sheets were, they felt stiff. The ground was stable, unmoving, and it made her uneasy after being at sea for ten days. Syra wondered if Zane or Roman felt the same way.

It had been nearly thirteen days since her walk in the Soul Realm and fleeing from Sekar, but the dream felt as vivid as the night she'd had it. She hadn't dreamt of the realm since, but every single night, Syra prayed that she didn't return. To return meant facing the God of Darkness, and she didn't think she'd be so lucky this time in escaping his grip.

It was dark in her room, and her thoughts wandered without restraint. The night hours always did this to her when she wasn't asleep. Everything felt overwhelming. Her thoughts raced between the screams of the slaughtered passengers on the ship and the clash of metal from the assault in the Nighthunter palace—her actions laid bare to her and without mercy. Syra could have done things differently, acted differently, and perhaps innocent lives would have been spared.

Her heart felt like it was going to burst from her chest. Syra had failed to protect Dryl, her father, and Jared. The Demon Killer—the one thing she'd poured her purpose into—was gone. Kar would be unstoppable with that cursed blade, and he would kill hundreds, if not thousands more, in her name.

Zarek's arrival had not put her mind at ease. Now, lying here, she couldn't help but think the worst of him. Perhaps his self-proclaimed grieving was an act, a way to manipulate them all into letting him in. He could be a ploy to distract them, or worse, partnered with Kar himself. The thought made her chest tight.

The floorboards creaked again, this time closer. Syra exhaled, listening. She had gone to bed with Death's Sword unsheathed and lying against her. It was a habit she had started at sea—safer, especially since she didn't know when or if Kar would show himself again.

Even the sword didn't feel like enough against him.

Her right hand was wrapped around the hilt under the bedsheets, and she gave it a squeeze as her heart skipped an impulsive beat. The steps were closer.

Syra opened an eye in the dark. She was facing the wall, away from the door, but she didn't want to move and take her hand off the hilt.

She needed to sleep, to get some rest before she was summoned for the final watch, but she couldn't. No matter how hard she tried, she could not give herself over to slumber.

A footstep reached her room, and she stiffened. "Roman?" Her voice was strained.

No one answered.

Syra looked up just as she heard a blade pulled from its sheath. Frightened, she flipped the sheet off and bared the sword, just as she felt the cold sting of metal slice her arm. She gasped at the bite and stumbled to the side. A man hissed in frustration in the dark.

"By the Gods," she murmured just as he lunged at her. Syra lifted the sword and deflected a strong blow. Sparks flashed in the air as the edges of the blades collided. A boot struck her in the chest, sending her backward into the wall. Her elbow collided first, taking the brunt with an agonizing impact.

Her ribs were on fire, and from somewhere, Syra thought she heard more footsteps. Dread filled her. They were being ambushed.

The man grunted, and she heard the distinct hiss of metal slicing through the air. Rolling, Syra felt the wind of the blade pass her shoulder. Any closer and it would have cut right through muscle and bone. She struck out with the blade, letting it swing freely, but it struck nothing. Heart pounding, she could hardly hear anything else but the sound of the beating muscle.

The flat of the assaulter's sword hit her abdomen, and she cried out in shock. The strike could have been fatal. Syra couldn't afford another mistake. The next time the man swung, she wouldn't be so lucky.

Lifting the blade, she drove it forward, hoping to catch him by surprise. She did.

The tip of the sword felt the familiar resistance of armor and muscle but kept cutting through. It was Death's Sword—it would cut through anything given the chance. The strike was pure luck, and Syra heard the man's breath catch just as the clang of metal echoed through the room from his sword dropping. Taking initiative, she shoved the blade deeper and twisted.

"Syra!" Zane called from down the hall, his steps slamming into the wood flooring. Roman's voice followed second, accompanied by several others that sounded hushed and surprised.

Without thinking, Syra yanked the sword out of the man's chest and heard him collapse. She narrowed her eyes on the faint silhouette. "Who are you?"

The only response was a final wheeze.

Zane barged into the room and looked around. "Syra?" It was too dark to see her standing in the corner with the dead man.

"Over here," she replied with a slight tremble. As Zane began to enter, she added, "Watch your step. There's a dead guy on the floor."

Roman entered right after, his silhouette lit with a single candle. "What happened?"

"Attacked," Syra answered. "Where's Zarek?"

"Right here," the Guardian answered from behind Roman.

She nodded as Roman entered, holding the candle out to cast a low glow over the surroundings. He stepped toward the first lantern next to the door and lit it. Slowly, he continued until three lanterns were aglow, casting warmth and lighting up the body that now lay on the floor next to her bed. The fitted armor was black, slick, and etched with gold veins.

A Nighthunter.

Bright crimson pooled underneath the man where she had landed the fatal blow—just below the heart. Syra swallowed as she stared at him. It had been a lucky strike, alright. Any other location and she may not have been so fortunate. She dropped her eyes to the cut on her arm. It was a clean slice, but shallow. Blood dripped down to her hand, yet she couldn't even feel the cut. Her senses were on overload, numbing the pain completely.

Roman let loose a string of curses and walked down the hall, yelling for someone. How in the world had a Nighthunter managed to get inside the home without anyone knowing? That left Zane and Zarek, who stood across from her. She eyed the Guardian suspiciously.

"A damn good strike," Zane observed, nudging the body with his bare foot. "And to kill a Nighthunter, no less."

"I wouldn't necessarily compliment the killing blow," Zarek stated. His red eyes drilled into Syra. "He could have had information for us."

She raised an eyebrow at him. "Oh? Sorry, I'll remember that the next time I'm attacked in the dark—don't go for the killing blow. Got it. Thanks."

The sarcasm in her voice made the Guardian raise his brow. "Wonderful."

"He was probably sent by Grit," she explained, looking at the bloodied sword. She leaned over and wiped the metal along the fabric of the bed sheets. It was crude given this wasn't her home, but she didn't have another option. When she was done with that, Syra reached for the sheath and slid it back in its casing. "I'm wanted from the disaster with Grit. I'm sure the Nighthunters are all over us."

"Or someone else wants you dead," Zarek suggested. "But again, we'll never know now that you've killed him." His tone was challenging. The Guardian was upset about this, and that annoyed her. She returned his glare with her own heated stare, not in the mood for such petty arguments.

Zane inhaled and broke into the conversation. "What matters is that no one is dead."

"Snuck in through my study!" Roman called from down the hall. His steps were making their way back to the room. "The windows on this floor weren't locked. My staff apologizes profusely, but they haven't locked these windows in nearly three seasons."

Syra nodded at the statement, unsure of whether to scream or cry as the adrenaline began to peter off. What remained was the bruised discomfort along her ribs and the burn of the cut. "They didn't know," she said, and looked at the body. "But we must be careful from here on out. We're obviously being hunted, and they are closer than we anticipated."

"We should get you cleaned up." Roman motioned at her arm. "Don't know what his blade could've been dipped in."

Zarek held up a hand. "I'll take care of it."

Syra narrowed her eyes on the Guardian. She didn't trust him still. Zarek lowered his hand and raised his brow at her. Silence passed between the two. Clearly, he knew what she was thinking.

Zane looked at them, oblivious. "You can use magic?"

"Energy," Zarek corrected. "If you want to sound like an idiot, you use the term magic. If you want to sound like you know what you're talking about, say energy."

Even in the heat of the moment, that comment forced a wry half smile out of Syra.

"Oh don't blow that crap at me." Zane turned to Roman. "We've got to get rid of the body. Got a backyard and some tools? I'd suggest burning, but that would bring unwanted attention."

Roman sighed, and for a second, Syra thought he might go back to bed. The man looked as exhausted as she was starting to feel. Based on the lines under Zane's eyes, he hadn't slept either. Nobody had found comfort tonight.

"Zane and I will get rid of the body. I'll have staff in here shortly to clean the blood." Roman looked over everyone. "I have a feeling nobody is sleeping for the rest of the night, so I'll ask for coffee and snacks to be made for us." He motioned for Zane to go to the Nighthunter's legs while he went to the top half. "On the count of three. Ready? Okay—one, two, three." They hoisted the body up with grunts and began trekking down the hall. Bits of blood splattered onto the polished wood as the body swung, leaving a trail.

As they left the room, Zarek closed the gap between them; his steps were light, hardly traceable against the floorboards. "Your arm," he insisted, and raised his hand.

Syra looked up at him. "Was it you who sent the Nighthunter?"

A muscle in his jaw ticked. "Is that what you've made me out to be, Light Bringer? A traitor like Kar?" Zarek kept his hand out for her arm, even as his tone dripped with disdain.

Startled, she stared. A thousand things raced through her head at once, all arguing for a place to be heard. His tone indicated that he found no humor in her judgment. In the end, she obliged and gave him her arm. His touch was warm but firm; he held no sympathy for her wound based on his grip. "How can I trust you?"

As he turned the limb in his hand, surveying the cut, he spoke. "Was my story not enough to you?" Blood stained her porcelain skin around the open laceration. The wound still shimmered with fresh crimson, but it had slowed to an ooze. "This will sting," he told her, and hovered his other hand over her arm.

On cue, she felt a sting touch her skin. She gritted her teeth. "I've heard a lot of sob stories. I'm sorry for it, if that's what you want to hear, but that doesn't make me trust you."

The grip on her wrist tightened, and he yanked her closer, even as the skin stitched itself together and sent a tingling sensation up her arm. "If I wanted your sympathy, I would have asked for it," the Guardian hissed. They were close enough to kiss. Too close.

He blinked and let her go, pushing her away. Syra swallowed down the bitter taste of fury and glared at him. The dull sensation of an itch remained where her wound had been—that and the blood stains. Her ribs still hurt, but she wouldn't tell him that. "Noted," Syra mumbled, and rubbed her upper arm, careful to avoid the blood. If they were on better terms, she would have questioned him on his energy harvesting ability, but that thought barely breached her mind.

Zarek eyed her up and down. "Do you know how to swing a sword?"

"Huh?" She raised an eyebrow. "I mean, I'm fine with it."

"Hm." The Guardian walked over to her bed and pulled the sheathed sword up to observe it. He wrapped a hand around the hilt and pulled the blade out just enough to show silver. She watched. If this was his time to strike, he'd do it now, while a weapon was in his hand.

"You will have to trust me eventually, Light Bringer," Zarek remarked softly as he slid the sword back in. "We have a lot to discuss." He turned and faced her, weapon in his left hand.

"Like?" Syra pressed, ignoring the first comment.

"Excuse me?" The sound of a woman's voice interrupted them, and Syra looked over to see a maid standing in the doorway, holding a wooden bucket in her hands along with some cloths. The woman's gray hair was tied up in a bun, and her simple dress was covered with a white apron. "Is it alright if I step in?" Her accent was thick—thick enough that if they were to converse, Syra would need to strain her ears to understand everything.

"We were just finishing up," Zarek answered, moving toward the doorway. "You may do what you need to do." He looked over at Syra. "Coming?"

Taking a sharp inhale, she followed. Now was not the time to start an argument, but she wasn't done with this conversation either. "Thank you," she told the maid earnestly, and gestured to the sheets. "I, um, got blood on the bedsheets, Miss. I'm sorry."

The lines in her skin scrunched as she gave a warm smile in return. "Do not worry, it isn't the first time." The woman stepped past the two and set the bucket down. It sloshed with water and she knelt to begin her work, pulling up her dress as she did.

Syra stepped into the hall with the Guardian. Her sword—or rather, Dryl's—was still in his hand. They fell into step, but it was a slow walk down. "Don't call me that," she voiced in their privacy. "Light Bringer."

He glanced down at her. "Why?" Syra returned his look but didn't need to answer. "Nobody else knows, do they?" Zarek asked.

"No, and I want to keep it that way," she clarified.

After a moment of silence, he spoke up again, keeping his voice even lower. "How much do you know, Syra?"

"I know about the story—your legend—about saving the Soul Realm or what not," she said. When he didn't answer right away, she felt her stomach drop. "Why, is there more?"

Zarek exhaled as they reached the stairs. "We have far more to discuss than I thought," he whispered. "You're in danger, Syra, and Kar is the least of your worries."

The angst in his words caught her by surprise. "What do you mean, Zarek? Do you mean Sekar?"

He stopped her dead in her tracks just as she was taking the first step down the stairs. Syra gripped the cool railing to keep herself from falling as the Guardian cut her off by grabbing her shoulder and swinging her back to face him directly. "How do you know about Sekar?" His words were sharp.

The grip on her shoulder was bruising, and she grimaced. "I saw him in the Soul Realm when—"

"When were you there?" he pressed.

"Um, just recently, by accident, but he was there. He—"

"Hey, you two good?" Zane called up the stairs. Syra and Zarek looked down to see him at the base, staring up. "Coffee and snacks are about ready." Even as he said that, Syra could feel Zane's eyes drilling into her soul. He wasn't dumb—he knew something was up.

"We're fine," Syra called back, and forced a smile. Her heart slammed itself against her tender ribs, demanding to be let free.

"Later," Zarek muttered quietly. "We must speak later." He let go and shoved the sheathed weapon into her hands. She gripped the engraved leather as quickly as she could before he let go and trudged down the stairs without waiting for her. Syra rolled her shoulder as she followed behind, the weight of Death's Sword mocking her. She'd been on land for less than a day and was already covered in bruises. Perhaps she should have stayed at sea.

As she descended, she could see Zane waiting for her at the bottom. The Guardian brushed passed the man without looking and disappeared behind a wall, likely into the galley. Syra came to a slow stop, knowing she wouldn't be able to avoid the burning question on Zane's tongue.

"What was that about?" he asked, hands planted on his hips, covered in dirt.

"Aren't you supposed to be burying a body?" Syra asked. It was too obvious of a deflection, but the question slipped before she could help herself.

"Roman asked me to come inside and grab something," he answered without missing a beat, and crossed his arms. "Then I heard you two at the top of the stairs and couldn't help but note the flattering tone."

She slowly nodded. "I see. Well, we just had a bit of a misunderstanding," Syra lied. "Guardians are a bit . . . dramatic. I'm used to it."

The look Zane gave her meant he wasn't entirely sold, so she quickly added, "The Nighthunter. He's pissed I killed the guy."

"Hm." He turned around then and walked out toward the back. "I'm here when you want to tell me what's really going on," he called back, but he didn't wait for a response. Disappearing outside, Zane let the door fall shut behind him.

He had walked out with nothing, she noted. Perhaps Roman had never sent him in for anything all—maybe it had just been curiosity.

Part of her hesitated walking into the galley, but she knew she didn't have a choice. The sword remained firmly gripped in her hands, but she lowered them slightly as she stepped forward. When she rounded the corner and saw Zarek leaning up against the counter, she stopped.

"Why'd you grab the sword?" she asked, letting one hand fall free from the oiled leather.

He eyed her. "A Guardian sword is extremely valuable. Never leave it out of your sight, Syra. People kill to get their hands on weaponry like that."

"And you really think that lady was going to steal this sword?" The question was innocent, but in her current mood, it had come out challenging.

Zarek didn't flinch. "Roman is a master thief. Do you really believe he doesn't have thieves working for him?" She opened her mouth to speak, but he waved her off. "First lesson—assume everyone has an incentive, no matter how much you like or trust them. Everyone you meet is driven by underlying goals."

Now she was being ridiculed, but she bit her tongue. She walked over next to him and set the sword down on the counter before reaching for a copper mug. A kettle was set upon a large, folded cloth to protect the counter from the heat. Syra grabbed the small wool pad and wrapped her hand around the kettle handle with it. The drying blood caught her eye as she did. She would need to bathe after this. When she poured the steaming coffee into her mug, she saw that it was black and bold.

"So what are your incentives?" Syra asked without turning around. She set the kettle down and looked on the counter. There was some bread and butter, and a cake that smelled thickly of cinnamon, but no sweetener or milk to add to the coffee. She'd have to settle for black.

"To protect you," Zarek answered without hesitation. "It guarantees the Soul Realm's survival."

She nodded, but it was to herself. Turning around, she leaned against the counter. The Guardian walked around until he was across from her. She sipped her coffee and did her best to ignore the bitter flavor.

There were a dozen questions she wanted to ask, and she was sure he felt the same. But they couldn't. Not here in the open, with so many prying eyes and curious ears. They would have to wait.

The lanterns burned in all four corners of the galley, the flames dancing. The curtains of the home were drawn down, shutting out the night. Above them, Syra heard several pairs of steps walking. But they did not speak. All Zarek did was watch her, and she him. A growing tension filled the air between them, unavoidable.

One thing was clear to her. Zarek knew something she didn't, and she was dying to know.

Instead of asking, she remained quiet, and the Guardian didn't offer any information. From anyone else's perspective, it would have looked like they were in a standoff, for someone to break. To Syra, they were merely unsure of each other.

She sipped her coffee in silence.

A KING'S PROMISE

"He's right in here, Your Majesty." The woman's voice shook as she spoke, and she wouldn't stop kneading her hands into her simple indigo dress. She looked up at him, her blue eyes accompanied by tired creases along the corners. Her braided hair was splayed with small gray fly-aways around the crown of her head—the woman looked as if she hadn't rested in days. "Can you help him?"

Morei pursed his lips as he regarded her. All he'd ever wanted was to be a king to his people, someone that the Geral citizens could look up to and feel safe with. He hoped to give that to her and her dying husband.

Outside, the people continued on their way, oblivious that the king of their crumbling city stood inside this home. Voices still carried between the walls, but they were muffled. That didn't stop Morei from reliving the gruesome scenes and the hideous letters written against him. In the silence of this home, those thoughts were louder than he liked. His heart beat with a fierce anxiety—the people were looking for a scapegoat, a reason for their demise, and he had become it. Of course he had wondered about this, but to see it in person, real, was an entirely different perspective. It made him realize how fragile rulership really was.

The doorway was lower than Morei was used to, so he ducked his head to save himself from hitting the wood. The home appeared to be made for people of smaller stature. He removed his gloves and stuffed them in his pockets, finding no reason to wear them here. It was disrespectful to be inside this home and dressed as if he were preparing to run, and he would be damned if he didn't show this woman the respect she deserved.

Their boots creaked along the old wood floor. The narrow hallway made Morei itch—he hated the feeling of confinement—but he remained where he was, awaiting the woman's directions. Old, weathered paintings hung along the stone walls. At first glance, he saw the woman with a man in their younger summers. Between them stood a young girl—their daughter, no doubt.

But she was nowhere to be seen now, and he was in no place to question where she was. Some things were better left unsaid, and given the state of the city, he could already surmise their daughter's fate.

"I can't promise anything," the king told her. Morei held her gaze, hoping to convey as much sympathy as he could. "But I can try to give him peace."

"That is all I ask," she admitted, and lowered her eyes. "We have spent nearly thirty-six summers together, Your Majesty. To see him now . . . he is a shell of the man he once was." Her voice broke in the final sentence, and she inhaled sharply.

Morei's heart shattered at her words. Love was a tragic game, but he still yearned to play it. His parents had been together for nearly twenty-six summers before fate had stepped in. He flinched at the memory, and as quickly as he could, he locked it away deep in the chambers of his thoughts. He hoped to forget that horrific day altogether. In time, he would.

Before the woman could make any suggestive comments to his response, Morei reached forward and grabbed her hand. Her skin was crepe, weathered like the house, but warm to the touch. He gave it a small squeeze. "I will do what I can, but please, call me Morei. I am no stranger to you, and I don't want you to think I seek formality in a time like this."

A single tear fell from a blue eye, and she blinked it away. "Thank you."

The king forced the faintest of smiles. "Do you have a name I can call you by, my lady?"

The woman reached up and gave Morei a motherly pat on his shoulder. "Call me Skye." The touch warmed him in ways he wouldn't ever be able to explain. She didn't see him for anything but what he was—a man. Or if she did know the rumors circling about him, Skye chose not to speak or acknowledge them, even with the obvious ailment painting his skin.

"Skye," he whispered, and nodded. "What a beautiful name for a woman like yourself."

The woman gave the tiniest of laughs. "Oh, I certainly appreciate that, but I am not the woman I once was. Time has taken a lot from me." She gave his hand a squeeze back. "Now, let me take you to see Kalan. He will be honored to see you. Come."

At that, she turned and slowly made her way down the hall. The floor groaned with each step, and around them, it was as if the entire house responded to their presence. The walls hummed with life—there was an energy here that would have been subtle to the normal eye, but not to Morei. And something else, but he couldn't place his finger on it.

They passed several more paintings, these of distant forests and wildlife. The canvases were younger looking, the paint shinier. As if on cue, Skye spoke. "Kalan painted everything and anything. He'd take them down to the market on his off days and sell them. It was his favorite thing to do."

"They are gorgeous," Morei remarked. He kept his voice low. It suddenly felt intrusive to speak any louder, and he wasn't entirely sure why.

She smiled back at him. "Kalan is a stubborn man—never was satisfied with the canvases. Took me the longest time to convince him to sell them. Ah, here we are." Skye halted at a cracked door and turned to face him. "Stay as long as you need, Morei. This was Kalan's final wish, to see you in person, and it will give him peace to pass into the Afterlife now that you are here."

Morei wanted to scoff and tell her Kalan's final wish should have been anything but to see him, but he didn't. This was not the time to condone or challenge requests. A man lay dying in the other room. People often did strange things when faced with death—Morei was no exception.

"Of course." He nodded. "I will call if I need anything."

"Good. I'll be in the galley." Skye reached up and gave his arm another pat before turning and making her way back down the hall. Her steps were lighter than his, but the wood still cried out to her weight with each passing step. After a few seconds, she disappeared around a corner.

The king stood there in silence. He stared at the area where Skye had just been, half tempted to walk away. While Morei had faced Death in the eye and smiled, that still didn't make it easy to bear witness to the tragic suffering that destiny wrought. He had no idea what to expect, and he frankly didn't want to know.

But he was a king—the king of Geral—and that meant doing things that made him uncomfortable for the people.

He laid a hand down on the knob and gently pushed the door open. It creaked on old hinges, but the noise was lost to Morei. The room before him was mostly bare, save for the ancient dresser in the far left corner, the vertical mirror positioned across the room, and the bed that looked out of place to his right. There were no windows, no chance for air to circulate through, and the rich scent of rot and body odor bombarded him with its putrid scent.

Morei blinked and wiggled his nose. The smell didn't bother him as much as he had thought it would. But that only made him more uncomfortable in his own skin. He was changing. Everything about him was shifting, evolving into something that he no longer recognized.

Swallowing down that revelation, he stared at the frail figure in the bed. A single sheet covered what was left of the man, but what remained visible to Morei was horrific. Along the skin that was visible were rotting black blotches—decaying by Cu'cel's touch. The blotches shimmered with pus and what he could only decipher as blood, but it was blackened, dead.

A chair sat next to the small bed. Morei closed the door, wanting privacy, before he crossed the room, acutely aware of every creak the wood made from his weight. He took a seat, the chair groaning in protest. A fleeting thought passed through the king—that the chair would crumble under his weight—but it held, and after a moment, he let himself relax slightly.

Suddenly, the world around him disappeared—there was only the person next to him and this room. The noises faded, the problems slipped further away, and the king became acutely aware of how fragile his life was.

The silence that followed was broken by the shallow inhale of the man next to him. Morei glanced over and saw that his dark eyes were open and he was staring at the ceiling. He tried to move his hand, but the king watched as the man grimaced with discomfort before giving up.

"Skye tells me your name is Kalan," Morei said, keeping his voice soft. He was afraid to startle the man—afraid to disturb Cu'cel's next victim. "She told me you're a painter. The work I saw is outstanding."

Kalan inhaled and tilted his head just an inch toward Morei, enough to make eye contact. "Your Majesty . . ." His voice came at barely above a whisper, as if it pained him to speak.

"Please," the king chimed in. "Call me Morei. I am here as a friend and an ear, nothing more." He smiled, hoping to reassure the man. "Is there anything you wish to speak of? Or perhaps of me to share?"

Kalan wheezed and moved his head back to stare at the ceiling again. His chest barely rose before falling. "I am . . . sorry."

The king leaned forward. "For what? You have done nothing wrong, Kalan." He searched his face for any change in expression, but none came.

"For what . . . this city has become," he finally whispered, then took another breath, this one as shallow as the last. Kalan's chin quivered. "This is not the city . . . I remember."

Morei pursed his lips. "Nor is it the city I remember. The people have changed, but they are afraid. It is not something I can control."

Kalan didn't reply. He appeared to be struggling more. Morei leaned forward, resting his elbows on his thighs and clasping his hands together. The chair groaned in response. He felt an overwhelming need to continue to speak to Kalan, as if the silence between them was a direct invitation for Death to step in.

"When I was little," the king began, letting his thoughts take the lead. "I used to run along the streets and weave between the market stands." Morei smirked at the memory. "I would steal fruit and pastries off the tables when the owners weren't looking." He heard a noise in the back of Kalan's throat—one he could only decipher as a weak laugh. "My parents never knew, which was for the better. Could you imagine if they knew I was a thief as the sole heir to this throne?" Morei chuckled. "I'd ruin the family name."

In his eyes, he already had, but he didn't tell Kalan that. Destiny had ruined the Geral name the moment he had been born.

"I was a rebellious child, though," he continued. "I'd always pick an argument if I could—I loved the debate, the challenge.

My mother used to grow so upset with me. She felt as if I was unruly and unteachable, but let me tell you something, Kalan, and I guess it'll stay between you and me." Morei dropped his voice an octave. "I was a bitter child. My childhood was nothing but promises and good fortune, yet my father was a busy man. What can you expect from a king? But as a child who wanted their father's undying attention, I did anything to get it, even if it was only to be yelled at."

Morei dropped his head and shook it. He had no idea why he was telling Kalan this. Part of him felt like a fool, but the other part yearned to talk and share these memories. It gave them a place to go, because he no longer wanted them. All they did was drag him down and remind him of a life he once took for granted.

"The night before my parents were killed, we had gotten into an argument. Well, my mother and I—we were very similar, and it was easy for us to get into small arguments from time to time once I was older. As stubborn as steel, as my mother used to joke." He stopped then and rubbed his hands together. Emotions he hadn't planned for reared their ugly head and deafened his thoughts with a howl. He blinked and strangled those feelings before he continued.

"When I left that night to go out, I never anticipated it would be the last time I spoke to her. Sure, we had made up and laughed it off, but I will always beg for it to be different. There are so many things I wished I could have said that I never got the chance to." He scoffed. "I guess what I'm trying to tell you is that death is something we never prepare for, and yet it is the most familiar thing to us."

Morei stopped. Swallowing, he stared at his right boot. There had been no intentions of sharing so much about himself, especially to a stranger, but nonetheless, he had. The king was desperate for others to understand him, even if he didn't want to admit it.

Silence followed. It was as if the entire house had shushed, and after a deep breath, Morei raised his head to look at Kalan. The man was staring at the ceiling still, his gaze distant, glassy. Glancing at his chest, the king waited for the familiar rise and fall, but it didn't come.

Kalan was dead.

Morei sighed and leaned back in his chair. Another victim to this fucking game, he mused. He should have gotten up, pulled the sheet over the dead eyes, but he didn't do a thing.

Instead, he sat there, listening and feeling his surroundings. It felt as if the entire world had stilled. Even his own thoughts ceased, and for the first time today, he found peace.

After some time, Morei decided it was time to go. He wasn't sure what he would tell Skye yet, but he assumed he would figure it out as he spoke. Morei was good at that—weaving together a conversation, a story, a debate, all on the spot. He supposed it was what made a good ruler. Someone who could think on the spot and create something out of nothing.

But as he turned, his eyes fell on the mirror, and he felt his entire body tense.

A woman stood behind him in the reflection, her face concealed by a thick layer of wet hair. Her pale skin shimmered under the lantern's light. Morei watched as droplets of water rolled down her shoulder before disappearing from his sight.

Heart pounding, he licked his lips, captivated. "Hello?" It was weak.

The woman hardly moved. An icy sensation snaked its way over Morei's skin, and when he exhaled, his breath came out in a large plume. As quickly as he could, he whirled around in his chair to face her, but she was no longer there.

Morei's breath caught in the back of his throat, and he stared at the space where she should have been for a heartbeat too long. Slowly, he turned to face the mirror again, the sound of his own heart in his ears.

He saw her again. This time closer. He could practically feel her presence behind him now, and it unnerved him.

"What do you want?"

The woman shuddered, her hair swinging. A frigid droplet hit the back of his neck, and he flinched. "You must protect her." Her voice was so sharp that Morei started and nearly choked on the very air he breathed.

"Who?"

"Protect her," she repeated, louder this time. It was like a thousand voices were molded into a single one, echoing off each other as the woman spoke. "It's the only way."

Morei had no clue what she was talking about. "*Who?*" he insisted. "Who am I supposed to protect?"

She didn't reply, and that pissed him off. Agitated, Morei turned without thought to try to face her once more, but a cold hand grasped his throat. He inhaled, feeling the breath cut short as she squeezed. The king panicked and grabbed at her arms. They were slick and frosty to the touch.

Before he could fight her off, she hauled him out of the chair, lifting him as if he weighed no more than a feather, and tossed him backward. Morei's spine met the ground first, the muscles screaming out in protest from the impact. Shooting up, he reached for his neck and scrambled back, feeling nothing as his eyes fell on no one. She was gone—the room was empty, save for Kalan's body.

Unsatisfied, he sat up and turned to face the mirror. As he did, his eyes found their own reflection.

Blood-red orbs stared back at him, his skin pale and webbed with black veins that covered his face and stretched down his neck. Morei gaped at himself. The man before him was unrecognizable. A monster. A creature of death.

"Stop this," Morei whispered. He couldn't do this, this fucking game that toyed with him like some prey. He shook his head and looked at himself again. The same monster was staring back. Images of him running his tongue over a bloodied blade bombarded him, and he hissed through clenched teeth. He could *taste* the metal on his tongue. "Stop it," he ordered.

But the person in the mirror remained unrecognizable, gawking. Rage boiled in his veins, suffocating out all other emotions. Morei balled his hand into a fist and sent it into the mirror. The glass shattered in a deafening song that shook the king out of the trance. He blinked and pulled himself away from the shards that scattered the floor. Looking around, he waited to see the woman again, but she was nowhere.

The creaking of floorboards met his ears, and the king remembered Skye. Frantically, he reached forward for a large shard of glass. The edge of it sliced right through the palm of his hand, piercing the skin with a nasty sting. He ignored it and raised the glass to his face.

A normal man stared back at him.

The door opened. "Morei, is everything—oh my, are you alright?"

He waved her off as he pulled the sleeve over his cut. "I'm fine. Just—" He cursed to himself silently, realizing how much of an idiot he was going to sound. "I tripped."

Skye knelt next to him and wiped at his shoulders, as if she could see something on the fabric that he couldn't. "Oh, I am so sorry. These floors are so uneven. I am so embarrassed."

"Don't be," he insisted, and grabbed one of her hands with his good one. He didn't want her to see the injury. "This was me. I wasn't paying attention." He forced a smile. "It should be me apologizing. I broke your mirror."

"Oh, that?" Skye helped him up, her grip never lessening as they rose from the floor. Morei wanted to commend her for her strength. She was aged with time, but tough and firm. "Kalan always had that thing. It was the most outrageous item to keep around here. Said it was a family heirloom, and what could I say to that?" She chuckled and shook her head before letting go of his hand. "I just can't tell him to toss it out. It would crush him."

Everything struck him at once. Kalan's passing, his rambling, the strange woman or ghost, the vision of himself. He swallowed. It was unlike him to look or be so out of control, and especially in front of a woman such as Skye, who had already seen more than she should have. It aggravated him. The king couldn't let her see his failures. He was her leader still, and as shaken up as he was, he needed to be tough for this next part.

Morei took a deep breath and fully faced her. "Skye . . ." He reached up with his good hand and tucked a strand of copper hair behind her ear. Her blue eyes didn't leave his. "I am so sorry, but Kalan passed while I was in here."

Skye ripped her eyes from his and dropped them on the still figure that was once the embodiment of her husband. She didn't move, and for a moment, the king believed she had become paralyzed, but then she took a deep breath and faced him once more. Her eyes were rimmed with fresh tears.

"I guess I shouldn't be surprised." Skye dabbed at her eyes with the hem of her dress. "Yet I am, like a fool."

"You are not a fool," the king admonished. "Death is still a stranger, even to the most seasoned person." He reached up and wiped a rogue tear that had escaped between her dabs. "Can I help in any way?" His mind still raced, his heart still slammed against his ribcage, but he couldn't let any of it show.

She took in a breath and shook her head. "You have already done enough, Morei. You gave Kalan his final wish and gave him the permission to cross over. All I wanted was for him to be at peace and not in so much pain."

What should have relieved the king only made him more anxious. His skin crawled with the anticipation of the woman returning, or Skye looking at him and screaming. But none of that happened. Instead, she reached forward and wrapped her hands around him, embracing him into a hug.

The act caught him off guard, but he didn't push her away. Skye needed this, and Morei would deliver, for if he didn't, he would be abandoning her in this time of need. Wrapping his arms around her, he hugged her back with a firm grip, keeping his injured hand smothered in the sleeve to subside the bleeding. A single sob escaped her lips, and then she fell silent.

Morei didn't rush her, even though he wanted nothing more than to bolt from this house. This place made his skin crawl—it was saturated with strange energy. He couldn't stop thinking of the monster in the reflection, the man he would become when his ailment reached its worst, and he couldn't stop thinking about the woman and her haunting words.

The faint memory of the metallic taste on his tongue echoed in his mind. It made him want to scream, but as hard as he tried to get rid of the vision, he couldn't. That day on the battlefield had unleashed the true force of his demons, and in their ecstasy, Morei had felt real power. He would be a fool to not admit the potential of his abilities if he submitted himself to their control.

Perhaps he was already the monster.

DINNER UNDER
THE STARS

yrus tugged at the sleeve, uncomfortable.

The blue, embroidered shirt was thick, embellished with black threading around the sleeves and collar. It was a shirt of royalty, something Cyrus had never once dreamed he would be wearing, yet here he was. He was dressed like a prince, but all he wanted was to return to his lightweight tunic and pants. At least in those, he could move freely, without the constriction or the eyes of the people around him. The outfit made him stand out, and he hated that.

And to make matters worse, he didn't have his sword or sack. Both were back in his new chamber, tucked away behind the threaded pillows. The chamber was large enough for a family, with a bathroom attached to a living area and bed, but it was all his. Frankly, it was the largest living space Cyrus had ever had in his life. Clothing was ready in the giant walk-in closet for Cyrus to choose from, but for the dinner that would be held for him, this specific outfit had been presented. The queen had insisted he dress the part as a Rider, and to make her point clear, he had even received a pair of new, freshly oiled calf-high boots that fit perfectly.

He had complained silently to himself as he dressed. After a nap and a bath, Cyrus had grumbled the entire time he was messing with the buttons of this outrageous shirt, but when he was preparing to leave, a knock echoed through the room.

He opened the door to find Zorya standing there, dressed in a blue silk dress embellished with gold. Her hair was curled loosely around her face, and a slight pinkish hue touched her cheeks. As grumpy as he had been about being awoken for the late dinner and dressed in stiff fabric, it all quickly faded at the sight of her. And he had been put into an even brighter mood when she explained that she would escort him to the feasting hall.

The hall was massive, with a vaulted ceiling decorated with extravagant crown molding and landscape paintings scattered across the walls. The ceiling was painted as the night sky, with Eazon's Hammer, the Heart of the World, and even the Bell. It seemed all the notable constellations had been captured. Green and gold banners hung in all four corners of the hall, bearing the East Razan crest of the moons.

All around, people of royalty bustled. Some danced with each other, some drank, while others ate at the table Cyrus was at now. Before him sat a half-eaten chicken with a small serving of stuffed pasta. He ate some more of the mushroom-filled delight, enjoying the creaminess and hints of truffle. It had been a long time since he'd had pasta, and after the travels, it felt like the finest meal.

Lords and ladies surrounded Cyrus at the table, but he didn't know any of their names, having heard some but quickly disregarded them. Reaching for the silver goblet of wine, he took another drink as the music shifted into an epic song of adventure, love, battle, and conquering. To his immediate left sat Lorelei, dressed in blue with her hair pinned up. To his right was Zorya, her cheeks flush from the wine. On several occasions, Cyrus hadn't been able to help but stare. When she looked over to him, he averted his gaze, scolding himself all the while. Her laugh was sweet, her smile captivating, and like a fool, he couldn't help but return to her.

There was something so different about her, but he couldn't place it. Whatever it was, it didn't matter—Zorya was gorgeous.

The smells of baked sweet goods wafted through the air, indicating dessert was near. They had been eating for what felt like an eternity, and Cyrus was eager to excuse himself from the public. Never had it taken him so long to eat a meal, but then again, he had usually eaten hunkered in a mine shaft somewhere deep in the mountain, not like this. When he'd first entered the grand hall, everyone had stared at him—even the most royal couldn't help but gawk. And they had lost it when Sozar had entered. People gasped and applauded, cheering as the dragon walked down the middle of the hall and toward his spot, where Cyrus already stood. It had all felt unnecessary.

Now, Sozar lay behind him on a large, royal-blue cushion. The dragon simply observed the crowd, letting people wander close, but nobody ever touched. Without permission, they knew better then to overstep.

Kyllian clapped a hand over Cyrus's shoulder, returning from a conversation. "Well, isn't it amazing?"

Cyrus looked up at the tall man and nodded. "The food is unbelievable."

"Good." The king walked over and sat back down next to the queen, taking a large gulp of his wine. He was dressed in silver, with black-threaded sleeves. He wore no crown nor any indicator of his title, only the pristine fabrics like everyone else here.

"Is Sozar enjoying himself still?" Lorelei asked, leaning in to be better heard over the noise. Her cheeks were flush from the wine.

Smiling, he nodded once more. "Yes." Sozar had been enjoying himself much more than he was admitting, that much Cyrus knew. The dragon was relishing the attention and free food.

Zorya made eye contact then. "What was your childhood like, Cyrus?"

He swallowed, not wanting to admit to his feelings of abandonment from being raised parentless. "It was busy. All kids were expected to adhere to a strict schedule." At her curious gaze, Cyrus felt the information ripped from his mouth. "I was raised in an orphanage and put to work in the mines at fourteen. It's all I can remember."

Zorya raised an eyebrow as the queen patted his arm. "A cruel upbringing for a child. I am sorry."

Turning his gaze to her, Cyrus replied, "It is what it is. I don't know anything different, so to me, it was normal."

"Child labor is outlawed here," Kyllian chimed in. "That is inexcusable."

He wasn't sure what to say, so he didn't respond. What Cyrus had grown up with was normal to him. Dingy rooms, tiny cots too small for growing boys, stale bread and salty stews—it was what he knew. What was abnormal was sitting with royalty and being dressed in outrageously expensive fabric, but Cyrus wouldn't tell them that.

Smart, the dragon commented, having read his thoughts. *Some things are better left unsaid.* Cyrus eyed Sozar over his shoulder, surprised he had been tuned in to any of that, but he didn't reply. There was no need too. The dragon knew he appreciated the support.

But what he really wanted to do was excuse himself from the table. He had sat far too long, and he was feeling antsy to move about. This all felt strange to him—sitting here, stuffing his face, music playing, all these people just for him. No, he didn't like it at all.

"Excuse me," Cyrus said, and pulled the cloth napkin from his leg, setting it on the table. "I just need some fresh air." Before anyone asked further, he added, "I'll be back."

"Don't miss dessert," Lorelei called, her words fumbling over one another as the wine hit her. "It's butter cake."

That made him cringe, but he didn't let it show as he started out of the grand hall. Evander had made butter cake, and it had been divine. And in payment, Cyrus had taken the man's life.

His stomach lurched, threatening to discard the contents of his dinner.

As Cyrus neared the exit, a young woman stepped up to him and brushed her fingers over his hand. "Your eyes are extraordinary," she hummed, dark skin glistening under the lights. She batted thick eyelashes at him.

Cyrus was beyond uneasy with the accolades and attention, but he managed a small smile. "Thank you."

"Where are you going?" The woman leaned into him, obviously drunk.

"To the bathroom," he lied. The last thing he wanted was for her to follow him. To make it clear, he stepped away from her and toward the exit.

She turned and stared up at him. With her high cheekbones and rich amber eyes, she was stunning, but Cyrus wasn't in the mood for flirting. "When will you be back?"

"Soon." It was all he could manage to say as he turned and escaped the clutches of the party. As Cyrus walked down the hall, he kept his gaze lowered to the handful he passed, hoping they didn't acknowledge him. They were either too drunk or didn't outright recognize him, because nobody said anything. Cyrus had never been so relieved to avoid the attention.

He followed the path of the hall, hardly paying attention to the extravagant stone carvings and outrageous paintings that stared down at him from the ceiling. It all felt like too much. How could anyone live a life surrounded by so much gaudiness? It made his skin crawl.

Almost as if fate mocked him, he tripped on his own foot and nearly stumbled onto the floor but then steadied himself on one of the stone carvings. When he righted himself, he caught the eye of a man dressed in red robes. His skin was pasty white, and a black mark was branded into his forehead. The man gave him a slow nod but didn't stop as he continued to walk. Cyrus cleared his throat, embarrassed. Regardless of how weird he looked, the guy probably thought he was drunk—the Dragon Rider, stumbling around these halls. The robe, the mark, the mannerisms all felt religious, but he had never heard of such a practice.

With his boots echoing off the silver marble, Cyrus steered his way until he found an exit that led out to a patio. He took it without thought, welcoming in the night air, the crisp breeze that teased his skin. Blinking, he looked around. Before him, the city was still alive, and the sound of laughter and chants followed. There was a party in the city tonight, likely for his arrival, as Cyrus was now certain Kyllian had told his soldiers to spread the word. It unnerved him to think the entire city of East Razan would know about his presence. When would the rest of the country find out?

Where have you gone? Sozar's voice rumbled through his head, breaking his thoughts.

Cyrus turned his attention to the massive mountain range to the north. *To get some fresh air,* he answered, and then, unable to stop himself, added, *I thought you would have known.*

Sozar grumbled in response and retreated backward from their bond. The dragon must have sensed Cyrus's need for privacy, for he let him be.

If Cyrus remembered correctly, the massive mountain range was one of the largest in the world, competing with the Releuthian Mountains. He couldn't remember exactly, but he believed the range to be called the Beutóne Mountains—he would have to ask to be certain.

Walking over, he laid his hands on the stone railing and closed his eyes.

Cyrus stood there, listening to the world and shushing his thoughts. It brought him a small level of peace to just listen. He heard the wind, the whispers of the palm trees rustling, the thrill of the citizens' voices as they carried, and from somewhere, he thought he heard the distant cry of the river as water moved. He wanted nothing more than to retreat into the forest and embrace the isolation of that world. At least there, his actions would not be judged. There, he was free from the obligations that mankind tried to chain him to.

The only thing he'd come here to do was find answers about his lineage. Everybody wanted to cheer and celebrate his arrival and existence, but no one wanted to discuss the elephant in the room—Cyrus could only have these silver eyes if he'd been born from Dragon Rider parents. At least, that was what the letter Kyllian had written Evander had mentioned. At this rate, he was certain that most, if not all the citizens of East Razan knew this.

Tomorrow, he would speak with the king on the matter. He wanted to see the records for himself. And then, once he had the information he desired, he would—

What would Cyrus do? Leave? And go where?

He was running, but it had been from Sorréle, and now that he had escaped the country's clutches, Cyrus suddenly felt at a loss for purpose. Sozar was inside, safe, and the people had welcome them in as one of their own. Yet all he wanted to do was run, and he didn't know why.

"I see you're enjoying the party." The voice startled him out of his brooding thoughts, and Cyrus turned to see Zorya standing there. She raised an eyebrow. "I mean that sarcastically."

The comment made him smirk. "Thanks."

Zorya looked around. A breeze rustled her hair. "Royalty can be outrageous, can't it?" She walked over to the railing next to Cyrus.

He stared at her, surprised. It was the last thing he had expected from the daughter of the king. "What makes you say that?"

She laughed, her voice bright. "As I was sitting there tonight, I thought about how this must all look to you." Zorya looked up at him and shrugged. "Probably ridiculous, huh?"

There was no point in lying. "You could say that."

"What *is* it like, Cyrus?" Zorya asked, keeping her voice low. He didn't like the way she had shifted her tone—it put thoughts in his head that he needed to avoid. "To come here after running for your life, hunted, all of it—father told me about it all." She stopped and shook her head.

Cyrus sighed. In a single heartbeat, he felt as if he had relived everything—the anguish, the fear, the thrill. "You want to know the truth?"

The princess nodded.

He had expected nothing less. "I hate it." Cyrus leaned against the railing, using his forearms to prop himself up. "I've spent almost an entire season running for my life, trying to protect Sozar, learning to abandon everything. Before that, I was punished for being different, for speaking out, or when I was late to a shift in the mines." He bit his tongue, not wanting to ramble. "All I have ever known is that, and now, being surrounded by so many welcoming people, it feels . . ." Cyrus trailed off, unsure of what to say.

"It feels wrong," Zorya finished for him.

He looked at her and nodded. "Exactly."

There was no need to continue moping about how much he disliked the party—it made him look like he was complaining about having a bed to sleep in. "My gratitude is beyond words, though," he added. "I appreciate the hospitality and warmth of your family and the people."

Zorya smiled. "It's not every day a Dragon Rider walks down the street."

Cyrus nodded but didn't say more.

For a moment, neither spoke. Cyrus soaked up the silence after the noise of the party, and while he wouldn't outright admit it, he appreciated her comforting presence. There was a warmth and peace about her that shoved his anxieties away.

Zorya leaned onto the railing next to him. She was close enough that their arms touched. "What's your plan, Cyrus?"

The question wasn't threatening, but under her gaze, Cyrus felt embarrassed to admit that he didn't want to stay. "I don't know."

"Be honest." Zorya nudged him in a playful manner. She was trying to keep the conversation light, but it wasn't helping.

Meeting her dark gaze, he answered, "If we're keeping secrets still? Or no?"

She raised an eyebrow. "I won't tell anyone if you don't."

Cyrus rolled his eyes. They were in this game, and he loved it—loved the way she toyed with her smile every time she knew she had gotten what she wanted. "Truthfully," he said, and lowered his voice, "I never intended on staying, Zorya. I don't belong here."

"And what makes you so certain of that?"

Cyrus shrugged. "I've never fit in, and when I tried, it always blew up in my face. I do better alone, and with Sozar now, it's safer that way."

"So," the princess exhaled, turning her gaze onto the city. "You've been here less than a day, and you've assumed we're like the rest of the people that have let you down."

The statement stung for reasons he wasn't sure how to explain, and he shook his head. "I haven't been wrong yet about that, and the last time I tried to see the best in someone—" Cyrus bit the inside of his cheek, remembering Evander. "Well, I was wrong about that too."

"Huh."

Cyrus stole a look at the princess. She was still staring ahead. "What?"

Zorya didn't reply right away. "The Dragon Rider who wants nothing to do with the world, and yet"—she looked at him—"the world wants everything to do with you."

"I never asked for this," Cyrus protested.

"And neither did the victims of the Diyrǎllian Massacre ask for their lives to end, but here we are." The statement was cold. "Cyrus, one day you will have to embrace the world for what it is. There are cruel people out there, but there are good people too—people who are victims to the monsters." Zorya took a deep breath. "You might not have asked for this, but the Gods see something in you, whether you do or not. There is a reason you were chosen to be a Dragon Rider, and one day, you will have to see that."

With that, she turned and walked away. When she got to the entryway, she added, "Dessert is coming. If I were you, I'd head back in. Not for yourself, but for the people."

And then she was gone.

Cyrus pursed his lips and dropped his head. Maybe she was right—maybe there was a reason he was selected to be a Dragon Rider, but right now, he had no idea why. All it had done was consume his life and complicate things. Nothing good had come out of this. Nothing except blood on his hands.

Hatchling, Sozar intruded, gentle. *Do not pester yourself with such worries when you are tired. Tomorrow is a new day. Rest, enjoy the evening.* The dragon's voice faded from Cyrus's thoughts, leaving him alone. If Sozar had eavesdropped on that entire conversation, he felt violated.

Did you hear all that?

A grumble echoed across their bond. *Only the second half. Dessert is here, and the king is looking for you.*

He exhaled. Zorya was right, and Sozar too. He needed to return to the party to be respectful, no matter how much he loathed going back there. And when he could, he would retire himself and get much-needed rest.

With one final look toward the Beutóne Mountains, Cyrus turned and left.

PRAYER

It was a big day, and Syra couldn't have been more thrilled. The sun was low in the sky, the morning still young, but already so much had happened. Packs were filled with food—nonperishable items, like jerky—and their cloaks were laid out, all forest-green except for Zarek's with his iconic Guardian attire. His black cloak was embroidered with silver at the bottom, symbols of the Old Tongue.

The Guardian had his sword strapped to his hip, and he was already dressed and ready to go. The belt he wore was just like Dryl's—the leather was engraved with patterns, as was his sword sheath. He dressed in slick black leather armor, something neither Kar nor Dryl had done on their travels with her. They had worn simple clothes underneath their cloaks, but he was dressed for battle. It made Syra wary.

Zane and Roman dressed mundanely, as did she—in tan pants and a white tunic, keeping it loose as she strolled around the house, helping anyone who needed it. On several occasions, she had caught herself in a mirror and jumped.

Her hair was no longer the beautiful fire red that she had become accustomed to all her life, but rather a dark brown. Earlier, everyone had dyed their hair to minimize attention on their travels. The dye had consisted of plant material and smelled thickly of soil, but she had been assured the smell would fade. She had grown used to the organic scent now, but not the look.

Roman looked ten summers younger, and Zane . . . well, the man looked better blond, but she couldn't say she was any different. She looked better red too, but there was nothing they could do about it. The dye would wash out in a couple of washes, so they would have to make their travels quick and be careful not to get their hair wet.

Last night felt leagues away already. The tenderness of her ribcage still ached at any sudden movement, but for the most part, it remained unproblematic. Like everyone else, she had bathed one final time before the long road ahead. Nobody was certain when they would see the inside of a home again.

The Nighthunter had been buried but not forgotten. Everyone seemed to walk with a bit more care and caution when entering rooms. If a Nighthunter had been sent to kill Syra, then there was a good chance there would be more.

She wasn't sure she'd get such a lucky strike next time.

Syra needed to grab her boots, but she had been hesitant to put them back on. That would mean she was ready to tackle the next challenge in her life, and frankly, she wasn't sure she was—but she didn't have a choice, either.

She double-checked her belt around her hips. The sword was there, clipped in with its sheath, and the pouches remained tightly sealed. The Infernol ring and note still lay snuggly inside. When the time was right, she would present it to Zarek. She wanted him to have it. Regardless of his attitude, he deserved it if it was one of the last of his brother's possessions.

From the galley, she heard Zarek laugh at something Roman said. The noise sounded weird—he had been so serious since his arrival, she hadn't even been sure he was capable of laughter. It fit him, though. The travels would be grueling and risky, so she needed to make friends fast. Syra couldn't go on forever being standoffish. He might be the person who would end up saving her life.

Still, she wasn't ready to trust him yet.

Turning, Syra walked up the stairs. The stone was cool against her bare feet, and she made sure to relish the feeling. It would be a while before she could do this again. As she reached the second level, she paused. Rushed whispers caught her attention.

They were coming from her room.

Syra inched forward and strained her ears. The whispering belonged to a lady. It sounded like it was a chant, perhaps, and she continued forward, curiosity grabbing ahold of her manners. As she approached, she noted the increased intensity of the whispering and stopped at the door's edge.

She peeked in.

The woman was the maid who had cleaned the blood from earlier. Ryshal, if she remembered the name correctly. Her back faced the door, but beneath her was the bucket of blood and water. The woman's hands moved, the skin stained red. Next to the bed, as expected, were her black leather boots.

Syra felt the hairs on the back of her neck rise. Whatever Ryshal was doing, it involved energy. She could feel it tingling her skin, taunting her.

Ryshal hummed loud and then stopped. She spun around so fast that Syra had no time to react. Her face lit up. "Syra, my dear! Just in time, come here." The old woman stepped forward and reached for her, pulling her into the room and to the bucket. Bits of blood splattered the maid's white apron, giving her a horrid look.

The energy was thick, the air chilly. It reminded her of when Raven, the Soul Speaker, had read her future in that small room. Except this time, Syra didn't feel safe—she felt like she was being watched.

"Ryshal—is that your name?" Syra asked, keeping her voice low, afraid the dead might hear. The woman nodded with a warm smile. "What are you doing?"

"I am simply wishing you luck on your travels, my dear. Roman has been kind to us all these summers. I want to return it by offering protection and safe travels. Dip your hands in, dear."

Syra startled. "Excuse me?"

Ryshal gestured to the bucket. "Your hands. It is how we pray. It is the Crystón way."

Words failed on her tongue, and she just stared at the maid. She didn't entirely understand the culture of Diyră or the religion the maid referred to, but this felt wrong. "I don't think I'm comfortable with that," she confessed weakly. "Where I grew up, praying over blood meant something dark." And more specifically, Sekar. The last thing she needed was to pray to the same God that wanted her.

"This is not a blood ritual," Ryshal admonished. "This is an old practice my family has done for generations, when we were still bound to the northern lands. Now, please, I insist." She held her hands out expectantly, brown eyes bright.

Syra hated being rude. "This isn't something for the Dark Lord?" she asked weakly. Even as the words came out, she regretted it. Ryshal's smile dropped, and her hands faltered. She looked completely crushed.

"I'm sorry," Syra said, and held out her hands. "That was out of line. Why don't we start fresh?" She was in no place to accuse the maid of praying to the evil God.

Ryshal studied her, unmoving. She was about to apologize again when the woman wrapped her hands around Syra's with a firm hold and nodded. Her touch was calloused, aged. "Alright, fresh start. Just follow along. You don't need to say anything."

"Okay." Syra shoved her worries aside. People had different cultures, she reminded herself, and that meant they did things differently. It didn't make it wrong, just strange sometimes. If they were in a different situation, she would have taken the time to ask more about the maid's religion.

Ryshal started whispering quickly under her breath once more. She knelt, taking Syra with her, and plunged their hands into the bucket together. The bloody water was cold, and thicker than Syra was prepared for. Her stomach turned at the undeniable stench of copper. She held her breath, not wanting to insult the maid any further by gagging.

Ryshal kept her eyes closed and started caressing her hands over Syra's in the bucket. Bloody water stained her wrists and forearms. "Grace our dreams," the maid chanted. "Show us mercy through your patience." The words fell from the woman's lips faster, as part of a prayer. "All children born to the dark are bound to crave the light." Ryshal dragged the bloody water higher up her forearms. "Punish the dreamless and preserve the pure."

Syra watched and listened, ignoring the growing panic at hearing the scriptures. She had wanted to feel nice, to be respectful, but now it was starting to look like a terrible idea. All the warnings of her culture, of her upbringing, were demanding to be heard, but she swallowed them down as best as she could. As the low chant took over the silence of the room, Syra's thoughts began to disappear. The room around her washed out, and suddenly she could no longer hear the maid or see the room.

The vision in the Soul Realm grew louder and louder in her head. The chase, her breaths, and the fall—all of it felt so vivid. Above, the sky pulsed with the dying heartbeat of an animal, purple and otherworldly. In the distance, creatures screeched with savage hunger, hunting. The slimy ground smelled rotten and coated her hands and legs with an icy sensation. Behind, the footsteps of her assailer, Sekar, stopped. He was upon her once and for all—she couldn't wake herself. This time, he had her.

Her heart skipped a beat as cold fear strangled the breaths out of her. She couldn't escape him, no matter how hard she tri—

"Syra?" Ryshal's voice shattered the vision, the memory, and she blinked. The room came to life around her, and she looked down to see her hands still submerged into the bucket. The maid was staring at her, crouched, the lines around her eyes crinkled with her frown. "Are you alright?"

Syra swallowed and adjusted her feet. "I—I'm fine. Just got lost in thought." She let a shaky laugh escape her lips, hoping to reassure the woman. She was eager to be out of this room for good. "Are we done?"

Ryshal smiled, but it was weighted, as if she sensed there was more going on that Syra refused to share. "Yes, dear, we're done. Here—" She offered her apron for Syra to wipe her hands.

She obliged without argument, desperate to get out. The room felt like a tomb. She would rinse the blood stains off once she was out of here. This had been a mistake. All of it had been a mistake. Ryshal was trying to be nice, but Syra should have known herself better. It was too far outside her level of comfort.

When she was done, she exhaled and stood. The maid followed after. "Thank you," Syra told her, and forced a smile. "I appreciate your time."

The woman reached forward and took her wrist with an iron grip. Her brown eyes were paralyzing with their intensity. "May all your dreams come true, Syra," Ryshal whispered, and nodded. The maid let go then, and stepped back before gesturing at the door. "Your future awaits you."

Syra opened her mouth to reply, but nothing came out, so she shut it. The words were probably harmless, but they made the hair on her arms stand on end. This was one of the strangest interactions she had ever had; the one with Raven felt like child's play next to this. She shook free the chills that coated her skin and simply nodded. Without another word, she reached down next to the bed, snatched up the boots, and walked out.

As she crossed the threshold of the door, she took a deep breath. The air felt lighter, free from the weight of whatever

Ryshal had conjured up in that room. Syra assured herself it wasn't sinister. It hadn't really felt that way, after all. Yes, there had been energy, but she knew what evil felt like, and that hadn't been it.

"Syra?" Zane called from downstairs. The sound of his voice was a relief.

"Yeah?" she yelled back.

"Just seeing where you're at. We're going to do a final run-down on the plan."

Syra exhaled. "Just give me a moment!"

Without further hesitation, she walked down the hall toward the washroom. The boots hung at her side, lost to her. She clung to the memory of the Soul Realm, unable to help but revisit the details. Things had felt similar, the details close, but not identical. Perhaps it was her mind contorting the small things. That was what she told herself, but not even she could convince herself entirely that it was the same vision.

Sekar terrified her. There was no denying that fact now.

When she reached the wash bowl and set the boots down, Syra saw that her hands were shaking. She couldn't let the others see this. And more importantly, she couldn't allow herself to submit to this fear. Closing her hands into fists, she took a deep breath over the basin.

Fear would not control her. It couldn't.

She just needed to convince herself of that.

COURAGEOUS
AND CRUEL

The cut had become a dull ache, only reminding Morei every so often that it was still there. Keeping the sleeve pressed against the palm of his hand, the king had gladly gotten out of that house and retrieved Sunny. As expected, the Shire had waited patiently for him, only moving once he saw Morei approaching. In quick succession, the king mounted and bolted for the palace, taking no time to pause or to let citizens pass.

Everything about this visit had been wrong. The city was haunting in a terrible way, and to make matters worse, the citizens were blaming him for their downfall. Morei couldn't outright blame them, but he was bitter about it. This wasn't what he had been raised to deal with, and he surely hadn't been raised to become the Demon King.

Skye's home made him shiver, even under the sun's brutal heat. The chill that had crept under his skin from the bizarre events had made itself at home, and even as he descended Sunny and handed his reins over to a staff member, the chill clung. He rubbed his neck, certain he could feel cold fingers tickling the skin, only to find it wasn't there. There was nothing there—only his growing paranoia.

His time was running out.

If he hadn't been certain before, he was now. The city was growing more and more hostile toward him. Even the dead didn't want him here.

Maybe that was for the better.

Smells of cooked meats wafted through the hall as he stepped into the palace. The sun was shut out, saving his skin from the direct touch, and he took a deep breath. He should have felt better in the halls of his home, but instead he felt even more isolated.

Morei rolled his shoulders and began to walk. He mustn't think this way, not now. There were far more important things that required his attention, and one of those was to find a cure for Cu'cel. It had to be out there, he knew it. Geral could not be the first city in all of Vorelian history to fall victim to such an illness.

But there was also the matter of what the ghostly woman had said. *Protect her.* The forcefulness of the request could not be ignored. Who was this woman? And whom was he supposed to protect? The thought made him scoff—Morei could hardly protect his own city.

Yet, he couldn't shake himself of this. He was not one to believe in signs from the divine—quite the opposite, actually—but neither was he foolish enough to ignore the obvious. The ghost was real. After all, she had tossed him like he weighed nothing more than a feather, a feat no normal man could accomplish.

He couldn't shake the idea that maybe the ghost was referencing to the only woman he could think of—Syra Castello. She was the one who had come into possession of the Demon Killer. There was no way to validate it, though, and despite his concerns, he couldn't bring this up to the council. They would laugh at him, thinking this was all part of a grand scheme to keep power. Simply put, they no longer trusted him, and anything he said would likely be met with trepidation.

He could not ignore it, though.

The council meeting from earlier felt leagues away as he strode through the palace, making his way closer to his study. There, he could pull from a handful of books he had on hand and then retrieve any more from his personal library in the upper level. He hoped to spend the rest of the day researching previous illnesses recorded in Vorelian history.

"Your Majesty!"

The voice made him cringe as he slowed to a halt. He didn't need to turn to know whom it belonged to. Kiren. The last person he wished to see right now when his thoughts were so scattered. A jealous man, he had concluded, desperate to have the queen for himself, but Morei had instead bed her, albeit in the heat of twisted desires. If Kiren wasn't so hung up on pleasing his queen in every possible way, Morei was certain the commander would have attempted to kill him by now. And that made him an enemy.

He waited until the very last moment before he was forced to face Junok's commander. The king nodded in greeting, noting the man's green tunic and freshly trimmed, dusty-blond hair. "Hello, Commander. Is there something needed of me? I am in a bit of a rush."

Kiren's hazelnut eyes dropped down, as if taking his attire in for the first time. "Going somewhere?"

"Just getting back." He forced a pleasant smile.

The commander nodded. "Ah, I understand. I heard it's quite dangerous to be walking around out in the main city due to all the deaths."

"If you're ignorant enough to believe Cu'cel spreads that simply," the king said, the smile still hovering. He was in no mood for these formal antics, and he knew Kiren had found him for a reason. No one ever wanted to just have a light conversation.

There was always an incentive, a hope, a dream, anything but an easy chat.

Kiren cleared his throat and crossed his arms. In an instant, the attempt at respect drained from the commander's face. "Understood. I suspect you're aware then of the rumors circling about you."

This would be good. "I am aware."

"Then I suspect you are also aware that my duty, as well as that of my men here, is to protect the queen." Kiren raised his chin, a challenge. "Do I need to explain myself?"

Morei's lips pulled upward in amusement. If he wanted, he could break this man's neck without lifting a finger. The energy that was his to control was always there, waiting, begging him to call upon it. While the bravery was commendable, it ended there, smothered by the distrust. It was evident from Kiren's body language and the threat between the words. He thought Morei was going to harm Emerald, whether intentionally or not.

If the commander wanted to be tough, Morei would gladly put him to test.

"Let me explain myself to you," the king whispered, holding his gaze. "I was raised with one purpose in mind, to protect and serve my people. No matter who steps into Geral, thief or not, they are my people, and I will do as I see fit for them." He took a step forward and dropped his voice into a threatening hiss. "Do you think I am responsible for the atrocities?"

The commander swallowed as a handful of heartbeats slipped by. "I think you're not what you say you are, King. The man I saw on the battlefield was bloodthirsty, merciless." Kiren inhaled, his nostrils flaring. "Men with that hunger never do good by the people because they want to, but because they have to." Barely audible, he finished, "So why are you trying so hard to mask the real you?"

Agitation flooded Morei's senses. He wanted nothing more than to put an end to Kiren's life, and to make sure it was done with methodical slowness. The tongue would go first, followed by a slash to his throat, so that he wouldn't be able to scream while the king peeled his nails off one by one.

Instead, Morei straightened and flashed one of those charming smiles that nobody but royalty could pull off. A smile of a thousand meanings. "Because the real me would scare even the Gods, Commander." The response made Kiren flounder for a moment, and the king took it as his chance to leave. "I must go, but your attempt at courage is well respected. I'll remember it, if ever we are meant to cross paths differently."

Brushing past him, he made his way down the hall, not looking back to see if the commander watched him go. If Kiren had more to say, he did not try, and it was best that way.

The only noise that met his ears was the pounding of his boots against the marble and the distant conversations of staff members, laughing and gossiping about one thing or another. For just this sliver of a moment, he enjoyed the sound. It resembled the normalcy of a time he once took for granted. The first season as king, he had been disoriented and mourning the death of his parents, but the peace had been there, a calmness that had been brought on by his father when he ruled. The citizens of Geral respected that man, and Morei had no doubt that the entire city would have died for him if given the chance.

But the king could not say the city would do the same for him. Truthfully, they were just waiting for an excuse to storm the palace and raise a blade against him.

If he could find a cure, a way to end Cu'cel and bring back peace, then maybe the citizens would accept it, despite the rumors that he was the prophesized Demon King or that he had struck a deal with the vile God Sekar. The people would finally see everything he was doing for them and give their thanks. This city stood because of him, and Morei would be damned if the people did not soon understand that.

It was only a hope, a fleeting one, so small he nearly lost it in the growing blackness of his thoughts, but he reached for it nonetheless. It was the embodiment of what humanity remained in him, and he would not lose it without a good fight.

If he failed, though—well, Morei did not want to consider the consequences.

SUMMONED

yrus yanked a boot on. It was morning, and he had slept horribly. Exhausted by the evening, drained of all reserves, he had stumbled back to bed and slept in his clothes. At least he'd been coherent enough to take his boots off before falling face first into the bed.

But Cyrus's dreams had been riddled with horrific tales, and he had awoken in a cold sweat.

The hooded man had been there, the same one from before, where he couldn't see his face. All around, destruction ensued. It was a terrible dream, one of blood, fire, and strange, black-eyed people. As Cyrus stood there, he saw his sword dripping in fresh crimson. Innocent people lay in every direction, slain by his hand. Above, screeches from some unseen beast echoed, and when he looked to the side, the hooded man was approaching. Try as he might, Cyrus couldn't see his face. A shadow covered his features, making them unreadable.

As the man grew closer, Cyrus's heart pounded against his chest. Fear turned his limbs cold as a strange sensation washed over him—a complete loss of control. Cyrus's body was no longer his, and as the man stopped before him, his knees buckled.

Then a gloved hand grabbed his hair and lurched his head back, but Cyrus didn't see the sky or the man. He suddenly found himself in an underground tavern. Stone surrounded him, and water ran freely through a canal to his left. Voices bounced off the walls, but Cyrus cringed as the voices pierced his skull, bombarding the sanctuary of his mind. He stepped forward, drawn that way though his legs were weak underneath him.

He traveled deeper into this bizarre chamber, the voices calling him to some unseen end. Sigils of the Old Tongue and fissures gouged the stone of its once-pristine condition. As he neared the end of the chamber, the voices hushed, and Cyrus found himself looking at an old oak door. Its frame was cracked, the metal rusted. At the sight of it, he felt confusion but familiarity—he knew this place, knew this door, but from where and why, he had no idea.

"Thank you."

Those words were the last thing he'd heard before being jolted from the dream in a cold sweat. Cyrus had no idea what time it was when he woke—the curtains were pulled over his windows to hide the night sky—but it didn't matter. Cyrus had lain awake for the rest of the night, unable to fall back to sleep after the dream. As tired as he was, the dream had unsettled him. It had felt too real. He could still feel the hand lace through his hair and rip his head back, his neck stiff.

He tossed and turned for hours, and when morning came, Cyrus reached out to Sozar. The dragon had slept in the courtyard, where the holds were. As the queen had told Cyrus, there would be Razan soldiers there throughout the night to ensure no unwanted guests arrived to pester the dragon while he slept. It hadn't been comforting to think Sozar was alone, but the dragon had reminded him that they were separated by only a couple of walls, not leagues of distance.

Last night had been the first night since their departure from Evander that they had slept apart. It felt weird, and as exhausted as he'd been, the separation had screwed with his sleep. Cyrus blamed the strange environment as well, and the idea that there were so many people. Whatever the reason, he hoped to sleep better tonight. His body still felt drained from the travels, and sore this morning too.

Cyrus looked over at his sack on the round table. The book was still in there, calling to him with a curious pull. Standing, he walked over and grabbed the bundle. The salty air of the sea had devoured the fabric and left the strings tattered. Pulling the strings loose, he peeked inside.

There it was. The strange *Book of Liral*. He hadn't understood why he had taken it, yet he'd felt the need to, just like with the sword. The energy that pulsed from it was rich. It was the only energy he could feel besides Sozar's without trying. It was simply there, never dwindling, like a beating heart. The Rider's Sword hummed, but ever since he had taken the weapon, the noise of its life force had ceased, though he knew it was there. If Cyrus had been better trained or stronger at energy harvesting, he could have tapped back into the power of the sword. His skill as a Dragon Rider was pitiful, and he felt ashamed of himself.

The book glared up at him from the confinements of the tattered fabric. Shoving the pity aside, Cyrus realized he could steal a few moments to take a peek at the pages. He had waited days for this, and now that he was alone and awake, he wanted to look.

Letting the sack drop to the table, Cyrus ran a thumb over the old leather of the book. The initials *HJ* that he had seen before were etched in the upper right corner, gouged with a knife. The pages were yellowed but for the most part intact. He flipped through, not entirely looking at the lines, until he saw bold black ink that stood out against the rest of the words. Turning back until he found it, he found the large words scrawled over the original writing. *Light Bringer.*

Sozar, he called to the dragon through their link, *does the name Light Bringer ring a bell to you?* It was a long shot, considering the dragon was not even a summer old, but sometimes he felt Sozar knew more than the oldest man.

The dragon grumbled. *No, although I'm sure it has something to do with ancient traditions. Perhaps the king may know.*

Cyrus stared at it, rereading the two words over and over, as if an answer would reveal itself if he stared long enough. Nothing revealed itself to him. He had no idea what that meant or who this *HJ* referred to. Maybe he was in possession of some lunatic's journal, someone who believed in fairies and shapeshifters, just like Evander. The thought made him chuckle.

Knocking broke the silence, and Cyrus yelped in surprise.

He closed the book and dropped it back into the sack. Then he tied the strings and stuffed it behind the pillows. The sword looked up at him, and he pursed his lips. Zorya had told him last night that he shouldn't wear a sword when walking the halls of the Razan palace—it showed he did not trust the soldiers or family. While he wanted to protect the Rider's Sword from unwanted attention, he also didn't like the idea of just leaving it here.

The knock came again, and he grimaced. "Coming!" With one final look, Cyrus shoved the pillows back in place, made sure it all looked natural, and turned.

He crossed the room, his boots echoing off the marble, and opened the door. Zorya stood there, dressed in fitted leather for fighting. Her ashy-blond hair was pulled back in a braid with loose strands falling around her face. On her hip was strapped a sword, with a beautifully designed hand guard that was both elegant and fierce.

Cyrus raised an eyebrow. "Going somewhere?"

"Usual morning routine," Zorya replied with a huff. "Some of us like to have an early start."

"Some of us haven't crossed the sea," Cyrus pointed out. "Last time I checked, you were cozied up in bed every night while I slept on tiny islands and ate dried meat."

Zorya crossed her arms with the faintest smirk. "Excuses, excuses."

He rolled his eyes. "Did you come here to berate me?"

"As fun as it is, I actually didn't. Father has requested to see you." The princess looked him up and down. "I see the staff found you fitted clothes. Do you like them?"

Cyrus looked down at his green button-up and black pants. The clothes were more relaxed than what he'd worn last night, but he still felt out of place in such nice attire. What unsettled him the most, though, and what he couldn't shake himself of, was how her observance of him made him feel. His thoughts swam with things he'd do to her. "They're nicer than anything I've ever owned."

"Hm." Zorya turned, heading right, her hips swaying deliberately. "We might not be so bad after all, the Razan family. Head left and down the hall. Then turn right. It should be self-explanatory from there."

Then she was gone around the corner.

Cyrus shook his head, smiling. Zorya was playful, too playful for her own good, and it was going to get him in trouble. The last thing he wanted was to disrespect the very king housing him because he couldn't keep his cool. With a deep breath, he shut the door.

Sozar chuckled in the depths of his mind. *I like her.*

Rolling his eyes, Cyrus headed down the hall, the sun's early shadows painting the wall from the windows to his left. *Yesterday in the courtyard. What did you say to her?*

I told her the truth, the dragon said. *Your life is now in her hands. If she fails you and something happens, she'll answer to me.*

Cyrus choked on his own breath, but he couldn't find a way to be angry at him. After everything they had been through, Sozar's response was justified. Although, that meant that in less than a day of being here, the princess of Razan had already been threatened twice. Cyrus wasn't thrilled about that, but he also didn't regret any of it. In these times, nobody was safe. He just wished she weren't so damn beautiful. An urge to turn around and run to Zorya filled him—going out and training with her sounded far more enticing than sitting in a stuffy room.

But the king had his answers. All this time, this was what he had been waiting for. By the afternoon, he could know his heritage, know everything. That idea made his breaths quicken and his heart skip a beat. This was it.

He picked up the pace.

THE HEART
OF THE WORLD

eath came in many forms, and Syra had come to accept that. Still, Zarek's steed was not something she had been prepared for. Uyul was solid black, with large red eyes and short horns that jutted out along her jaw; she was bony, but not in a skinny way, just how the strange horse like beast was built. Bones with sharp edges along the hips and shoulders protruded at a ghastly angle, and she stood as tall as a Shire.

What made Syra uncomfortable was how the Guardian's horse looked at everyone. At one point, Uyul had looked right at her, and it felt like she was meeting the eyes of another person, not a beast. It was as if Uyul understood everything going on around her. On several occasions, Zarek had mumbled something to the creature.

Roman had said his farewells and dismissed every staff member. When they asked questions, he told them that he wouldn't be coming back to this home ever again. Not even to this side of the country. He gave them the option to stay in the home if they so choose, but he advised that they leave Raveer territory and go seek living arrangements elsewhere.

When he had gotten on his steed, Roman had wiped his eyes and nodded. "This was my father's home—where I was raised."

"Then why part with it?" Zane asked.

"Because in order to change the future, I must first let the past die."

Nobody said more, and with a few nods, they'd set off on their travels.

Now, lanterns and torches were lit along the streets as Syra and the group passed by. Many villagers were retiring for the evening, but the few still out stole glances at the group. There was little they could do save for keep their hoods drawn up and their heads down. They kept distance between each other, hopeful this would keep anyone from recognizing them, and Zarek traveled on a different street altogether. His beast of a horse would draw enough attention as it was. The mutual decision was that the Guardian would meet up with them outside the village.

This was their best option. Leave now or be cornered. It was them against an army, and they had to move quickly. Soldiers would no doubt be on their way from the main city of Raveer. They had left the ship in shambles and with an Onye onboard, more than enough to alert authorities that their village, and the city, were under threat.

When they reached the outskirts of the village, it was dark. They reconvened with the Zarek and let Guardian take the lead, as he and Uyul had perfect night vision. The dirt road was well-traveled, the ground packed tight and the gravel minimal. For now, they would stay on the road since few people if any would be traveling overnight.

Above, the night sky was dotted with the brightest stars Syra had ever seen. They weren't threatened by any light from the ground. Here, on this road, they were scattered proudly. Even the faintest star was visible. The constellations were clear, and to the west, Syra noticed Eazon's Hammer. Directly above her, stars clustered together, staining this part of the sky purple and white.

It was the Heart of the World, or so the stories told. Syra had never seen the constellation before, not when she had been in

Caster or even traveling across the Merrél Sea. It only showed itself once in a season, and to see it, everything had to align perfectly.

Looking at the beautiful spectacle above her, Syra felt a wave of remorse fill her. Dryl would have loved this. The smallest piece of her knew Kar would too, despite his hideous actions. The story he had shared on Jared's porch felt like it had been lifetimes ago, but he had spoken with such beautiful appreciation of the world around him. Those times were chaotic, but they'd been much easier than now.

That thought turned her bitter, and she dropped her head, overwhelmed. Regret filled her, regret for where she was now, and that made her ashamed. She was alive, and she should be grateful. She was accompanied by people who had given up their lives for this adventure of hers, and yet she wanted nothing to do with it. All she wanted was to be back home, back to the coast and watching the sea. Syra wanted to reverse time, return to a simpler and dare she say duller world. Gone were the times when she used to complain about working on the port or when she used to gossip about the boys of Caster with her closet friend, Kaeyle.

"Syra."

The storm of thoughts dissipated at the sound of Zarek's voice. "Yeah?"

"Come here."

Zane and Roman didn't speak, remaining behind as she nudged Hazel forward until the petite horse was side by side with Uyul. Hazel flicked his ears but didn't appear uncomfortable to be next to the beast. She was certain she could feel Zane's eyes drilling into her from behind. He had unanswered questions, and he wouldn't remain quiet forever.

But that would have to wait. Now, she and Zarek were separated enough from the group that she could finally ask her burning questions—about the monsters he had mentioned only last night, and about her. Most importantly about her. She needed whatever answers he had.

"I'm sorry," he said finally, his voice low.

The apology caught her by surprise, and she swung her head toward him. "For what?"

"For all of it." Zarek looked at her, and under the night sky, his pale blue skin and red eyes were illuminated in a ghostly fashion. "You've had to navigate all of this extremely fast and without clear guidance. In the spiraling order of the Soul Realm, there was failure in preparing you properly."

Syra swallowed down her apprehension. "I don't understand."

"This story about your involvement with the Soul Realm was given to us by a Soothsayer. They are long gone these days, having been few to begin with. They died out with time." Syra refrained from asking questions about Soothsayers. She had no idea what the Guardian was referring to, and there was too much else to know.

Zarek gave her a quick glance and smirked. "Soothsayers are messengers of the Gods. They were able to see into the future and identify patterns of history and the present that would impact the future. There is cause and effect for everything—energies that shift and evolve as fate dictates our reality. My cause for telling you this will create an effect unique to this path, and if I hadn't told you, a separate path would have been created from the effect of that action. Soothsayers could see all of this. Do you understand?"

Syra nodded.

"We were given information about you by a Soothsayer nearly five centuries ago. You can imagine how then, when our realm was alive and beautiful, we didn't quite understand the impact of her words. But we also thought highly of Soothsayers. So we listened, and we documented what she said."

Zarek leaned forward on Uyul and looked up at the Heart of the World. "The Soothsayer explained that if we didn't act when you were born, we would set our path for devastation. It would create a cause and effect that would bring only mayhem and intertwine with another dark prophecy—that of the Demon King, whom you know as Morei Geral. This was so long ago, Syra, that it sounds foreign on my tongue speaking about it."

Zarek looked down at her now. "Our realm is dying, but in it, an evil has been born that is likely incurable, and in time will infect the living too. Monsters rule the dead now, not us. We failed ourselves, and as a result, we have failed to prepare for the destruction ahead of us."

Syra stared, waiting. When he didn't continue, she licked her lips and stole the silence to ask a question. "What was supposed to happen?"

He smiled, but it was sad. "We were supposed to bring you back and help you prepare to take the throne of the Soul Realm." The statement tore the air from her lungs. "But the queen, Shevana, despised the idea."

"Why me?" Her voice came out barely above a whisper. Syra was certain he hadn't heard it and was preparing to repeat the question when he spoke.

"Syra," he mumbled. "What I'm about to tell you will scare you but please, be patient. The mistakes of the past must be corrected, and it starts with you. Do you understand?"

Numbly, she nodded.

"Shevana had a sister," he quietly explained. "She was born when Shevana was twelve. It was a fluke, and unexpected, but nonetheless she was welcomed. Time went on, and when Shevana took the throne, her younger sister, Nala, grew tired of the Soul Realm. This was especially true when the realm began to lose its beauty. Nala wanted to leave, to explore, and with nothing holding her in the Soul Realm, she did so. We thought she would come back when she grew tired of exploring the living world, but she never returned. We were ordered not to search for her."

Zarek shrugged. "Centuries passed, and Nala became a memory, until six summers ago, when her soul wandered into my line of sight one evening in the Soul Realm. She was as beautiful as the day she left, as if time had stopped itself." He smiled and looked down, and Syra was certain she saw a single tear fall. "I guided her to the Afterlife that night. Nala told me she had been poisoned by Shevana, but I couldn't hear it—I didn't for the longest time. But she told me so much more." He met her eyes. "You are the daughter of Nala, Syra. Blood touched with the damned and destined to rule the Soul Realm."

Words died on Syra's lips and instantly, her world ceased in a heartbeat.

"I don't expect you to understand. Not now," Zarek rushed to say. "And when you are ready, I can answer questions to the best of my abilities. I didn't know as much as Dryl did, but I can try."

Syra swallowed bile. "Dryl knew?"

"Yes," Zarek admitted, looking at her now. "He knew and tried to tell me because he wanted to protect you from Shevana, but I wouldn't hear it. I didn't believe Shevana would kill the only family she had left, and I certainly didn't think she was cruel enough to kill her sister."

Syra grasped the reins as tight as she could, steadying herself. Her head spun. None of this made sense. Her mother had aged like anyone else, like a mortal, not as a member of the Soul Realm. She blinked back a sudden wave of grief as she relived those last few days—she had her mother had been so sick and weak. But her name had not been Nala. Her mother's name had been Rose.

She reeled. That name felt foreign in her thoughts, as if it knew it didn't belong. Her mother had been Nala—everything about it clicked in her, as if her soul understood better than she did or ever dared too.

And for Dryl to know . . . it felt like betrayal that he hadn't told her. She was growing real tired of people knowing things about her that she was unaware of.

Syra had no idea what to say. She sat there, eyes forward, as a war raged inside her, tearing apart the very fabrics of her reality. Anger boiled, denial turned her limbs cold, and confusion drowned her thoughts into nothingness. It felt unreal, all of it.

Syra took a shallow breath, unsure of how to move on from this information when she wasn't even ready to process it. So, she didn't. "Dryl had the last book of the Soul Realm." The statement gave her thoughts an outlet from the storm inside her. It was the only thing she knew to say.

Zarek leaned so far over that he clamped a hand on her shoulder. "What?"

"He said it had some of the oldest information known," Syra whispered, acutely aware that Zane and Roman were probably staring at the scene unraveling in front of them. Zarek must have sensed the same, because he let his hand fall to his side. "He took it when Shevana burned the records of everything. Dryl had been trying to take it somewhere when he was"—she swallowed the guilt down—"when he was killed." Her voice was hoarse. "The book was gone when I found him. I think it was taken."

Zarek swore under his breath. "Leave it to Dryl to get his hands on something not even I could touch. He didn't say anything else about it?"

Syra tried to recall, then shook her head. "No."

"Then I can't say for sure what book it was," he confessed. "But I assume it was probably the *Leangé*." Before Syra could ask, he added, "It is the oldest book ever known. There is information in there that I dare say predates even the Guardians of Death. I never got the chance to look at its contents—it was prohibited by Shevana for anyone to access that book. But I did see it." Zarek shook his head. "The *Leangé* was guarded by vile creatures. Winged beasts with fangs and horns—they are the Einhër, souls that are damned to pass into the Afterlife and must pay their debts through servitude."

"By the Gods," Syra mumbled, staring at the Guardian, eyes wide.

"It's a cruel world for even the sick," Zarek commented dryly, and then exhaled. "I am at a lost, Syra. Really. This information scares me."

She raised an eyebrow.

"This information stays between us. Okay?" he added. "I trust the other two, but what we are dealing with could unravel their reality. This is the kind of information only the Gods know."

Syra opened her mouth to speak and then closed it. She wanted to ask more questions, demand answers, but their time was up. She could sense it as one would sense an approaching storm. "You have my word."

"Good." Zarek took a deep breath and rolled his shoulders. "It's going to be a long night, I think. We'll keep our eyes on the horizon." He pointed just to her right. "That is where we will see soldiers. Shy of dawn, we'll cut off the main path and head north toward the meadows and camp there. Sound good?"

"Yes."

Zarek nodded and fell silent, his eyes ahead. She let her own eyes wander, unable to keep them off the Heart of the World. It was beautiful in a way that made her feel so small. If she closed her eyes and pinched herself, maybe she would wake up and this would all be just a dream.

Her world was gone, the life she knew charred and left in ash. A part of her had always hoped that she could run and find freedom in the shadows of the world where no one would find her. But tonight, that small hope died with Zarek's words. No matter how hard she tried, Syra was destined to belong to the dead.

The Soul Speaker's words danced across her mind, now making more sense. Raven had believed her blood was royal, and Syra had shaken it off as irrelevant—it had felt like the right thing to do. Now, she wasn't so sure. If she had brought the fortune telling up, perhaps Kar or Dryl may have confessed the knowledge that Zarek now shared with her.

Syra swallowed the growing dread in the back of her throat.

It was becoming increasingly clear that losing the Demon Killer and running had been a fatal mistake for not only her, but the world.

A COLD EMBRACE

Morei closed the book and slid it out of his way to the growing pile beside him. They were all determined to be of no help. He reached over and grabbed the goblet of Kendell's Milk that he had been slowly drinking through his research. When he found it nearly empty, he poured another full glass from the decanter to his right, which was now half gone. His high tolerance made it impossible to numb the voice. All it did was remind of how different he was from the people he was supposed to protect. The memories of the dreaded night—the night his entire life had changed for the worse—flashed across his mind, as if to mock him.

Wincing, he set the goblet down and took a deep breath. He hated that night.

The day's events had caught up with him, which only soured his mood. In so many words, he had been requested to identify a new heir to the throne in a day's time. His lineage was being sacrificed for a new ruler the people could trust. Nobody cared about the rich bloodline of Geral rulers anymore. They wanted peace, and that meant forfeiting traditions that had kept this city standing for centuries.

Nobody could just take the throne. Morei had spent his entire life preparing to rule. Every day, every moment, was a lesson to make him a proper king. A stranger with no experience would surely fail the citizens, but if he remained a king without the title, transferring it over to the new ruler to appease Caster's threats, then maybe the city had a chance.

A fire danced to his right, the flames a rich orange, snapping with delight as they engulfed the wood. Frankly, it was too hot for a fire, but the flames had brought him some level of comfort. He didn't feel the heat, only the energy, and it caressed his skin with a cold touch. It hummed with a song only he could hear.

The song of a thousand voices. Voices of the damned, of the forgotten, of the unforgiven.

His thoughts lingered there, listening to the song that he had come to know as Dark Energy. Unable to help himself, he caved. As dangerous as the melody was, he couldn't ignore how hauntingly it captivated him. If he listened closely enough, he could almost make out what the voices were trying to convey.

The king shook his head and reached for the next book, dragging it closer. The sound did little to distract him from the fire's song, even as he opened the cover and read the title: *Herbs and Ancient Practices of the Vorelians.*

He couldn't shake the thought that was growing in the back of his head. That if he could master the Dark Energy element of fire, then he could master more. And if he mastered more, he would be unstoppable. Nobody could or would dare to challenge him. An empire in his hands.

He dragged his eyes over to the flames, their whispers growing louder. Morei stared, captivated. An entire world within those flames that could be his to control. He had manipulated it, become a conduit, but he was unsure if he could claim to have truly mastered Dark Energy.

The flames cracked as if in excitement—no, they *responded.* He could feel it in his bones as one would feel fear, grief, or love. An instinctive sense of Dark Energy was living, listening, and it knew what he was thinking.

This was true power before him. Raw, untamed, and untouched. Uncontrollable.

The voices grew deafening in his mind, blocking out everything else. The king listened, certain he could now hear what they had finally wished to say all this time. "Chaos," "freedom," and "relinquish" were just a few words that jumped out at him. The more he listened, the more at peace he felt—no, relieved. Deep within him the heat of the power grew, starved, ready to consume him. It stormed his limbs and grabbed at his fraying control, and he gave in, curiosity dragging him under.

His entire body shuddered just as a wind howled in his head, so loud that he cringed. It was the howl of the dead. Morei's head grew heavy, and his vision blurred. Tingling started in his fingers and feet, crawling up his limbs as the heat was sucked from his body and a chill replaced it.

The voices stopped just as his entire being was enveloped in a frigid grasp.

Morei felt Death's embrace rush over his consciousness like an old friend, fretting over his decisions since he had last seen her and shushing him as he tried to speak. It was the peace she brought that gave his soul a chance to rest, if only for a moment, from the demons that were tearing it apart.

Then she pulled away, abandoning him, and the voices bombarded him with frustration and rage. His own fury blossomed immediately in a hiss between his teeth, and he cursed and extinguished the flames with a single command of his hand. The voices couldn't even give him the peace he so desperately wanted.

Smoke rose in place of the flames, the charred logs unfinished by the fire, their wood blackened like the thoughts that stirred in his mind. They were cold and horrific, built from the pain of yesterday and alive for the torment of tomorrow.

Morei lowered his gaze to his hands. The black veins stared back at him, mocking. The demons were both his salvation and damnation. The king was alive today because of them, but they would also be why he crumbled.

He stared back at the books. There was no answer that would resolve what was happening to Geral in there, no herb or practice to alleviate the malevolence of this disease. That much he knew. Every book thus far about diseases didn't mention symptoms like the rotting black spots on the victim's flesh or the madness that took them. Cu'cel came from a sinister force, not something natural. There weren't cures for darkness, only ways to minimize the torment. There was no fix for the wicked.

A knock ripped him back into his surroundings. Morei glanced at the door, having forgot about its existence entirely. He stared, caught between his tragedies and the understanding that he needed to address whoever was there. Again, he found himself alone and at the mercy of his demons, lost in their world and falling from his.

He cleared his throat and repositioned himself in his chair before grabbing the goblet of Kendell's Milk. "Come in!" he called, and took a massive drink. It was tasteless.

The door cracked, hesitated for a moment, and then opened all the way. Ezra stepped through, his amber eyes lowered, so that Morei couldn't see the face of his emotions. Dressed in green, he looked like a prince in the making in all but the name—a prince, he realized, that the people of Geral might be able to grow to respect as their king.

"Ezra," the king acknowledged as the man lingered behind the chair. The air had tensed to his arrival, permeated by the fury that seeped out of the Energy Harvester's skin. The king could almost taste the emotion on his tongue. This was not going to be a pleasant conversation. "Can I help you?"

Chest rising and falling, Ezra looked at Morei, giving him a glimpse into his troubled soul. "I was hoping we could talk, if you're not busy."

The king forced a smile. "Not at all. I'm glad you've arrived. Please, sit." He motioned at the seat and then at the half-empty decanter. "Do you want a drink?"

"Um, no," the young man replied as he took his place. "I won't be long."

"Are you sure?" Morei pressed, raising an eyebrow as he lifted the goblet to his lips. "You are troubled, that much I can tell."

Ezra seemed surprised. "You can?"

The corners of Morei's lips twitched. "You couldn't fool a blind horse if you tried." Lowering the drink, he rested a hand over his forearm on the desk. "Your eyes tell me more than I think you expect too. You're angry, so spit it." The last words came out cold and abrasive, a reflection of his deteriorating mood.

Ezra stared at him, his gaze hardening as his anxiousness melted away and resolve replaced it. "Julian and Hank are dead because of you."

"Don't forget Yaz," Morei chimed in darkly, and took another swig.

"Do you have no guilt?" Ezra challenged. "They burned alive, all because of you and your little trick. You can tell everyone that you don't remember anything, but I don't believe it. You knew what you were doing. Damn the consequences so long as you can save yourself, hm?"

The demons inside him stirred with aggravation, feeding into his temper. The urge flared—the compulsion to draw blood, to control the situation. "You think I lied about that?"

He gritted his teeth. "Yes."

Betrayal coated his next words. "After what you saw with Yaz, you have the nerve to think I intentionally killed my men?" The king knew what he would say, but he needed to hear it verbally.

"I do." The words came out in a sneer. "The big hero of the day."

Morei inhaled, trying to keep his emotions restrained. He needed to be mature, collected, and balanced, not a volatile king who gave in to his compulsions when things got tough. "And do you think my last ten days were a hoax? You think I made that up?"

Instead of responding, Ezra's eyes flashed down to Morei's demon-touched hands. The king rolled up his sleeves to bare more skin that had since been consumed by the curse. Black veins traced up his forearms, disappearing under the fabric of his shirt. "You think this is a fucking joke, Ezra? You want to see the rest of it?" He pulled down the collar of his shirt on the left side, exposing more. "You think I've asked for this? You want to know what I did those ten days?"

When the Energy Harvester didn't reply, Morei continued, voice raw. "I wanted to die. I wanted nothing more than to die. The torment . . . the voices. The power wanted to consume me, and I nearly let it, but the demons wouldn't let me go. How do you think that feels, Ezra? To have your soul torn apart and at the mercy of those damn monsters? It changes you. Every piece of me has changed because of what happened. Do you think I wanted that?"

The apple in Ezra's throat rose and fell. "No," he managed to say, voice strained.

"I didn't," the king confirmed, thinking about what Kiren had said earlier. "And the last thing I need is to have people like you question what is happening to me, as if I have a choice. Do not make me out to be the monster here, Ezra. I will not tolerate it."

"Then what happened, Morei?" The question was spoken in a hiss, as if Ezra still didn't believe him. "Forty of our men burned to death because of that stunt you pulled, including two Energy Harvesters. I think an explanation is warranted."

Morei felt a chuckle bubble up between his lips. Already, the man across from him spoke like royalty, desperate to protect the very people who had also shunned him because of his gift so recently. "I already said, I don't remember. What more do you want?"

Ezra leaned forward. "I want the truth. Is that so hard to ask for from you? So keen on being honest, yet you can't even stand by your own words."

The insult burned, but Morei didn't show it. "I was surrounded." The memory danced behind his eyes as clear as if it had just happened yesterday. He could still smell the dirt and blood mixing on the ground and the growing thunderstorm that would wash the mark of man away from the soil. Sweat permeated the air. "I had an episode right there, just when I needed to fight. I could feel my control waning, and the next thing I knew, there was a blade against my cheek. I knew then that if something wasn't done, Geral would fall. This was it."

He trailed off, trying to recall what happened next, but he couldn't. Getting the rest of the memory was like trying to pull teeth. "Everything went blank after that. The only thing I remember after that blade touched my cheek is waking up yesterday and feeling the sun on my face. Everything between that is blank, besides the nightmares."

Morei slid the goblet closer to him, eyes dropping to the little that remained of Kendell's Milk. "Does that suffice to answer your question, Ezra? Or do you want me to lie about it and tell you I remember that day like the back of my hand so that you can find some peace in the men you slayed?"

The question caught the man across from him off guard, exactly as the king had intended. Words tumbled from the Energy Harvester's tongue without direction. "What? No, I mean. It was necessary to do what we did." Ezra rubbed his hands together and took a deep breath, clearly uncomfortable. "Don't turn this on me."

Downing the rest of the drink, Morei was still not satiated. He reached over and poured more into his goblet, now having nearly drunk the entire thing. The third glass would hopefully shut the damn voices up.

Ezra watched but didn't speak, and an intentional silence fell over them. Morei looked over at the dead firepit, now wishing for the fire's return, but calling upon Dark Energy in front of Ezra would likely trigger another argument. The man was haunted by the murders he had committed on that field, and based on the dark circles under his eyes, he had likely lost sleep over it. Throwing insult at the king was just Ezra's outlet.

When he finally spoke, Morei let his words trickle out at a snail's pace, making sure each one was heard. "It's alright to feel guilt and shame for your actions that day, Ezra. It means you have a conscience, but do not let it devour you. There is nothing else you could have done that day. The men that fell were destined to fall. You were merely a conduit to fate's ploy."

He could see that Ezra was struggling to keep himself together. The man was broken, which surprised Morei more than anything. Ezra had killed his father to protect his mother, and he bore no shame about that. Yet he went to battle and struck down soldiers attacking his homeland, and he was tormented. Again, the thought that the man before him could pass for a prince presented itself. He looked down at his full glass of Kendell's Milk, not wanting to share when it could grant him his silence but knowing Ezra might need it.

With a sigh, he slid the glass over to Ezra, deciding he'd get more later. "Drink," he ordered.

Ezra looked at the goblet, his jaw moving as he fought back what could likely be tears and grabbed it. He took a large swig and inhaled sharply at the bite of the drink before setting it down and slumping back in his chair. His amber eyes were glossy.

A pang of remorse filled Morei, but as quickly as it arrived, it was gone.

His heart could not bear the burden of the deaths of those men. There was simply too much it already had to deal with. More than anything, he felt bad that Ezra was so torn over this when in reality, thousands more would die for an inevitable war. Why fret over the past when so much was still to happen?

Morei couldn't say this. Before him was a man with morals and a heart, and he knew he had to be sensitive about it. There was a time when he too used to feel the same, before the murder of his parents had suffocated that part of him.

"My father had a choice," Ezra whispered. "Those men didn't."

Morei nodded and took a drink from the goblet, letting Ezra mull over his thoughts out loud.

"Those men I killed . . . every single one of them was afraid. They were brave—they fought—but none of them wanted to die." The Energy Harvester looked down, picking at the hem of his sleeve. "I took their lives because I was ordered to, not because I wanted to."

"You did the right thing," Morei acknowledged.

"For who?" Ezra looked back up, meeting him in the eyes. "For the city? For you? For your bloodline? Because it wasn't for me. I would have laid my sword down if I had been given the choice."

"Why didn't you?"

He snorted. "Because then I would have been hung, and that is no way to go."

The answer sat between them like ice, chilling the room to a deathly cold. Morei swallowed. Ezra was right. Any soldier who refused to fight was punished accordingly. It was barbaric and part of the old laws from when war was more prominent, but nonetheless, it was still enforced.

"What if you could change the law?" Morei countered. "What if you had the power to be an influence on the city and help legislation? Would you do it?"

Ezra raised an eyebrow. "What are you getting at?"

"Geral. Ezra Geral," Morei said, letting the words sink in. It had been somewhere in his mind ever since meeting Ezra, knowing he was without a name, a family, and a lineage after the death of his father. The king had been tasked to find an heir to the throne, and he was now more certain than ever before that the right ruler sat across from him. Ezra was cunning and clever, and based on his behavior here, he had heart, which was hard to come by these days. It felt more appropriate than ever before to induct Ezra into the family. He would be a brother, a trusted ally, and could help secure the bloodline further.

"I don't . . ." Ezra shook his head. "Why?"

"Because you've proven yourself, Ezra. There is no namesake you leave behind. You would have a lot of say over how things run, including the treatment of Energy Harvesters, as we discussed a fortnight ago. You would have power over how things were ran, and could see fit to do what you want, so long as it is reasonable and agreed upon by the majority of the council. And I think, most important to you," Morei added, "your mother would have a place here and could live in peace."

The fight died in Ezra's eyes. He stared at Morei as if lost. "How can you even trust me?"

"I don't," Morei answered honestly. "But I trust the man you are, and that makes you a strong addition to the Geral family." Leaning back, he crossed his arms and took a deep breath. He was dreading saying the next part out loud. "The council wants to replace me, and I could sit here and tell you a hundred different things about why I'd ask you to join the family, but the truth is that Caster has threatened to cease all imports and exports if I remain with my title. A new king is to be appointed by me, but I will continue to make decisions from behind closed doors." With a shrug, he finished, "You are the only person I believe can hold the Geral name and title with honor."

In time, Morei could learn to trust Ezra, but until then, he would have to go off his instinctive belief that the man before him had an honorable heart and a keen eye for politics.

"Your city is falling apart, and you ask me to join the family," Ezra voiced aloud. "I'm not sure if I should be insulted or honored."

A snicker escaped between the king's lips. "You may find purpose in it. All I ask is that you think it over. A lot happens when you are brought under a royal family—legalities, politics, duties, and the ceremony. You have to be certain this is what you want."

"The ceremony?"

"Well, yeah," Morei replied, and slid the goblet back to Ezra, who took it without hesitation. "You think you can sneak into the namesake without a special party? That doesn't fly by Geral standards. It will do the staff and council good to enjoy themselves a little."

Ezra took a swig, downing the rest of the drink. When he set it down, his amber eyes flashed with a spark of excitement, but he gave nothing away when he spoke. "I can't decide yet. I have to speak to my mother and ensure this is what she wants."

Morei nodded in acknowledgment. "Fair enough. Take all the time you need." If he still had his mother, he would have done the same thing. Mothers were staples in families. Nothing passed their ears or eyes, and anyone with the right mind knew that. It was considered a direct insult to make any major decision without the mother's consent. That was Sorréleian culture.

Ezra stood with a sigh. "I need to go." He turned and walked to the door but paused just as he laid his palm on the handle. He glanced back at Morei, and a heartbeat passed between them. A shared understanding. Something had clicked. A bond—even if it was miniscule, it was still there. "Thank you," Ezra said with the faintest of nods. Those two words held more meaning in them than he would likely ever admit, but he didn't have to.

The king only nodded in return. There were no need for words. Ezra had already decided on what he wanted, but his respect for his mother far outweighed what he chose. By tomorrow, he would likely have an answer, and until then, Morei would wait.

It was a gamble, he knew, given the state of the city, the strange plague, and the rumors circling about his involvement with Sekar and being the Demon King, but hopefully Ezra's mother was smart enough to know this was the only chance to saving their family. To be inducted into a royal family was the highest distinction a citizen could ever be given—and not just as a member, but the future king? This was as honorable as it got. Once the documents were signed, Ezra would be considered a full-fledged Geral, and treated as such too. His blood would be considered Geral property and strong enough to carry the Geral name.

Morei sat there, letting a thought bloom in his mind. What he had given the man was a chance to a new life and recognition. Ezra had only ever wanted recognition, and he finally had it. In Ezra's eyes, he was finally seen with potential and as an equal to the rest of the world.

That was their shared understanding. In that moment, they had both realized just how similar they were and how the world both saw them. While it was in varying degrees, they had both been ostracized from the world they were born into because of their nature. The Energy Harvester had understood such a revelation today, that much Morei knew. They might never speak of it, but they didn't have to.

The king glanced back at the firepit as a wave of anguish filled him. They might be extremely similar in that sense, but Morei did not wish his reality on anyone else but himself. In that sense, they would remain different. It would destroy Morei if he had to watch anyone else succumb to the same cruel fate that had been handed to him. In truth, he had no idea how anyone could live on as he did, with the daily torment. Morei was strong, but he wasn't sure how strong he could remain.

Only time would tell.

A SECRET FIT
FOR A RIDER

"I'd let that tea settle a bit," Kyllian said as he arranged himself in the chair across from Cyrus. They were in the king's study. "The ladies know I like the drink hot, but it's usually too hot for anyone else." He flashed an apologetic smile before grabbing his cup and lifting it to his lips, taking a small sip. "Perfect."

Cyrus glanced down at the cup before him. The steam was thick, wafting up to his nose. It was cinnamon black tea, and if Cyrus wasn't so nervous with what he was about to do he'd have been more inclined to try it, but his stomach lurched with anticipation. "Thanks."

The king nodded and took another sip.

Cyrus inhaled to steady himself. He knew what he needed to do—what he had come here for, what was keeping him. He licked his lips.

"Did you sleep well?" the king asked, his tone light.

Cyrus cleared his throat. "Yes." When Kyllian didn't say more, he said, "I want to thank you for your generosity. Last night was incredible." From the depths of their bond, Cyrus could hear the dragon snort. If Zorya had been here, she would have laughed too. If he never was a part of a fancy royal dinner

174

ever again, he would be a happy man, but he couldn't tell the king that.

The man nodded. "It was necessary, Rider of the Sea. You are a miracle to the people and will be celebrated as such."

This was his chance. "When I was in the Releuthian Mountains . . ." Cyrus took another deep breath and rubbed his hands together underneath the desk. "The man who rescued me, Evander"—again, Kyllian didn't flinch—"I was snooping through his study. I know it was wrong, but I couldn't help myself," he added. "But I found some letters. Letters from you." Cyrus watched Kyllian stiffen. "Were you two brothers?"

The king set the cup down and tapped a pointer finger on the desk. His expression was stoic and unreadable, but Cyrus didn't take his eyes off him. The sound of his heart pounded into his eardrums. It had been a bold way to start the conversation, but he also wanted to test the king. If he was an honest man, it would show.

Based on the satisfaction he felt from Sozar, he knew the dragon approved. They could not afford to beat around the bush for the sake of manners and royal code. If the king didn't have answers, then it was time to move on. But if he did, then it was time to get them.

When Kyllian finally spoke, his voice was soft and his eyes were distant. He was lost in some memory. "I guess I should say I'm not surprised Evander kept those letters," he began. "Evander is . . . sick. I thought when he left, he would get better, but as you probably realized in those letters, he quickly deteriorated. I loved him for as long as I could, Cyrus. You must understand that, but—" Kyllian looked at him fully now, and his tone hardened. "That's not what interests you, does it?"

At that, Cyrus felt his breath catch in the back of his throat. Either the king did not wish to speak of his brother, or he was not in the mood to play games. Regardless, the less they spoke of Evander, the better. The more they brought him up, the more risk there was that Cyrus would divulge the truth, and he didn't want the king to see him as a murderer.

Or maybe Cyrus was a coward. Maybe he wasn't strong enough for this world or for the horrors that awaited him. Perhaps he was better off in the mountains somewhere, where he wouldn't ever be forced to take another life with his hands.

"I, um," Cyrus said, yanking himself from the depths of his thoughts before he could drown in them. "There was a letter. One about Dragon Riders and their silver eyes. You said you had records from the Rider Federation that showed first born children had the silver eyes." He stopped there, hoping he didn't have to explain himself.

"Ah," Kyllian replied with a half smile. "I think your interest is validated, given your circumstances." Cyrus felt a wave of relief wash over him. "We have patiently waited for centuries as a family, a city, a country, for the presence of a Dragon Rider but were left with no indication any still existed. You are the first we have known in nearly eight centuries, or so the records say." The king bared his hands. "Your silver eyes indicate you had Rider parents by history's standards, but who or where or why ... I'm sorry, Cyrus, I have no idea."

He hadn't expected Kyllian to know his family, but hearing the words still hurt. Deep down, Cyrus had wanted to be wrong. Adjusting himself in the seat, he cleared his throat. "The records that you have. Are they detailed?"

"I'm afraid not," the king replied, his voice soft. "I can show them to you though, if you would like?"

Cyrus nodded. "Please."

The man stood gracefully and walked over to his overfilled bookcase. Without hesitation, he shoved some books aside to reveal a pile of rolled parchments, yellowed and cracked. Carefully, he pulled two rolls out and walked back over to the desk, where he sat and exhaled. "These are some of the remaining records of the Rider Federation. Almost everything was burned when Aythen destroyed it in her rage."

Cyrus lifted an eyebrow. "The stories about the dragon destroying the Rider Federation are real?" He had always considered them works of fiction—it had seemed preposterous that a dragon of all creatures would destroy the federation. The stories of Aythen had been shared over drinks between miners on late nights. They were always followed by laughs and rumors. Some had even mentioned that the Rider Federation was all a hoax, the greatest fiction ever told. Cyrus never believed that part, but he hadn't been keen to believe a dragon would destroy the only home it had ever known.

"Oh yes." Kyllian untied a weathered leather string from the parchment. "Aythen and her rider, Vikter, were among the last of the federation. When Vikter was killed in a political dispute, Aythen went mad with rage—they had been bonded for nearly two centuries. She flew to the Rider Federation, blaming the crumbling politics, and toppled the palace. With it, the city fell. There was no one that was willing to take the place of their fallen leaders because to do so would be fatal against a dragon. It is a ghost town now. You didn't know that?"

"I don't understand." Cyrus leaned forward and ignored the question. "The Rider Federation wasn't led by Riders?"

"In its early days, it was. There was a council of Riders—they were the rulers of the federation, hence the city's name. But as power grew and minds became warped, Riders became fewer as the numbers dwindled. Their family members took their place in the council to fill the void. The city was crumbling for decades prior to Aythen's destruction." Kyllian rolled out the parchment, the paper crying out in protest. "Does that story align with what you've heard?"

Cyrus nodded. "Yes, just more detailed." He scooched forward in his chair and laid a hand down on the desk, wanting to get a better look at the document. Not wanting to risk damaging the historical parchment, he moved the cup of tea to the right. "So, this is a family tree, but . . . the names?"

"Are scorched," Kyllian finished with dissatisfaction. "I know. Frustrating, isn't it?"

Before him, the yellowed parchment was blackened where the names of Rider families should have been, as if someone were hiding something or didn't want their names to be known. Branches stretched away to varying parts of the paper, some with a sigil drawn over. Studying it more, Cyrus realized there was a pattern to these sigils. They were signifying families who had children—the one who would carry the Rider name. But with the names scorched, all he could see was the branch lines and sigils, nothing more.

"Wow," he whispered, touching the edge of the parchment. He was afraid he would ruin it if he pressed too hard, so he quickly retreated his hand and looked at Kyllian. "Who would damage the document?"

The king shook his head. "Someone who wanted nothing more than to watch the Rider Federation burn," he breathed, and grabbed the other rolled parchment. "This one is an old letter. For the life of me, I've never been able to figure out what it means. It's clearly written by someone inside the federation— perhaps a councilmember before the destruction." He undid the leather tie and laid the parchment out slowly before he slid it over to Cyrus. "My guess is that it was written before the fall. The parchment is older and far more damaged than the family tree. Just look at the edges."

And Cyrus did so, carefully laying several fingers along the base of the letter. The edges were so dried that pieces of parchment had actually broken off. "You should protect this more," he whispered as he looked over the short letter. The ink was so faded that he had to scrunch his eyes to make out the words.

"I should," Kyllian agreed, but he didn't say more, and Cyrus didn't press.

There were a handful of words he couldn't make out, where time had taken the ink and dissolved it into nothingness, but Cyrus read the letter as best as he could.

Strange that I must be writing this but here I am. It feels fitting really, given the lies you've fed me. Dark, cold, and . . . that is where you'll find it. Ha! But it doesn't matter anymore, does it? After all you've done . . . The end has already begun, don't you see? The . . . have infested the minds of everyone . . . You won't even know until it's too late. Ah, I am enjoying this much more than I thought I would . . . look on your face when it—

Cyrus looked up to Kyllian. "This is it?"

"Yes." The king shrugged and began to wrap up both pieces of parchment. "It just ends."

"Like the writer was interrupted," Cyrus whispered, and leaned back. "But if they were, why would the letter still be in the Rider Federation? If something happened, then why hold on to it?"

"Exactly my question." The king nodded. "I believe it may have been written during the last days of the Rider Federation, before Vikter was killed." With delicate fingers, he picked up the parchment rolls and walked them back to the library. Cyrus watched, and as he laid the rolls back in their spot, he noted several other scrolls that looked just as aged tucked in the back.

"What are those?" Cyrus asked. The parchment looked to be in the same condition as the ones Kyllian had grabbed.

The king glanced back his way and gestured at the other rolls. "Those? Those are Razan documents. Royal family lines and such, nothing extraordinary." Without waiting for another question, he walked back over and took a seat, grabbing the tea.

"Some of Razan's documents are so old that they're too weak to be hung or messed with by curious hands. The oils of our touch damage parchment that old, so I figured it would be best to keep them here, where only I could see them when absolutely necessary."

Cyrus nodded, although he had his doubts about the king's honesty. The letters that he had read in Evander's home had made the king sound like he had quite a bit of information on the Rider Federation and the Dragon Riders in general. While he wanted to believe Kyllian was being truthful, he couldn't. The king was withholding information. Intuition told him so, but he couldn't outright call the man out for that. If he was keeping information from Cyrus, there was a good reason.

"Help me understand." Cyrus shook his head. "All this happens here, in Eiyrằl, and yet, I find Sozar's egg in the Releuthian Mountains in Sorréle. Why?"

Kyllian looked at a loss for words. "Honestly, I have no idea. It's bizarre. There was nothing else around the egg?"

Recalling the moment he had stumbled on Sozar's egg, Cyrus remembered how hollow it had sounded, and how the gold had peeked through the hardpacked dirt in the mine. The surrounding area had been untouched until he had dug at it to reveal the egg. "No. Nothing."

"Hm." Kyllian took a drink and swallowed. "Drink your tea before it gets cold."

Without thought, Cyrus reached forward and lifted the cup to his lips, trying to look calm, but deep down, his mind was racing. The lukewarm cinnamon tea was gross, but he forced himself to take three large gulps. They both sat there in silence, brooding over thoughts, but Cyrus was dissatisfied. So far, nothing was going to plan. He had never intended on being housed by the Razan family, yet here he was. He hadn't gotten any decent answer from this conversation, which had been the entire reason he had agreed to stay here to begin with. All Cyrus wanted was answers, and he'd barely gotten any.

"You say the Rider Federation still stands though?" he asked, doing his best to sound indifferent about this blossoming prospect.

Kyllian cleared his throat. "For the most part, yes. It is a ghost town, as some would say." The king narrowed his brown eyes. "While I envy your ability to cross a country in a matter of days with your dragon, I do not recommend traveling to the federation."

Cyrus cleared his throat and set the tea down. The cup landed against the desk with a sharp tap. "Why?"

"The city may be abandoned by people, but word has traveled to my ear that there are creatures inhabiting the area now. Beasts of bizarre origins—things we've never seen before. And the strangest part is that these creatures won't leave the city. It's like they're stuck there."

Or protecting something, Sozar chimed in. The dragon's sudden intrusion startled Cyrus, but he didn't let it show. He had been so engrossed by his own thoughts, he had forgotten that Sozar was also listening.

"My people used to go there all the time," Kyllian continued. "There is a shrine at the city's main gate made by the Razan and Kalic citizens—a place that allows people to go and give their thanks to the once-mighty dragons. But the last time the shrine was visited, there was an attack. Many of the citizens didn't make it, but the two who returned told me they had never seen a creature like the one they saw. More had swarmed the gate too." The king shook his head. "These are strange times indeed."

The door opened behind them, startling Cyrus. "Your Majesty, I do not mean to interrupt." The voice belonged to a young man with pale green eyes. He was dressed in a gold robe.

The king nodded. "Go ahead."

He looked between Cyrus and Kyllian. When their eyes met, the man slightly bowed his head to Cyrus, which made him want to squirm, but he held his ground. "The council requests your presence immediately."

"Is this an emergency I should be concerned about?" Kyllian raised himself from his seat, hands splayed out on the desk to hold himself up.

"Not necessarily."

He looked to Cyrus. "While I do not wish to cut our conversation short—"

"It is not a problem." A part of him was relieved for the interruption. It would give him time to think about what they had discussed.

"I appreciate your understanding." The king clasped his hands and looked around his study as if searching for something. Cyrus watched, trying to note if his eyes halted anywhere, but they landed on him. "Are there any other questions you have?"

He opened his mouth to say no but then caught himself. There was one. "Does the name Light Bringer ring a bell to you?"

Instantly, the air shifted, and Cyrus regretted asking. Something flashed over the king's dark gaze, but his expression remained unchanged. "No," he answered. "I am unfamiliar with that term."

The councilmember cleared his throat, and Cyrus took it as his cue to leave. "Thank you for your time," he told Kyllian, and side-stepped around the chair. "I'll get out of your way." Eager, he approached the exit and flashed a smile to the councilmember. "Good day."

The man dipped his head in Cyrus's direction. "Son of Greve," he replied in return.

That statement nearly forced him to stop in his tracks, but he kept going. Never in his life had he heard of such an acknowledgement, but he was too desperate to get out of the king's sight to turn around and ask. His skin crawled, and his instincts were screaming for him to run. That had not gone as planned.

If you are the son of Greve, then what of me? Sozar teased. It was the dragon's attempt to lighten the mood.

Turning the around a corner, Cyrus stopped, looking around at the marble and the extravagant decorations. *What do you think the councilmember was really doing there?* He peeked his head around to get a view of the king's study. There he was, Kyllian, exchanging words with the man, but the kindness in his eyes was gone. His look was serious, and cruel.

Hm, obviously something he doesn't want others to know. Shall we fly?

Cyrus watched Kyllian close the door and walk the other way with the councilmember, their heads close and voices so low that not even a whisper made it to his ears. *He's hiding something, and I intend to find out.*

And get yourself in trouble? The dragon was unamused. *You barely survived a run-in with one lunatic. What makes you think it's a good idea to sneak around under a king's nose?*

That stung, and Cyrus felt the abnormal flare of annoyance toward the dragon. *You're not curious what Kyllian might be hiding from us?*

I'm curious, but I also would prefer you to stay alive. Cyrus could feel the dragon stir from his spot in the courtyard. *You are all I have, hatchling. Do not forget that.*

He pursed his lips. Sozar had a point, but if the king was keeping something from him, he would be damned if he didn't try to find out. *I'm going to investigate the pala—*

"Are you looking for something?"

Jumping, he turned and saw a man approaching, dressed in a purple-and-gold robe. Gold rings decorated his fingers, and his short red hair was styled to the side with a well-clipped beard that shaped his jaw. Dark, sea-gray eyes studied Cyrus as the man halted. He smirked, as if amused by some unseen joke. "Are you looking for something?" he repeated.

Cyrus swallowed. "Just exploring."

"Ah." The man looked around the hall. "One must be careful. The palace is massive, and it's very easy to get lost, especially in the underground taverns."

That caught his attention. "Underground taverns? Like tunnels and such?" The dream danced behind his eyes. Maybe it had been a vision.

The man chuckled. "Tunnels that were built out well over fifteen hundred summers ago. They were used during battles and other such times but have long since been abandoned. There are leagues of tunnels underneath these floors."

"Do people still go down there?" Cyrus tried to withhold his excitement. If he was to go searching for the tunnels, he needed to make sure this guy didn't get that impression.

"Hardly, and if they do, they are doing so in hopes they don't return." That answer gave Cyrus the chills. "Do not hesitate to call on me if you need anything, Rider of the Sea." The man stepped passed him. "I am needed in the council chamber. Have a good day." With that, he continued his trek down the hall, passing the king's study.

Cursing silently, he looked behind him to make sure no one else was watching. A councilmember had caught him spying! And now, he was heading to that meeting, whatever it was. All he could hope for was that the man hadn't assumed Cyrus's intentions. Hopefully he thought he was lost, and nothing more.

None of that mattered now. What mattered were the underground tunnels. Adjusting his shirt, Cyrus adopted a relaxed stride and started to walk down the hall in the opposite direction from where the king had gone. Hopefully no one would stop him on his exploration. From his bond, he could tell that Sozar was unsatisfied, but they didn't argue. One thing they had learned about each other was that once either had his mind set on something, there was little point in trying to change the decision.

He wasn't worried about getting lost in the tunnels. Cyrus had spent summers in the mines of mountains. By now, he was comfortable walking along dark corridors with little light, and deep down, he was thrilled to return to what he knew best— exploring untouched tunnels. It was practically second nature. So long as he tracked his steps, all would be well.

Determined, Cyrus knew he would find the entryway to the tunnels. There was not a doubt in his mind that a door lay somewhere in this palace.

If the king didn't give him answers, he would find them himself.

TOUGH LOVE

The sun hung low in the sky, but the heat was still intense from the day. The group had gotten off the main road and headed north to avoid any unwanted attention once dawn had crested. They found a spot between the rolling hills that dipped lower, giving them more shelter from any wandering eyes. Soldiers were spotted just shy of dawn, their torches filling the horizon, but they were leagues away. It had been one thing to acknowledge that Raveerian soldiers would be sent to Jasper Village for them, another entirely to actually see them. Syra was relieved to finally be off the main road and hidden by the rolling hills.

When they stopped, each of the four took turns keeping watch while the others slept. Sleeping in the day disoriented Syra, and she found herself awake for most of the time, tossing over and trying to hide her eyes from the unwanted sun's attention. She was certain everyone else felt the same, but no one discussed it. They only mumbled curses when they got up from the hard ground.

Her thoughts still raced from her conversation with Zarek. Her mother's name, Nala, danced around her head without mercy, jarring her thoughts every time she thought slumber was near. Being the daughter of the dead wasn't something she knew how to process, and it only left more questions the more time passed. Syra was angry about it all, and yet numb. Her last living family member had murdered her mother in some cruel ploy to keep power, and Syra hated the woman for that, regardless of who she was.

She had eaten a fine meal of dried meat, a pear, and a piece of bread. The bread would be short-lived, but for now, she enjoyed the extra food. When she was done, she sat there and rested while Zane took his turn.

The rest sat around their encampment now. The horses were staked, except Uyul, who stood there, flicking her black silky tail and munching on the grass. Seeing the beast eat a mundane meal forced a double-take from Syra. It looked unnatural, as she anticipated Uyul to munch on bones, but she refrained from asking about it. Zarek seemed particularly protective of the beast. He always remained close to Uyul, even when resting and eating.

Syra twirled her fingers around the long grass, breaking a piece off and playing with it. The air was dry, the sun unforgiving. She kept the hood drawn over her head to protect herself from the sun's brutality, stealing a glance over at Roman. He was lying on his back, one leg crossed over the other, while he picked at his nails. The man hadn't said much since he'd gotten up from his rest, and Syra figured it was because he was tired.

Zarek was studying his sword. His hood was drawn down, legs crossed. Syra took the chance to steal several glances at the weapon without staring. It was marked up with sigils along the metal and shined as if it had been freshly polished. The handguard was an intricate design of thorny vines, the steel blackened. It was a beautiful piece—different from Dryl's in the handguard design and perhaps even the sigils, but the style was similar. And while Death's Sword looked oversized in her hand, this looked like it had been made for him.

A wind rustled the grass around them, and Zane stirred. He kept his arm over his eyes and adjusted his legs. The man didn't get up, but based on his disgruntled breaths, he was annoyed by the lack of sleep too.

It was incredibly quiet, save for the munching of the horses.

Her thoughts turned inward as she toyed with the blade of grass between her fingers. The more Syra considered Zarek's words, the angrier she became. It was a world she hadn't asked for, and yet she had been thrust into it without warning, preparation, or information. She didn't want to be the daughter of Nala, didn't want to have the weight of saving the Soul Realm on her shoulders. She had wanted freedom, a chance at a new life. This wasn't it. This was bullshit.

Syra swallowed that bitter revelation and tore the blade of grass in half. She wasn't ready for this, but more importantly, she didn't want anything to do with it.

"Something on your mind?" The words came from Roman. She looked over to see his head turned toward her, watching.

Zarek looked up just as she did, and they made quick eye contact.

"Just thinking about how delicious that meal was," Syra replied bitterly.

"We could pick up some sour ale," Zarek remarked. "Might round the meal out a little better."

The comment made her snort. "Perfect, and some moldy cheese too."

Roman repositioned himself, dropping his leg. "It's going to be a long trip."

"That it will be." Zane sat up and rubbed his face. He grabbed the bundled blanket he had been resting his head on and stuffed it into the pack next to him before standing. Then he walked over and sat down next to Syra. "Damn sleep," he added with a flare of annoyance.

"You're not alone," Syra replied softly.

"Do you sleep?" Zane asked the Guardian. "For real. Is that a thing for your kind?"

Zarek looked up from the blade. "We aren't entirely dead. We do sleep, but we don't require the same amount." He shrugged. "Or some of us find the less sleep there is, the less chance you get of having nightmares." Zarek smirked, but his face remained dark. "The choices we must make."

"Charming," Zane remarked, and dropped his head. He grabbed at the long grass and tore several pieces off to mess with. "When do we leave?"

"At dusk," Roman answered. "We can't risk the attention. It'll be night traveling until we are past Raveer."

Syra sighed and dropped the broken blade of grass. Traveling was already grueling, but doing it with little sleep was about as torturous as peeling nails off.

"How well can you use that sword?"

The question forced Syra's eyes back up to Zarek, who was staring at her. "Huh?"

The Guardian gestured to Death's Sword strapped to her waist.

She glanced down at it. "I did just fine when the Raveerian ship was ambushed by pirates," she replied, sounding defensive. Sure, the sword was heavier, but she had some training from her younger days.

"Show me," Zarek told her, and stood. He maneuvered his sword gracefully to his side, as if it were an extension of his arm.

Roman and Zane looked back and forth between them. Syra swallowed. "Now?"

The Guardian raised an eyebrow. "Got plans?"

She rolled her eyes and stood.

"Over here." Zarek motioned past the encampment, farther down the hill. Syra followed and unsheathed Death's Sword. The weapon was heavy in her hand, and she adjusted to get a better grip.

When they stopped, he faced her. A twinkle touched his eyes. "Did Dryl or Kar train you?"

"No, but I had training from my home city."

The corner of his mouth twitched upward, and she gritted her teeth. Apparently he found her answer humorous. "Let's see how that holds up then, shall we? Take your stance."

Syra took a deep breath and settled herself in a fighter's position. She watched Zarek study her, and he gave the slightest shake of his head before charging without warning.

An unintentional yelp broke from her lips. Syra ducked as Zarek dropped his sword where hers should have been. The blade cut through the grass where she had stood. The Guardian was twice her size and incredibly fast—Syra knew immediately that she couldn't hold up in strength against him. She rolled and jumped up swinging, but her blade met Zarek's instantly. With a flick of his wrist, he shoved her sword aside and took a winning step forward, lowering the blade to her throat. "Dead."

Syra turned and took several steps away before turning back and positioning herself again. "You gave no warning. I wasn't ready."

"Excuses," he replied, and twirled his sword. In his grip, the metal looked as light as a feather. Her muscles were already protesting from the weight of the sword. It felt like she was hauling a bag of stones. "Ready?" Zarek asked with a hint of sarcasm.

Annoyance flared. "Just go."

Again, he charged her, and again, Syra ducked and tried to catch him by surprise, rolling in the opposite direction, but the Guardian was too quick and deflected her blow with ease. He swung at her a couple of times, which she parried, but her movements were clumsy, and she knew the Guardian could tell. With a quick jump, he dropped the blade to her side before she could defend herself. "Dead."

Syra ground her teeth. "Again." He was fighting like an ass, and she knew that he knew it. This wasn't training, this was humiliation.

So again, Zarek defeated her, and again, Syra demanded to be refought. The Guardian's style was elegant, clean, and agile. It was unlike anything she had ever seen before. Her training had consisted of basic formations, defensive blows against certain strikes, but every time she thought she saw a pattern, Zarek changed his step and caught her off guard. The weight of the sword only hampered her further.

Zarek flicked her blade aside and swept his foot, knocking her clean on her ass. Syra tried to save herself but was unsuccessful and instantly found the tip of Death's Sword meeting her eyes.

He eyed her too long. "Dead," he said with a hint of disappointment, then lifted his sword and sheathed it.

His tone unnerved her. "That's it?" Syra hauled herself up, sword still in hand. Her muscles ached from the fight, and her arm felt like it would fall off at any moment, but she refused to show it. "We just started!"

Zarek kept his back turned to her. "An enemy only needs one lucky strike. You've had four chances, and all four times, you've failed."

"I've never—"

"Excuses," Zarek retorted, looking at her now. "Stop making excuses for failure. If you don't get a sword shoved through your chest, you'll have your tongue cut out by your enemy."

The Guardian's words stung, and she snapped her mouth shut. She wanted to explain herself, wanted to prove that she wasn't a moron—she wasn't dead yet, and that was something to be proud of. She just hadn't ever dealt with this kind of fighting style before. But it was useless. Zarek wouldn't hear any of it, and it pissed her off.

"How's your energy harvesting?" he asked, tone sharp.

"My—what?" Syra stumbled on her words, unprepared for the quick subject change. "I can't harvest energy."

The Guardian raised an eyebrow. "You can't?"

"No."

Walking toward her, Zarek closed the gap and looked down, his crimson eyes scrutinizing. He pinched her chin and forced her gaze up to meet his. "*What?*" He kept his voice low, but to Syra, it felt like he was screaming at her, and she flinched.

"I've never harvested in my life, Zarek," she said, and pulled herself free from his grip. Kids showed their gifts at young ages, but not her. She had been normal.

"Or you've never tried," Zarek retorted, leaning down. He picked up a round pebble and handed it to her. The pebble was hot to the touch from the heat of the sun. "First lesson. Energy is everywhere. Everything, down to this pebble, is made up of energy in varying degrees. With each object, your concentration will differ to meet the needs of the energy." Zarek motioned at the grass. "This is all energy that when called upon, you can manipulate. Do you know what energy is, Syra?" The question sounded on the edge of being cynical.

She bit the inside of her cheek and whispered, "No." It had never been important to learn.

Her answer must have been expected. Zarek continued to speak, his words dripping with disappointment. "Energy is the life force of the world. If everything is made up of energy, then everything has a life force." The Guardian turned and placed a finger against her chest. "You are a life force, just as that pebble possesses its own life force, even if it is faint compared to yours." He pulled his hand away. "Your goal is to finetune your concentration and identify the life force of this pebble, Syra. When you feel it, tell me, and we will work on manipulating that life force, or energy."

Before he could turn, she piped up, "How will I know?"

A smile touched his lips. "Think of it like a beacon of light in a dark room. You will know when you find it."

"But what if I can't?" When he raised his brow, she added, "What if I can't harvest energy at all?"

192

He lowered his voice even further. "If you can't harvest energy, then we're all damned, Syra. I'd like to be optimistic and think you've just lacked the guidance needed to even know that side of you exists."

His words made little sense to her, and she dropped the hand that held the pebble. "Why all this? Do you want to make a fool out of me, or are you going to help me?"

The Guardian dipped his head to regard her. "If Dryl were standing here, I'd kick his ass for not training you sooner, but I'll have to settle on the fact that he thought he was doing the right thing." He met her eyes. "All due respect, Syra, if your friends die, the world will go on. If you die, then we're all fucked, including the dead. So, yes, I am going to train you because there is a lot more out there than drunk men with a dull sword. There are monsters out there—creatures so vile that even the strongest Guardian cannot escape unscathed, and one day, they will cross into the living." Zarek leaned in then, his words harsh. "You've been chosen for a reason to be the Light Bringer, so you might want to start acting like it."

He turned and walked toward Uyul, stopping next to the beast and giving her a good scratch behind the ear. Syra tore her gaze away to Zane and Roman, who were staring at her. They had no idea what had just been discussed, and it was safer that way. Still, right now, Syra felt like the entire world knew she was a complete idiot.

Agitated and flustered, she turned her back and sat down right where she had been standing. She wanted to be alone from everyone else after that humiliation. His words had stung, but she didn't want to show it. Holding up the pebble, she stared at it. The wind tousled her hair, and she shoved it out of her line of sight and behind her ears. This damn pebble was supposed to have a life force like her, and she tried to concentrate on it. She was staring so hard at the rock, her eyes started to hurt. Exasperated, she snapped her hand shut and dropped it to her lap. It was a rock—it wasn't supposed to be anything more than that.

Syra blinked back a wave of tears. Frustration boiled in her, and she wiped her eyes, not wanting anyone to see her cry. This was not the life she had asked for.

She sat there until it was time to move. Thankfully, nobody bothered her.

THE CURSE
OF THE SNAKE

Morei stared at the stars. They twinkled and danced before him, their light undiminished by the moon. Thousands dotted the sky, some larger than others but all beautiful in their own right.

There, above, were a million stories he would never know. Stories of loss, tragedy, beauty, rebirth, and death. Stories that only the oldest star knew. The world was complicated, yet simple. Man made it complicated, that much the king knew. In all his summers, he had never been trained for handling the types of problems that now faced him.

He scoffed. Perhaps the world was better without the Vorelians.

One thing Morei was grateful for was the view before him, of the Hazar Desert, and not of the burning bodies to the north, where he had no doubt the embers of the dwindling flames cracked with delight, eating away at the flesh and organs of Cu'cel's victims.

Forty had been piled and lit on fire this evening alone, based on the report by Peter. Forty lives lost between last night and tonight. What would tomorrow's numbers be? With no cure, he had no idea how long this would last. Maybe the sickness would run its course, take out the weak and compromised, and then the stronger would live to tell the tale.

Yet Morei couldn't help but fear that this illness would spread to the rest of the country, and if it did . . . A citizen of Sorréle, of Geral, could even carry it across the sea. That made the breath in the back of his throat catch. There was no denying that if Cu'cel captured the rest of the world in its clutches, it would not let go.

And it would be his fault.

There was no wind tonight, saving him from the worst, but the lingering scent was still there, permeating everything with the sobering stench of death. All was quiet save for the dozen who chanted in the city center, their voices carrying to the palace in a haunting melody. Their desperate pleas to the Drügale Gods were heard by everyone save for the Gods themselves, for they were nothing but man's desperate attempt to find purpose in a life so grueling and yet so precious.

The king took in a sharp breath and straightened. It was his first day back as ruler, and already he was tasked to hand his crown over. Instead of receiving thanks, he was being blamed. Morei could not deny the growing resentment building in him, despite the oath he had taken to protect these citizens. Lifetimes of Gerals had ruled this city, pure blooded, and now he would hand that name over to a man with no family name. Ezra was a good man, albeit hotheaded. And the king could sit there until he was blue in the face and claim to have the same heart, but the council and citizens would never listen.

It was because of what he was—or rather, what he was willing to become to protect his city. Not a decision he considered lightly or one he accepted, but as king, as a Geral, he had been raised with one thing in mind: the people always came first.

Peter had been accepting of Ezra's ascension—in fact, Morei would have almost said the chancellor looked thrilled.

A knock on the door broke his trance, and he rubbed his face with his hands, hoping to shake himself free from the soured attitude. It didn't work, and he was instead forced to swallow the thoughts and turn away from the Hazar Desert.

"Come in!"

With no idea who it could be, the king stepped back into the living space he called home. Although, glancing around at the furnishings, the décor, and the space that had once belonged to the previous king and queen, he felt like a sham. If able, he would have turned and run far from this world. Instead, he stood in place, eyebrows raised in surprise, as Emerald stepped in and closed the door behind her.

She was dressed in a pink silk wrap, barefoot as always, her rich, dark hair billowing around her strong jawline and dark green eyes. The queen of Junok was sexy as ever—dangerously so. When he met her gaze, she smiled. "I hope you don't mind."

The king nodded, understanding. "I don't remember inviting you." Just like the first night, she barged in whenever she so damn pleased, but tonight, it irritated him, regardless of her looks.

Emerald didn't react like he expected. "Your first day back, and I imagine you've had a stressful one at that." She shrugged and stepped toward the decanter of wine that sat on the table to his right, snuggly pressed up against the wall. "Drink?"

"I am not looking for company," he whispered, eyeing her as she poured herself a drink. "If you came here for a good laugh, a story, then you will not have it."

Glancing over her shoulder, she raised an eyebrow of her own. "And what if I came here as a friend?"

"Then I would still ask that you leave."

"That's too bad," she replied, and poured the second drink. "Because I don't intend on leaving."

The king scoffed. He couldn't even rule his own people, and now Emerald wouldn't respect his wishes. With a dismissive wave, he turned and walked back outside, needing fresh air.

His temper was fried, and if he stayed in this room any longer, he was certain the walls would cave in on him.

The air hugged him with a cool grip as he laid his hands back on the stone railing, eyes locked ahead. Focusing on his breathing, Morei told himself that with her here, he could ask the questions that most bothered him.

He heard her approach from behind. "Here," the queen said, and handed him one of the goblets.

Taking it, he stirred the wine with a motion of his hand. "Shall I trust you didn't drug this one?"

Emerald raised an eyebrow at him. "I have spoken my piece, Morei. Do not dig up old graves because you are short-tempered." Then she took a drink, keeping her head forward.

The king gritted his teeth, knowing she was right but not wanting to admit to it. Instead of saying more on the matter, he took the goblet. The wine did little to wash away his sour attitude.

When he lowered it, she asked, "Better?"

"No."

Nodding, she leaned up against the railing, placing the vessel on the flat surface of the stone. "Want to talk about it?"

Morei didn't look her way. "No." But before she could say anything more, he spoke again. "Why did you stay?"

Out of the corner of his eye, he saw Emerald glance toward him. "It was the right thing to—"

He scoffed, cutting her off. "Emerald, we both know you have no concept of what's right and what's wrong, only what's best for you. You proved that the night you drugged me for a child. Shall I ask, have you bled? Are you carrying the child you forced from me?"

Now, he looked at her fully, watching her eyes harden and her mouth become a thin line. For a moment, she didn't speak, but when she did, her words were harsh. "I don't know, if you want the honest truth. I won't know for at least another moon cycle."

"Hm." Morei took another swig. "So, why did you stay?" he repeated, and leaned his forearms onto the chilly stone, looking at her. "And don't give me your royally humble answer. I want the truth. You have a city, a council that awaits your return, and yet you choose to stay here while my city becomes a living nightmare."

Emerald huffed, her fingers playing with the neck of the goblet in what the king could only interpret as a nervous habit, one that she likely kept well-hidden in the world she came from. "I stayed because I had to." The queen met his eyes with her own captivating gaze. "And you might not believe me, but I stayed because it was the right thing—a way to right my wrong, if you could call it that." She tilted her head at him, then finished, "So yes, I do know what's right and wrong, believe it or not."

The king eyed every aspect of her—her beauty, the curves hidden underneath that pink robe, her lies, her secrets, and her unquenchable need to save her heritage, despite the world falling apart around her. In so many ways, they were one in the same—caught in a storm without cover but too stubborn to ask for help. Too similar for their own good.

But the difference between them was that Morei was destined to become the enemy—the enemy of his people, of this country, of the world.

And as for Emerald, she would go on to be the queen everyone wanted, needed. No one would know or understand just how far she would be willing to go to secure her bloodline or just how cruel she would be to prove a point. Nobody would know because no one would care to find out, unlike him.

He loathed her for it. He also couldn't help but lust for her because of it.

Morei took a drink of his wine, acutely aware of how bitter it was against his tastebuds. The slightest of breezes brushed up against him, and he caught a whiff of the queen's sweet scent. She smelled like honey.

"Kiren told me what you said," Emerald whispered. "He wasn't entirely fond of the situation."

Morei raised his brow. "Did he suspect that I would get on my knees, beg that he see the best in me, and pledge myself to you?"

Emerald rolled her eyes. "No, Morei. You're in quite the mood tonight. Must have been a good day."

"As I said, I was not looking for company."

The queen snorted. "Have you ever realized that you might be the very reason people turn on you?" The question forced his eyes to look back at her, and she continued. "You wonder why the people are pointing the blame at you—and don't you worry, I've heard *all* the rumors—but have you stopped to wonder why?" Setting the goblet down, she crossed her arms. "Maybe because you do nothing but push everyone away. The great king of Geral, ruthless, merciless, willing to do just about anything for a reaction"—Emerald laughed, a shrill sound—"but guess what? You're still the same man at the end of the day, and I'm starting to think you hate him."

Audacity was the only word that came to mind to match the shock that slapped him cold. The king couldn't comprehend Emerald speaking about him in such a way, as if she had known him all her life. It was not her place to speak of his rule, his people, or whom he believed himself to be. It simply wasn't acceptable. Anyone else would have lost their head for such a statement, but she stood there, chin held high, as if challenging him to make a move against her.

She seemed to have some sort of death wish.

Morei clenched his teeth, enraged. "You have no right to speak to me in such a way when you have spared no detail about your life," he hissed. "You are a queen on the run, no? Abandoning your people for the sake of some unborn child, some dream of yours? If you stayed because you thought you could fool me into marriage, some sort of arrangement to save your city, you're wrong. I would never marry you." He leaned in. "The answer is still no."

Emerald stared, and if it was possible, the king saw the faintest flash of pain cross her eyes. He held his ground, determined for her to understand his point. She was foolish, outrageous even, for holding on to such a dream when he was in no place for marriage or even a child. The queen was a fool, and she should have left the moment she could.

Taking a deep breath, she came to life. "You've made you're point very clear, Morei. You are despicable, you know. Dragging me back to your room the night before Diemon with that look in your eye, making me believe you forgave me." The queen shook her head and scoffed. "But it's clear you've got issues. The city is the least of your problems. My advice? Make up your mind and choose a path—this is not a mistake I will make again."

At that, she turned her back to him and started to walk. The king watched, annoyed that she'd had the final word. This was his city, his rules, not hers. Morei was done with people walking all over him. One day back, and the council and city had already treated him like he was some disgrace to the throne. This would not be how he ended his night.

Swiftly, he set the goblet down and closed the space between them, latching his hand onto her arm and forcing her to face him. Emerald glared up and tried to yank herself free, but he would not let her go. Not now, not until she acknowledged him.

"If this—"

"Listen, and listen very closely," he whispered, keeping her eyes on him. "There are few things that I will never tolerate under my rule, and one of those is being challenged about who I am as a king." His grip tightened, and he saw her grimace, but he didn't loosen it. "You want to know what happened to the two people who questioned my rule, my authenticity?" Morei leaned in, dropping his voice, knowing he had her full attention. "I killed them. Don't think I won't do the same to you."

Lady Dail and Lord Rodrick had died because they couldn't see what Morei was willing to do for his people, what he was willing to sacrifice. He would not tolerate the same behavior from Emerald.

But as she stood there, staring up at him, he could not ignore the desire that turned his blood hot, flooding his senses. It was as if she had worn the robe intentionally, making his thoughts scatter at the mere thought of untying the simple knot that kept his eyes from seeing the rest of her.

His gaze danced over her lips—plump, beautiful, pink. The king could not ignore his needs, not when having her could help him blow off steam and satisfy him.

Emerald must have sensed his shift, for she attempted to pull herself free, but it was weak, futile. If anything, it was a plea for more, a way to test his resolve.

Without further hesitation, he closed the gap and parted her lips.

The tension of the night melded into the intensity of the kiss. Morei pressed into her more as she flicked her tongue over his, drawing him in. Rage and lust collided, and he dropped his hands to her robe, pulling the knot free and pushing the silk off her shoulders. She wore nothing underneath, as he quickly discovered with his hands. It was clear now that she had come here with the same goal. All he wanted was to touch every part of her, to feel her skin against his.

He shoved her back up against the stone wall and pulled the robe free from her body. It fell in a heap at her feet, exposing every part of her to him.

Morei hummed against her lips in satisfaction, feeling her body with his hands, from her breasts to her hips. He explored, letting her tremble against him, as he ventured deeper into *her*.

The more he felt her, the more aroused he got. His breaths went shallow at the thought of tasting her.

Morei dropped both his hands to her thighs, breaking the kiss. "Grab on," he ordered. Emerald obeyed and wrapped her hands around his neck just as he hoisted her up. He felt her legs twist around him as he walked back inside.

Her lips met his ear. "I want all of you, Morei," she rasped, breath hot. She nipped, and he nearly took her on the ground, unable to wait any longer, but the bed was right there. Emerald whispered more, turning him on and making him weak as the heat of her breath traveled across his neck. He shuddered as she ran her tongue over his skin, teasing with her teeth.

Morei laid her on the bed, falling on top of her. He pressed his lips against hers, kissing as hard as he dared without hurting her, unable to restrain himself or the surge of emotions that coursed through him. The same ones he would have slaughtered a man with given the chance. They needed an outlet, and she was it.

Emerald's hands unbuttoned his shirt, pulling the fabric apart so that she could explore his skin. Her touch burned with delight, making him moan. It was as if the heat of the sun were concentrated in her body, intoxicating him. And he let it, captivated.

He broke the kiss and allowed his lips to explore her, tasting every part, but he did it slowly, ensuring he could take care of her in every way possible. His tongue explored her breasts as he let one of his hands caress her body, desperate to feel every curve. Emerald's skin was so soft—it smelled like roses but tasted like the honey. Her hands traveled over his shoulders and intertwined through his hair, divine.

As he traversed down her body, he heard her breaths go shallow, and to tease her further, Morei nipped the inside of her thigh. She cried out, and he smiled against her skin.

Morei kissed until he had reached his desired destination, and as he tasted her, he moaned. She tasted just as he remembered, letting his tongue roam over every aspect of her. She moaned in pleasure, satisfying him, but he wasn't done with her yet. He wanted to make her tremble.

And so he continued, and the more he did so, the more roused he became, wanting nothing more than to take her as his. Emerald's breaths quickened just as her body shuddered underneath him. His entire being burned with stimulation, and he moved his lips to her thigh, biting her tender skin. He couldn't help himself. He wanted to make her scream.

She nearly did, but it wasn't enough. Emerald trembled underneath him, and Morei undressed himself, shaking the shirt off and slipping off his pants as she lay in bliss. Done, he dropped his lips back to her, letting them ascend back to her own. As he got closer, he felt her hands grab on to him, one laced through his hair, pulling him to her.

Emerald met his lips with a fierce passion, flicking her tongue over his and nipping his lip in the process. Morei groaned, feeling his body go weak from the intensity of her. He kissed in return, letting the passion build and basking in the heat of her body. Every piece of him, even the demons, wanted her, grabbing at his control until he caved. The intensity of it all reached a peak, all molding into one goal.

Dropping himself, he found her with ease and pushed himself inside. His body shuddered in delight as he thrust. Morei grabbed one of her hands and laced his fingers through hers, placing it next to her head, holding it as tight as he dared.

Intertwining his other hand through her hair, he pressed his lips against her temple. Emerald's hands dug into his back in response to his rhythm.

Morei gave his body over to her, no longer in control, as euphoria shushed everything else out, even the voices. He let his lips tease her neck and ear, using the hand through her hair to move her head as he saw fit.

Everything about her was exquisite, down to the sound of her breathing, as it quickened and she whispered his name against his ear, sending a shiver down his spine. Her body was made for his, as his was for her. Morei felt alive and at her mercy, captivated, under her control.

For the first time that day, he was able to forget about the nightmare he was living in.

GODS AND PRINCES

Cyrus never made it to the tunnels because as he neared, he was sourly interrupted. A maid found him behind one of the three galleys he had stumbled upon.

Whether she determined him to be sneaking around or not, the woman did not say. She simply clasped her hands, smiled, and asked if she could escort him back to his room. Cyrus told her he was fine and didn't need to be escorted, but she insisted. The woman wasn't rude, but she made it clear that she was not about to leave without him. At last, he relented to the search and followed her.

The maid was short and stumpy, but she carried herself like she had been doing this for countless summers. Cyrus felt like he was in the presence of a mother preparing to scold a child for acting out, so he made sure to make respectful conversation in hopes of lightening the mood. Even though he towered above her and was a Dragon Rider, he had zero doubts that she would lay a hand on him if he acted out.

Careful with how he spoke, he was able to make small talk with her. He learned that her name was Rosarie, and she had served the Razan family for nearly thirty summers. As they walked, she told him about the various palace chambers, pointed out statues, explained portraits, and even spoke of Zorya and her unruly behavior, especially as a child.

There were massive washrooms that could host entire parties, several chambers dedicated to rituals and prayers, countless rooms used by staff members and guests for living, chambers dedicated to historical artifacts, and many other rooms that Cyrus did not see. Statues of every single God, including the vile Sekar, were chiseled out of various stones. Helyna was a deep purple, perhaps Jamunia, but her eyes had been done with a yellow stone that Cyrus had never seen before. All the Gods stood as tall as he, captured in perfect detail, their expressions all unique—Sekar had a mischievous smirk, Helyna was lost in laugher, Greve appeared serious, and Hyle brandished a sword to the sky. And at last there was Eazon, who held a majestic bird on his wrist with its wings spread out wide, ready for flight.

"The Gods were all once mortals," Rosarie explained as she gestured along the statues. "Many believe their home was right here and that they were part of the Great Crossing, when Kera guided ships to this land all those summers ago." Rosarie grazed her fingers along Helyna's stone dress. "They say in an act of defiance, after learning she would be arranged to marry a cruel soldier, Helyna jumped from the falls south of here, but when she awoke, she found herself a Goddess and not among the dead in the Afterlife." Rosarie retracted her fingers and looked up at Cyrus, the lines framing her blue eyes. "That is why it is called Helyna's Falls. Come."

Before she could lead him away, Cyrus pointed at Sekar. "Why celebrate him? He's nothing but bad luck. The stories about the Releuthian Mountains—" He shook his head, now feeling foolish under Rosarie's critical gaze. He was obviously missing something. "I just don't understand."

The maid tsked and motioned for him to walk with her. "He was once a mortal man, like you. What has happened to him is not our place to judge. His soul was chosen for a reason to serve, and we must respect that." She spoke sharply, as if it annoyed her to have to explain the Razan's choice of worshipping the God of Darkness, so Cyrus bit his tongue, not wanting to insult her any further if he had.

Then Rosarie laughed and nudged them on their walk. The sudden change in her demeanor unnerved him, as if she had two entirely separate personalities. "They say Hyle was a Dragon Rider. It's why his eyes are silver and the others aren't."

"That's impossible," Cyrus said. "Nobody could know that."

Rosarie waved him off. "Don't be ridiculous. Many could counterclaim the events of the Gods, where they came from, how they come upon their powers, but there are certain things that remain consistent among the people." She eyed him. "And one of those is that Hyle's eyes are silver."

Cyrus couldn't argue that point. "So because he has silver eyes, he was a Dragon Rider? Where's his dragon?"

"Dead." Rosarie indicated for them to turn right, so he did. "But they believe that Hyle always returns to the remains of where his dragon lay, which is said to be in the Dark Forest. Ah, I believe this is where I leave you."

The abrupt end to their conversation startled Cyrus, and he looked up to see his chamber. The door was closed, as he had left it, and no one was there waiting for him. He gave Rosarie a suspicious look. "Did the king ask you to bring me back?"

The maid rubbed her hands over her dress. "I was instructed to bring you back to your room so that you may prepare for another dinner. That is all." She walked away quickly, her sandals echoing against the flooring.

Had he been followed after the conversation with Kyllian? Cyrus felt violated suddenly, and a shiver ran down his back. Maybe he wasn't really being welcomed after all.

We will have to investigate after dark. Sozar's voice hummed in his head. *Until then, do not draw attention to yourself.*

Cyrus snorted into the empty hall. *Easier said than done when I'm what everyone is talking about.*

He was about to turn when a man stepped out from around the corner. The man was bald, and dressed in silver, his complexion the color of leather, his eyes a rich amber. He had silver bangles and rings, as well as metal piercings running up both ears. A grin touched his face at the sight of Cyrus, but while it may have been intended to be welcoming, it made him uncomfortable. A malevolent air surrounded this man.

"Ah, you must be the Dragon Rider!" He spread his arms wide, his robe flapping as he strode before stopping, eye-to-eye at Cyrus's height. "I've heard all about you."

Slowly, he nodded. "And I've heard nothing about you." At the faltering grin, Cyrus smiled, unable to help himself. "You are?"

Sozar growled across their link. *Do not make a fool of yourself.*

The man lowered his arms and raised an eyebrow. "I am Prince Shunera of Kalic, here to see my future wife, Zorya Razan." The words dripped with smugness, but while it was Cyrus's turn to be taken aback, he didn't let it show. The idea of the princess being married off to *this* was repulsive. Like shoving a fire into the ocean and wondering why the flames sizzled out.

"Ah, lovely," he remarked. "Although she hasn't mentioned you. Will you be at the dinner tonight?"

"Dinner?"

"Must be a special event," Cyrus retorted, letting his words sink in. "Well, I must be off." Laying a hand on the door handle, he opened his room and stepped inside, leaving the prince of Kalic standing there. Still feeling rather annoyed, he closed the door right in Shunera's face. Satisfied, he nodded to himself and slid the lock over.

But his pride was completely stepped on by Sozar. *And what will you do when you must face him later?*

Cyrus grunted in response and walked across the room until he reached his bed. He pulled the pillows back to ensure that his precious items were still there, and they were. Satisfied, he sat down and ran his hands over his face. The reality of his situation was setting in. The one woman he liked was arranged to marry another man, and an ass at that, based on the smug expression on Shunera's face.

It had been a day since Cyrus had arrived, and deep down, he knew he wouldn't stay longer than necessary. The attraction he felt toward the princess would be nothing more than a memory by next season, or so he wanted to tell himself. Regardless, it was better that she be married off to a man with the title and power a royal member deserved. Cyrus certainly couldn't offer her anything more than some stale bread, a strange book, and a bit of company, and she deserved far more than that.

Soured by the prince's arrival, Cyrus lay back on the bed and stared at the gaudy ceiling. He was not meant for royalty, structure, or a normal life. Already, he had a running list against him for all that he had done since arriving. It was just a matter of time before he pissed the king off and outstayed his welcome.

But first, he would get answers. Once he had those, he would set his path elsewhere.

REALM HOPPER

They traveled through the night once again. Above them, the stars twinkled, but tonight, the Heart of the World was faint. Straight ahead, a massive thunderstorm blasted the sky with purple lightning. It was far away but added a dazzling view to the landscape. The smell of moisture was faint as a breeze swept the group.

Syra rode in the back. Hazel was strolling at a leisurely pace, and she wasn't about to speed the horse up. Zarek's words were still charred in her thoughts, turning them black, and she hadn't been in the greatest of moods. The Guardian had not been warm to her since their training, and she couldn't help but conclude it was because he was disappointed in her.

On top of that, having tried to locate the life force of the pebble had turned into one of the most frustrating tasks yet. A tiny stone was outsmarting her, and she had thrown it after becoming so frustrated, only for Zarek to turn around and hand her another pebble that looked almost identical.

Lightning flashed, basking the land in a deep purple light. It was sunning, otherworldly. Never before had Syra seen such a dazzling display from a storm. Ahead, Zarek rode next to Zane, and Roman followed just slightly behind the two. They were following the main road once more, having tracked their way back to it once the sun had fallen. To the south, slightly behind them, the torches of the soldiers were distant. The armed forces were trekking to Jasper Village and would likely arrive there by sometime tomorrow afternoon. It was a relief to know they had passed the Raveerian forces without issue, but it didn't mean they were safe.

It would be another day before the quartet arrived at the outskirts of the city of Raveer. And that was only if they continued to make impeccable time.

As Hazel strolled on, Syra dug the pebble out of her pouch again. She rubbed her fingers over it, feeling it chill to the touch. If she could just focus, she could sense the life force and prove to Zarek she was capable of *something*. That was all she needed to do. Everyone had a life force, which meant it couldn't be impossible to feel the energy.

Syra closed her eyes, holding on tight to Hazel's reins with her free hand. She was far too experienced a rider to grow off balanced, so she wasn't worried about falling, only if the horse became startled. Her body swayed from side to side as Hazel sauntered forward. Syra slowed her breathing, keeping her fingers wrapped around the pebble as she concentrated.

She narrowed her thoughts and then focused on the sound of her own heart as it beat slower against her ribcage. She listened to the rustle of the grass as a small breeze teased the air and the crickets sung their nightly tune. A headache had already started in her temples, but she ignored it. Syra refused to be beaten by a pebble no larger than her thumb.

She focused as hard as she could, shushing out the wandering thoughts that threatened to break her concentration. Several times, Syra's attention was lost as she found her thoughts on something else, like the itch on her forearm. Cursing silently, she returned her attention to the pebble and let her frustration drive the nail into concentration.

A flicker of light flashed behind her eyes. It was so faint and quick that Syra gasped, feeling the buzz of excitement fill her ears. It was exactly what Zarek had explained—a light in the dark—and she opened her eyes to tell him.

The world was gone, replaced by the decay of the Soul Realm.

Above her, the purple sky pulsed. It was just how she remembered it—the heart of a dying animal. Around her, slimy black trees stretched upward, their leaves gone, and beneath her, the ground sighed as she took a cautious step. Screeches pierced the air, so close that her heart fluttered and her blood ran cold. Demons.

"Terrible, isn't it?"

Syra startled and spun around. There he was, the man she had been running from, the man who had taken the last bit of trust she had and burned it. The person who had betrayed her and killed Dryl. Kar.

He stood with his hood drawn, revealing his Guardian features and piercing crimson eyes. Kar's lips were turned upward in a smirk, his hands clasped behind his back. He stood there, relaxed, as if he had been enjoying the nature prior to her arrival. Beside him was a large tree, its branches twisted outward in a ghastly fashion, the trunk covered in slime.

They were in a small clearing.

Anger surged, and Syra bolted for him without thought. She would punch him, stab him, anything to get back at him for everything he'd done to her. But as her steps sank into the mushy ground, the trees around her elongated. Kar was farther away, but the smirk did not falter. She hesitated, confused. It didn't make sense. They were no longer in the same clearing that she had arrived in. In the blink of an eye, the dead forest around her shifted.

"What . . ." Syra glanced around, trying to recognize pieces of the clearing, but she couldn't tell. The trees all looked the same. The sky was still purple, the ground still piled high with dead leaves and grime. It sighed with each step she took.

Once more, the demons screeched from the distance, and her heart fluttered in response.

She wanted to ask, but instead she bolted once more for the Guardian. Then the ground jolted underneath her, and she tripped. Her hands landed in a soppy mess; the leaves were slimy and cold to the touch. She coughed and stood, angry, only to find Kar right in front of her. Now he wore an arrogant smile, as if her demise amused him. Syra lashed out, intending to punch him square in the jaw.

She watched as her fist went right through him.

Kar's form rematerialized. Once more, he looked as real to her as anyone else. "Are you done?" he asked, voice soft.

She faltered, not wanting to admit defeat but knowing she was never going to beat him at his own game. "Are you even here?" Her voice echoed, while his remained clear.

Kar dipped his head to regard her. "I am as real as you want me to be." He reached out with a gloved hand and brushed the cool leather against her cheek. Syra slapped it away from her face, surprised when her hand connected with his. This was her chance, but as she prepared to hit him with her other fist, his fingers took her throat with an iron grip.

His eyes ran cold as he squeezed. The air was ripped from her lungs, and she grabbed at his hand with her own, trying to tear his fingers free from her neck. Pain flared, and she grimaced. Kar didn't react to her attempts to break free—his expression remained stoic.

She wheezed, her lungs screaming for air. "Please . . . let me go."

Kar's lip curled upward in a sneer. "Are you done?"

The words failed on her tongue, so she nodded. Her head was growing light, and her vision blinked in and out as she began to slip into unconsciousness. The pressure released suddenly, but her legs buckled underneath her. Syra collapsed onto the ground, coughing, heaving for air. Her hands shook, and she wiped at her mouth.

"Don't think I enjoyed that," Kar told her, his tone bitter. "But I hope I got your attention."

"You could . . . have just asked," she bit back between breaths.

"Mm, live as long as I have, and your tolerance lessens."

Syra ignored the comment as she stood. Looking around, she felt incredibly vulnerable. She was weaponless in the Soul Realm with Kar, her belt gone. He could kill her if he wanted to. But he hadn't. Still, she was at his mercy, and she would need to play by his rules.

"How did I get here?" she asked, then cleared her throat. Her voice sounded scratchy.

"I would think by now you would have figured that out on your own," Kar answered, and looked at her fully. "Or did Zarek tell you?"

Her blood ran cold. He knew. He was watching them, just as she'd suspected. "How . . ."

"Syra," he whispered. "Did you really think I was done with you?"

She swallowed. "The Demon Killer. I thought—"

"You thought wrong," he cut in. "The blade is only a sliver of my intentions, and I would have let you hold on to it, but I couldn't trust the people around you. That is not why I wanted to meet you, though. Look."

As the word left his lips, he swept his hand over their surroundings. The screeching of the demons vanished in an instant, and the blackened ground and dead trees gave way to greenery. The branches sprouted orange and blue leaves; flowers sprang to life and took exotic shape all around. Above, the sky hummed with life, casting a sizzling purple hue. Ahead, a butterfly with three pairs of wings fluttered, each a different color.

It was the most beautiful sight she had ever beheld.

"This is the world I remember," Kar mumbled. "This is the Soul Realm."

The grass beneath her swayed as a warm breeze rushed by. The air smelled sweet, almost like honey. "What happened?"

"The Gods are what happened," the Guardian hissed. "They intermingled in a world where they did not belong. Their presence upset the balance. Gods are born from Chaos, enslaved to the power, but that power belongs to the living, not the dead."

Syra opened her mouth to ask a question, but Kar continued before she could speak. "The Guardians were made not only to guide souls to the Afterlife, but to protect this realm from sinister forces. Where there is good, there is evil. Such is the balance of Chaos."

The vision shifted. A tall creature stepped out of the forest before her. It stood on two legs and had two arms, like any man, but its face was grotesque. The mouth was filled with razor-sharp teeth with no lips, its eyes a solid black apart from a white slit of a pupil. Its nose was slitted as well, and its head spotted with short horns. Black-tipped tusks decorated its jawline and jutted from its shoulders. The monster was dressed in simple gray armor that was molded to its body. A curved sword hung at its side.

It moved ahead, oblivious to their presence.

"Honuyál," Kar stated. "Do not be deceived by their appearance. They are powerful Energy Harvesters and can manipulate souls. Souls are not meant to be manipulated. In this realm, they are volatile balls of energy, but the dead don't know this about themselves, and Guardians keep it that way. It's safer. Some souls do not pass into the Soul Realm and instead become chained to the living—these are what feed Dark Energy. A story for another time."

He let the image shatter, replaced by the Soul Realm—dead, rotted, and cold once more. Demons screeched, and Syra flinched. The Guardian turned to her, his eyes soft, as if oblivious to the world around them. "You are the daughter of Nala, and it is you alone who can change the future of this realm. The blood that runs in you is the only blood that will bring balance. You are the future, Syra."

She shook her head, overwhelmed by it all. "No—no, I'm not," she retorted. "You stand here as if you are something special, but what have you done?" Syra curled her lip up at him in disgust. "You are a murderer, a traitor—nothing more than a Guardian with a sour attitude."

She wanted to leave, to escape this nightmare, but that hope crumbled as she felt Kar grab her arm and yank her forward. His grip was bone-breaking, but that wasn't what scared her. It was his look. Hate coated his expression. "You think I killed him, don't you?"

With a single yank, she broke herself free from him. Syra swallowed down her growing dread. "It had to be you," she mumbled. If it wasn't, then she would have no one to bear the weight of her anger.

All around, her surroundings shifted, turning into mist. The change happened so fast that she had no time to react. Kar dissipated before her as well.

Syra started and blinked. She looked around, disoriented, but then saw stars above her. The smell of rain met her nose, and she took a large inhale. Faces came into focus above her. Zarek, Roman, and Zane.

Zane's eyes were wide. "You passed out—"

Zarek took her firmly by the shoulder and hauled her up like she weighed nothing. Syra barely had time to react and get her footing before the Guardian was in her face. "What was that, Syra? What in the world was that?" His voice was raised, heated.

Immediately, she was defensive. Her heart was racing, and she was still trying to catch her breath. The storm boomed in the distance. "I was trying to practice my lesson, just how you taught me. And then I wasn't here anymore, I—"

"Was he there?" Zarek interrupted.

"Kar was—"

"How?" The Guardian turned on his heels. He asked as if she would know the answer, as if she had facilitated all of this. It enraged her.

She took a step toward him. "You think I want any of this, Zarek? You think I just decided to have a visit with that traitor? You think I want to run with my tail tucked, like some pathetic moron?" Her voice was rising. This was it. She had reached her wits' end, no longer caring about who or what heard her. "I don't want this!"

Zarek was in her face before she could take her next breath. "You're marked, Syra," he said. "You can't run from any of it. You think this is running?" He gestured at their surroundings. "This is buying us time, because you're ill-prepared." He shoved his finger into her chest with a bruising force. "*Marked*," he repeated with disdain. "The dead know who you are, but you obviously don't."

He turned around and hauled himself up on Uyul. "Let's move," he ordered. "I'm done."

Syra gulped and approached Hazel, ignoring the glares of the other two men. The time was nearing. There was no way she could keep information from them any longer—this blow-up had slaughtered that goal.

If they wanted answers, they did not challenge her for them. Instead, Zane and Roman got on their steeds without a word. Syra ignored them and motioned for Hazel to start walking. The horse flicked his ears in annoyance, but obeyed. She bit the inside of her cheek, fuming. Her thoughts wandered back to the vision, visit, whatever it was.

"Zarek," she called. The Guardian's head tilted in the slightest toward her. She took that as her sign. "It was Kar. He was in the Soul Realm, and he did things—"

"Silence!" He ordered and spun on Uyul to face her. "What good will it do to talk about this now? Who can change what happened?" He waited, and the only response was the hooves of the steeds as they walked. Syra felt heat rise to her cheeks in humiliation. She could fix it. She could change it if she was prepared—she didn't need him to tell her to know that. This was her fault.

Zarek turned to face forward again with a huff. "Like damn cattle waiting to be slaughtered," he mumbled, and fell silent. Roman and Zane hung behind her, and rightfully so. Syra wanted nothing to do with the Guardian, and she was pretty certain nobody else did either. The group fell quiet, and she couldn't shake the feeling that the two men behind her were watching, whispering things that only they could hear.

She shoved the worries aside. Not for right now.

Kar had been furious with her assumption that he was the one who killed Dryl. She had gone all this time believing he had slaughtered the Guardian in cold blood, but maybe she was wrong. Maybe she was wrong about everything. His fury had cracked her beliefs, and now she wasn't sure about anything at all.

The creature stained her thoughts. It was a vision she couldn't shake free from, no matter how hard she tried. It was hideous, otherworldly, and massive. If these were the monsters Zarek had referred to, she now understood why the Guardians were afraid. With dwindling numbers, and only some possessing the skill to harvest energy, they stood no chance against a force of that nature.

But the vision of the once-beautiful Soul Realm stayed with her too. She could vividly recall the sweet smells and the crisp colors. In all her life, she had never seen anything as perfect as that.

Syra had so many questions, so much she wanted to say, but she withheld. The only person who stood a chance at answering her questions was Zarek, and she wasn't going to speak to him right now. The Guardian was ahead, his back to her. The silence was deafening, the air thick with tension, even in this open space. It made taking a full breath nearly impossible.

When the time came, she would ask her questions, but until then, she refrained. Zarek had a lot of explaining to do, and she expected an apology on top of that.

For now, she focused on her breathing. Syra needed to get her anger under control, because her hands were still trembling. Now was not the time to talk. She feared if anything was said that pissed her off, she would pop.

In the distance, thunder bellowed.

LATE-NIGHT CONFESSIONS

Morei could see the flames lick the metal of the soldiers' swords just as they screamed. The fire's heat filled his body—not with distress, but with a thrill. Dark Energy moved *within* him, devouring the souls of the fallen. All around, he watched as these men's eyes flashed with that final moment, that instant where their entire life passed in front of them, where they either saw the monster they became or the hero they dreamed to be.

It was euphoric to see a man die—to have their entire life in his hands. With a flick of his wrist, a simple gesture, they were gone. That was true power, real control.

As he watched the final man fall before him, the voices screeched in his head, unsatisfied and hungry for more. Morei roared in response, wanting to take back the sanctuary of his thoughts. The Dark Energy had had enough, yet it was being greedy, wanting to take even more lives.

There were none to give. They had all been slaughtered, and what lay before the king was a landscape of bodies, bloodied and ruined.

Hot power surged through him, driving him to his knees, as his control was stolen from him. His sword fell from his grip, clanging against the ground just as his lungs cried out for more air. Throat constricting, he could no longer breathe. Panic flared abruptly, consuming him, just as the energy did. Suffocating was no way to go, and yet it was exactly how he would die. Dark Energy was never satiated. The more it was fed, the hungrier it grew—the stronger the impulses became. It was an undefeatable battle, and the king had already lost.

Morei jolted awake, gasping for breath, body shaking as cold fear stabbed at his pounding heart. The air was moist against his bare skin, and he blinked in the dark, hearing a torrent of rain outside. He looked over at the door, which he'd left open, just as lightning filled the sky with a white light. A late-night thunderstorm. These were some of his favorites, when the volatility was at its peak and the world at its mercy.

Slowing his breath, he looked to his left. Emerald's back lit up from another flash of lightning. This one was accompanied by a low rumble that crawled its way across the sky. He watched her breathing—slow, steady, at peace.

Morei was overcome with the nightmare he'd just awoken from. Perhaps it had been a memory, perhaps a vision. He didn't know, and frankly, he didn't want to. There were certain things better left to the imagination.

Because if he accepted what he had seen as reality, then he was a monster.

Emerald stirred, and instinctively he reached out and wrapped an arm around her waist, pulling her closer to him so that their bodies touched. Underneath the sheets, her skin was hot, chasing away even the strongest of chills.

When they had made love, the voices had stopped. If only for the moment, the king had found peace. That was not something he knew how to explain, or where to even begin. But as he lay here now, they were there, prodding at the back of his mind. Their whispers were incessant, incoherent, and there was only one way to make them quiet—to give them life.

That would require him to spill the same blood he was ashamed to want.

"Is it raining?" Emerald asked, her voice soft. She slid her hand down, wrapping her delicate fingers over his.

"Yes," he answered her, his face tucked up against the back of her neck. Her hair smelled sweet, and he took a deep breath in, trying to place the scent.

"We left the glasses outside," she told him.

Morei chuckled at her words, remembering how quickly things had escalated. "Your robe too."

Emerald laughed, her voice music to his ears. "By the Gods, we're wrecks."

He laughed harder, surprised by her words, and burrowed deeper, finding her neck and kissing it gently. Emerald rolled over onto her back, taking her hand and tracing it over his arm.

Raising his head, Morei gave her a mischievous stare. The heated conversation from earlier felt leagues away. Here, the king felt free. "I prefer the terms stubborn and passionate," he replied, and reached forward, drawing her hand up to his lips. As gently as he could, he kissed it.

Lightning flashed, filling the room with a white light and painting her features with a delicate brush. Emerald took her hand from his and caressed it over his face. Her fingers sparked against his skin, full of life. "Come here."

As she pulled him down to meet him, she kissed him affectionately. Morei wrapped his arms around her and moved himself over. Lying atop her, he broke from her lips and showered her in kisses along her cheeks, jaw, and neck. As he did so, the king could feel her smile and giggle.

Moving down to her ear, he whispered, "You could rule the world with looks alone."

When he heard her scoff, he repositioned himself so that he could lay his head against her chest. The sound of her heart met his ears, and he smiled. Life. How much he wished he could listen to this sound forever. A beating heart knew nothing but to continue onward, despite how cruel life was. As he listened to the song, Emerald's fingers played with his hair, tugging and lacing their way with methodically slow motions.

They lay there for a while, basking in each other's touch. Emerald's breathing had slowed so much that he was certain she had fallen asleep. He was about to move when she spoke, her words breaking through the noise of the storm as if it were nothing more than dust.

"My twin brother is Nerius and my younger sister Jasmine," she whispered into the dark. Her heartbeat quickened to his ear, but he did not speak. "Both named after our great-great-grandparents on my mother's side. My mother was Cora, and my father was Derik. On the outside, we were the family everyone wanted to be. Perfect, as some used to call us. But we were far from it."

Emerald fell silent, her breathing unsteady now. The king lay still, certain that if he moved, she would forgo the rest of her story.

After what felt like lifetimes had slipped by, she continued. "I never saw it until I was a little older, but Nerius resented me from a very young age. I was the child my parents always turned to, you see. I was, in their eyes, the perfect one who never did wrong. I excelled in everything I did and obeyed their every command. As a child, you can imagine how much that influenced me. They loved me, but they didn't let me breathe—let me be a kid—and so I spent my whole life bending to their will, because it mattered most to me that they were happy, even at the cost of my own freedom."

Her hands groomed his hair as thunder boomed. The rain lightened from a torrent to a steady drizzle, and in the midst of Emerald's confession, Morei thought of the giant firepit to the north, where the victims' bodies had hopefully been devoured before the storm came. He could see it now, the mush of ash and decay, blending to create a gray mud stinking of burnt flesh and metal. Bone jutted out from spots in the mud, catching the light of the storm. It was a horrific thought, but he couldn't shove it away.

"My father was on his deathbed when he proclaimed I'd take the throne," the queen mumbled. "By then, it was obvious Jasmine would not be selected, for she was younger by four summers. I never had interest in the throne though—by the Gods, it was the last thing I wanted. I had been raised to be so exceptional that I loathed power and fame. More than anything, I wanted the throne to go to my brother, because at least then he would feel accepted."

Emerald's voice dropped even lower, and her chest shuddered underneath him. "I can still remember when Nerius and I sat at our father's side, awaiting his decision. I remember the look on my brother's face when we heard my name—Nerius was so angry at me. He had wanted nothing more than to be accepted, and he weighed that entirely on that single decision. Our relationship died that day. Nerius left while Jasmine and I slept. I haven't heard or seen him since. Before the next summer, my sister was swept away by one of the princes of Assane. And I've been alone."

Emerald stopped talking, as if slapped into a silence. The king waited. She had shared such an intimate piece of herself that he hardly knew how to react. All along, he had wanted information about her, yet the mysterious Emerald had remained exactly that—a mystery. Finally, after all this time, he had gotten the key to understanding her.

Morei took a deep breath. The silence that hung between them was marked by the occasional thunder and the thin rain. After a long moment, the king finally found the right words, but it was not what he had planned to speak of.

"I have been tasked to identify someone to take the crown," he confessed, the words tasting even more bitter than before.

"And I have done so, and to some degree I understand why. The people are afraid, and they think that a new king will give them a profound sense of hope. Caster will continue to supply Geral if I step down too, which is critical to the city's survival." Morei let the last sentence fade before he finished, "But I'm beginning to resent the people I swore to protect."

In all honesty, he wasn't sure how to process these developing emotions. The king hadn't ever been trained to deal with hatred toward his own city. There had ever been one goal, and that was to protect his people. Take that away, and he wasn't anyone. He would be a man without purpose.

Emerald's fingers twirled through his hair without interruption, as if to tell him it would all work out. "It's because they are afraid of you," she whispered. "That is no way to rule."

"I would remain at the council table, but they would never view me the same," he added. "I would be a reject and certainly have no respect from anyone." Morei held on tighter, confident that if he let go of her, he would drown in his own thoughts. "The moment I hand the crown over, I've failed my family name."

"No," Emerald replied, firm now. "You could say Henry Junok failed our family name. By the grace of Greve, he outright destroyed our name, but we did not let that deter us or what we stood for. You could do the same. A city is nothing more than some buildings, territory, and people. The ruler defines what that city becomes, not the other way around."

"What are you suggesting, Emerald?"

A handful of heartbeats passed between them. "I'm . . ." The queen trailed off, and by the shift in how her fingers were playing with his hair, he knew she wasn't sure about her next words. "If you find yourself no longer the man you want to be, or the king you deserve to be, you have a home in Junok."

Whatever thoughts Morei had wanted to say were swept aside with a strong hand. Leaning up, he stared at her in the dark. "Don't make promises you don't know if you can keep."

While the idea of running far from this city sounded divine in every aspect, he was still the king of his people. Plus, he doubted Junok's council would welcome him in with open arms. It wasn't like he had made a heroic name for himself.

She obviously didn't see him in that light. "I'm serious, Morei. I know I came here on a mission, and I'll eventually have to leave, but when I do and if things are no better here, you are welcome to join me."

The king leaned back and rested his head against the pillow, eyes locked above him. It felt like in an instant, his life's purpose had been shattered and replaced with ultimatums. If his rulership went down in flames and the people completely turned on him because of Cu'cel, he could leave. But if he left, abandoned the only world he ever knew, then he wasn't sure what that made him. A coward?

"Perhaps," was all he could manage to say. It seemed to put Emerald at peace, and she pulled the cover over, tucking herself back to sleep. He listened as she got herself comfortable.

"Thank you," the queen muttered, words already slurred.

There was no point in a response, so he held his tongue and listened to her fall back into slumber. When he was certain, Morei rolled over and sat at the edge of the bed. Holding his head between his hands, he sat there for a long while, his mind its own storm. The humid air from the rain coated his skin as he remained motionless.

Freedom would be his if he left Geral behind. Morei would no longer be tied to the obligations of being king. But running only made him a deserter—if he walked away from it all, he was certain it would haunt him. That was not the man he had been raised to be. Geral might be falling apart, but it was only temporary. Once they found a solution and peace returned, all this tension would fade, and soon, the people would forget that they had ever turned on Morei in the first place.

By then, though, he would no longer be king.

Above all, he couldn't ignore the sour attitude he felt toward the citizens, toward this city. If he ran, they would never understand. More than anything, he wanted to march into the city and demand the respect he so rightfully deserved.

Yet he didn't trust himself. Even as he sat there, captivated by his own thoughts, he couldn't ignore the growing impulses that scattered his logic. It had been nearly half a moon cycle since he had drawn blood, and it was becoming increasingly clear that the longer he waited—the more he refrained—the stronger the urges became. If he thought about it, he could practically taste the warm, metallic flavor he had experienced dragging his tongue over the bloodied blade.

The impulse was a symptom of his illness, which he hadn't asked for and couldn't rid himself of. While he had been unconscious, the ailment had intensified, and he now looked worse than ever before. There was no point in denying that the people didn't see a king they could trust, but rather one they feared. How could he ever regain their respect when he would only become sicker?

It was impossible—and perhaps the council had seen that long before he had.

A single tear escaped, running down his cheek in a mad dash to get away from him. The king let it, surprised and ashamed. It was not royal to cry, and it certainly wasn't something a man of his stature should be doing over a few thoughts, but he couldn't help it. Everything felt like it was falling apart, and if he didn't do something drastic soon, all that his family's lineage had worked for would have been for nothing.

Morei wanted to do the right thing, but it was becoming increasingly clear that that might be impossible.

A NEW ERA

inner was over, and night was here. The stars twinkled, proud, oblivious to the world beneath them. Cyrus lay in his quarters, basking in darkness. The only light offered was that of the rising moon. He watched it climb, waiting for the right moment to leave. Stress tickled the nape of his neck, and he rubbed it with his hand. It was never easy outright betraying anyone's trust, but this felt different.

Kyllian was Zorya's father and the princess had taken a strange liking to Cyrus that he could not shake off, no matter how hard he tried. She was dangerously beautiful but also betrothed to Prince Shunera. However, based on the interaction he saw at the dinner tonight—because, yes, Shunera had ensured his place at the table—he had concluded that Zorya wasn't thrilled with the prince. The man was loud, obnoxious, and pompous, while the princess carried herself with grace and consideration. She was charming, clever, and funny, but she held herself with an air that only royalty possessed.

Cyrus couldn't say he remembered the taste of the food, not because it wasn't delicious but because his mind was elsewhere. It was in the tunnels, waiting for him. The princess had pulled him aside at one point and asked what he was thinking. When he had told her nothing, she snorted and rolled her eyes. "I've spent my whole life studying people for when I become queen, do you think I don't notice how you're withdrawn from the conversations? Is it Shunera?"

Cyrus gritted his teeth at the prince's name but didn't tell her the truth—that he was eager to return to exploring this palace and its secrets, and that he was certain her father was keeping secrets from him.

Now, standing here, he glanced back at his bed. The *Book of Liral* lay in its sack under the pillows, but the Rider's Sword was strapped around his hip. He would not be wandering strange tunnels without it. For all he knew, some bizarre cult lived underground and was using the tunnels as their resting place. Perhaps that was why people who ventured there never returned.

Sozar would wait in the courtyard, because if he moved, that would bring about unwanted attention. As much as the dragon despised being left to just wait, he understood. They were walking on a dangerously tight rope, and one wrong move could create an enemy out of an entire city. While Cyrus had come to the conclusion that another city added to the list was not much to worry about, he really didn't want to keep making enemies.

He had gone his entire life trying to befriend everyone and anything, avoiding confrontation, bowing out of arguments if they steered toward unchartered waters. Now, in a season, he had turned an entire country against him—particularly the cities of Geral and Diemon—and risked turning another. All those summers trying to make friends suddenly felt pathetic.

Cyrus sighed and shook himself free of those thoughts. He couldn't afford to care what strangers thought of him. What mattered was figuring out the truth and staying alive.

A sensation washed over him, making the hairs stand on end up his arms and down his body. Then came an icy wave, and he shivered in response. Dragging a hand across his face, he peeked back, suddenly feeling exposed, but nobody was there.

Sozar spoke. *Did you feel that?*

Cyrus let his eyes continue to scan the dark room, now wishing he had kept the lantern on, but it would have attracted unwanted attention at this night hour. *Yes,* he answered. *What was that?*

I don't kn—The dragon stopped, and Cyrus could feel Sozar tense.

What is it? Cyrus's tone dripped with urgency. The dragon had never before reacted like this, not even when he was captured by Geral soldiers. Their mental link wavered, as if a force had just slammed into it, threatening to sever their connection altogether. Crossing the room, he was prepared to barge into the courtyard and fight the Gods themselves when Sozar spoke.

We are not alone.

Confused, Cyrus shook his head at the door. "What are you talking about?" he asked aloud.

I will meet you at your room. We must go. Sozar's words were full of excitement. The dragon's energy shifted. To Cyrus, he felt like a hatchling again, bouncing around and eager to go exploring, regardless of risks. Sozar could hardly speak to him as he clambered out of the courtyard's dragon hold and launched himself into the sky. From their bond, Cyrus watched it all, feeling the wind take hold of the dragon's wings as he unfurled them and flapped to gain altitude. Then he steered toward the other side of the palace, where Cyrus's room lay.

Without hesitation, he ran over and flung open the door to get out onto the patio. The wind was chilly, and it tickled his skin through the black tunic he wore. Closing the door, he stepped out until he was at the railing, then looked about. On cue, Sozar was already arriving. The deep thump of his wings jarred his bones and danced off the stone walls of the palace.

I can't get close because of my wings. The dragon dipped underneath the patio. *But you can jump.*

Cyrus had already had that in mind and was pulling himself over the railing. The stone was rough to the touch, but he hardly noticed, keeping his eyes locked on the dragon beneath him. If he didn't screw up, he would land on Sozar's haunches, but if he missed, he'd either be freefalling to his death or impaled on one of the dragon's horns.

He wasn't worried, though. After their trust fall in the Releuthian Mountains, this felt like child's play. He leapt, and the air filled his clothes for several long heartbeats before he landed hard on Sozar's left thigh. Immediately, he gripped one of the horns and pulled himself up. *Go,* he told Sozar, and began his small trek to the gap in his shoulders. The dragon pulled himself up just as Cyrus plopped himself in the spot he had spent so many days in. There was no saddle, so he made sure his legs were comfortable and gripped the horn in front of him as Sozar climbed to escape any eyes.

The city was beautiful from this height, a spectacle of stars along the land, where people scurried with their lanterns or homes were still awake. The moon sat over the horizon, bathing the lake behind the city in white light. Hyle's Lake, as he had learned from passing conversation, and the river that cut through West and East Razan was the Frynian River. Snuggled up against the lake were the Beutóne Mountains, with Craygon's Crater. Razan itself was huge. It had to be the largest of all Vorelian cities, but he didn't have time to ponder, for Sozar turned and they were flying out east, away from the city and toward the untouched land.

To his right stood the Ashen Sea, calling for his return. To his left, an unexplored world north of the Razan city. Helyna's Falls lay to his right, where the Frynian River met its fate with the edge of a vertical cliff. All of it basked in the light of the moon, making it appear otherworldly. It felt like Cyrus was traveling the underworld.

Then his attention turned ahead, in the direction Sozar was flying. Something else moved there with bulk and speed, bright, even for the night. It was as if the moon itself were traveling through the sky.

The revelation slapped him hard, and he suddenly understood Sozar's comment. He had been so eager to get to the dragon that he hadn't spared a moment to grasp what he meant. Not that he would have understood it, even if Sozar had explained himself right then and there, because what he was witnessing right now stole the breath right from his lungs. His limbs froze, eyes wide. He'd all but stopped breathing. Even the world fell silent.

A dragon.

And Rider, Sozar added, sensing Cyrus's realization. *We are not alone.*

A yell was bubbling up in the back of his throat. He could hardly contain himself. The excitement was overflowing, and he raised a fist in the air and yelled as loud as he could. Damn the city that lay behind him, this was fate! Sozar dipped his head and let a burst of flames erupt from his jaws. The bright orange nearly blinded him, the heat kissing his legs before it was swept away and sizzled out.

In response, the dragon coming toward them blew fire as well. The yell of a man reached Cyrus's ears right after. His heart raced, and it felt like the entire world had melted away in an instant.

They weren't alone.

The Dragon Rider ahead dipped, and they followed suit, looking to land. The wind rushed past as they descended at an incredible rate. The noise deafened everything around Cyrus save for the flap of Sozar's wings as he flared them in preparation to land. As the dragon planted his legs onto the ground, Cyrus was already jumping off. The impact jarred his bones, but he hardly minded, only caring about meeting another Rider like himself. So desperate was he to meet the mysterious man, he barely noticed the mud that splashed along his pants from Sozar's tail.

Before them stood a glorious, pearl-white dragon. The scales of the beast glittered under the night sky. Horns jutted along his jaw, curved sharpened to a deadly point. The dragon stood taller than Sozar, but leaner, and he blinked at them with bright red eyes. As if knowing he was being studied, the dragon snorted and sent a plume of fire and smoke into the air. On the beast's back lay a custom onyx saddle, the leather well polished based on the way it reflected light. Pouches were tied along the front of the saddle and on several of the horns. By the looks of it, they were traveling.

The man descended, and he appeared to be no older than Cyrus. The moonlight painted his features, revealing dark hair and a rich tan complexion that gave away his ancient heritage. The Rider stood tall, meeting Cyrus's gaze, and he wore a metal mask that wrapped around his jaw. It looked intentionally tattered and gave him a menacing look, as if he belonged on the battlefield. The man's eyes did not leave Cyrus's as he reached up and unsnapped the metal mask before removing it completely.

They stood a dozen paces apart, surrounded by their dragons. Cyrus opened his mouth to speak, but his tongue failed him. A sword was attached at the man's hips, and he was suddenly overcome with the belief that perhaps they had been lured out here to be attacked.

If that was the case, though, then they should have attacked from the air.

The Rider hooked the mask's strap over a horn and spoke, his accent thick. He was not from Eiyrằl or Sorréle. "Up here, the air is drier and less forgiving than what my body is used to." He smiled and stepped forward. "I have traveled long and far to finally meet you, Dragon Rider!"

The white dragon stepped forward and dipped his snout so that hot air washed over Cyrus. A foreign but familiar presence forced its way into his mind, the voice deep like Sozar's. *Greetings, Mountain Flyer.*

Cyrus opened his mouth to speak, then closed it. He was at a loss for words and instead reached up to touch the warm, soft scales around the dragon's snout. Laying a hand on Sozar had become habitual, normal, but to be in the presence of a new dragon made him realize just how extraordinary these beasts were.

The Rider laid a gloved hand onto the white dragon. "Ashtir," he explained, and smiled. "And I am Dameon."

Sozar brushed his snout over Cyrus's hair, standing nearly on top of him. "I'm Cyrus," he answered, then gestured back. "Sozar here." Licking his lips, he added, "Your accent. Are you from Diyră?"

Dameon snorted. "That cursed land? No, no. Saveen, the city. I am from Creitón. Rumor has it you're from Sorréle. Is that so?"

Nodding, he replied, "Diemon. How'd you know?"

Dameon slapped Cyrus on the shoulder, which startled him, but he didn't let it show. "Some of us are better at hiding, eh? Word reached my ear that a Dragon Rider was last spotted fleeing the gem city nearly a season ago. Ashtir and I had been planning on heading north to the Rider Federation and decided to place our bets the urge would fill you too, that you would come to Eiyrăl. And you did!"

Cyrus could sense Sozar's confusion as much as his own. "The urge? We came here because . . ." He trailed off, suddenly unsure of himself. "Because I wanted answers about my heritage."

"Nonsense." The Rider flashed a grin up at Ashtir, as if a conversation had just unfolded between the two. If he was anything like Cyrus, then he wasn't used to people watching. Dameon looked back at him. "You may not have realized it, but there's a call, an energy, that we Riders are all joined with. Ancient energy, from the stories I've heard. It draws us to the Rider Federation, but its source is unknown." He shrugged.

"Probably buried after the Great Fall. I am rambling. You must forgive me. It's not often us Riders find one another."

Cyrus laughed, understanding, but his voice came out weak, even to his own ears. While Dameon might be rambling, he was in shock. "I—" He shook his head. "Back there, Sozar and I felt something. Did you feel it too?"

"Aye, it's a trick Ashtir and I created. Sort of a pulse we put out to the world in hopes of reaching another fellow Rider and dragon." Dameon nodded toward Sozar, eyes hovering above Cyrus's head. "Dragons have a powerful life force, one that we can tap into with practice. It was what you felt, and what drew you out." He grinned again. "Glad to know it worked. We have been using it for several moon cycles now, unsure if we were harvesting the energy right."

Slowly, Cyrus nodded, lost. He and Sozar had spoken relentlessly about what the dragon might be capable of, but Sozar had yet to uncover it. Cyrus couldn't even harvest energy, but he felt insecure speaking on that matter. The last thing he wanted to do was let this Dragon Rider know he was damn near useless.

"Tell me about you," he said instead. "How did you come upon Ashtir? Do you have the same scar?"

And like that, the conversation was off. If Dameon had noted Cyrus's sudden topic change, he thankfully didn't show it. Soon, the insecurity was lost as the two shared stories and commonalities. Sure enough, Dameon had the same raised scar at the base of his left thumb. It was red like Cyrus's, but a shade pinker because of his skin tone.

Dameon had stumbled on Ashtir's gold egg by accident, much like Cyrus with Sozar. Down in Creitón, there were three ports to the three cities. His city, Saveen, had imported a shipment from Diyrå of golds, jewels, and rare oddities. With his family the receiver of the goods, they had eagerly dug in to find a chest that held the dragon egg. It was supposed to be a dud, a fake, nothing more than a showpiece, and for a few summers, that was all it was. It sat nestled in its chest with the lid up, on display for anyone willing to pay. Dameon's father was particular about who cared for the more unique artifacts, but on one afternoon, Dameon had been sent to polish the egg while the staff member had been unreachable.

That afternoon had changed the rest of his life. For, much like Cyrus, Dameon awoke to the sensation of being watched, and stumbled for his light. Only when he lit the lantern and found a small white dragon staring at him from the edge of his bed did Dameon realize just how much his life and everyone else's would transform. With the same draw that Cyrus had felt, he had reached out and touched the powerful beast, locking in his fate.

Unlike Cyrus, Dameon had eagerly approached his family, thrilled and wanting to share this historical event. But his father chained him and separated him from Ashtir, demanding that he and the dragon would serve the city—a cruel part of the story that Dameon quickly skipped over, clearly uncomfortable. By a stroke of luck, he had been freed by a bystander and slipped away in the middle of the night with his dragon.

Ever since, Dameon had been on the run.

"The saddle." Cyrus gestured at it. "It's stunning. Where did you get it?"

A sheepish smirk touched the Rider's lips. "I—shall we say borrowed? It was part of the collection my father had. I took it when I escaped." The Rider scuffed his boot. "One could say it was payback for what he did to me. Ashtir will grow out of it soon, but it has been good to me."

As the story had gone on, Cyrus had quickly learned that Ashtir was a moon cycle younger than Sozar. Both dragons would likely double in size once they reached full maturity, but they would each be unique in their own way.

Now Cyrus retold his own story with as much detail as Dameon had provided. The Rider listened with respect, only asking questions when needed, but he was quick to react when the recount of the capture at Geral was told.

"You saw *him?*" Dameon pressed. "The Demon King?"

Cyrus laughed. "From behind bars, yes. But not for long. He left soon afterward, and I broke out after that."

"The stories about him are everywhere," Dameon replied, sounding eager. "You can't turn a stone over without *some* mention of that bastard. I would have flown out to see him myself, but rumor has it he's mastered two elements of Dark Energy. He's ruthless, and cuts the heads off anyone who disagrees with him."

Raising an eyebrow, Cyrus couldn't necessarily say he didn't believe the rumors. Although, two elements of Dark Energy seemed outrageous.

Compared to what Kyllian had shared, this all sounded much more relevant.

"What do you want?" Dameon asked suddenly, his voice going softer. "I mean, you came here looking for your heritage, and I'm assuming you've found nothing."

He pursed his lips and reached up to where he knew Sozar's snout was and gently rubbed it, relishing in the heat. The night air was catching up to him, and his adrenaline was beginning to fade. "Nothing, but your parents weren't Dragon Riders. All the stories I've heard talk about first-borns." It was becoming increasingly clear that he would never find his family. Perhaps they were dead after all.

"When Ashtir hatched for me, I thought the same." He glanced around and dropped his voice, as if afraid someone might hear even though they were so far outside the Razan city. "I think a new era of Dragon Riders is happening, and you and me? We're the first. We're going to lead it."

Cyrus swallowed. "Lead it? How can we? It's not like there's eggs just lying around." And truthfully, he still didn't know what he wanted to do.

As if sensing this, Dameon grabbed his arm with a firm grip. "I know what you're thinking—how could we do this? But let me tell you a little secret. Something I learned while I was scavenging around the Rider Federation."

"I was told it was inhabited by strange beasts," Cyrus interjected. He knew Kyllian had been keeping information from him, but was the king trying to keep him out of the Riders' home?

Dameon waved him off. "Sure, there's some wild things there. I can promise there are creatures you've never seen, scurrying among the debris and hissing when you get to close. But with a dragon by your side, they leave you alone. The small ones are pretty harmless, and cute, too. I'm getting off topic, though. Listen, in the debris of the palace, there are items still. Scrolls of various trades, imports, deals, court orders, all of it. Most of it is pretty damaged, but I stumbled on a deal that was made between Razan and the Rider Federation almost eight hundred summers ago." The Rider's eyes shimmered with such ferocity that it looked as if he might scream. "Dragon eggs, Cyrus. The court handed over two dragon eggs to the Razan family in some deal."

The information just about knocked him right off his feet. Even Sozar had tensed behind him. "What?" Cyrus licked his lips, breathless and overwhelmed. "Are you certain they weren't Ashtir and Sozar?"

"More than certain," Dameon answered, clearly proud. "The description said silver eggs. Females."

"The last Dragon Rider was seen about eight centuries ago," Cyrus whispered, putting the two together. "That would mean whoever struck that deal was trying to protect the next generation of Riders."

"Exactly!"

Ashtir snorted in agreement.

Kyllian's withholding that, Sozar blurted out, satisfied. *Now we have our answer.*

Cyrus stole a glance up at his majestic dragon. *They must be hidden somewhere in the tunnels.* The dream danced behind his line of vision, and he couldn't help but recall Rosarie's behavior. All the signs were there. They had to get back to the tunnels.

Agreed. The dragon let a rumble radiate through his chest.

"You came from Razan, didn't you?" The hunger in Dameon's voice was there. The Rider already knew the answer.

"You want me to go look, don't you? You want me to find the eggs and bring them back."

"Think about it," he insisted. "We could take these dragon eggs and raise a new generation. Cyrus, we were chosen. Can't you see that? We will drive the new world, build an empire. We will be unstoppable."

Again, purpose. If Destiny was trying to mock him, she was doing a fine job at it. Cyrus bit the inside of his cheek and inhaled deeply. Perhaps he didn't understand, but he did not wish the dragons to be obligated to war. Dameon didn't strike him as a man who would sit passively while men fought for power, not based on the way his eyes lit up at the idea of him being in charge.

These eggs, Sozar, and Ashtir if the dragon so chose deserved a life in peace, not a life chosen by man. Who was Cyrus to say what ancient beasts should and should not do? It was not his place. It was no man's place.

"What if we take the eggs and disappear?" he countered. "We can slip away to some place. I know the west of Sorréle is uncharted. We can fly there, set up a place, and raise the dragons without war."

"And in a matter of summers, the war would be brought to our door." Dameon straightened then, as if filled with some unseen force. "I do not seek bloodshed, Cyrus. I seek to win the war that will end all future wars. I want peace."

Peace. The idea teased Cyrus. Of course he wanted peace among the lands. The idea of flying wherever he went without the fear of a king or queen hunting him down filled him with indescribable joy. As of right now, he was a nomad, belonging to no city, and the thought of being able to land somewhere and call it his made him smile.

"See? You want it as much as I do." Dameon looked up at the white dragon. "The pair of us? We could go anywhere we want, be anything we want."

But as quick as the smile appeared, it slipped from his face. The bloodshed it would cost would be irreversible. No, Cyrus would not have it. "I'm sorry, Dameon, but I can't. I can't be a part of this."

The cheer in the Rider's eyes fell instantly, replaced by a cold rage that made his features monstrous. Without hesitation, he shoved his hands into Cyrus's chest, knocking him backward. Sozar growled as Cyrus fell, the scales digging into his back. The dragon snaked his head around and forced Dameon back, lips curling upward. Ashtir stepped up to shield his rider, pushing his own giant head between Sozar and Dameon. With one glittering red eye, the dragon held his ground, separating the two riders completely.

Seconds passed, marked only by the breeze that caressed the grass beneath their feet. The dragons stood still, ready to pounce on whoever moved first. Cyrus swallowed, feeling foolish and angry. He wanted to trust Dameon and Ashtir, wanted to yell in delight and celebrate the existence of someone else who was just like him, whose life had been torn away because of what he had become.

But they weren't the same. Dameon wanted war, and power, and he wanted Cyrus to do his dirty work and steal the eggs. There was no guarantee that Dameon wouldn't backstab him either once he had done what he wished.

It occurred to him then that the Rider didn't know where the eggs were located. He also didn't know that Cyrus had an idea. If he refused, Dameon would try to sneak in himself and find them.

The plan became clear: find the eggs before he did. At least in Cyrus's hands, they would be promised a life of peace, the life they deserved.

Dameon moved suddenly, but he retreated onto Ashtir instead of forward. As he yanked himself up onto the saddle, his sneer was replaced with a calm, flat expression. "Two nights from now, we meet here, when the moon breaks the horizon. Then you will tell me your final answer." The white dragon stepped away and unfurled his leathery wings. "I was once uncertain like you, but my family betrayed me and taught me just how cruel the world could be for power. There's only one way to defeat that—become just as cruel."

At that, Ashtir launched himself into the sky. The gouges in the ground were the final reminder of what Cyrus has just done—turn away the only friend who could ever fully understand him. It left a hole in his heart the size of this country, and he watched the Dragon Rider go, listening as the beat of Ashtir's wings faded.

Sozar nudged his arm and blew hot air over him. *Hatchling, the choice you made will one day grace you with its benefits. I believe you did the right thing.*

I know. Cyrus turned and pulled himself onto Sozar. The familiar rough scales and gap in his shoulders settled his nerves some. He knew it had been the right choice, but that hadn't made it easy. There was no way he could agree to such a wild plan when he hardly knew Dameon or his true intentions. The dragon eggs were just the beginning.

What was supposed to be an amazing meeting had officially soured his mood.

Sozar sensed his desire and launched himself into the night, and they quickly disappeared among the stars. Instead of turning to the city, however, the dragon veered toward the sea. Cyrus noticed immediately, inhaling the salt from the waters and feeling the familiar humid air brush over him.

"What are we doing?" he asked. The words were torn from his lips and tossed behind him. Still, the dragon had heard.

I will not return so quickly. For now, we fly. The world can wait.

Sozar dipped lower until the land gave way to a steep cliff and impressive waterfall. Helyna's Falls, no doubt. The sound met Cyrus's ears but was quickly replaced by the howl of the wind as they dove. He gripped the horn in front of him, tensing his body in preparation for the dragon's next move. Sozar's wings unfolded and caught the air, halting his dive and dragging them up. All the muscles in Cyrus's body felt like they were being pulled downward, as if he himself were being summoned by the sea. But the pull of the water dissipated, and they were soon soaring over like they had only days prior.

Cyrus gave himself the chance to watch the sea glitter as it shifted under the moon's gaze. It was a beautiful world, he reminded himself, but it was scratched and dirty from man. Right now, though, he could enjoy the purity that the waters offered him. Out here, no one could tell him what to do or who to be.

But he also could not run from the thoughts that were growing stronger every day. The Rider's Sword was pressed up against his leg, providing a constant source of fuel to his increasing worries: that no matter how hard he tried to run, destiny was going to find him.

Sooner or later, Cyrus would have to become the Dragon Rider the world needed him to be. Even if he wasn't ready.

AWAKENED AND AFRAID

"**A**gain!"

Syra heaved herself up from the ground and barely had a foot down before Zarek charged her once more. She lifted Death's Sword, muscles burning, and felt the metal collide. The impact jarred her arm. She ducked, turned, and tried to land a blow on his arm, but the Guardian was too fast.

"Trust yourself," Zarek advised as he stepped away, switching the blade to his right hand. "You're too cautious, overthinking and questioning every step you take."

The sun fell behind a cloud, but she hardly noticed. They had stopped in the morning and rested only half the day before the Guardian had forced her to her feet. She was exhausted, sore from yesterday's training, and distracted from last night's disaster. Her lungs were begging for more air than she could give, and her entire body ached. Zarek was driving her harder than she had ever gone before, but she refused to say anything to the Guardian—she refused to look weak. Syra was unable to speak between panting, so she nodded instead. A drop of sweat rolled down her cheek, leaving a path chilled by the breeze.

Zane and Roman were watching. Zane looked like he was itching to have a go, but he hadn't spoken up, and as bad as Syra wanted to hand the reins over to fresh meat for Zarek to squash, she was also desperate to prove herself.

The night before hung heavy over the group. No one had brought it up, but it was obvious everyone was thinking about it. Zane had eyed her all day between resting and eating. Roman had spoken to Zarek on several occasions, but the Guardian was short and tense, and the conversations never lasted. The tension brewing between Syra and Zarek had officially permeated the entire group. They hadn't spoken, except for Zarek demanding she train, but the Guardian's actions spoke loud and clear. He was pushing her as hard and as fast as he could.

"Switch arms," Zarek ordered once they had done a half circle around each other.

She stared. "I've never fought with my left hand."

"And when your enemy cuts your right off?" the Guardian said, directing Death's Sword at her. The metal shimmered just as the sun broke free of the cloud. "Switch."

This was outrageous, but Syra obliged, biting back a string of curses. If she couldn't defend herself against him with her dominant hand, then there was no way she could fight him off with her bad hand. The weapon felt foreign in her left, and she weighed it—the sword even felt heavier.

"Ready?" Zarek took a fighting stance.

She wanted to distract him, even if only temporarily. "Can we talk about last night?" The question came out in a pant.

A muscle in the Guardian's jaw twitched, visible even from her distance. "Ready?" he repeated, dismissive.

Syra rolled her eyes. He was ignoring her. She did her best to mimic her fighting stance with the opposite leg. The muscles in her forearm were already angry at the weight. "Sure," she puffed.

Zarek lunged once more, but at the last second side-stepped to her unarmed side. Syra swung her weapon and met the edge of his sword just in time. She jumped out of the way, instinct kicking in, and raised the blade to deflect his next strike.

"Faster!" Zarek yelled as he pushed her backward.

She grounded her teeth and deflected another blow, but it was too slow. The Guardian struck the edge of her sword and shoved it aside before swinging his boot under, knocking her on her bruised ass. That was the fifteenth time today.

"Get up," Zarek ordered, and turned to reposition himself. Frustration molded into fury. "No."

The Guardian halted in his steps. "What?"

"I said no," she spat. "Let me rest." Her back was on fire, the muscles in her arms ached, and her pride was broken. In all their fights, she hadn't even landed a scrape on the Guardian.

Zarek turned toward her. "Is this all a joke to you?" he hissed.

"Give her a break," Zane interjected. Syra shot him a warning glare. This was not his battle.

"Sit your ass down and stay quiet," Zarek snapped, pointing the sword at the man. A challenging moment passed between them before Zane met her eyes. Then he lowered himself down next to Roman, who raised an eyebrow.

The Guardian faced her again. "Okay, let's change it up. Stand."

Syra gave him a hard look. He didn't return Death's Sword to its rightful sheath, so she leaned over for her blade.

"Don't," he said. "You won't need it."

"But you—"

"Stand."

Syra swallowed and obliged, leaving the sword on the ground next to her. With him across from her, weapon already drawn, she felt hopeless. "Now what?"

Zarek switched the blade back to his dominant hand, his expression stoic. "Since you don't want to fight, you'll defend. Your goal—stop my blade."

Her jaw went slack, and her heart skipped a beat. "With my hands?"

"Energy," he grated.

"You can't expect me—"

The next words were replaced by a cry as Zarek charged her, sword raised. Syra felt the cold touch of fear grab her heart, and she rolled. Adrenaline pumped through her blood—there was something primitive when one was weaponless like she was now. The aches and discomfort evaporated from her muscles, even if it was only temporary.

"Come on, Syra," Zarek admonished as he turned to face her. "If you can hop realms, you can deflect my sword."

She tried to steady her breathing, but she felt like she was suffocating. "I don't know where to begin," she wheezed, and wiped her brow. The back of her hand came away coated in a fine layer of sweat and dust.

The Guardian readied his lunge. "The energy you are pulled to when you realm hop is the same energy you use to deflect me. This is all about control, Syra. Focus on the energies around you—feel that same energy in my sword. Ready?"

Zarek was intentional—he was testing her to see how fast she could learn, if she could at all. Syra had spent her entire life thinking she was ordinary, and now, in a matter of days, she was being forced to face a side of her she hadn't known existed. It all felt unnatural, and yet she had never felt more alive than right now.

Syra took a deep breath and nodded. If she couldn't manipulate the energy, then she'd roll, but she had to at least try. Zarek was right—if she could hop between the dead and living realms, then she had the power to defend herself against a sword.

She watched him dig his boot into the ground and tried to focus on her surroundings. She thought of the pebble, which was in the pouch on the belt around her hips, and how she had seen that flicker of light in the dark. All around her, energy pulsed. She just needed to tap into it.

Eyes focused on Death's Sword, Syra tried to concentrate as the Guardian broke into a run toward her. The pounding of his steps neared, and her heart fluttered in terror as Zarek became too close for comfort. At the last second, she rolled.

Now behind, Zarek cursed and spun to face her. "What was that? Did you even try?"

Annoyance flooded her, and she gritted her teeth. "Hard to focus when I'm being charged by you." Syra positioned herself, ready for his assault once more.

"Cute." Zarek sneered. The Guardian was agitated, which only made her angrier. "Will you tell your enemy to wait while you prepare yourself too?"

"Fuck off." Wind tousled her hair and cooled her skin from the heat of the sun. Syra took a deep breath, remembering to focus. "Go."

"More like it," Zarek said, and charged her once more. Syra bent her knees and readied her roll as she focused on the sword coming toward her. The metal glimmered, and as she curled her hands into fists, she felt it—the light. It flickered just behind her eyes and moved through her with the warmth of a hot summer day.

But it was too late. The fleeting sensation disappeared as she realized Zarek was upon her, and he wasn't slowing his sword. Syra ducked, and in the last second kicked out to knock him off his feet. It worked, and the Guardian fell.

Syra smiled, satisfied to see Zarek on his ass this time. She stepped away and repositioned herself. "Well, come on. I'm waiting on you."

The Guardian scoffed and stood, but she thought she caught the faintest of smirks flash across his face. "Very well," he replied, and readied himself. "If you can't harvest energy, you resort to playing dirty. I can accommodate that."

Syra's heart sank a sliver before she swallowed and nodded. She put her attention on Death's Sword and focused on the feeling she'd had—the warmth. It spoke to her in a language she didn't understand, but it didn't matter. What mattered was deflecting the sword.

The Guardian tilted his head and hesitated. "You feel it, don't you?"

"Go," she ordered. Syra didn't want to lose the feeling.

Zarek charged her, and Syra closed her eyes. She dropped to one knee instinctively just as the warmth consumed her. She could *feel* the sword lift, and the ground around her hummed in anticipation. Syra tapped into it, willing the energy to protect her as she crossed her forearms above. The life force radiated throughout her entire body, interacting, molding, and constructing a shield that nobody could see, only feel. Her entire body fell into sync with the steady pulse of the energy, and Syra felt a flutter of excitement as she heard Death's Sword ricochet off the invisible shield.

"By the Gods!" Zane yelled. Roman cried out in delight, but Syra hardly heard them.

What she did hear were the whispers of something else, something sinister. Every part of her knew they were wrong, evil, desperate. The heat of the day drained away, and a cold chill raced over her body. The hair on her arms stood on end, and her heart fluttered from the sudden grip anxiety had on it. She wanted to run and get as far away from those voices as possible.

They broke her concentration, and before she could react, she felt a boot meet her ankle. Pain flared, and she fell over, her elbow catching her fall. Zarek's shadow fell over her, and he looked down to meet her gaze. He raised an eyebrow. "I expected better."

The voices were gone, but she could still hear their echoes in her head. The insult went unaddressed—it didn't matter. She gulped air down, feeling exhausted; a low-grade headache pounded. "What is that?" She eyed Death's Sword. The voices had come from that.

The Guardian glanced down at the metal before sheathing it. "There are reasons the blade gets its name, Syra." He held a hand out for her to hoist herself up with. She did, though cautiously. The last thing she wanted was to hear those voices again. They made her skin crawl.

"Dark Energy," Zarek added with a slight nod. He chewed on his words a moment longer while Syra watched, waiting. "What you heard were the trapped voices, Syra. Voices of souls that will never pass into the Afterlife—sucked into this void of darkness that fuels the power of Dark Energy. It is an unfortunate consequence of wielding this weapon, but without it—well, it wouldn't be the blade it is." He offered a sympathetic smile, but Syra was too appalled to see it or care.

Kar's words danced at the edge of her mind. He had mentioned the lost souls tied to Dark Energy, but to know now that it was this very force that fueled the Guardians' weapons disgusted her. They were supposed to protect the souls, not take advantage of those chained to the living.

"How can you stand here and preach your philosophies about guidance and protection when you're using Dark Energy?" Syra challenged. She gestured at the sword on his hip. "You are a walking contradiction."

Zarek raised an eyebrow at her. "And you think you're pure?"

"No, but I certainly thought higher of your kind."

"Can we not do this right now?" Zane piped in. He came up next to her, running his hand through his dyed hair. "Some of us still don't know what's going on." The statement came out icy, annoyed, and Syra cringed.

Roman had risen from where he had been sitting as well, but he had not approached. The man had his hands planted on his hips, regarding them. To Syra, he looked like he was judging them, as if he had better things to do.

Zarek held his hand up to Zane. "You'll get your story soon enough, but not now." He didn't take his crimson eyes off Syra. "I'd like to finish my lesson first."

Zane was not having it. "No, I think I'd like my story now, Death Seeker." He stepped between them then, staring at the Guardian. "I'm getting pretty fed up with being toyed around with. You've practically got Roman and me roped like livestock, dragging us around like we're nothing more to you than a nuisance."

"Zane," Syra warned. She was not done with her conversation with the Guardian. "Move."

"No." He glared at her, fists clenched. "I want answers—"

Zarek's fist connected with the man's jaw before he finished, throwing him to the side. Zane landed on his shoulder and yelped in surprise. It all happened so fast that Syra reacted without thought. She closed the gap and shoved Zarek backward. "How dare you!" The Guardian stumbled but kept his footing. For once, his expression faltered in shock.

A loud bang shattered the argument. On instinct, she cowered. "What was that?"

Roman turned on his boots and sprinted up the hill before dropping on his hands and knees. Everyone waited, tense. The exchanged words dissipated instantly. None of it mattered. Even the wind hushed. Long seconds ticked by, but no one moved, waiting on Roman's word.

He swung around and bolted down the hill, his blue eyes wide. "We'd better go," he said.

Zarek grabbed his arm. "What is it?"

Zane was up and already tossing supplies that had been out back in the two sacks on the ground without waiting for the reply.

"Tribal hunters," Roman explained. "They've got an Energy Harvester based on that arrival."

"Unbelievable," Zarek cursed. "We'll head north, stay off the road and behind the hills." He was already turning and approaching Uyul. The steed was standing ready, her red eyes unblinking. "Let's go."

Syra dipped her hand and hoisted Death's Sword up, no longer caring about the blade's origins. Stories of tribal hunters were savage—they followed a different philosophy of life, cruel and unforgiving. Her muscles were sore and protested against the weight, but she ignored them and sheathed the weapon. Now was surely not the time to complain. Running over to Hazel, she hoisted herself up and grabbed the reins.

Zarek was already heading away from the small encampment. Syra dug her boots into Hazel's side, and they were off. Her heart was slamming against her chest, forcing her breaths shallow as her hands trembled.

She got close enough to the Guardian to ask the burning question. "Are they coming for us?" Even with the distance between the hunters and their group, she still kept her voice low.

Zarek glanced her way and then at the others behind. "No, or so we want to hope. But we don't want to be seen by them either."

"The outer edge of Raveer should only be a half day's travel," Roman added. "With Eazon's luck, we'll be there this evening, just after dark."

"My cousin lives on the outskirts," Zane replied. "If he's still there, he'll keep us hidden overnight. At least long enough to let the hunters pass. He's a good guy, if just a bit odd here and there."

Zarek nodded. "Then we head that way."

Another resounding boom followed them, and Syra kept her head low. The group fell silent. For once, she was relieved to have the dark brown hair dye instead of her natural fire red. She stole a peek behind her to see Zane and Roman following on their steeds, heads low.

To be captured by tribal hunters would mean certain death. They could hold their ground against a few attackers, but tribal hunters traveled in packs, so there would likely be a dozen or more on horseback. And if they had an Energy Harvester . . . it was a losing battle. Syra knew the stories—the terrible, gut-wrenching stories—and nobody escaped alive once they were in the hands of a tribe. Kids were told these stories to keep them from disobeying their parents. Never did Syra think she would be living one.

The wind whispered to her as they trotted onward; the group was careful to avoid the high points in the rolling hills. She refused to listen to the wind, for it spoke of nothing but bad luck. She instead focused on the beat of the hooves their steeds made.

Nothing mattered except staying alive.

THE START OF THE END

Morei finished the water and pushed his dish aside. It had been bison and steamed vegetables—delicious, the meat delicate, cooked just to perfection and seasoned with salt and pepper. Wiping his mouth and hands clean of anything that remained with the red cloth, Morei glanced at the door just as a knock rang through his chambers.

The morning was still incredibly young, and while the king should have gotten up, dressed himself, and gone to perform his duties, he didn't. Perhaps it was because he was cherishing this rare and raw opportunity with Emerald—his way of hoping that the confrontations were behind them—or perhaps it was because he no longer cared like he used to. If the title was going to be transferred, assuming Ezra accepted, then the people, the council, would not miss him if he skipped out. In fact, they would likely wish for it.

Last night had taught him at least one thing—that he could not control everything.

"Who do you think that is?" he asked, and raised an eyebrow at Emerald, who sat next to him in the chair. Dressed, the queen looked exquisite. A maid had been ordered to go to her chambers and pull a green dress, light and with a halter neck, layered in gold glitter. Morei had given her space to wash herself and get dressed but hadn't wasted the chance to get another peek at her tasteful curves.

"Perhaps more food?" Emerald inclined.

He laughed and stood. "If I have more food, I'll be bedbound the rest of the day," Morei joked, and walked to the door.

"You're the one that ordered it all," she remarked through a mouthful of grapes.

Morei eyed her, hoping she wouldn't see the concern that hung over him. Nobody ever bothered the king unless something was important. "I happen to remember someone who said they were starving earlier, no?"

As she swallowed, sweet laughter bubbled up.

Even such sweetness would not protect him from what lay on the other side of the door, so with one final breath, he opened it.

Peter stood, fist raised in preparation to knock again. "Oh," he stammered, and dropped his hand. "My apologies for interrupting anything, Your Majesty, but this cannot wait." The chancellor's blue eyes flicked around to where Emerald was sitting before coming back to Morei with an embarrassed look. "I can come back if you prefer."

"If this is so pressing, then that would be foolish of me to turn you away." The chancellor was fidgety, and it was making Morei uncomfortable. "So, what is it?"

Taking a deep breath, the chancellor rubbed his hands together, as if cold despite the heat of the day, letting his shoulders slump a little when he dropped his hands. "It's Boris. He's requesting to see you down in the dungeons. He says it's urgent."

* * *

Morei noted the cracks in the stone leading down to the dungeons. They were new and shallow, but in time, they would break the stone apart further and tear at the very foundation of Geral. It felt morbidly fitting.

"Has anyone noted these?" Morei asked Peter. Two Geral soldiers accompanied them from behind, their steps four paces back on the staircase, but he said it loud enough that everyone could hear.

The chancellor glanced over at the cracked stone. "Um, I don't know, Your Majesty, but I'll make note of it immediately. Tryv?"

One of the soldiers grunted in return, dark skin glistening. "I'll report it to Drew, Your Majesty."

"Very good," he replied with a slight nod.

They made it to the bottom of the stairs, and Peter gestured to the right, down a low-lit stone hall. The king noted no cracks, which relieved him, but he was overcome by the scent of rot. "What's that smell?" he asked.

Peter cleared his throat. "There was some run-off from the storm last night. It flooded the cell at the end of the left hall."

"You're telling me we've got a crack big enough to flood our dungeon that hasn't been fixed?" the king clarified, annoyed.

A moment of hesitation. "Yes, Your Majesty."

"Damn the Gods," he cursed. "That is unacceptable." Flooding was common in the desert, especially with the massive thunderstorms and little vegetation, but never had the rainwaters swamped the underground dungeon. "We're better than this, Chancellor. Tryv, make sure Drew knows this too. This needs to be fixed immediately."

"Yes, Your Majesty."

They came upon a cell that was lit far better than the rest. With only a few current prisoners, Boris had been given two torches instead of one, and he stood with his hands clasped behind his back, dressed in a plain tunic and pants. He looked well taken care of, which relieved Morei some. They had never been enemies until Boris had spoken against him, and deep down, he still had a soft spot for the man who had served his father.

It had been almost thirteen days since that dreaded day in the council, and Morei could still hear Lady Dail's scream ring through his ears as if it had just happened. The only problem was that it didn't make him uneasy, it only fueled his need for more.

A single cot to the left was well dressed with sheets, and a small stone desk to the right was covered in parchment that held drawings and words that from here, he couldn't decipher, since they were piled untidily over one another. Boris stood next to it, looking down at whatever he had just written.

Morei looked over at the soldiers. "You've given him supplies that he could use to harm with if he so wished." It wasn't an insult, it was a point. No prisoner got this kind of treatment, especially the violent ones. As the soldier left of Tryv opened his mouth to speak, the king shook his head. "I don't care, so long as Boris is satisfied. But do not make a habit of it."

They both nodded, and Morei looked around them all just as Boris glanced up, as if only then realizing they were here. "Leave us be."

Peter looked as if he might protest but decided against it. They all nodded and started to trek back down the stone hall. As they receded, their voices fading, the king crossed his arms and looked back at Boris. His ebony skin glistened under the torches' light, and his green eyes had a fierce twinkle. Even imprisoned, Boris still managed to look more courageous and emboldened than half the soldiers Morei knew.

When it was certain they had the place to themselves, Morei inhaled, ignoring the rotting stench. "I see you've done quite well," he acknowledged, keeping his voice low. He trusted Peter, but he didn't trust anyone else not to take the opportunity to eavesdrop.

Boris picked up on this cue and replied with the same soft voice. "I have been grateful for the kindness. I know these men mean well, so do not punish them for my requests. This"—he motioned at the desk—"keeps me sane. A chance to journal and express emotions I would otherwise keep locked away."

With a nod, the king replied, "I understand and am relieved to know you've been taken care of, Boris. It was never my intention to keep you here this long, but circumstances prevented me from coming sooner."

"As I've heard. But you're the reason this city stands still, if I am correct?"

"That you are, but it came at a price. One that I fear will only grow steeper."

Boris didn't reply right away. He took a deep breath and dropped his gaze instead. The king remained quiet, sensing there was something on the man's mind. Whether it was why Morei had been summoned down here or not, he did not know, and he was not going to ask. It was time for him to shut up and listen. Boris deserved that much after what Morei had done to him.

The ex-commander had more respect from these soldiers than Morei could ever dare to grasp. It was a way he had with the people. He was their rock in unsteady times, a powerful force when he entered the room. And the king had ripped away his title and tossed him here in a fit of rage like a fool. But Boris's public refusal to back him could not have gone unpunished. If he had dismissed him with a wave of his hand, he would have become a laughingstock.

Sometimes, being a king meant doing what wasn't easy.

Finally, Boris lifted his eyes back to Morei. He took several steps forward, and the king now noticed boots, another item prohibited in the dungeons. "I failed you, Morei," he admitted, and shook his head. "And before you go and say something formal, let me speak."

Taking a deep breath in, he held his tongue. What he really wanted to do was tell Boris that he hadn't failed, that he had been an acting commander with a desire to keep the people safe, no matter what. And because of that, he had been willing to stand up against the king of Geral. That made him braver than most men out there.

"I failed you as a friend," Boris continued, giving the smallest of smiles. "In this time down here, I've had a lot of time to consider my actions, words, and how you may feel. You are a man and still capable of emotions, which means you still fear, grow anxious, and love like the rest of us." He shook his head and scoffed. "I was incapable of seeing you as you always have been because all I saw was a threat."

"Things change," the king offered. "I do not expect everyone to understand what's happened to me."

"But don't you see? I *want* to know. I *want* to understand, Morei." The accentuated words held so much emotion that Morei felt his heart skip a beat. The man might as well have screamed them. "I might have had responsibilities, but that was no reason to turn my back on you when you needed me as a friend and a support. You didn't ask for this." Boris motioned at him, his voice so low that it was barely above a whisper. "Who am I to decide who is right and who is wrong? That is for the Gods, not me."

The Gods. That was a sore topic for Morei, but he didn't address the claim. As far as he knew, the only judgers were those around him—the living, mankind, thieves and beggars, whores, and soldiers. "I didn't come here for an apology, Boris, but I accept it."

Boris nodded, his shoulders slacking a little. "Is it like the stories? The ones we grew up on?"

Morei couldn't help but let a thin smile touch his lips. Old stories about evil men doing evil things because they were possessed by a sinister force, or the Dark Lord. They were used to scare people into believing the Gods, to be good, upstanding citizens. Loyal.

259

But it wasn't that simple, was it? People weren't inherently evil. Good and evil were defined by man, and man decided who was punished and who was praised, not the Gods. Evil was only as cruel as man wanted it to be, just as being good was only as genuine as man defined it to be. There was no true right or wrong. There was only the matter of perspectives.

Standing here before the man who had once stood by him while he had been crowned despite the council's nasty words made Morei question who the real monsters were. "Worse," he confessed. Damn formalities and political correctness, the king would have a real conversation, regardless of the prison bars that separated them. "What I've become scares me more than anything else, Boris. The more I fight it, the stronger it becomes. The more I cave, the uglier I become."

His voice shook, and he scolded himself for it, not wanting to look as weak as he felt but grateful to speak on the matter. To admit his fear out loud made it real, and a wave of anguish washed over him, momentarily paralyzing his thoughts. Repulsed by his own weakness, he shook himself free from the pressing reality and eyed the man. "I don't think I came down here for you to apologize."

With an exhale, Boris turned away and walked back to his table. "You're right, I didn't." He paused as he lifted a piece of parchment up with a shaking hand. "Last night, I had a dream. I know we all have dreams, but this one was different." As he looked back at Morei, there was no denying the torment splattered across the man's face. "It felt as real as you are to me right now."

The hairs on the back of Morei's neck stood on end at the uneasiness of the man's voice. "What was it?" One thing Boris had never been was superstitious. To squirm over a dream was unlike the man, and *that* made Morei uncomfortable.

Boris licked his lips, true fear reeking off him. He glanced between the parchment and the king before speaking. "There was a man—or I think it was a man. I couldn't tell, because he was in this black cloak and wouldn't look at me, but it was only him and me. We were in a field that was covered in black soil, and I mean as black as you can think of, okay? There was fog, so I couldn't see my surroundings—" Boris licked his lips again, his voice shaking. "He spoke to me, but he sounded like he was in my head—"

He suddenly stopped speaking, and Morei was startled to see Boris so unnerved. His hand trembled, shaking the parchment, and his breaths came in short bursts. He was petrified.

"Boris, what did he say?" Morei asked urgently. He leaned forward, grabbing on to one of the metal bars in front of him. Now he wished he had the key to open the damn cell.

"The message was for you," Boris answered, and lowered the parchment to his side, eyes on the king. "He wanted me to give you his regards."

Morei stared, dumbfounded. "What?"

"That was all he told me to say." Boris shook his head, defeated. He dropped the parchment on the desk. "I tried to ask what he meant, but it was like my tongue was tied and the words wouldn't come out. Frantic, that's how I felt. And then I woke up. I'm sorry, I know this sounds crazy, Morei. I feel crazy telling you this, but it was so real to me that I had to." Meeting his gaze, he added, "I think something bad is going to happen."

The king took a deep breath, gathering his thoughts and trying not to look as shocked as he felt. It was like a cold, serrated blade had just been thrust into his chest. His hands shook, and he was grateful for the metal to hold on to in order to steady himself. "I don't understand. This was just a dream, right?"

"That's what I wanted to think, but I woke up with such a strong need to tell you this." Boris approached him cautiously. "It's all I can think about." He shook his head. "It was like he was right here."

"Does Peter know?" Morei asked.

"No. Nobody does. I—I know it's crazy."

"Good," he breathed. "We keep it that way." He raised his eyes to the ceiling, unsure how to proceed or how to feel. If anyone else had told him this, he would have laughed it off. This was different, though. When Boris had something to say, it was serious.

This was not something to shake off, no matter how much the king wanted to—the terror in Boris's expression told him that. "I know this sounds crazy," the man repeated, wrapping a hand around a bar.

"It is not crazy," Morei mumbled as he scuffed a boot against the stone, trying to figure out his next steps. There was nothing he could do about this dream, yet it unsettled him more than Cu'cel or the failing trust of the citizens. It unnerved him to no end. Because somewhere, the idea that perhaps this dream was linked to everything happening breached his thoughts. The cloaked man, whoever he was, was toying with Morei, but why? Only recently, he'd had a similar dream, or at least the vision of someone in a cloak.

Here he was, trying to make meaning out of a nightmare. A half moon cycle ago, the king had been face-to-face with a demon, yesterday he had spoken to one of the dead, and now, dreams were starting to link up. This was a sign.

He needed more information.

"Boris, I am going to go, but I will send someone down here to release you and take you to a room in the palace. Does that sound alright to you?"

The statement must have caught him off guard because he stood there, staring—a moment that felt like a lifetime slipping by. When Boris finally stirred, his voice was slow, halting. "Are you sure that's what you want?"

"Yes," Morei rushed to say.

Guilt ran cold in his heart for a quick beat as he saw the troubled look in the man's eyes. "I'm sorry," Morei whispered.

"I know my ailment is no excuse for what happened that day, for what I did." Boris had watched the king murder two councilmembers in a blink of an eye before turning a hand on him. It was inexcusable behavior. But it had been exhilarating.

The man sighed. "I understand, but the council . . . You will be seen as indecisive if you let me out."

Leave it to Boris to fight to stay behind bars, so that Morei's reputation could stand strong, but now was not the time or did it matter anymore given the spiraling view the citizens had on him. The man had no idea about the upcoming changes to the throne, and this didn't feel like the place to speak about it—rather, it was the last thing he wanted to do. "Damn the rest, Boris. I will not have you spend another night here. It's an order, got it?"

The man chuckled and dipped his gaze. "Alright then."

Morei nodded, satisfied but troubled. "In an hour's time, you will be served food and mead, so I hope you're hungry." He exhaled and pulled back from the bars, ready to tackle the pressing matter at hand—the dream and its meaning. "I'll see you later."

Whether Boris would reclaim his title as commander once Morei was no longer king was outside his power. Ezra, if he accepted, would have the right to reinstate the man if he so pleased, which the king would silently approve. He couldn't do it, for if Morei went backward on his decisions, it would make him look unreliable. Boris had already pointed it out—how the council would see him as indecisive—but it didn't matter. In the end, none of this would matter, because in the end, when he was no longer king, it would no longer be of importance. It would be Ezra's problem.

Regardless, he didn't want to dwell on it when all it did was sour his attitude. The people of Geral would never understand what he had done for them or what he was willing to do. But if they didn't understand, then perhaps he would make them understand. If they wanted a monster, then they would get one. One day.

What mattered now was finding an answer about this dream. The king was not a superstitious man, but he was also not an idiot. Dreams had once been considered powerful messages from the Afterlife to the ancient Vorelians. While the significance of that had faded long ago, the ideology had not been lost to royalty. Books upon books that captured the ancient cultures were stored in the library that was his and his alone. He would start there and hope to find some key, because deep down, he was more certain than ever before that this was all tied together to Cu'cel. The dream would lead to some answer that would inevitably lead to some cure. It had to. The king could not accept any other option, regardless of how wild it sounded.

As he rounded up the stairs, he saw Peter standing there, reading a book that he hadn't had before. It was on herb medicine. "You told Boris about what happened to me," he stated simply, without animosity. There was no reason to question him. Morei knew the chancellor was the one responsible for it.

Peter's eyes widened. "I felt it was necessary. I, um—"

"Still respect him," Morei finished. "I understand. I do too." At that, the chancellor looked relieved, letting his large stomach relax. The buttons of his shirt strained in protest but held their ground. "He will be joining us in the palace. Will you see to it that he is released immediately and brought to a proper room? Then given food and mead?" The king waved at him, already walking by. "Prepare him a feast."

The chancellor smiled broad and shut the book. "Of course, Your Majesty."

"Good," Morei acknowledged. He continued on, keeping his pace steady but brisk. He was eager to get to the library, but he didn't want to run and unnerve anyone. The people already held unlikeable opinions about him for something he was not responsible for. The last thing they needed was another excuse to talk about him, for they had already said enough. Inexcusable rumors that, if they were more isolated, the king would have delt with personally, mercilessly, but he could not kill an entire city. The only thing he could hope for was to beg for their forgiveness and hope that by relinquishing his title and finding a cure for Cu'cel, he could retain some sort of respect with the Geral citizens.

But he didn't need to prove himself to Boris, and for that, he was grateful. The man had spoken his piece, and so had the king. They were on neutral terms, albeit in cruel circumstances, and that put him at ease.

At least he had done something good today.

A MINER AT HEART

yrus wandered the halls of the Razan palace. His fingers grazed over old shields, plants, and the polished gold stone walls. The marble underneath his boots echoed with each step he took, giving away his location. Several times, he peered back to see if anyone was following him. It was becoming a habit of his, given how little comfort he felt around so many strangers. And now, with the belief that Kyllian was hiding the eggs from him, he knew maids were likely instructed to fetch him if they saw him wandering.

The windows along the hallway were open, allowing the warmth of the day to seep into the walls and the wind to whisper past his ears. Cyrus inhaled several times as deep as he could, hoping to gather some clarity.

It was time to find the tunnels. If the king wasn't going to be honest with him and give him the information, then Cyrus would tear it out of him. And he would do so with knowledge of the eggs. Then Kyllian would have no choice but to divulge what he knew.

It was a dirty trick, and not one he was eager for, but it was the only option he had left. Once he had the information he so desperately deserved, then Cyrus would leave, but he would take the eggs with him and Sozar. It was the last thing he wanted to do, to be considered a thief, but no other option lay before him. The dragons did not deserve to be used for war, and he would be damned if he didn't at least try to find them and take them—before Dameon did.

Last night hung heavy over his head. If they were playing a game of secrets, Cyrus was certain he'd win. Eggs were outrageous, but another Dragon Rider? It would upset the entire world. If the king believed his age-old family secret was protected, he was wrong.

Dameon wanted war and power. After the conversation and long flight, Cyrus had come to the conclusion that if he didn't become the man he was supposed to be—the Dragon Rider the world needed—Dameon would cause havoc. That man would stop at nothing to get his hands on the eggs, and if he was anything like Cyrus suspected based on their brief conversation, he would raise the dragons to be weapons.

A part of him hoped that if he found the eggs first, he could speak some sense into Dameon, and perhaps Kyllian too. The king's possession of them may have protected them for all these summers, but it was time to let the past die. The ancient Dragon Riders had given the eggs over in hopes of a new era of Riders, when war and politics did not obligate them to act against one another.

There was no point in denying that he was disappointed to not have learned anything about the families of the Riders. The names had been scorched, the parchment looking like it was on its last leg. The small sigil indicating firstborn children was all that Cyrus had to validate that he was indeed someone. Yet that parchment was centuries old, so the families listed there—or the ones that had been listed—were likely all gone by now.

And last night, as Dameon had stated so confidently, perhaps they were selected for a reason—Destiny herself had played with both their lives, transcending traditional expectations and molding them into the new era of Dragon Riders. If this was true, then his family may truly be dead or have abandoned him. Or both.

Frankly, Cyrus didn't like any of this.

It didn't add up in his head. The letter to Evander had been thought out, detailed, and Kyllian had indicated there were multiple records about the silver eyes, not just a half-finished letter and scorched family tree. The realization of this made him halt in his steps.

Sozar's presence nudged his mind. *Perhaps there is another place in the palace where he holds more records?* So the dragon was thinking the same thing.

Quickly, he double-checked that he wasn't being followed, then turned down the right hall. He wanted to find a door, a staircase, *something* that looked out of the ordinary—and less traveled. Damn being polite, Cyrus would not be lied to or have information held from him. He didn't doubt Kyllian's honesty, but he did doubt whether the king was telling him the entire truth.

And he didn't blame the king for that. Kyllian had a responsibility and had been upholding his duties for a number of summers now, but Cyrus also had a responsibility—to learn about his heritage. He would stop at nothing to have the answers he wanted.

One thing was for certain, he had until tomorrow night before the Dragon Rider would expect anything from him. Until then, he would gather as much information as he could within these walls.

A hall branched off that caught his attention. It was narrower than the others, and on instinct, Cyrus turned down it. The walls here were bare, untouched. Several doors were decorated on each side, but ahead, just to the right, was a door that looked slightly different. Instead of the standard polished gold handle, it had a brass one that looked worn out. Slowing to a stop, he checked behind him. Still no one. Chances were low that this door, but one thing that Cyrus had going for him was a knack for finding things.

He laid a hand on the cold, warped door handle. A strange sensation washed over him. It was accompanied by a flutter of his heart and a tingling that rushed up his arm, making his fingers feel numb. Withdrawing his hand, he shook it and frowned.

"Going into the tunnels?"

Cyrus jumped at Zorya's voice. She wore a green dress that stopped just above the ankles with a tattered cut. The halter neck was studded with gold that continued down in a V-cut. The style dragged Cyrus's eyes exactly where they shouldn't have gone, but he couldn't help himself.

"Just exploring," he replied, and pointed at the door. "You said this leads to the tunnels?" That was exactly what he wanted to hear. They had made it, but now he had the princess to worry about.

"The entire city of Razan, including the western side, is linked by a network of tunnels. I've never been down there, but I hear the tunnels continue north for some time."

Narrowing his eyes at her, Cyrus asked, "You're telling me that as a kid, you didn't try to explore these?"

The princess rolled her eyes. "Okay, fine. I did once, but that was it. I got too scared and came back before my parents knew."

The hint of a smirk in her expression made him laugh. "Well, did you find anything?"

"Just a bunch of old chambers and water—lots of water." She shrugged. "There's a canal down there that I guess was built to help channel the ground water."

The information made Cyrus's breath catch. The dream last night had shown him next to a canal and approaching a door. "Mind if I go looking around?"

Zorya raised her brow and gestured at their surroundings. "Instead of exploring all this, you want to go down there?"

Cyrus waved her off. "I've spent the last ten summers working in the mines. Dark and dingy tunnels don't scare me." He grabbed the door handle and raised an eyebrow at her. He knew Sozar would be unhappy if she tagged along, because they still didn't know if they could trust her, but he couldn't waste more time. If this was where the eggs were, then they needed to know. It felt like the future of the dragons was weighing down on his shoulders, and if he didn't act now, then he would be too late.

If he was to go now, then Zorya would have to follow. He doubted she would let him go down by himself or without raising alarm. Or maybe she was trustworthy. There was only one way to find out.

"Coming?" Deep down, he hoped he could rely on her— hoped that she wasn't her father.

She looked behind them before turning her dark eyes back up at him. "If my father finds out—"

"Yeah, yeah. Blame it on me and my curiosity." Cyrus turned the handle and opened the door. The smells of mildew and moisture met his nose, but it hardly bothered him. The mines had their own unique smells, and this was no different. Cyrus was so eager to find if his dream matched the tunnels that he nearly ran forward, but he kept himself restrained in front of the princess. Desperate was the last way he wanted to appear, even if it was exactly how he felt.

You sure you want her tagging along? Sozar pressed. *If you find the eggs—*

You're assuming she's knowledgeable about the eggs, Cyrus countered. *I can't wait any longer. I have to find out if they are here.*

Cyrus knew the dragon had a point, but he also didn't want to turn her away. It would only make her more determined to follow. Besides, this gave him time with her—not ideal, but then again, Cyrus already wasn't in an ideal situation, sneaking around a palace in a strange city. And with the daughter of the king, no less.

Zorya let a large exhale out and started following. "Fine, but don't hold this against me if he finds out."

Cyrus laughed. "Too late."

The door closed behind them, and Cyrus saw a lantern hung to his left. The light flickered, casting a warm glow over the stone staircase. While he grabbed the lantern off the rusty hinge, grateful for the light source, he couldn't shake the thought of how odd it was that there was a light. It was as if the tunnels themselves were waiting for him. "Any idea who was down here before us?" he asked, knowing Zorya wouldn't know the answer, but he still wanted to test her.

She rubbed her arms and looked at the lantern. "No. As far as I know, no one comes down here."

"Hm." Cyrus turned and started the trek down the stairs, hearing her fall into step behind him. Carefully, he descended, not sure if the stone would crumble or hold against his weight. Thankfully it held, and he continued, staying slow, so that Zorya could follow with the light.

"How far down does this go?" Cyrus asked, keeping his voice low. His words bounced off the narrow passageway, fading below.

Zorya was a step behind. "We're almost there."

"I thought you said you've only been down here once," he said, not turning to face her.

"Part of my studies as the future queen was to know these tunnels," she explained. Her words were swift and strained, as if she was upset that he would question her integrity. Guilt squirmed inside him, but he didn't apologize for being curious. If anything, it validated that the king was keeping secrets.

Taking a deep breath, he caught a hint of copper. He wrinkled his nose and kept going until they made it to the bottom. But just as he hit the landing, he heard the princess curse and stumble. He turned just as she reached out and grabbed his arm, catching her fall. Zorya's grip was strong—a fighter's grip—and she straightened herself as quickly as she could. "Dumb stone."

Cyrus rolled his eyes. "Sure." He turned toward the tunnel and raised the lantern above his head. From what he could see, the tunnel was aged. Cracks ran along the stone walls, where water crept through and made the stone glisten. The ground was covered in dirt, but from the sturdiness, Cyrus assumed it was stone underneath. As they stood there, he noted one thing that the mines of Diemon and these tunnels shared: silence.

"Your father," he whispered, and looked at her. The warm glow danced off her features delicately, casting her in the light that only a Goddess could possess. It was dangerous. "Did he mention anything to you about why you had to know these tunnels?"

For a moment, she didn't speak, but she frowned. "No," she said. "When I was young and he would put the maps in front of me, he'd say"—the princess dropped her voice in a futile attempt to mimic Kyllian's voice—"'Zorya, one day you'll have to know these tunnels by heart.'"

A smile tugged at Cyrus's lips. "That was it?"

"Yeah. I always used to fall asleep studying them because it was pretty boring." Her eyes glanced around. "Why do you want to explore these so bad? It can't be because you were a miner."

A fleeting thought slipped through his mind—that he should tell her the truth. He was an honest man, or at least he told himself so, but then he shut that idea down. If there was truly nothing down here, telling her his motives seemed like a terrible idea. And if she was as clever as he decided she was, Zorya would understand that he was sneaking around here underneath the king's nose. No. Better to not say anything and then hope for the best.

"A miner has an insatiable curiosity for dark places," he remarked. "I'm simply fulfilling that desire." The response he got was a raised eyebrow, so he took that as a good sign and turned.

They continued forward, following the tunnel deeper into the network. Cyrus was in his element. He had zero doubt that he could track their way back to the door no matter how far they went—all thanks to the countless summers working in dingy mines. Small details were what he looked for, like the patch of green algae that filled the stone to his left or the large crack crossing the floor. Cyrus was great at noting these details and retracing his steps. It had saved his life one too many times in the caves.

Down here, he was at complete peace.

They came upon a round chamber, and when Cyrus stepped ahead, he caught glimpses of three other tunnels. The ceiling was low and unimpressive, the chamber itself small. All the tunnels beckoned to be explored, but he would have to be satisfied with one, with no idea how long they would be down here or how far any of them went.

"Want to choose which one we go down?" he asked Zorya. The dream hadn't given him a clear direction here, so he was going to leave it to fate. She lifted an eyebrow at him and looked around. Cyrus sensed she was uncomfortable, but that didn't surprise him. Most people were uneasy in these circumstances. It was why miners like him were so valuable—no dark hole scared him.

"If I remember correctly, the one farthest to the left leads toward the west city, so we should probably avoid that one. I didn't dress for a long hike, and last I heard, water from the Frynian River was leaking heavily. But—" She breathed and looked between the center and right tunnel. "I think the other two are fair game."

Cyrus chewed on his lower lip, considering his options. "Right?"

She nodded and turned toward the tunnel. Cyrus quickly fell into step with her, walking side by side. For a minute, she didn't say anything, but as they made their way deeper into the tunnel, she cleared her throat. "What are you looking for?" The question was more direct than her first attempt.

Cyrus looked down at her. "What do you mean? I'm just exploring."

Zorya scoffed. "Exploring the underground tunnels of an ancient city. Sounds innocent enough."

Her tone was obvious—she didn't believe him.

"And you wanting to accompany me is a gesture of concern and friendship," Cyrus countered. When she stared at him, he shrugged. "Come on, Zorya, did you really come down here because you're just wanting to have some fun? Or are you responsible for making sure I don't find something your family is keeping secret?"

"By the Gods," she mumbled, agitated. "I'm not my parents' pet, Cyrus, I actually can think for myself."

"So?" he pressed. "You could be Shunera's."

The princess went quiet, their steps echoing in counterpoint to each other's. Cyrus didn't need Sozar's opinion to know that had been the wrong thing to say. In fact, if he could have turned back time, he would have said anything but bringing up the pompous prince. It was not his place to judge Zorya and where her loyalties lay, not like this.

"I'm arranged to marry the prince of Kalic, Shunera," she answered quietly. Inhaling deeply, he decided not to tell her that he knew that. He would let her speak. "With old culture comes old traditions." Zorya shrugged. "I guess you could say I'm wanting to soak up the last bit of fun before the marriage is formalized."

Cyrus swallowed, choosing his words with care. Suddenly, the tunnel felt like an impenetrable sanctuary that he was terrified to lose, for it would mean returning to the real world.

The world where the princess was obligated to be someone she so clearly wasn't, where Shunera existed, and where Cyrus was supposed to have some sort of purpose. "Do you like him?"

She scoffed. "Does anyone really like someone they're forced to marry, Cyrus?"

"I would want to hope that you were at least engaged with someone decent," he muttered.

"Decent if you like your husband to be a controlling ass," Zorya said.

"Then why are you arranged with him if it's obvious you disagree?"

"It's an old law," she explained. "Kalic and Razan would exist symbiotically so long as when the cards aligned right, the heirs to their family would marry. As I am a woman and their heir a son . . ."

Cyrus shook his head. "That's outrageous, Zorya. That's ancient practice." The sound of water was growing louder, and despite the direction of the conversation, he couldn't help but be excited. Perhaps they were going the right way—maybe the dream was real, after all.

She hummed but didn't reply right away. Cyrus was about to press on the matter more when she said, "Your turn, Cyrus. Why are we really down here?"

He swallowed and glanced down at her. He hated the fact that she was so beautiful and persistent. It was like every ounce of logic was torn from him when he beheld her. And to hear she was arranged to marry a man she wanted nothing to do with angered him—not because of the practice, but because Cyrus was ignorant enough to fantasize about what it would be like to settle down with a charming woman like her. He was not one to overstep, but his desire to see her happy made him want to storm into the council and demand Zorya have her choice.

But a settled life was out of the question for him, and that meant she was out of reach. That understanding shouldn't keep him from sharing a piece of information with her, though. It was only fair.

"I had a dream, and I want to know if these tunnels look the same as what I dreamt about." He could no longer ignore the excitement building in his chest from the sound of rushing water.

The princess frowned. "So, we're going off a dream? Was there anything in it?"

"A door," Cyrus answered, but the words died on his lips. To his left, a waterway opened up. Water piled out of the opening and rushed down the channel ahead of him to some unseen exit. This was it. He was in the right place.

He inched forward, then turned his eyes to the stone on his right. "It was on this side," he told Zorya. "The door."

The water rushed beside them, filling the tunnel with a melody that put his racing heart at ease. Cyrus was anxious about the man he had seen in his dream. If this was all real, then the man had to be too. Maybe he was down here, waiting for him all this time.

They kept walking. The temperature was warm, the air stifling after being trapped for countless summers. Perspiration beaded his brow, and he wiped at it. Just when he was going to say something, the light from the lantern danced off a door.

They froze. Cyrus could practically taste the bitter bile in the back of his throat as he beheld the door that he had seen in his dream. It was made of oak, the metal rusted just like he remembered, the frame cracked. There was only one thing missing.

Cyrus turned his attention to the surrounding stone. Taking his boot, he rubbed the dirt away from the floor and lowered the lantern. There it was—a sigil of the Old Tongue.

The princess whistled next to him, clearly surprised. "Was that in your dream?"

Cyrus was overwhelmed but excited. "Yes. Do you know what it means?"

Zorya knelt closer and brushed a finger over the stone. Her blond hair fell around her features as she studied the sigil. "I do." Her tone was troubled.

"What?"

The princess rose and looked at him, her dark eyes haunted. "It means death."

For the first time since entering the tunnels, Sozar stirred, his presence shattering Cyrus's concentration. *There is Dark Energy attached to that sigil. I can feel it. Be careful.*

Instinctively, he dropped a hand to the hilt of the Rider's Sword, but it was gone, left upstairs in his chamber, along with the *Book of Liral.* The uneasiness in the dragon's voice now made him wish he had carried the weapon. *I have to see what's behind that door,* he told Sozar, but as the words faded from his thoughts, he realized it wasn't the dragon he was trying to convince, but himself. The sigil had unsettled him. Never once had he thought he might be walking into a trap.

Don't get yourself killed.

Cyrus stepped toward the door, but a hand grabbed his arm and halted him in place. "Are you serious?" Zorya asked. "That sigil is a warning. We shouldn't be here."

Nothing would stand in his way. "If you don't want to see, then turn around."

"I—" Zorya stopped and pursed her lips. "I just don't . . ." She was at a loss for words.

He raised an eyebrow. "Concerned about me?" His lips twitched as he watched her try to say something in return, and when she failed to, she sighed.

"Fine. Go." The princess motioned for him to open the door. "Well, don't keep me waiting. If we're going to die, might as well get it over with."

Cyrus laughed, his voice ringing through the tunnel. Zorya's tone was sarcastic and playful, devoid of the previous concern. It helped him shake off the foreboding feeling that he wasn't supposed to be here. Stealing a quick glance down from where they had come from, he found nothing, but he couldn't deny the feeling of eyes on the back of his head.

Laying a hand on the door handle, he found it ice cold, sending a chill up his arm, and he became acutely aware of the sudden temperature change. It felt like they had just gotten caught in a snowstorm; even the thick humidity they had breathed earlier was gone. "It's unnaturally cold, am I wrong?"

Zorya nodded, hot breath sending a plume of mist into the air.

Validated, he turned the handle and found it catch. It was locked, but he wasn't surprised. "Hold on," he told her, and rammed his shoulder into the frame. His muscles protested, but he heard the door groan. One more would break the lock.

"You're going—"

Zorya's words were lost as Cyrus slammed his shoulder against it one last time. The frame cracked and gave away. The wood scuffed against the stone floor, filling the tunnel with a screeching sound that made him cringe.

"Break it, I know," Cyrus finished for her. Lifting the lantern, he felt tendrils of magic slither into his mind. There was power in this room, and it made his skin crawl.

The lantern painted the space in an orange glow. It was a small, round chamber. The ground gave way from stone to tile that once had been a vibrant color. Now, it was faded, muted, covered in dust.

Ahead, Cyrus saw a podium that was made of polished stone. On top of it sat a large chest. The lock was broken and laid on the ground, but based on the metal, it had been lying there for a long time. He stepped forward and heard Zorya follow closely behind.

"Was this in your dream?" she asked quietly.

"No," he whispered, but he couldn't look away. As they stepped up to the chest, it dawned on him that the carvings were nearly identical to the chest he had found the Rider's Sword in. Swallowing, he glanced over at Zorya. "Recognize this chest?"

She shook her head. "No."

Taking a deep breath, he knew he needed to open it. No matter what, every ounce of him knew that he was being led to this chest. If he didn't, he would be failing himself. Deep down, he already knew what lay inside. The dream and Dameon's information had given him all the proof he needed. "Hold this," he said, and handed the lantern to Zorya. She took it without hesitation.

Setting his hands on the side of chest, Cyrus took a deep breath. He could feel Sozar's presence pressing so hard into his consciousness that he almost told the dragon to back off so he could concentrate, but he decided against it. Sozar was desperate to see as well.

"Here goes nothing," he whispered, and opened the lid.

HOME SWEET HOME

Terror clung to Syra's thoughts well after they had lost sight of the tribal hunters. She constantly checked over her shoulder as they rode, firmly believing that if she didn't, they would sneak up on them. But every time she looked, she was reminded that it was just the four of them.

The grass danced to the growing wind. It tore at her clothes and whipped her hair with a warm touch. The stars would give a dazzling display tonight—not a cloud in the sky.

They had hardly spoken since they'd taken off. For what felt like leagues, the resounding booms echoed. When she had asked what it was, Roman told her it was a tribal call. A call for the hunt, as he stated bluntly. The answer made her skin crawl. It sounded final.

Ahead, the edge of Raveer was visible. Farmland with homes and barns scattered the surrounding area. Farther north, ahead of them, were the stone buildings of the city itself—massive, even from this distance.

She swallowed at the sight. It was eerie being this close. They were wanted, and every piece of her screamed that it was wrong to get this close, but they had no choice. The tribal hunters were far too dangerous to ignore. If the stories were true, then their group would become targets if the hunters spotted them. And if they were caught . . . Syra shuddered.

No. It wasn't safe getting this close to Raveer, but it was safer than being out here with those savages.

"Zane." The Guardian's voice tore her free from her thoughts, and she glanced up to see Zarek eyeing him. "You know where your cousin is at?"

"Aye." Zane squinted his eyes and gazed at the farmland. "Let's stay on the path we're on. If I remember correctly, he'll be on the outskirts, closer to the village."

Zarek nodded and didn't say more. Syra watched the Guardian run his gloved hand over Uyul's bony neck. She had so many questions about the strange beast. Zarek mumbled something that was lost in the wind and then looked in her direction. Syra averted her gaze, hoping he didn't catch her staring.

"Hey," Zane spoke up. He rode up next to her and flashed a smile. "Having fun yet?" A faint bruise had blossomed along his jaw where Zarek had struck him, the area swollen, but the man didn't give any signs that it bothered him.

Syra snorted but remained tense. The last thing she wanted was to be questioned by him again. It felt like every time she turned around, someone was demanding information from her. Information she didn't necessarily have, but everyone expected her to know.

Zane must have sensed her weariness. He tilted his head and raised an eyebrow. "No questions, just normal chat," he clarified. "I'm just curious how you're holding up."

A wave of relief washed over her. "Truthfully? I have no idea what to expect, Zane. I had a better idea about my life on the ship than I do now." At that, she spied Zarek glance her way. If he was listening, he made no attempt to interrupt.

Zane chuckled. "Want some advice?"

She eyed him. "The great commander who's committed treason against his own city wants to give me advice?" When he didn't reply, she raised an eyebrow. "I'm listening."

That forced Zane to smile. "Stop trying to fulfill the expectations of everyone else." He shrugged at his own words. "Who do *you* want to be, Syra? Do you want all this? Do you want to be something spectacular to the world? Or do you want to be . . . just Syra?"

The question stumped her. She fumbled for the right words, but when she opened her mouth to answer him, she stopped herself. Truthfully, she had no idea who she wanted to be. A part of her wanted to be no one, able to disappear into the shadows of the world without a trace. Another part of her knew that was completely impossible. If the dead didn't find her, Kar would.

"You don't have to have an answer," he told her. "I don't expect you to." He laughed, his voice light despite the weight of the conversation. "If you had an answer that quick, then I'd be worried."

With that, he gestured his steed forward until he was closer to Zarek. "When we get closer, let me do the talking, alright? Joshua has a thing with, uh"—he licked his lips—"your kind."

The Guardian snickered. "Fair enough, Commander."

Syra stole a look at Roman. The older man's head was facing the horizon, his eyes distant. He was lost in his own thoughts, but what about, Syra had no idea. She didn't feel like it was right for her to ask either, given she was withholding her own information.

The night was nearly upon them, she realized. Exhaustion had a firm grip on her, her muscles were sore, and the headache that had started earlier had never left. It was the result of too little sleep. At this point, she could have curled up on the cold stone floor of a dungeon and been happy.

Syra couldn't wait to close her eyes.

* * *

"Remember, let me do the talking, alright?" Zane said, but his eyes were fixed on the Guardian. They had dismounted their steeds and were standing on the outskirts of Joshua's property. Livestock roamed in a large fenced off area, just next to a worn-down barn. The cousin's home didn't look like it was in much better shape either. A cloth hung over one of the windows, the wood warped and shabby, and a part of the roof was caved in. It looked nearly abandoned, save for the lantern that hung on the porch, its flame flickering lazily.

The night was still young, but the sun was gone. The thick smell of livestock wafted through the air, and she wrinkled her nose. They stood in the dark, unmoving, as Zane trudged across the property and toward the home. Roman held Zane's steed in his other hand. The older man sighed. "I really hope this works," he said.

"If it doesn't, I'll kick his ass," the Guardian retorted dryly. "And he knows it."

Syra raised an eyebrow at Zarek. "Has anyone told you that you have zero boundaries?"

He eyed her with those deep crimsons. "Give it a season and let's see if you still say the same thing."

"Hm." Syra looked around, avoiding his stare. She wasn't done with him, but now was not the time to start. Their primary goal was to get coverage. Ahead, Zane was on the porch, and he stole a quick glance back at them. He nodded, his features orange from the warm lantern glow. Then he turned around and knocked.

The door opened, and a young man stepped out with a large beard. Even from here, his shocked expression was visible. A conversation quickly started between the two. Syra watched, anxious. In the back of her mind, she couldn't shake the idea that the tribal hunters were toying with them, ready to pounce.

"How do we know those hunters aren't after us?" Syra blurted out, looking between the two men. "What if they're following us?"

"If they were after us, we would have never made it this far," Roman answered. "Oh, the cousin looks annoyed."

At that, everyone turned to watch as several tense moments passed. The exchange was heated, but she couldn't hear what they were talking about. Although, she didn't need to hear to know it was about them.

She couldn't shake her concerns. "Am I the only one concerned we're just being stalked by those people?"

Zarek snorted, the sound cold. "No, but you are the only one talking about it."

Before she could reply, Zane's wave caught everyone's attention. He was motioning to the barn. Joshua's eyes danced between him and the group in the dark before he shook his head and turned back into the home. The door remained open.

Roman was already off, leading both horses. Syra fell into step just beside the Guardian. Their feet crunched the gravel, the steeds snorted, and from the livestock, a cow mooed. The sounds were deafeningly loud against the silent night, and she cringed.

"When we're settled, we'll talk," Zarek said. Syra looked up at the Guardian just as Uyul snorted.

"Took you long enough," she mumbled. Zarek did not reply.

They crossed the land, passing several cows in the process, who stuck their heads over the wood posts. Hot air blew on Syra's neck, and she started, stumbling against Zarek's form. The Guardian laughed. "Jumpy?"

She straightened herself and stole a quick glance his way. "I'm exhausted, that's all."

They continued their trek until they reached the barn. Zane was opening the barn door already, the hinges squealing as he did so. "Joshua will bring us food, but we can rest here tonight." He flashed a grin. "Home sweet home."

Zane was the first to enter, followed by Roman, and then Syra. Zarek followed behind. The hooves of the steeds echoed against wood flooring. A lantern was lit to their immediate left, and Zane grabbed it. "Let me light the place up," he told everyone, and disappeared further into the barn. The small lantern wobbled around, and Syra watched the place creep to life with a handful of lanterns. The light was low, but it was better than nothing.

The barn was larger than she'd anticipated. Simple wood stairs to her right led to a second floor, a place likely used for storage. The main floor was covered in straw, and toward the back, four stalls were closed up with massive horses. Their heads poked out the top at the new arrival, and several whinnied. Syra's horse, Hazel, replied with his own whiny.

Zane came back and hung the lantern on its hook. "Alright, we'll have to tie the horses and, uh"—he motioned at Uyul—"I'll let you deal with her, Zarek." He looked at everyone. "So, let's get comfortable."

With that, the group broke off and began to make the barn their temporary home. Syra took everyone's sacks and piled them next to some straw. Roman and Zane tied the horses up, while Zarek investigated the upstairs. Uyul stood there next to Syra's makeshift spot and flicked her ears.

She eyed the beast. As much as she wanted to tell herself it was a horse, she knew that was wrong. Uyul might look like one, but she was in no way a normal horse. Uyul looked at Syra then with one of her large red eyes, unblinking. The gaze was eerie, *knowing*, and a shiver ran down Syra's back. She cleared her throat and looked away, choosing to reposition the sacks.

As she did so, she listened to Roman strike up a lively conversation with Zane about living in barns. The man used to do it during his travels to minimize being seen. He'd sneak in after dark and sleep on the second floor. If owners visited in the middle of the night, which sometimes occurred when an animal grew upset, then they wouldn't see him—a lesson he explained he had learned the hard way. In the mornings, he would pack up and leave before the sun crested the horizon.

Syra smiled to herself, satisfied. This wasn't home, but it felt like a piece of paradise after sleeping in the open with the sun beating down on them.

Tomorrow was a new day. Tonight, she would rest and relish having a roof over her head.

DREAM WALKER

When the door was shut, Morei let his nerves take hold of his senses. It had taken nearly all of his control to not run as fast as he could to get to the library. As if fate mocked him, he had been stopped three times on the way by various staff, as well as one of Emerald's. The man had wanted to know how to get a custom sword and the cost. Without much regard, the king had told him to find the chancellor and say that Morei had cleared all expenses—it was not a matter he wished to concern himself with.

Once he had reached the grand staircase, the king had taken two steps at a time, ascending to the library's massive doors. It was times like these that he realized how large this palace was. The architecture glared at him, reminding him of the centuries of dedication the Geral family had put into this place.

Those centuries mean nothing if he could not find a solution to Cu'cel.

He crossed the large room as quickly as he could, his boots echoing off the marble floor, and began to search madly through the titles on the fifth shelf. He knew the works on dreams, ancient Vorelian culture, and the Gods were here because he had often avoided them in his earlier summers, when he was fearful of the very idea of Gods. The simple thought that someone knew more about himself than he did had unnerved him to no end, so he'd avoided the concept altogether.

The firepit to the left was dead, having not been touched in days. This was the Geral family library, restricted from the public unless Morei allowed someone in here under his or a soldier's surveillance. Books were prized possessions in every country, regardless of culture. The pages bounded by hard work and leather were keepers of the most intimate words, of history and the future, of man's fears and greatest achievements. They were irreplaceable. This library had to have over a thousand unique volumes, some single editions, others copies.

Ezra would have access to this library if he accepted the offer—*when* he accepted, because it was not an opportunity even the uneducated would pass up. The thought stabbed Morei with a strange possessiveness. This had been his library all his life. His father used to sit in the chair that now sat behind him and read with a drink by the dancing fire. It had always rightfully been Morei's in inheritance, but now, it would be Ezra's too.

He yanked an old book out, *Strange Phenomenon and Dreams*, at least five centuries old from the date on the first page. Without moving, he started flicking through it, trying to catch phrases about Gods and symbolism. Several words caught his attention, but they weren't directed toward the Gods. Morei kept sifting until he was on the last page. Then he slapped it closed and shoved it back into its spot.

"Your Majesty?"

The voice nearly killed him, and he spun on his boots to stare at the young maid who had poked her head through the door. At the sight of her, he relaxed some. "Yes?" He had been so engrossed in his search, he hadn't even heard the door, which he scolded himself for. For all he knew, Hyle himself could have walked through the doors and he would have never known.

She gave a sweet smile, one that screamed innocence in a time of violence. "Just checking to see if you need anything? I know this room hasn't been used in a bit. I could bring a drink or food? Maybe a fire?"

Her care made him yearn for simpler times, and he couldn't help but smile, though just barely. "None of that will be necessary, but thank you."

The woman nodded. "Of course. Let me know if you change your mind, Your Majesty." At that, she closed the door with a soft thud. Before Morei continued his search, he ran over and slid the metal bar across to lock it. He tried to make it quiet, but the metal screeched against the hook, and he cringed. If she was still standing on the other side, she would have heard—anyone within the vicinity would have, but there was nothing he could do. What was important to him was to not have interruption. This was his time and his alone, and he would not explain himself to anyone. Not yet.

Satisfied, Morei crossed back to the shelves and continued his search.

He yanked a book off the fourth shelf titled *Meaningful Dreams*. Scanning the table of contents, he found a section on the supernatural, so he quickly flicked to that part of the book. Holding it with one hand, he scanned down the first page, but felt frustration boil up. This was on ghosts and the dead, not Gods—ancient cultural beliefs about the Afterlife that would not answer his burning questions.

"Damn you, Greve," he mumbled, and shoved the book back into its spot.

Morei continued to search, but he found nothing in the dreams section, which infuriated him. After five more books turned to be unsuccessful, he moved his gaze over to the section that consisted of all the Drügale books, down to the philosophies, teachings, rituals, and history of the religion for Vorelians. He should have been eager that his hunch might be right, but instead, it only brought cold terror that forced the air from his lungs.

Because if the Gods were real and he had been sent a message . . . he shuddered at the thought. It would mean Cu'cel was more than some ailment, but rather an omen. Perhaps he was being punished after all for turning his back on them.

He took a deep breath and stepped over to the next bookcase. It towered three shelves higher than him, with up to twenty books on some. He began his search, feeling an intense array of emotions wash over him. All this time, the king had renounced his faith, certain that no God would stand for such heinous acts against someone as faithful as he had once been. But in a matter of days, he could no longer ignore that maybe, just maybe, the Gods were real—and crueler than anyone would have expected. Slower, the king scanned the titles, letting his fingers graze over the imprinted letters along the spines. What he was looking for would be specific, and he knew it.

Despite the circumstances, he loved the old leather and the smell of countless summers. He breathed in deep, hoping to calm himself, but it did little good. So many hands had brushed over these books. There was a monument of answers here, and yet he was still like the rest of them—foolish, ignorant, and scrambling for an explanation to his life when things were no longer going the way he wanted.

As he reached the bottom two rows, he sat and crossed his legs. Morei continued his search, more methodical now that the books were thinner and harder to make out, reflective of their age. He had no idea how much time passed and didn't stop to check. If anyone was looking for him, they hadn't attempted to find him here.

At the last shelf, his fingers stopped as he read the title of a book, its leather spine worn and shredded on the top half, seemingly held together by mere luck. *Understanding the Dream Walker.*

With his heart in his throat, Morei pulled out the book. The black leather on the front was scratched, and at the bottom, someone had carved *Forbidden* in hideous scripture, likely with the head of a knife. Hands trembling, he swallowed the growing dread that threatened to suffocate him where he sat. This book was older than Sorréle and had only been mentioned in passing on several occasions when he was but a boy. It had been brought over from Eiyrạl by none other than a Dragon Rider, or so he had been told. A handful of books had been a part of that trade, but this was the only one that had ever scared him.

Sekar was once known as the God of Dreams or Dream Walker, before his malevolent behavior had turned his brothers and sister against him and cast him out of their family. Sekar's history was brutal, cruel, and complicated. His old title was as ancient as Vorelian history, yet he was only known for his mischievous and sinister personality. Some cultures acknowledged his original place among the Gods, while others, like Sorréle, saw him as nothing more than an exiled God—if one didn't acknowledge him, then he simply didn't exist.

Morei stared at the book, afraid of what he might discover, but knowing he had to do it. Taking a deep breath, he opened the cover and let his eyes graze over the old words. There were Old Tongue sigils drawn into the corners of the page, as if by someone hoping they could cast the evil God's existence from the world by destroying this original work.

If only it were that simple.

Morei skipped the history of Sekar, not interested in learning what had happened to the banished God; it was all stories and theories. Nobody would know how or why or even *if* Sekar had been banished unless they spoke to him directly. And that was if the God was real. He continued to carefully groom the pages, taking care in how he handled each ancient piece of parchment, yellowed and dried with age. He continued until he reached the portion of the book that he was most interested in: *Messages from the Dream Walker.*

The king halted at the title and carefully brushed his fingers over the edge of the book, sweeping his thumb across the corner, where another sigil was drawn. A part of him wanted to close the book now, turn and walk away, cast aside these outrageous ideas, but he couldn't—he wouldn't. His eyes scanned the page without his permission, soaking in the words that would unravel him.

"*... take one's dreams and alter them ... known as the Dream Walker.*" Morei held the book tighter in his hand. "*Sekar will give his warnings and fortunes in the realm of slumber, where man's guard is lowest and his messages can be received or easily manipulated ...*"

Morei leaned forward more, as if he couldn't see the words clearly enough already, and read the next part. "*Journals from the experimentation have proven fruitful. Sekar seeks out those desperate and afraid . . . he thrives off these emotions. It is no wonder he was cast out by his own family . . .*" He turned the page. "*He has consistently been identified as the voice in one's head when they dream ... never seen but always there ... he takes all his victims to the same place before he strikes ...*"

Morei read further, trying to figure out what the writer meant by the "same place," but the author never described it, even when explaining the experiment, which had consisted of a handful of participants who willingly conducted rituals. Flipping the page, he found that when Sekar became known as the Dark Lord, people claimed to have horrific nightmares of death and would experience sleep paralysis. Their souls and minds would be stuck in the Soul Realm and their bodies back in the living. It was in this state that Sekar enjoyed keeping his victims, where he tortured them, both mentally and physically before taking them to the unknown location. This altered consciousness allowed his presence to go unnoticed by his brethren, while also giving him the ability to use his power as he desired. He was a mysterious God, one of violent tendencies and a past that no one knew for certain.

But none of that entirely mattered to Morei, at least not yet. What mattered to him was that Sekar did use dreams to deliver messages. He was the only God who had been documented to do such things, assuming he was real at all. But Morei was focused on gathering information, not on what was and what wasn't real. Some could have argued the enigmatic Guardians of Death weren't real, or that Soul Speakers were frauds, but he knew better. The king had seen and experienced enough to believe in the otherworldly. And yet, he was hesitant to believe in Gods. He swallowed and turned the page, and what he saw there made his blood run cold.

"Grënyl, the Mark of Death, is believed to originate from Sekar. The illness begins with patches of rotting flesh, followed by mental deterioration, which is how the God infiltrates his victim to begin drawing upon their life force—"

Morei slammed the book shut. He didn't need to read more. Trembling, he shoved the book back into its place between the rest on the bottom shelf and stood. Boris's words rang through his head, crystal clear. *"He wanted me to give you his regards."*

The pieces of his reality crashed around him and he inhaled sharply, taken aback by their force. Cu'cel—no, Grënyl—was no coincidence, and Boris's dream solidified that. Whatever Morei believed, he was not foolish enough to ignore the signs. As much as he wanted to think the Gods weren't real or that he was exaggerating, grasping onto threads that made nothing, he knew he was wrong. They had all been wrong.

Morei thought of the woman he had been brought to before the battle of Diemon. How she had been so deranged, and her warning. He thought of the letter, of the Nameless One and their threat. That letter had started it all—the day he received it was the day his life changed forever. Ever since, he had been scrambling for a break. Everything that could go wrong had gone horribly, horribly wrong.

Cautiously, almost fearfully, the king peeked around his shoulder, expecting to see someone, perhaps Sekar himself. If the God had been standing there, laughing, pointing a finger with a cold gleam in his eye, he wouldn't have been surprised. He could nearly hear the God's laugh in his own ears, raking over every part of him with a serrated edge. It was a laugh he was certain he had not made up, and it made his blood run cold. With a weak hand, he reached up and wiped away the perspiration that had sprouted from the strength of his anxiety. Heart pounding, he slowly scanned the whole room. The silence that fell over him was deafening, like the entire palace had ceased to exist around him.

There was only one thought blossoming in his mind, taking control of his senses, smothering his confidence and making him mad. It was a thought he hadn't ever been prepared to acknowledge, let alone accept, but nonetheless it was there, and it was not going to disappear. If anything, it was going to consume him.

He needed to prepare for the worst.

PART 2

"When you give the shadows fire,

they become indistinguishable to the sun."

~ Vorelian Scrolls

AND MAY DREAMS
COME TRUE

Two dragon eggs.

Cyrus gawked at them. Two silver eggs sat nestled up against each other on a blue cushion. Everything looked untouched—not even a speck of dust coated the inside of this chest. It felt so unnaturally out of place in the dingy chamber that Cyrus had to look around to remind himself this was all real.

"Are those . . ."

Zorya's words stabbed him with the reality that he wasn't alone. He looked at her and opened his mouth to speak but then closed it again. He couldn't find the words, so he simply nodded and turned back to look at the eggs.

Sozar? Cyrus prodded the silent dragon, but Sozar withdrew completely, overwhelmed, shutting him out. It had been one thing to fantasize and think they were real, but it was another to see the eggs for real. And females, no less. If they hatched in Sozar's and Ashtir's lifetime . . . the dragons would be reborn.

"How could that be?" Zorya leaned in and tentatively touched the one closest to her before pulling her hand away, as if it had stung her.

"Zorya," Cyrus mumbled, his mouth dry. "You had no idea?"

"None," she answered. "This is huge information, Cyrus. We need to tell my parents."

He shot her a glare. "We aren't handing these eggs over to them."

"Why not?" the princess challenged. "They can help."

Cyrus felt possessive. There were innocent dragons stuck inside these eggs. If they stayed in the hands of Kyllian and Lorelei, there was a good chance they would either never hatch, or would be forced into servitude if they did. They deserved freedom, not to be bound by royal law.

But he couldn't explain that. "What are they going to do, Zorya? Are you telling me that neither of your parents knew of these eggs?" His tone was far colder than he had expected, but he didn't retract his words. He needed answers, and more importantly needed to know that Zorya hadn't known.

The princess opened her mouth and then closed it again. Her dark eyes hovered over the chest, and finally she shook her head. "I don't know, Cyrus."

She was unconvinced. And if she was, that meant that deep down, she had always known that information was being held from her.

Cyrus swallowed and looked at the eggs. Tentatively, he reached out and laid his hand on one. It hummed against his touch. There was no doubt the dragon knew who Cyrus was— that he was a Rider.

Nobody would take these eggs without his permission.

"How long do you think they've been down here?" Zorya asked, her voice barely above a whisper. She reached out and ran her fingers over the other one, but this time she didn't pull away as quickly as before.

Cyrus scoffed. "Likely centuries, based on these chambers."

She nodded, lips pursed tight. "I want to thank the Gods, but I am not so sure what to say."

The words escaped before he could think. "Your father was withholding information from me, about these eggs. He lied."

"What? How are you so certain?"

The familiar emotions of betrayal rose in his throat. Yes, Cyrus had known Kyllian was keeping information from him, but never had he believed a king would be foolish enough to hide dragon eggs from the first—one of the first—Dragon Riders in nearly eight centuries. If anything, his arrival should have been the king's chance to come clean. Together, they could have worked together to promise a peaceful life for these dragons.

Instead, Kyllian had held on to this, trying to prevent Cyrus from stumbling on them. "You didn't know?" he repeated, his voice more sinister. Suddenly, her eagerness to accompany him felt weighed down by different motives.

The princess took a step back, her face contorting into something dark, pained. "Who do you take me as?"

"You are the daughter of the man who lied right to my face," he hissed. "Who would I be if I didn't think you had some knowledge of this? Is that why you found me in your city? You know, now that I think about it, the timing was impeccable. Truly. I commend you and your family for reeling me in like some animal for slaughter."

Zorya shook her head furiously. "That is not what happened!" Her words came out in a shrill yell. Her cheeks were flush with rage, eyes glassy.

He didn't believe her. "How can I trust you? How can I believe anything you've said or will say?" Cyrus snorted to himself. "Maybe your father didn't want to come down here himself, and I just happen to walk in at the right time. Lo and behold, the Dragon Rider who found the missing Razan eggs." Narrowing his eyes toward her, he finished, "How *thrilled* you all must be to have me here."

Tears streamed down her face. It shook Cyrus to his core. Never had he been so cruel to someone without reason. All the emotions he had felt for the last season—the anger, guilt, betrayal, loneliness—it all had bubbled up at once, and she had taken the brunt of it. And while he was furious, there was no real evidence about how much she knew. Inhaling deeply, he was about to speak when Sozar stirred between the link. *The king just passed the courtyard. I advise speaking with him before I destroy this entire place with my talons.*

The statement came out so calmly that it took him a moment to digest those words.

Kyllian. The man of the summer, it seemed. With one final look at the eggs, Cyrus snapped the lid shut and turned. The princess followed, steps scuffing against the floor. "What're you going to do?" she asked.

The lantern still hung in her hand, but he didn't need it. He knew exactly how to get back, driven by rage as much as instinct. Maybe the king even had information about Cyrus's heritage that he was withholding. The scrolls that he had seen on the bookshelf, the king's expression when he had brought up the term Light Bringer, his coy smile as if he knew exactly what he was doing and thought he had gotten away with it. It all flashed across his mind.

For the first time since he had stumbled on Sozar's egg back in the mines of Diemon, Cyrus felt like he had purpose. True purpose. He had always known he had the responsibility of protecting Sozar, but that had only filled a part of him. Memories danced behind his eyes as he strode, memories of the dungeon in Geral, King Morei, the trek across half of Sorréle with a young dragon, fleeing from Diemon once the people had learned of his secret. So much had happened to him in a season. So much of his life had been torn away from him, and now, in an instant, it felt like everything was falling into place.

The princess hurried behind him, sending light dancing over the stone in quick and frenzied flashes. "Cyrus, what are you doing?" she repeated.

"I'm getting answers. What's it look like I'm doing?" he snapped back. They reached the chamber, and he turned left, back where they had come from.

A hand grabbed his arm and forced him backward. Zorya was facing him now, lantern raised to paint both their features in a warm glow. Her eyes were fierce, a warrior's gaze. "And what will you do when you get the answer you want, Cyrus? What happens next? Do you kill my father and leave my city without a king?"

The question tore the air from his lungs. "I am not a murderer." Even as the words left his mouth, he felt the cold pang of shame stab him. He was a murderer, but not in the way Zorya expected him to be. He couldn't admit that to her, though. By the grace of Greve, he couldn't even admit that to himself.

"I can't stand by while you make a scene that could ruin my family's reputation," she shot back. "We've lived in peace for centuries, and if you upset that—" She broke off and shook her head, sending waves of blond hair bouncing.

He could feel the dragon's growing agitation, but he swallowed it down, not wanting to be crueler than he already had been. "Zorya, it's never been my intention to hurt anyone or mess up anything. It was never my intention to even show my face to this many people, let alone meet you." Stepping closer, he dropped his voice. "My goal? I was supposed to sneak into your father's study, get answers without disturbing anyone else, and leave. If I had intended to commit any sort of crime, I would have done so once I had you alone."

The grip on his arm faltered, and he took it as a chance to remove himself from her completely. "If you intend to follow, then keep up."

Without wasting another moment, he turned and continued toward the exit.

TIME TO MAKE PEACE

he stew was old, but after the recent meals of dried meat and turning fruit, it was the best thing Syra'd had in days.

She inhaled her soup, only stopping when she was certain Zane was going to choke on his own. Nobody said a word as they ate. Joshua watched them, keeping himself next to the barn door and his arms crossed. He was shorter than Syra had expected. From the distance, he had looked larger, but when he approached with Zane by his side, carrying the bowls of stew, she'd found herself sorely mistaken. The man was a head shorter than his cousin, but his broad shoulders made up for it. He was a farmer, a man who had spent countless summers out in the field, and it showed.

When they were done with the stew, they stacked their bowls. Syra tried to thank Joshua, but he simply grunted and eyed Zane once more. A silent conversation passed between the two before Joshua grabbed the stacked bowls and left.

He hadn't said one word. It was clear he was not in total support of the plan.

Once he was gone, Syra sat silently, listening to the men speak. It wasn't that she didn't want to speak herself, but it had been a long time since she'd felt comfortable enough to simply listen. Her stomach was full, the barn was warm, and the low light teased slumber. At one point, she was certain she had dozed off with her face resting in her hand, because when she came to, she couldn't remember anything that Roman had been speaking about. Her wrist was numb, the muscles annoyed. She shook out her hand and was bombarded with the tingling sensation that she loathed. It was uncomfortable, but after a few moments, it settled.

Zane was engaged in a story, his hands going left and right, when Syra stood. She didn't interrupt his story, which was a tale from his time in the ranks and some outrageous situation about a man missing an eye. Her belt was still firmly around her hips, with Death's Sword strapped in. They might be hidden away from the world for the night, but that didn't mean they were safe.

She wandered over to the stairs. Uyul was standing next to them, sniffing the ground. The creature raised her head at Syra's approach and exhaled loudly. She flashed a small smile and passed by carefully—the beast still freaked her out. Zarek seemed particularly fond of her, though. Syra had known countless riders who loved their horses like a family member, and the Guardian was no exception.

Zane and Roman's voices drifted as she climbed the old stairs. The wood creaked underneath her steps, and on several occasions, she repositioned her weight when the step felt weaker. As she came to the second floor, she saw a single lantern toward the back. Next to it, Zarek sat with his back up against the wall and a book in his hand.

At her arrival, the Guardian raised his head. Syra approached, careful to avoid hitting any of the crates, which looked to hold a little bit of everything. Likely pieces of Joshua's life. It smelled of dust up here, of a lost lifetime.

"Where'd you get the book?" she asked, sitting down to his left. She drew her knees up and rested her arms on them. Moving had helped awaken her senses, but sit here long enough and Syra was certain she could fall asleep again. That wouldn't happen—she was determined to have the conversation that was well overdue with the Guardian.

Zarek closed the aged book and looked it over, as if seeing it for the first time. "Some old recount of Saveen and Creitón," he answered. "I got it from the crate." He set the book aside. "Probably shouldn't be snooping in the man's stuff, but curiosity got the best of me."

She chuckled. "I won't tell. I've got a bad habit of doing the same." It was how she had found the book of the Soul Realm, the *Leangé*, in the first place. The memory forced Dryl into her thoughts, and she swallowed. "Find anything interesting?"

He shrugged. "A lot of false information about the royal family of Saveen. Things about serpent wranglers, deals with pirates, stuff like that. The Saveen family is eccentric, by all means, and perhaps a handful had chosen snakes for pets, but they've got good heads on their shoulders."

Syra raised an eyebrow. "I take it you know them personally?"

"From time to time, I visited. I haven't been in quite a few summers, but the family had a good relationship with the Guardians. Many of us would stop by on our travels, have a drink or two and share stories, catch up. It was a bit of an expectation, actually." Zarek smiled, and for once, it was warm. His entire face lit up. "I met with their son for a number of summers, even when he was just a boy. He'd tell me about his training, studies, life, everything he could, and I just listened. About seven summers ago . . ." He trailed off and shook his head, the smile slipping from his face. "I hope he is well."

"What's keeping you from visiting?"

Zarek inhaled. "Guilt, time—what would I say?" He looked at her fully now. The lantern's light danced against his crimsons. "What could I say? What we had was a season, nothing more."

She shrugged. "Maybe to you. Perhaps to him, it was more than that."

"Perhaps," Zarek whispered. For a moment, neither spoke. Syra rested her head against the wall, her eyes locked ahead toward the stairs. The Guardian laughed softy. "Uyul finds your wariness of her amusing."

That caught her by surprise. "She can talk?"

Zarek tapped his head for emphasis. "Mentally, we are linked. Much like a Rider and Dragon. It is a power only ancient creatures possess."

She licked her lips. "Is it because of Dark Energy?"

He snorted. "Oh, by the Gods, no. This is purely power. You see"—he motioned with his hands as he spoke—"those who lived well before our time were the true masters of this world. Creatures unlike anything you've ever seen. Strange, stunning, and extraordinary. They had a special link to this world—to the mother of energy, Chaos—and it is that link that gives them such incredible abilities. A dragon or Uyul is not so different, yet one found sanctuary in the realm of the dead, and the other died out as the living grew . . . *complicated*."

Syra slowly nodded. "So, why didn't the dragons or the others go to the Soul Realm? Why stay?" The few times Uyul had met her eyes . . . the horselike beast had known exactly what she was doing and could understand everything. A shiver ran down her back. The world was growing stranger by the day.

Zarek bared his hands and shrugged. "Who knows."

When he didn't continue, she took it as an opportunity to say her piece. It felt like now or never. She dug into the pouch on her hip and searched around until she felt the cold metal of the ring brush up against her fingertips. "When Dryl and I parted ways, he had something." Syra pulled the Infernol ring out and presented it to him. "I thought you should have it."

The air shifted immediately. Zarek fell quiet, staring at the ring. Syra kept her hand out; the reflection of the lantern's light shimmered off the gold metal and blue sapphire. It was a perfectly handcrafted piece, save for the scratch along the band. A scratch with a story nobody would ever know.

Carefully, Zarek reached forward and wrapped his fingers over the ring. His touch was hot, but as quickly as it brushed against her, it was gone. He brought the ring closer and examined it. Syra didn't say anything. There was no need. Instead, she watched a lifetime of emotions pass over his features. A storm raged in his eyes, but it wasn't anger—it was guilt, remorse.

Zarek wrapped his fingers tightly around the ring and brought his fist to his lips. His breathing came out uneven, and he closed his eyes, but not a single tear fell. Then he opened them and handed the ring back.

"He wanted you to have it," Zarek whispered. His expression was soft, his words heavy.

That was not the answer she wanted to hear. "It belongs to you, Zarek. He was your brother, not me."

He did not relent. The ring sat there between the two of them, in his hand. "There will come a time when you have to prove your relationship with Dryl. Keep it. You will have more use for it than I."

Syra wasn't entirely sure what he meant by that, but she reached for the ring and wrapped her fingers around it. It felt wrong taking it back. All this time, she was certain the ring would belong to him because it rightfully did. This was not hers. Her time with Dryl had been short—Zarek had spent lifetimes with his brother. Even if they were at odds, he still had a right to this item that she would never have.

Taking it felt like stealing.

"If there ever comes a time and you want it," she began as she rolled the finger in her hand, "it is yours."

Zarek smiled and leaned his head up against the wall. "The times are changing, Syra," he muttered.

The conversation had shifted. "What happens when we get to the Infernol? What do you do?"

He shrugged. "I will do whatever is needed of me—and what best suits the Soul Realm."

"Yeah, but how is being here doing any good for the Soul Realm?" she countered.

"You *are* the Soul Realm, Syra. Have you forgotten?"

She inhaled deeply. No, she had not, although she wished she didn't know. Life would be simpler, even with a target on their back. "Last night—What was that? I didn't know what would happen. I've only ever done that twice, and the first time I was asleep."

"What happened last night can't be a habit," Zarek replied. "Without control, a gift such as that will get you killed." He shook his head. "The two times you've gone, what have you seen?"

Syra jumped into a recollection of the events the first time and last night. She spared no detail, not even the spirit of the dead woman when she had visited Syra at Jared's. The Guardian listened silently, without question, only nodding here and there. It felt good to get this off her chest, to speak so freely about the events of her life. Only when she was finishing up did she realize that she had needed to vent more than she was willing to admit. And of all people, Zarek had been on the receiving end of it.

Syra took a deep breath as she finished. Her mouth was dry from all the talking, but she was satisfied, at peace, even if her life was in full disarray. Tonight had meant more to her than she realized. When she was done, she dropped her hands into her lap, her legs now outstretched, and waited.

Zarek's words came out slow, as if he had handpicked each one with considerate care. "Kar is more powerful than we know. I don't know how he was there last night, and you said he was there on the ship?"

She nodded. "It was sudden, too. One moment, I could see everyone; the next, I was on my knees and couldn't move. He was there, though. I could recognize his voice anywhere."

"By the Gods," Zarek muttered, and shook his head. "I don't know what he's done, but he's dangerous. Perhaps a deal with the Gods, but Eazon and Greve would never allow for such things."

Syra raised her brow. "Helyna would?"

He snorted. "She is a nasty woman. I've never met her, but there are plenty of stories among the Guardians about her. She is capable of giving love, but she cannot receive it. A cruel gift, don't you think?"

She opened her mouth to speak and then closed it, overwhelmed. Zarek spoke with certainty about the Gods, even as her faith dwindled. She had spent so many summers praying and doing her duties as a follower of Drügalism but had never once seen or met one of the Gods.

"How can you be okay with them?" When he looked at her, she added, "The Gods. They're supposed to help people, give them hope, but I've never seen one."

"Syra," Zarek breathed, "do you think the expectations of who and what the Gods are supposed to be are set by people or the Gods themselves?" His mouth twitched. "The Gods were once people, you know, just like Guardians."

She fell silent. He had a point, and she had never thought of it like that before. The rituals, prayers, the expectations . . . perhaps it was all manmade. The Gods existed, but maybe not for the people. Perhaps they were Gods to mortals like her and so many because they were special, powerful, immortal. They had everything she didn't.

"Do all the Guardians believe like you do?" she asked softly. "Did people like Dryl and Kar know what you know?"

He tilted his head and chuckled, but it sounded heavy. "I had special circumstances. Many in our order knew of the Gods and have plenty of information no mortal should ever have to know, but I . . ." He pursed his lips and stopped talking. Heartbeats passed like the changing of seasons. He looked at her, his eyes sorrowful. "I was Shevana's most loyal Guardian, and for many reasons."

He didn't expound, and Syra didn't ask him to. The look on his face, the weight of his words, it was all she needed to understand just what Shevana meant to him. She had questions, so many of them, but she bit her tongue. Now was not the time to poke for information. Instead, she swallowed and whispered, "What happened?"

"The Honuyál happened," he answered, and took a deep breath. Syra felt her heart drop at the mention of the creatures that Kar had only shown her last night. "They set free the enslaved Einhër and disrupted the dynamics of the Soul Realm. Shevana let the Honuyál in, believing they would offer something she lacked, something that would benefit the Soul Realm and the passing souls." He scoffed. "I advised against it, did everything I could to make her see they were manipulating her, but she waved me off. At the end of the day, it was her decision—no amount of advice from the Guardians would steer her."

"How could she do that when everyone told her no?"

Zarek's expression faltered, and for a moment, he looked destroyed. But as quickly as she saw it, it was gone. "Shevana is power-hungry, always has been and always will be. But in her desperation for more of it, she lost sight of everything she knew, including what the order stood for. When the Honuyál increased their numbers and began to interrupt the peace, we became divided. Many of us disagreed with the direction, but there was little we could do. The Soul Realm is all we've ever known."

He didn't continue, and Syra didn't press. The Guardian had shared more than she'd anticipated. His life had danced between each word, and while he didn't say a lot about his personal affairs, he didn't have to. Zarek had once been in love, and it had destroyed him. He had left everything behind in the

Soul Realm to be here. The least she could do was show him some respect.

"I'm sorry," Syra mumbled. He raised an eyebrow at her, as if he hadn't expected that. "None of this is easy, but know that I appreciate your training. You being here after everything I've been through . . . it's been tough." A small laugh escaped between her lips. "I wouldn't say I've been the greatest. But thank you."

Zarek laid a hand on her leg and squeezed it. "Let's call it a night, shall we?" The act was warm, affectionate, a shard of kindness in this disaster of their lives. "And a truce at that."

That made her laugh as she stood. "Deal." When the Guardian rose, he took the book with him and walked it over to a crate just to their right. Setting it back, he closed the lid and fell into step with her as they made their way back down to the main floor.

Syra smiled to herself as they walked across the old and dusty floorboards. For once, she felt at peace. This conversation had brought her solace and given her a reason to truly trust Zarek. It wouldn't be easy, she knew, but she could rely on him, and that was invaluable. She just hoped he felt the same.

Tomorrow was a new day, she told herself. With it, they would set off on their travels with a new understanding for each other. It wouldn't make it easier, and there was still much to talk about, but for now, Syra could rest knowing she was in good company.

And she could not wait to get some rest.

A PLEA FROM
THE SHADOWS

orei found Emerald in the seamstress chambers in the palace. It was a place dedicated to royally made clothing, where women worked around the clock to ensure the fabrics were taken care of, cleaned properly, and fixed, and also experimented with new outfits. On plenty of occasions, they would make new articles of clothing upon request, as they had done for the queen of Junok.

Dressed in a white slip, Emerald had her arms raised in front of a long mirror with three seamstresses. One stood behind the queen, placing her hands just underneath the breasts and explaining where the fabric would be tapered. One was cleaning a mark she had drawn on Emerald's skin along her shoulder with a cloth, while the final one was quickly sketching out the dress on parchment, brow scrunched in concentration.

The queen was grinning, her cheeks flush from what could have only been a good laugh prior to his arrival.

Behind her, along a long table, lay an array of fruits and breads. A decanter of something dark stood there, halfway gone—tea, perhaps. The windows ahead were open, letting the warm breeze sweep through the room. This part of the palace did not face the firepits, only the southside of the desert, where

Boldur Valley lay in the distance. The massive rocks were small from here, but for those daring enough to travel closer, some were taller than the palace itself, or so the story told.

As much as the king would have preferred to walk in and join in the laughter, he couldn't. He was here with one goal alone.

"May I have a word with Emerald?" Morei asked as calmly as he could. He had come straight from the library. Forcing his breaths to slow, he tried to calm his racing heart, but as the seamstresses eyed him, he could tell they were aware something was wrong.

The queen frowned as the ladies set their items down and filed past him to the hall. Once they were out, the king nearly slammed the door. In the silence that followed, neither spoke. Emerald stood there, her curves unhidden under the thin fabric that separated the rest of her body to his eyes.

As he stood here now, taking her in, the outrageous request he was preparing to make now felt smaller, unnecessary. The urge that had gripped him back in the library now felt petty, laughable even. But he swallowed down that trepidation, licked his lips, and began.

"You need to leave."

Emerald opened her mouth and then closed it again. Folding her arms across her chest, she regarded him, and he did not need her to speak to know she was as confused as he'd anticipated.

"Please just listen to me, okay?" The king stepped away from the door, closer to her, and continued. "I've been researching, trying to find anything that could be a solution to Cu'cel, but something's happened. I found something—" He could hardly speak now. It felt like his throat was constricting as he spit the next part out. "I think this all has to do with me. I think I'm the reason Cu'cel exists."

The statement sounded outrageous to his own ears, so he could only imagine how it sounded to the woman standing there, eyebrow raised. A criticizing gaze returned his own.

"Cu'cel is a sickness, Morei. You were unconscious for ten days, and during that time, it started. How could you be the reason for it?"

Morei clenched his fist and inhaled deeply. "I found a book, *Understanding the Dream Walker.* Ever heard of it?"

She shook her head.

"It spoke of Sekar when he was once considered a respectable God, theories about how he was banished and such, but it had a section about communicating with him—or how he communicates with you." The king swallowed, mouth dry. "It consisted of everything we're experiencing now, but back then, it wasn't called Cu'cel, it was known as Grënyl, the Mark of Death."

Emerald shook her head, sending the few strands that framed her face bouncing. "I don't understand how any of this relates to you."

It felt obvious, and he couldn't understand how she didn't see what he meant. "Do you remember when you asked me if I believe in Gods?"

She nodded.

"I told you no, that I couldn't when they had failed me on so many occasions. That it was impossible to believe in something or someone when they could do nothing but let you down." He snorted, mad. "But all this time, I didn't think of the obvious— that they were real but they were cruel."

"Morei," Emerald interrupted, expression scrunched in concern. "Cu'cel is not your fault."

She didn't believe him. The reality of that nearly took him to his knees right there. Finally, he was confessing to someone about what was happening, willing to admit the Gods were real, and she didn't believe it.

The queen approached him, cautious, as if he would lash out. "I know you blame yourself for the murder of your parents, but this—"

"Enough!" Morei yelled. He was infuriated. This had *nothing* to do with that fucking night, and he was tired of everyone blaming it for his motives. "You all scrounge for proof of the Afterlife, of Gods, but the moment I present it, you laugh it off—what could you all possibly be looking for other than this?" The king waved her off as she opened her mouth to speak. "I didn't come here to argue the point. I know what I'm saying sounds crazy, but Boris had a dream of a man, and I've had a dream of the same man. The writings in that book validate it all. This is Sekar we're talking about, okay? Cu'cel isn't some natural illness, it's supernatural, and it's meant as a sign—" He stopped and turned on his boots, overwhelmed. A thousand thoughts raced through his head at once. "It's a sign for me," he muttered.

A hand brushed over his shoulder, but he shoved the queen off, pissed. "Don't patronize me, Emerald. I didn't come here looking for sympathy." He faced her, now seeing her as nothing more than a liability. "You have a city, a council, people waiting for your return. Go home."

The last thing he expected was to see her upset, but there she was, obviously taken aback by his request despite his confession. "I stayed because I thought it was the right th—"

"And it was," he cut in, resolved. "But doing a good thing doesn't make you invisible to fate."

She reacted as if slapped. "I understand."

As much as he didn't want to be cruel, Morei also couldn't help but think about the bigger picture. She was a queen, and a city was expecting her return. The last thing he wanted to be was responsible for something happening to her, because it would forever tie him to Junok. He did not want those strings.

Perhaps she knew it too. She didn't argue.

"This isn't purpose," he whispered, and shook his head. "You may have believed you were doing right, and perhaps to some degree you were, but this"—he motioned around the room, to Geral—"this is not where you belong. You had a goal, Emerald,

313

to marry a man who could secure your bloodline and city, but I have refused, and that answer is still no. Our paths end here."

The queen stood there like a statue, unmoving. Morei didn't have the time to comfort her, let alone the tolerance. He had bigger problems. "Do I have your word? You will leave with your men as quickly as possible?"

Emerald's eyes hardened. Now she looked more like a queen, a figure of authority, than a woman who so desperately wanted to do right by her mistakes. "You have my word."

The relief that washed through him was overwhelming. He forced a deep breath in, feeling the slightest bit more in control. This was not her battle; it never had been. Sure, she had her own problems, but they were not the king's. No matter how much he wished to help, to guide, or try to be of service, he couldn't.

Hopefully, she finally understood that.

Without another word, he turned and walked to the door. Emerald had been a problem needing to be dealt with, even if he would have preferred her company. Still, he couldn't ignore the growing dread as he exited into the hall, passed the seamstresses, and made his way toward the chancellor's.

"Sekar is coming for me," he whispered to himself, but he might as well have screamed.

COURAGE

Cyrus had never felt so bold in his life, not even when he had confronted Evander about his bizarre behavior. To approach a king or queen without royal manner was grounds for punishment, and depending on the city, that punishment varied greatly.

He was willing to risk his safety for the sake of getting a point across. Kyllian knew damn well what he had done, and now he would answer for it.

Zorya remained behind him, having left the lantern at the door to the tunnels. She hardly spoke as they crossed the palace and headed toward the king's study, where he suspected Kyllian would be. Cyrus was grateful for her silence. He was certain he would snap, and he was done directing it at the princess. It was not her he wanted answers from. It was the king.

So much had happened in the last day that he could hardly grasp it all. Things were moving too fast, fate was pulling him in a thousand directions, and he had to prioritize what mattered most. The eggs, himself, and Sozar. Dameon and Ashtir no longer took the lead because he simply couldn't afford it. Tomorrow night, when he had to face them, then they would matter. For now, what mattered was getting the king to come clean and getting an explanation for it.

They passed a half dozen staff members, all of whom took second glances their way but didn't stop them. With Zorya next to him, he sensed the members of the palace didn't wish to interrupt whatever business they may be on.

On the final turn, Cyrus recognized the familiar red cloak of the man he had run into the first night there. The man glanced in his direction from down the hall, showing the branded mark between his eyes, and disappeared.

When he cared more, he would ask who that person was. If this was part of their religion, it surely made no sense. He had never seen people like that in Diemon or on his travels, and if he was correct, Eiyrǎl followed the same religion as Sorréle. The fleeting thought escaped as he turned the handle and barged into the study.

There, as expected, was the man he had been looking for, reaching for a cup of tea. His eyes danced between Cyrus and his daughter before settling back on him again with a smile. "My, what a surprise! To what do I owe the pleasure?"

"The pleasure is all mine, Your Majesty." Cyrus swallowed the white fury and stepped forward. Zorya's steps echoed behind him, and she closed the door. "Can we talk?"

Kyllian's smile faltered, and he set the tea back down. "For a Dragon Rider, absolutely." His eyes flashed behind him. "Zorya, are you alright?"

"I'm fine," she answered. Her words sounded unsteady, as if she were close to tears, but when Cyrus glanced her way, he found her expression stoic.

If he wanted to test her knowledge and loyalty, then now was the time, he realized. Walking past the king, he made his way straight to the bookshelf that had held all the scrolls. As he reached it, Cyrus saw that the scrolls were missing.

"Clever," he whispered, and turned to face Kyllian, who was no longer eyeing him with kindness, but with the look of someone who knew they had been caught. He didn't waste another moment. "When were you going to tell me about the eggs?"

All color drained from the king's face. He could have passed for a ghost. Cyrus looked over at the princess, who was watching her father with an intense glare. Perhaps she truly did have no idea.

Outside, more boots echoed, stopping at the door. The handle moved, and the door opened. Shunera peeked his head in. "Hey, I just—" He stopped when he saw Cyrus, and then his eyes landed on Zorya. "What are you doing here, Zorya? What's going on?" He opened the door further, but the princess quickly blocked him and pushed him out.

"This is a private conversation, Shunera." As she pushed the door closed, the prince's eyes darted back to Cyrus and darkened, but if Zorya noticed, she didn't say anything. "I'll see you later, okay?"

Then she shut the door in his face, making a piece of Cyrus smile, despite the disaster unfolding in front of him. When Shunera's face was gone, the princess slid the lock over to keep anyone else from barging in on their conversation. As she turned back around and crossed her arms, her eyes met his before settling back on her father.

The interruption brought the king back to life. Kyllian licked his lips and settled back into his seat before running a hand over his features. "How?"

"A little luck," Cyrus said, not taking his eyes off the king. "What did you intend to do with those? Keep them until the timing was right and then try to hatch them?"

"They've been in the family line for generations," Kyllian said with a shake of his head. "I wasn't intending to do anything with them. Not before I knew you were alive." He dropped his gaze. "They were gifted to us centuries ago. A peace deal of sorts, because as the Rider Federation struggled, animosity between the cities grew. At least, that's what I know."

"Then why didn't I know about it?" Zorya asked, taking a step forward.

The king looked her way. "Because you haven't taken the throne yet. Not even your mother knew until she took the oath upon accepting the crown." Meeting Cyrus's stare, he added, "What do you want, Rider?"

The question made him laugh. Sozar nudged his mind then. *Be careful,* the dragon warned. *This is unlike you.*

How right the dragon was, but Cyrus couldn't help himself. How many lies would he be fed before he would snap? He was so tired of fighting everywhere he turned. For once, he wanted to trust someone with all that he had. Instead, his very existence was grounds for betrayal.

"What I want are answers," he hissed. "I came here looking for answers, and instead, I've had nothing but secrets and lies shoved down my throat." Cyrus gestured at the bookshelf. "The scrolls. There were four of them, but you only showed me two and now they're gone. Where did you put them?"

The king raised an eyebrow. "You know I can't tell you that."

"Then tell me what they were."

Kyllian opened his mouth to speak but then closed it. Cyrus waited, trusting that the king would speak, and soon he did. "The other scrolls are documents from the court of the Rider Federation. They were found on an expedition three centuries ago." Sighing, Kyllian picked up his tea and finally took a proper drink. "It was all the men could return with, because whatever lives there killed over half of them in a single night. Out of twelve, only two returned, as the record states. Whatever other records that had been picked up had been destroyed with the slaughtering of the men."

When the king didn't expound, Cyrus crossed his arms. "And?" It felt like he was having to rip the answer out of the man's mouth, and it annoyed him.

"The records brought back discussed the banishment of two Dragon Riders. They had broken the law by marrying outsiders, non-Dragon Riders. The records state they had been requested to hand over material that belonged to the Rider Federation as part of the exile—things perhaps limited to an inner circle of power-holding Riders. There is no direct statement about what these materials are. However, it's stated that both Dragon Riders fled in the night, together. A court order was made up to go after them, but based on the timeline of the scrolls, it was right before the political fall of the federation. Aythen would have destroyed the place a summer later."

Slowly, Cyrus nodded. Wherever the Dragon Riders had fled to, they had taken valuable items that the Rider Federation had wanted in return. "You sound extremely knowledgeable for someone who only has four scrolls," he pointed out. It was his way of saying he knew the king still knew more than he was letting on. The Razan family had likely spent lifetimes collecting information wherever they could about the now-destroyed federation, passing it down from one ruler to the next. "Any idea what the material was? Any theory?"

"Handcrafted Rider Swords, for one," he said. Cyrus felt his blood run cold, but he didn't let it show. "The rest? I'm assuming amulets, dragon gear for riding in different weather, armor—" He shrugged. "All theories, though. Just guesses from what we know about the Rider Federation."

It felt like he was finally getting somewhere. "Then my big question. Why did you keep this all from me?" A part of him wanted to poke at the king's knowledge of perhaps another Dragon Rider, of Dameon, but he bit his tongue. Something told him that he did not know about another Rider, and he decided to keep it this way. It was not his place to divulge Dameon and Ashtir's existence.

Now it was Kyllian's turn to take charge. His expression darkened, and to Cyrus, he looked like the kind of man who would commit the most heinous crimes if it meant getting what he wanted. "Trust, Cyrus. You may be the first Dragon Rider in eight centuries, but that does not give you privileges that not even my daughter has." The king stole a glance over at Zorya, and Cyrus looked too, having forgotten she was here. She stood as still as a statue, frozen. "But now it seems you both know the truth." At that, he grabbed his tea.

Ask him about the eggs, Sozar insisted. *We must gauge his intent.*

"You said you had no intention to do anything with the eggs," Cyrus began, acting upon the dragon's request. "At least before me. What does that mean?"

Kyllian sipped his tea, eyes locked ahead rather than on anyone in particular. In between drinks, he spoke softly. "When the eggs arrived all those summers ago, you can bet my family did everything we could to make them hatch. We would elect children to be brought forth in hopes a dragon would choose one, we prayed, we even had an Energy Harvester try several rituals to break the eggs, but none of it worked. And the result of harvesting energy against the eggs cost my family their Energy Harvester."

He set the cup down and folded his arms along the desk, looking bluntly at Cyrus now. "That was well before my time. It happened for several generations, but it soon became apparent that none of it would work, so a deal was made to keep the eggs quiet and let the rumors die with time that the Razan family had them. They did, and it's stayed that way. So I ask you, Cyrus, what will do now that you know of them?"

It was a trick question. He was not foolish enough to think otherwise. The king wanted to know that he could trust that

Cyrus wouldn't speak about the eggs because if he did, it would disrupt the entire city. If word reached Kalic about this through Shunera, it would shatter the peace between the cities and could create war. Cyrus might be a Dragon Rider, but two eggs meant that if the dragons hatched at the right time under the right power, an empire could rise, because they would be moldable weapons.

On the other hand, if he intervened and took the eggs before they hatched, perhaps he could avoid a war.

Raising his chin, Cyrus spoke with as much confidence as he could muster. "I am not here to start a war, Kyllian. I came for answers and nothing more, and it seems you've provided them."

That seemed to please the king, and his shoulders relaxed. "And it is not my intention to start a war either. If this reached the wrong ears . . ." He let out a sharp breath. "I don't need to explain myself to you two. Cyrus, have I answered your questions well enough? I would like some time with my daughter before I am requested by the council."

He wanted to say no and demand more from the man, but he couldn't bring himself to, not when Zorya met his eyes. Already, guilt for how he had spoken to her itched his skin and made him uncomfortable. Yes, he had gotten the answers he needed. Or at least to start. The least he could do was give the princess this time to speak with her father. She probably had a dozen questions, questions that she wouldn't feel comfortable speaking about in front of him, a stranger. The kind that Cyrus would never understand because he hadn't been raised with parents or family.

"Very well." He crossed the room and approached the door. Zorya stood next to it, only coming to life to step out of the way so that he could open it properly. "Kyllian," he said, and met the king's eyes. "Thank you for being honest with me. I can assure you what was spoken here today will not leave this room."

That made him smile. "I suspect nothing less from a man like you."

Cyrus stole one last look at the princess. She was watching him, a hundred different things flashing over her eyes in an instant—things he could not decipher and did not have time to. All he managed was a quick nod, hoping to reassure her that he understood and didn't hold anything against her.

Then he was out the door. As it closed behind him, he looked around. The hall was empty, but he felt immediately like someone was watching him. A shiver ran down his back, making the hairs on his arms stand on end. He stood there for a long time, hoping to see someone walk around the corner on either side, but no one came.

Hatchling, Sozar said. The link they shared was flooded with affection, warmth. *Are you alright?*

"Yeah," he whispered. Before he could spook himself further, he turned right and toward his chamber. *I just need some time alone.*

He could sense the dragon wanted to say more, and Cyrus was relieved when he didn't. Right now, it felt like the entire world had been turned upside down for him. He could hardly grasp everything before the dragon eggs. Knowing those existed and everything Kyllian had spoken on, he was overloaded. All he wanted to do was seclude himself and disappear.

That was exactly what he planned on doing.

Fate was holding nothing back from him, it seemed. If this was his way of finding purpose, he would have preferred not having one. He didn't know what to think, how to decide his next steps, or what would be the best decision. Cyrus wanted to do the right thing, but he had no idea what that was. It was obvious that whichever path he chose would stir trouble. If he stole the eggs and slipped away, he had no idea if they would hatch, and he might just be creating a bigger mess. Perhaps they were safer underneath the city, but Kyllian gave him doubts.

Plus, there was still Dameon. The Rider would expect to see him tomorrow evening when the moon rose, and Cyrus needed to have a decision. Truthfully, he already did—as much as he wanted to be with another Dragon Rider and give Sozar the proper company a dragon deserved, he couldn't. Dameon was power hungry, and Cyrus didn't think the Rider would take the eggs and disappear in peace.

No. Dameon wanted war.

And if Cyrus didn't show up tomorrow night with the eggs, the Rider would break into the palace and find them himself. That meant tomorrow night, he would have to leave with the eggs in his possession. Deciding where to go would come next.

Satisfied, Cyrus got back to his chamber and locked the door. It was time for a proper bath.

BROKEN ILLUSIONS

Syra stirred. The ground gave no relief, and the stench of manure hit her first. She tried to adjust herself but found her body crammed up against the wall, though she had no recollection of falling asleep against one. Her shoulder ached, having supported her weight while she slept, and her neck was stiff. A piece of straw jabbed her cheek, and she shifted away from it as best as she could.

The room was quiet. A single lantern burned amid the group, but that light was fading as the oil ran out. In no time, they would be plunged into darkness. Syra had no idea what time it was or how long she had slept; frankly, she had no idea when she had fallen asleep. The last she remembered was walking down the stairs with Zarek to join Zane and Roman.

She wanted to continue lying there, but her shoulder had other plans. Its ache was growing and shoving off slumber with a growing aggression. Syra gave in and sat up, pushing her hair out of her face to get a better view of the group.

Zarek was laid out on his back, one arm over his face, with Uyul next to him, her bony face tucked up against him. Roman had his face resting on one of their sacks, although she wasn't sure whose. He grunted in his sleep and drew an arm up closer to his face.

Zane was missing.

Syra blinked, making sure she wasn't hallucinating, but when she shook her head, he was still gone. Careful not to wake anyone, she stood. Her head swam, mad at her for not continuing to rest, but she dismissed it. If Zane was in trouble, she needed to know.

She stepped past Roman, not bothering to put her boots on. If she did, the two would hear her, and she didn't want to wake them unless absolutely necessary. Her wool socks were with her boots too, leaving her bare feet against the old barn floor. Straw poked at her heels, but she ignored it and kept walking toward the barn door. The little bit of lantern light gave her just enough to see the faint outline of her surroundings.

When she reached the door, she fumbled for the metal hook. It was clumsy, the handle cold to the touch, but she was able to slide it back with minimal noise. She paused and looked behind her. Nobody stirred. Relieved, she opened the door just enough to slip through, then closed it without locking.

Taking a breath, Syra turned around and froze.

Zane was approaching with a lantern.

He met her eyes and grinned. "What're you doing up, fierce warrior?" As he approached, she could see the dust coating his cheeks. The hem of his cloak on his left hand was torn, and his belt was strapped on. He looked rough, but the smile on his face would have passed for that of someone who had just won a fortune.

"I should ask you the same," Syra replied, and raised a brow. She crossed her arms. "What have you been up to?" Her voice was low.

Zane stopped next to her and glanced down at her bare feet. "Comfortable?"

"Yeah, and you're avoiding the question." Syra had walked barefoot countless times growing up. Walking on dirt was nothing more to her than walking in her home.

He set the lantern down between them and sighed. "Well, you could say I was just paying my respects to Raveer." Zane laughed at his own joke and then shook his head. "You really want to hear?"

Syra raised her brow. "Unless you don't want to share?"

"No, no." He waved her off and leaned against the barn. "Just playing with you. I was breaking an old friend out from the barrack."

He said it so nonchalantly that for a moment, Syra just stared. "You what?"

"Dan," Zane said, as if that explained it. "Bastard got himself into trouble again. He's a bard, you know. Always got a story or a song. Guy is practically a legend to the thieves around here." He laughed into the night.

A warm breeze tickled her and chased the chill away from her bones. "How'd you know he would be locked up?" It felt like the only reasonable question at this point. All Syra could think of was the undeniable risk he'd just put himself and their group in. Agitation bubbled just under her skin, but she did her best not to show it.

He shrugged and crossed his arms. "Dan's always getting himself into a mess, and I'm usually the one breaking him out. We go way back, him and me. Our mothers were best friends, and we grew up together. It's a long story."

Syra gaped at him. "Yeah, but you quite literally just walked into a barrack in Raveer and broke someone out. Do you realize how much danger you put us in? All for a friend you guessed was in trouble?" Now the anger seeped out into her words. Her mind was going a thousand directions. There were so many ways this could have gone wrong.

The man looked down at her. "And guess what? No one is dead and no one got captured. *And* I got a drink out of it. Syra, I do this as a pastime—it's nothing new for me."

"And you could have been captured—or worse, killed," Syra retorted, and shook her head. "Why didn't you tell anyone?"

"Why should I?" Zane held up a hand before she could respond to that. "No, no, hear me out. I didn't wake anyone because this is normal for me, you see? Going out in the late hours of the night and breaking people out. People that don't deserve to be in there. It gives me purpose."

Syra swallowed. She recalled his love for this—he had shared it on the ship with her, but hadn't gone into detail. This wasn't—*shouldn't*—have been a surprise for her. But she hadn't expected him to do it while they had a target on their backs. It felt out of place, unnecessary to say the least.

"Just don't do it again without telling someone, okay?" Syra finally said. It was late, and she wasn't in the mood for arguments. He was alive. That was what mattered. "If something would have happened to you . . ."

"You wouldn't have been able to forgive yourself?" Zane finished. "Don't go there, Syra." He didn't say it with hostility. "This was my choice, my risk. It does not make it your responsibility."

She pursed her lips, not wanting to start this conversation. He had a point, and she knew it.

"So," Zane said with an exhale. "Couldn't sleep?"

"My shoulder," she answered, and rolled it. "I slept on it bad and woke up. When I saw you missing, I got worried." The breeze was back, but it felt colder this time. Syra looked up at the night sky. The stars stared back at her, dazzling, unperturbed.

"Hm." Zane nodded next to her.

She knew she should get back to sleep, but she didn't want to return just yet. The night air, the peace—it was beautiful.

"You're someone important, aren't you?" he asked softly. When she dropped her eyes to look at him, he offered a small smile. "Kind of hard not to think that when a Death Seeker shows up and basically pledges to protect you, eh?" Zane snorted.

"And that move you pulled earlier? *That* was cool. I've never seen magic. Ever."

That felt like lifetimes ago. Syra smiled in return and felt heat flood her cheeks. She hated receiving any sort of accolades. It made her uncomfortable. "Thanks. I didn't even know I could do that."

"And what was that with 'realm hopper'?" Zane continued. "Seriously, that's badass. When people sing about you in summers to come, they'll call you the Realm Hopper." He motioned with his hands. "I can see it now. Bards—particularly Dan, he loves his stories—singing about the girl with fire-red hair who could travel between realms. That is a story."

Syra rolled her eyes. "Okay, now you're being dramatic." Still, she couldn't help but giggle. It felt good to laugh and dream like this. Syra, the Realm Hopper, Daughter of Nala, Light Bringer. It felt . . . *good*.

As the laughter died between them, Zane raised an eyebrow. "I'm not mad, you know. About any of it. I get it. If I was so important that Death Seekers were flocking to my side—and hunting me, no less—I'd keep my lips sealed."

Syra didn't know how to tell him how much she appreciated his words. It had felt like she was carrying around a giant weight by withholding information, afraid that people would begin to resent her. Zane's attitude, his acceptance, even if he didn't quite understand everything, put her mind at ease. He didn't need to know, but he didn't respect her any less either.

"Just know that hit from Zarek earlier was rude," Zane remarked with a chuckle. He rubbed his jaw. "He got me good."

She laughed, but as she turned her head, something caught her attention: two glowing yellow eyes in the distance. They were low to the ground, unblinking. Syra felt the breath leave her lungs as she stared. She recognized those eyes. The Onye from the ship.

Her heart skipped several beats. "Do you see that?" she whispered, not taking her eyes off the beast.

"Huh?" Zane looked in the direction she was looking. "No, I don't see anything."

Syra couldn't believe it. "The Onye. It's right there." She pointed ahead. "It's looking at us."

He fumbled for words. "I, um—Syra, I don't see anything at all. I just see darkness."

She tore her eyes to look at Zane, frantically searching his glacier blues. "How can you not see it? It's right—"

She looked back. The eyes were gone. Syra felt her jaw go slack. No, it was impossible. They had been there. She took a step forward but felt a firm hand wrap around her arm. Turning, she saw Zane glaring at her.

"You should go back to bed," he advised. "I'm up for guessing games, but the last thing I want to hear is that beast stalking us." Zane motioned to the barn. "Let's go."

Syra wanted to protest, but the desperation in his eyes made her pause. He didn't believe her. She let a pent-up breath escape and ran a hand over her face. Maybe he was right. Maybe she was hallucinating. It had been days since she'd had a proper sleep. It was catching up to her, that was all.

"Okay." Syra nodded. Zane let go of her arm and turned to open the barn door. He was careful not to make too much noise, opening it just enough to let them slip in. Once inside, they were plunged into complete darkness. The lantern had finally run out of fuel.

She fumbled for Zane's hand, and once they had each other, they slowly moved across the barn until they felt close enough to sit down. Syra heard one of their steeds sigh. They made themselves as comfortable as they could, given their situation. Zane lay down just next to her, and she heard him push straw around before settling. She leaned over, using her hands to make a resting spot for her head, and closed her eyes. Slumber was already waiting for her, despite the illusion of the beast.

She could still see the Onye staring at her when she drifted off into sleep.

A DAGGER LACED WITH POISON

The knock made Morei cringe, but he did his best not to let it show as he stepped into Peter's study. The chancellor hadn't been in his designated space, and the king had been left asking questions to the soldiers until one of them had finally mentioned Peter had headed toward his personal study. At that, Morei had set off, not slowing, even as he passed Kiren, who waved.

Morei didn't wave back. He would have preferred to do something rather gruesome instead, but he shushed himself. Now was not the time to give in to his growing urges.

Soon, he had promised himself. Soon he could.

"Your Majesty," Peter acknowledged as the door closed behind the king. The chancellor was sitting, a handful of grapes in one hand while his other was splayed across an open book. Presumably research in hopes of resolving Cu'cel. Next to it lay a half-eaten plate of fruit-stuffed pastries. "I must say, it's not often you come this way. Is everything alright?"

Emerald hadn't believed him, had likely thought he'd gone mad, but he was placing all his coin on the chancellor. One person was all he needed, and he knew he couldn't rely on the council for support. Ezra was not an official Geral yet, and the last thing that man needed was to pick sides when he was going to be the face of the city—a city that would require he see it their way, no matter how much he may disagree. No, Ezra could not hear these problems. It could jeopardize his rulership; the council needed someone they were certain they could mold, not someone who had been persuaded by none other than Morei.

It would make enemies that Ezra could not afford to have at such an early stage of power.

The man who sat before him, the man who had supported his father's rule and watched Morei become the man he was today, he was the only person the king could rely on.

"I need to talk to you," he replied, and crossed the study to the chair that faced Peter. Sitting down, he was acutely aware of how uncomfortable he was—the leather was cold, the cushion stiff and unforgiving, the air stifling—but he refused to move. It would look far stranger if he stood right back up again and continued the conversation.

Leaning back, the chancellor held on to his grapes, his eyes flashing over the pastries before returning to the king. "You sound troubled."

The personal study Peter called home for most of his days was cluttered with books, scrolls, quills, and even the occasional horse statue. It did not look like a room that would not have belonged to the chancellor. There were no windows or firepit, only shelves of books and scrolls. It was confining, smaller than most of the rooms that even the staff members used for daily chores, and it felt even smaller because of the overbearing items. But if Peter liked it, then it was not his place to speak against.

Morei took a deep breath, his heart racing. The hands that glared back up at him from his lap were sketched with the curse—a curse that would undoubtedly be the end of him. Taking one final look at the chancellor, he nodded and began to explain.

He didn't hide the experience in Skye's home, explaining how real it was, and how he was certain this was tied to Syra Castello. At the mention of the fugitive, Peter's eyebrow went up, but the rest of his expression remained passive as he ate his grapes. The king did his best to explain his findings in the library and the book on Sekar, as well as the dreams. He even spoke about Boris's dream. Through all of this, the chancellor's only reaction was at the mention of Syra. He didn't even twitch when Morei stated that the God may be after him.

When he was done, his mouth was dry, his heart still beating at a quicker pace, and his hands were clammy. Carefully, Peter leaned over and set the rest of his grapes down on the plate next to the pastries before he turned, taking his chair with him, and sifted through what had to be more than forty scrolls stacked on top of each other. The sound of scraping parchment filled the silence between them for what felt like an eternity.

Then he made a triumphant noise in the back of his throat and straightened with a scroll in his hand. He undid the strings, which looked weathered, and spoke. "I keep bounties around for at least a summer, sometimes longer. Helps me keep a mental note about who's out there, threats, all that stuff." As he unrolled the scroll, he turned it around so that it faced Morei and laid it flush on the table, just shy of the plate. There, staring at him, was a sketch of Syra in black and white. Underneath, an exuberant amount of Krye for her capture alive and the note: *Armed and extremely dangerous. Treasonous crimes.*

"That's the Syra you are referencing too?" Peter clarified.

Morei brushed his fingers over the rough parchment, which had yellowed with age. She was a beautiful woman, even in the sketch, but they had done her eyes hard and angry, like she was a mean spirit. He hadn't seen that look in his dreams. "That's her," he answered, out of breath. The king had known that this bounty sketch had circulated and perhaps was still nailed to most of the announcement boards in the cities across the country, but he had long since forgotten it in the disaster his life had become.

Yet that was her. He was as certain as the sun was when it rose every day.

Peter let the scroll go, letting the edges fold in, and then leaned back, lacing his fingers over his large stomach. Those blue eyes narrowed. "Are you feeling alright?"

The question was so unexpected that Morei could do nothing but stare. Licking his lips, he took a quick glance around the room to ensure he was still in the same study, and when he realized he was, he looked back at the chancellor. "Excuse me?"

A heartbeat slipped by, then two, and then three. The king relived the entire conversation he had just had, and now, reflecting on it all, he felt like a fool. There was no way to prove how he knew Syra was involved in this all or why or even how, but she was in his dreams, and that *had* to mean something. It was too late to take back what he said, to tell the chancellor that he was joking or to forget about it. All he could do was wait while Peter gathered what he would say.

Raising one hand, the chancellor took a deep breath. "You've been through a lot, Your Majesty. By the hand of the Gods, you have been through more than a hundred men combined, and for that, I sympathize with you." He lowered his hand then, never taking his eyes off the king. "But this theory of Grënyl and Sekar and Syra is outlandish, and please, I mean no disrespect. Far from it."

He leaned forward and began to roll the scroll back up, speaking as he did so. "Syra is a thief, a traitor of her city, a defector of the country—she's like the rest of them. Do you understand what I mean by that?"

Numbly, Morei stared. The adrenaline of his earlier endeavors was slowly fading, replaced by a deep resentment that turned the air bitter.

If the chancellor noticed the shift in the king's demeanor, he did not speak of it. "Rike has already made progress on a remedy that has proven to have some level of effectiveness against Cu'cel. He should have the final version done by the day after tomorrow." Peter leaned forward and dropped his voice. "If Sekar was after you and this was all his doing, would he allow such a solution? A means to an end to this all?"

Again, the king did not speak. Couldn't.

"I suspect the stress has to be overwhelming," Peter continued. There was only concern as he spoke, like he was having a brother-to-brother talk, voice gentle. "And whatever happened to you in those days you were compromised has tampered with your mindset, and please, I say that with no disrespect. You woke up and jumped right back into the heat of it all, and it wasn't like you had a choice in doing so." Leaning back, he added, "You haven't had time to recuperate and process what's happened to you."

Morei found his tongue. "I have had all the time I need, Chancellor."

Peter raised an eyebrow, but again, it was not out of disrespect, rather worry. "I suspect the book you pulled was one of the ancient collections we have?"

The king nodded.

"The Vore people back then did not have the same knowledge we had about ailments, remedies, herb medicines and all that." A smile crept across his pudgy face, as if he found it all amusing. "Everything and anything was related to the Gods, even childbirth. Can you believe that?" He chuckled. "What I'm saying is that yes, this Grënyl and Cu'cel sound the same because they are the same. But unlike the old Vorelians, we have advances in our medicines and do not think it comes from the Gods, or Sekar himself."

Before Morei could point out the citizens and what they thought—their prayers to the Gods themselves and about the king's involvement—Peter raised a hand to stop him. "Syra is a common thief, nothing more. She has made a name for herself by stealing a prized possession of King Drexis, but that's all. She's a nobody, and she will die a nobody, like the rest of them." Offering a small smile, the chancellor said, "And a man in your and Boris's dreams? Well, that can mean a lot of things! A stranger can be symbolic of the unknown, and in our circumstances, can you blame anyone for having dreams about strangers?"

The compulsion struck him right then—the urge to kill Peter where he sat, and to do it slowly, carefully. It drowned out the rest of his senses with a loud ringing in his ears, and Morei became acutely aware of just how easy it would be to kill the man where he sat with a flick of his wrist. The eyes would bulge, his chubby cheeks would go red, then blue, and Morei would burn him from the inside out.

He forced a deep breath in and glanced at his boots. The ringing ceased, but the voices were there, whispering to him as they always were.

No matter what he said, he would not be heard. No matter what proof he presented that this was supernatural, an intervention of Gods, it would not be acknowledged. The king was a drowning victim, and nobody was willing to reach out and save him for fear of being dragged in with him.

Never had he felt so alone as he did in this moment.

"I advise you get some rest, Morei," the chancellor suggested. "You're exhausted, and it's no surprise you're seeing things. Poor Skye must have had quite a fright from you, hey?" He laughed just as the door opened behind them. It was a relief to the king, and he quickly turned to see who had rescued him from this pit of despair.

It was Ezra.

At the sight of the king and chancellor, the man's face contorted into surprise and then embarrassment. He hung at the edge of the doorway with one boot already turned outward. "Oh, I'm sorry. Was I interrupting?"

"No." Morei spoke as quickly as he could. Standing, he forced one of his charming smiles. "We were just catching up. Can I help you?"

The tension in the room was undeniable, but Ezra wouldn't say anything about it.

Stepping inside, the man closed the door and cleared his throat. He didn't seem to know what to do with his hands, so he dropped them to his side. Ezra was clearly nervous, and that made the king smile. He knew why he was here.

"I was trying to find you earlier, but nobody could point me in the right direction," Ezra explained. Amber eyes stared back at him, a storm of emotions. "I wanted to tell you my decision."

If Morei could have disappeared right there, he would have. It felt like the entire world had turned against him in a day and he was being squeezed out at all angles. Sure, he had been the one to offer to identify the new king, knowing he could not trust the council to make a balanced choice, but that didn't mean he had done this willingly. And when he had offered to make that choice, he hadn't anticipated that less than a day later, he would be faced with the debilitating revelation that the Gods were real and one had a target on Morei. Maybe he was being punished for turning his back on his faith, or maybe there was something bigger going on that he didn't fully understand.

Either way, nothing could have prepared him to be turned on by Peter, to be dismissed like some child and told to get some rest.

Now, before him, was the man who would undoubtedly destroy the king's reputation, even if it was nothing he ever intended to do. Ezra Geral, King, Bringer of Hope, the Ender of an Era, and Energy Harvester.

Taking a deep breath, Ezra grinned from ear to ear, eyes twinkling with true purpose. The king watched, no longer happy or accepting of what his life had become. The next two words he spoke took a dagger laced with poison and thrust it into Morei's chest.

"I accept."

WHEN THE SUN GOES DARK

obody had bothered Cyrus since he left Kyllian's study. The sun's rays stretched across his living space, indicating the day was slipping by, the doors to the patio wide open. It felt like an eternity had passed between this morning and now.

He stared at the pillows. The embroidered gold fabric was thick and uncomfortable, unforgiving. Counting the red ruffles had been his pastime. Each giant pillow had approximately a hundred ruffles. The decorative fabric was etched with crowns and different animals. Cyrus had no idea how anyone could sleep with these pillows. They were stiff and rough, and both nights, he had shoved all of them off the bed, bundling the sheets instead.

He glanced at the Rider's Sword, which lay on the bed next to him, sheathed. The majestic piece was one of two that had escaped the destruction of the federation when the two Dragon Riders fled.

Cyrus had spent the afternoon lost in thought. As he let the emotions of earlier diffuse from his limbs, he had grown more and more ashamed of himself. His reaction had been justified, sure, but he had put everyone in an awkward position. Cyrus was never one to lose his temper, but the man who had acted on behalf of him earlier was not someone he recognized.

Between the eggs and Dameon and Ashtir, he had been overwhelmed. Cyrus had spent the last season believing he was the first Dragon Rider in centuries, and completely alone. From that perspective, he felt like he had been owed the information kept from him—that there were eggs awaiting their Riders. Instead, he had heard from another Dragon Rider about what lay in this palace, not from the king.

For that, he felt betrayed. The more he considered it that way, the more he realized he couldn't trust anyone. He was a fool, and knowing he had fallen for the kindness of this family because he was desperate to trust someone only angered him more.

He understood why Kyllian wouldn't want the information of the eggs shared. In the wrong hands, the information that there were, in fact, dragon eggs still around would upheave the very order of the world. Cyrus wasn't entirely educated in the history of the Rider Federation, but he knew enough to know that the world would go to war for these eggs. Unnecessary bloodshed, that was what war was.

But if the king thought holding on to the eggs for the next eight centuries was a good idea, he was horribly wrong. Those two females might very well be the last of the dragons. Regardless of if they wanted any part in Cyrus's plan for peace, they still had a choice. And frankly, he was certain they were probably ready to travel the world and stretch their wings. At least he had known Sozar was when he had finally hatched and been able to communicate with him.

The best option was to take the eggs and run. Otherwise they'd stay locked away underneath Razan, or worse get taken by Dameon and become a part of some murderous plan. It would mean creating an enemy out of Kyllian, but hopefully, when there was peace and the dragons were free to choose their own destiny and Rider, the king would understand.

Cyrus grunted and glanced over at the double doors that led to the patio—the longer he sat here, the bigger the war got in his head. He had left the doors open to allow the sunshine in and fresh air, but from the shadows flickering across the stone, he imagined a storm was rolling in. He got up and walked over to the entrance and looked up.

Sure enough, there was a storm over the Beutóne Mountains. The bottom was dark, with massive white plumes sprouting into the sky. Lightning flashed, kissing the side of the massive volcanic crater. Cyrus had never seen an active volcano in his summers in Diemon or on his travels. The Releuthian Mountains held many mysteries, but they did not have visible craters, at least not where Cyrus had been. If the time permitted, he wanted to visit these mountains for closer inspection. That didn't seem likely, though.

He turned away just as the faintest rumble of thunder rolled across the land. As he did so, he caught the *Book of Liral* staring at him. When he had gotten out from bathing himself, he'd pulled the book out of its sack but hadn't done any more with it, choosing instead to leave it on the table for a later time. The book seemed to be waiting for something spectacular to occur, and Cyrus got the uneasy feeling that perhaps it was the catalyst to the strange dream. He quickly shook it off. It was a book, nothing more.

Still, it dragged him closer. The stone was cool against the bottoms of his feet, and the rich smell of moisture passed over him as a small breeze entered. Lowering his gaze, he stared at the book, the leather aged to such an ancient beauty that it felt wrong to hold it, but he did. Cyrus ran his fingers over the soft leather. He didn't know why he felt so awkward with this book. Maybe it was because he had stolen it from Evander after killing the man. Or maybe it was because there was something strange about the yellowed pages and old leather—an energy that made the hairs on the back of his neck stand.

A part of him thought about reaching out to Sozar, but he decided against it. Enough had happened already today, and it felt ridiculous to reach out to the dragon and pester him with small things. Based on what he could sense from Sozar, the dragon was in no mood to talk.

Sighing to himself, Cyrus snatched the book off the table and walked back over to the bed, where he sat down in front of the embroidered pillows. He was half tempted to kick them off but restrained himself.

Attention on the book before him, Cyrus grasped the cover, opening it carefully for fear of causing any damage. There it was, on the first page, the *HJ* mark that was carved onto the front of the book. The title was written in faded ink on the yellowed parchment, so he turned the page. It wasn't a thick book, but the dense pieces of parchment made it heavy.

The words that stared back at him startled Cyrus. They were written quickly, blending into one another across the page. It was difficult to read from a first glance. Whoever this person was switched between the Old Tongue and the current language. Cyrus only picked up on a handful of words across sentences, unable to translate the Old Vore language. It had never been important for a miner like him. Words like "era," "power," "beginning," and "king" jumped out at him, but he had no idea how they were all connected. The rest of the pages looked the same. "Beast," "forest," "god" . . . he couldn't understand their meaning because he had no idea what the sentences were trying to tell him.

He jumped ahead to where he had found "Light Bringer" scribbled across the original writing, but as he continued to search, he couldn't find it. At the end of the book, he paused, certain he had meticulously flipped through every page. Confused, he went back to the start and did it again. And again, the scribbled page was missing, but there was no damage to the book to indicate someone had torn anything free. To make sure, he checked the spine when he flipped through.

It was like the scribbled work had completely disappeared, but that was impossible. Cyrus had seen it, read it. He would have not known the term otherwise.

Frustrated, Cyrus closed the book with a loud clap just as thunder rumbled closer.

A soft knock caught his attention. He gripped the book tight, feeling his entire body tense.

"Cyrus?" It was Zorya, her voice faint between the thick walls and door. He recognized it as clear as day.

His heart skipped a beat, like a child getting a treat, and he stood from the bed immediately, all thoughts draining from him. He reached for the sack on the ground, tucked the book inside, and shoved it in the mess of pillows before he walked to the door as quickly as he could without running. Zorya might be the daughter of the king, but she hadn't known either. In that, he felt they shared a bond.

Cyrus took a deep breath to steady himself before he slid the lock back and opened the door. There she was, dressed in that beautiful green dress that hugged her waist, with her blond hair spilling over her shoulders and back. He traced his eyes over every curve, unable to restrain himself. The princess raised an eyebrow at him. "My eyes are up here."

Warmth flooded his cheeks instantly, and he swallowed. Meeting her dark eyes, he smiled sheepishly. "A guy can look." He couldn't remember the last time he had lain with a woman, but it had been a long while. Cyrus was and had always been a gentleman. Perhaps it got the best of him when he should have made a move or taken initiative, but he couldn't help it. It was engrained in his nature.

Still, that didn't mean he couldn't look.

Zorya took a deep breath and glanced around. "Can I come in?"

Cyrus stepped aside, letting her in. Long day or not, he wanted time with her. "Where's your handsome prince?" he asked sarcastically as he closed the door behind them. Without much thought, he locked it.

"I take it you adore him just as much as me," Zorya remarked. She was standing over by the open doors, staring out. "This will be a good one." Glancing back at him, she added, "The storm."

Cyrus walked up from behind and followed her eyes. Lightning flashed, cutting through the dark clouds with white. Thunder followed in a bellow, rolling through the city. From behind, Cyrus wanted to wrap his arms around the princess, to hold her and bury his head into her hair, but he restrained himself. He was being ridiculous, and deep down, his yearning for a settled life was him running from the life he knew was waiting for him.

"I'm sorry about what happened earlier," Zorya said quietly, without turning back to face him. She crossed her arms. "I didn't know."

"I understand that now," Cyrus responded. "This isn't your fault."

Zorya turned her head toward the chest on the bed. "I don't know what to even say."

"You don't have to say anything." The wind picked up, tousling her hair and filling his nose with a rich scent of mangos. Cyrus inhaled deeply. "Does Shunera know?"

She looked up to him and shook her head. "No, of course not. My father doesn't want anyone else to know about the eggs."

Cyrus raised an eyebrow. "I meant does he know you're here?"

Zorya contorted her face in disgust. "Shall I ask for permission the next time I go somewhere?"

Her remark shocked him. "I didn't mean it like—"

"Then don't ask what Shunera knows and doesn't know," Zorya snapped, turning back to face the storm. "I don't give a shit what he knows."

Cyrus nodded, biting his tongue. There was more he wished to say on the matter, but he knew better, so he opted for another pressing question. "Why are you here?"

She shrugged, even though she wasn't facing him. "I just wanted to check up on you."

"I'm doing fine," Cyrus answered, his tone colder than he anticipated. "I'm pretty used to people lying to me at this point, so that's nothing new."

Zorya sighed. "I know he doesn't mean ill toward you. My mother too. I'm not happy about it, but I'm not going to hold a grudge against them for it."

He scoffed. "You're a better person than me, Zorya." Nice or not, he didn't trust people like that, regardless of their justification.

"What about Sozar? How is he?" she asked, moving on from the topic. It was best that way. The last thing he wanted to do was insult her any further than he already had.

More thunder followed. "He is overwhelmed," Cyrus slowly answered. Even now, the dragon was preoccupied, not paying attention to their conversation. He could tell, their link strained and thinned by the dragon's distance. "I've given him space." When Sozar was ready, he would speak, but for now, the dragon preferred the distance, and Cyrus couldn't blame him. In less than a day, they had learned that not only was Sozar not the only dragon, but that there were two female eggs as well. They could save the dragon race if those dragons hatched.

Zorya turned to face him then, looking up between her thick eyelashes. "I am supposed to marry in ten days, Cyrus. Shunera arrived three days early in hopes of pushing the wedding closer. They are speaking right now—my father and him."

345

The confession startled him. He just stared at her, unsure of what she wanted him to say. After the discovery of the eggs, this was what she was worried about. It painted her expression with angst.

"I tried telling my father I didn't want this . . ." The princess shook her head. "But he says it's the only way. The deal the families made—" She took a deep breath. "My father needs this to happen."

Her shoulders slumped and she averted her gaze, wiping at her eyes. A wave of grief fell over him, and he reached out in hopes of reassuring her it would be okay. He hated seeing her cry.

Cyrus brought her into a hug. She immediately tucked her head against his chest and wrapped her arms around him. The feel of her touch, the sensation it provided, was enough to rip the air from his lungs. The feelings he had for her were outrageous and dumb, but her touch shattered that logic into a thousand shards. In response, he held her tighter and laid his head against hers.

They stood there for a while, listening to the storm. It was upon them, suffocating the sun and painting the world in darkness. Shadows fell over the stone on the patio, and the thick smell of rain filled his nose. Rubbing a hand over the princess's back, Cyrus relished in the touch of her skin.

He should have felt awkward holding an engaged woman. By the Gods, Cyrus should have been more assertive in keeping her at arm's length, but he couldn't help himself. He wanted to strangle Shunera and punch Kyllian. Before him was a woman being forced into a marriage she wanted nothing to do with—she didn't love Shunera or the future before her. And yet, no one cared. It was all about politics and power.

That enraged him. Cyrus hated royalty more and more every day.

Zorya took a deep breath then, drawing his thoughts back down to her. "Sorry," she whispered into his shirt. "I didn't mean to come here and cry. Not when there's bigger issues."

Cyrus gave her a squeeze. "You don't have to apologize for anything."

In response, the princess pulled away and looked at him. Her eyes glistened from the tears she had shed, but her expression was soft, delicate. Cyrus stared at her beauty—she was the most perfect, handcrafted gem he had ever seen, down to the curve of her lips.

Zorya's hands drew him in, and he didn't fight it. Her lips were as soft as they looked, and they tasted like berries. Her fingers caressed the back of his neck, her touch hot. Cyrus let his hands explore her body more, interlacing one through her hair and one across her back. The kiss was slow, intentional, and it awakened a side of Cyrus that he had nearly forgotten about. His body burned for her, desperate to have every part of her.

But he pulled himself away, breaking the kiss. It took every bit of strength to separate himself from her lips, but he needed to. They were destined to fail each other. Cyrus had no desire to stay here, and he surely had no intention to piss anyone off more than he may have already. As much as he loathed Shunera and the arranged marriage, Cyrus was in no place to provide safety or a home for Zorya. She was better off here with the prince of Kalic than with him, where he would undoubtedly let her down.

She looked at him, her cheeks flush. Cyrus pulled his hands away and choked out the next words. "We shouldn't, Zorya." They left a bitter taste on his tongue, but he couldn't toss aside his morals. Cyrus was not a man to take advantage of anyone, let alone a woman eager to be free of her future.

The princess took a shaky breath and removed her hands from him, withdrawing into herself. "Right. Because I'm only a liability." The words were harsh.

"Zorya," he pleaded, trying to catch her eyes, but she kept them lowered. "I've been here less than two days, and I've already pissed your family off. I can't stay here." At that, her eyes flickered over to him, stabbing him with remorse. "I never intended to stay," he finished, quieter. "What life would that be for you? Do you really want a life on the run, full of uncertainty?"

"I want to live," she snapped, meeting his gaze. "I want a life of my own choice, and if I choose you, does that make me wrong?"

Already, he could feel his reasoning breaking. Of all people, Cyrus knew best what it was like to finally be given the chance to live a life of his own making and not of others.

She must have seen his turmoil. "How dare you try to tell me what I can and cannot do, Cyrus. Of all people." Her eyes flared with fury, becoming darker. "You have abandoned your life, the world you knew, and all to protect your dragon. You chose this life, Cyrus. Can't I have the same opportunity, or must you protect me from myself?"

He gaped at her, the words failing his tongue. Confrontation was not his strong suit, and he knew he was in the wrong. He had spoken up in fear of letting more people down, when in reality, his biggest concern was hurting her. But he had done it anyway. "I didn't mean—"

"Enough." Zorya cut him off with a wave of her hand and a tone of authority. "You've made it clear to me what you want. I'll leave you be."

She brushed by him, but something overcame Cyrus—perhaps impulse or hopelessness, he wasn't sure, and it didn't matter. He latched on to her arm with a firm hold and forced her to look at him. "Zorya, listen to me. You don't want my life—*I* don't want my life." The words tumbled out of his mouth without consent. "How do you think it feels for me to look over my shoulder every time I walk by someone for fear they will pull a blade because of who I am? How could I ever drag someone else into this mess? Sozar never had a choice, and it kills me every day because of that." He loosened his grip, realizing how hard he was holding her. "At least give yourself freedom. I don't have that choice."

Their eyes remained locked for a moment longer before Zorya pulled away. He let his hand fall, hating himself. But she had choices Cyrus would cut his hand off to have—a chance to be free. No matter where he ran, he would never be out of reach of the claws of the world. Or his destiny.

At the door, the princess stopped and glanced back at him. All evidence of her tears was gone, but her pain was burrowed deep into her stare. "I've already chosen, Cyrus."

Then she was gone, leaving him alone.

Sozar's presence crossed their mental link as the door shut. Sympathy flooded him from the dragon—Sozar had heard the whole thing. Agitation washed over him. It felt like an invasion of privacy, but he couldn't even justify his annoyance. They were joined at the hip. The dragon had every right to listen in if he wanted to.

I don't want to talk about it, Cyrus said before walking back over to the bed. Smothering himself in the embroidered pillows, he hoped to find some sort of relief. Instead, he only felt dread and anger—Cyrus didn't want to turn Zorya away. Not when his body and mind yearned for that connection, that physical contact. He had spent his whole life alone, and granted, Sozar was his entire world, but the dragon couldn't satiate the undying need to have a connection with a woman.

Now he had destroyed the one chance he had for that connection. It felt like a serrated blade had just drove itself into his heart, and try as he might, he couldn't remove it. All he could do was relive every word in acute detail, ashamed of how he had treated her. He simply couldn't keep up. The last few days had done nothing but remind him that perhaps he was better off in the sky, away from people. At least he couldn't screw up like he had with Zorya.

Thunder rumbled, and rain pelted the stone outside, but he hardly took note. He didn't even get up to close the doors to keep the rain from splattering on the chamber's floor. Instead, he drowned himself in other thoughts of travel, adventure, and distant memories of when he used to work in the mines.

AND THE CITY
WILL FALL

Syra blinked, her head heavy. The barn was eerily quiet, and she sat up, confused. As she looked around, she realized she was completely alone. Their steeds were gone, Zane, Roman, and Zarek were nowhere to be seen, and based on the light peeking through the cracks in the barn door, it was daytime.

"What . . ." She fumbled around for her boots. The sword was strapped to her hip already, and it took her longer than she wanted to reach her socks and boots and put them on. Sleep still clung to her senses, but her heart was racing. Abandonment was setting in, making her agitated. If the guys thought this was funny, it wasn't. The last time Syra had been alone was when she had fled Caster city with the Demon Killer and soldiers after her.

Once the boots were on, she stood and swayed, struck by a nasty wave of dizziness. Syra waited until the wave passed and then continued toward the barn door. They had to be just outside, waiting for her. But why hadn't they woken her? Maybe they thought they were doing her a favor, but this wasn't a favor. Being left alone was not something she liked, and she fully understood that now.

At the door, Syra slid back the lock all the way. It screeched to a halt, and the hinges squealed as she pushed the door open. Ready to snap at the men, she was about to speak when she saw that no one was there. The sky was overcast but growing dark. A storm was upon them, and it would rain in no time.

The cows to her left flicked their ears lazily, undisturbed, munching on grass. Syra looked toward Joshua's house—the door was wide open.

A scream made her start, and Syra swung around. It had come from closer to the city. She stepped around the barn and saw in the distance, where the outer Raveer village stood, people gathered. Without thought, she broke out into a run. Something was wrong.

Syra ran as fast as she could, but as she neared, her heart sank. There were bodies scattered on the ground, next to the people, and blood—so much of it. The ground reflected crimson, with boot prints engraved into the soil filled with blood. The intense metallic smell met her nose. The scene was horrific, but no one seemed to care. They all stood, their backs to her, unmoving.

"Hey!" Syra yelled, hoping to get at least one person's attention, but no one even flinched at the sound of her voice. She was nearly upon the people—there was no way they didn't hear her. Lungs begging for air, she heaved for another breath—

And felt the entire world shift underneath her.

Syra collapsed hard on the ground, her hands taking the brunt of the impact. The ground underneath felt like it was going to erupt, engulf her whole, and she braced for it. The grass violently from left to the right, and she closed her eyes, preparing for the worse. It felt like the entire world was collapsing in on itself.

And then it stopped.

Opening her eyes, Syra no longer saw grass, but gravel. The ground beneath her was imprinted with the marks of boots and splattered blood. She inhaled and tried to gather herself. The people were around her, but she didn't know how. Just moments ago, she had been running toward them, but nonetheless, she could feel their eyes boring into her from every angle.

The sound of metal tearing through muscle and bone forced her eyes up. A blade jutted out from the back of a Raveer soldier's neck, coated red. The soldier's eyes were wide, dead, and his body lurched forward as the assailer yanked their weapon free. As the man dropped with a deafening thump against the ground, a familiar voice broke the silence.

"You've got to be cruel to be kind," Kar stated. He turned to face her, but it wasn't him. Before her stood a man with olive skin, midnight hair, and dark eyes. She recognized the voice— his facial structure and his eyes were inarguably the same, despite the color. Every part of her knew that. But it was impossible. It didn't make sense.

He smiled at her, holding the bloodied Death's Sword. "Something on your mind, Syra?" he asked, as if he knew exactly what she was thinking. And that smile . . . it was his. Kar's. It was the same charming and cruel grin he had given her a dozen times.

"I—" Syra swallowed and stood. She looked at everyone, their faces placid, before returning to him. "I don't understand."

"But you do," he whispered. "Deep down, you've always known, haven't you? But like always, you question yourself, doubt everything, and what has it done for you, Syra?" He tilted his head, his eyes softening. "Nothing."

"No, no." Syra backed up, overwhelmed. This was too much. "This is a dream again. Just like the other night. You're doing something to my head again." Her words came out frantic, desperate. Heart racing, she could hardly get a full breath of air. "Stop it," she begged. "Stop this."

Kar raised his brow. "You think this is a dream, Syra?" He broke from her gaze and walked up to the nearest bystander, a woman. She didn't budge as he thrust his sword through her chest, killing her instantly.

"No!" Syra screamed, stepping forward. That wasn't supposed to happen, none of this was supposed to happen. The woman's body slumped to the ground, her mouth agape, eyes wide, as Kar beheaded the man next to her with far too much ease. The head slammed into the next in line, blood splattering, but once more, the person did not move as the head struck them and then rolled onto the ground. The wide eyes stared right at Syra.

Her stomach turned, and she withheld a gag. This was a nightmare, a vision gone bad. "You're doing this on purpose. This isn't real."

Kar laughed as if she had just told him a joke. "Is it?" He reached between a group of Raveer citizens and dragged Zane forward. The man's eyes were distant, his form sluggish against the commanding force of Kar. "Maybe Zane can help you see that it isn't." He kicked him, knocking him onto his knees.

Zane came to life suddenly with a grunt. He spun around and crawled back on his hands, eyes locked onto Kar. "What the—*What was that?*" he screeched. The sound was hideous against her ears—he was terrified. Syra made to step forward, to tell Zane it was alright, but Kar was one step ahead of her.

"Why don't you tell your precious little warrior this is real, hm?" Kar asked Zane, voice dripping with black humor.

"Huh?" He turned his head, and his eyes went wide. "Syra! What—"

Kar kicked Zane in the ribs, knocking the next words out of him. "That's enough," he ordered. The man's form went weak, collapsing into the dirt, but his eyes remained open, vacant. If not for the rise and fall of his chest, she would have believed him dead.

The kick brought her to life. "What is this? What are you doing?" She quickly scanned the crowd, hoping to find Zarek or Roman, but neither were visible. "Where are the others?"

"Dreams are extraordinary, aren't they?" Kar asked, ignoring her. "They represent everything we are and everything we want to be." He walked over to a young woman and studied her features, moving her face around with a gloved hand. "In a blink of an eye, we can be exactly where we want to be, be exactly who we so desperately want to be, or face-to-face with the horrors of our mistakes." He let go of the woman and looked at Syra. "You should know this firsthand."

She had no idea how he had done it, how he could put these people in trances and completely remove them from the present. That would take an overwhelming amount of power. Mind racing, she reached for her sword, but it was gone. Syra glanced down. It was unbelievable. Impossible. The belt was missing. Syra grappled for an answer, lost for words. A raindrop struck her then with a cold slap. A breeze tousled her hair.

"May your dreams come true," Kar mocked. The phrase halted Syra's thoughts. She knew it—had heard it once before, just days prior, from the maid.

"Why—how do you know that?" Syra demanded.

Kar approached her slowly, intentionally. That smirk on his face told her he knew a thousand things, that he had been waiting for this. "The God of Darkness did not become who he was by choice, Syra. He was once the God of Dreams."

The shock, the finality, the revelation. It ripped the air from her lungs in a heartbeat. Words died on her lips, and her head spun. The memories rushed her at an unreasonable speed. Their laughs, stories, and travels, the kiss, his betrayal, all of it bombarded her at once. The things she had shared, the conversations they'd had, even about the Gods themselves. He was not a Guardian, he was a liar, a traitor, a monster. And he had played along and made Syra a fool. It was impossible, but here he stood in flesh and blood, real as Zane or anyone else.

Sekar.

"Impossible," she muttered, hardly audible.

The God waved her off. "You and countless others pray to our kind all your lives, but the moment you are presented with exactly what you've wanted—a God in the flesh—you're repulsed."

The audacity forced air into her lungs. "Repulsed? You—"

"Enough," Sekar interrupted, tone harsh and eyes hard. A force snapped Syra's lips closed. They tingled, and her entire body suddenly felt under attack. Unable to move or speak, she could only stare. He regarded her, just as rain began to pour in a torrential downfall. It was frigid against her skin. "A petite flower, that is what you are. So beautiful, soft, and divine. But your petals are poison." Lightning flashed, painting his features in a cruel light, casting shadows along his eyes and giving him a monstrous look.

He turned just as the ground started to tremble. Nobody moved, despite the violent shakes. A crack of thunder exploded as a dozen people fell from the sloshing mud and movement, devoured by the ground. Screams erupted as those who broke from their trance came face-to-face with the terrible reality unraveling.

Syra kept her eyes locked on the ground as it bulged and finally gave way to a massive serpent's head. Rock, mud, and dirt from well below the surface fell upon the bystanders. Some were struck head-on and knocked off their feet, unconscious. Others were dusted with the debris but remained unmoving in their trance. The beast flared its hood and bared its fangs with a skin-crawling hiss that rattled her bones. It towered above them, making Syra feel like an ant—its head as wide as a full grown man. Dark blue scales shimmered from the rain, and it flicked a forked tongue out. Most of its body remained submerged under the ground. With a final flick of its tongue, the massive serpent dropped a green eye on Sekar, the slitted black pupil dilating as it observed him.

"My dear," the God whispered affectionately, and reached his gloved hand out. Rain pelted him, turning the blood and dirt into mud. Next to him lay the body of the dead soldier. But none of that appeared to matter to him anymore. His expression softened; his demeanor changed in an instant. Time stood still.

The massive serpent lowered its head and blinked several times. The beast's snout brushed over his hand, and it flared its nostrils, letting a massive exhale escape. Syra was in awe. The giant serpent was supposed to be a myth, nothing more. To see it here before her . . . it was surreal. Even the storm seemed to quiet in admiration. No amount of stories had prepared her for its size and beauty.

"You have come," Sekar acknowledged. "I am grateful." The God looked down upon Syra. "The Firóle were nearly driven to extinction because of man and their greed. Yalana is one of the few that remain." He lowered his hand from her jaw. "And she will have her vengeance."

The serpent turned suddenly and dropped her head to the bystanders still stuck in their trance, wiping out a chunk of them with a single swipe of her massive head. A laugh escaped Sekar's lips as the entire world around came to life. Confusion erupted as the villagers and soldiers were torn free from their trance. Some screamed, some charged, others ran.

Syra's body returned to her in an instant. Stumbling backward, she lost her footing and fell, landing hard against an object. She looked and saw her belt on the ground, Death's Sword sheathed. Baffled, she grabbed it just as a soldier stepped on her hand, running away from the scene. The pain was numbed from her adrenaline. Syra pulled the belt into her chest, not wanting to lose it again.

The ground shook once more as Yalana slid her way out of the ground. Her body crushed anyone on the ground. Screams were silenced, and the serpent left a trail in the ground that was quickly flooded with water and blood. The Firóle moved with certainty toward the main city. Thunder cracked overhead.

Syra gaped in horror. The beast's size was even greater than she'd anticipated. Her body continued to slide out of the ground with ease, the scales stripping the skin of the victims as she slithered. When Yalana's tail finally revealed itself, it was jutted with a dozen horns, all curved inward to a point. Yalana swung the massive appendage as it exited the ground, and the horns connected with even more victims.

"Syra!" The voice tore her from her stunned position. She spun around, trying to locate Zarek. There was so much commotion that she couldn't see anyone clearly.

"It can all stop," Sekar told her. Syra looked up to see the God staring down at her. There was no smile, no humor. "All you have to do is ask." In all the uproar, his voice was the clearest.

She was cornered. She only wanted one thing—to protect Zarek, Zane, and Roman. This was not their fault, it was hers.

"Make it stop," she begged. When he raised an eyebrow, she repeated herself, louder. "Stop this. Make it stop."

Sekar smiled. Based on his pleased expression, it was exactly what he had wanted to hear, and she no longer was confident in her request.

It was too late. "Very well, my little flower."

With a wave of his hand, the entire world around her dissolved.

JUST LIKE OLD TIMES

The night was stiller than it had been in a long time, and the stars were dazzling. It was the perfect time to burn the victims of Cu'cel, when the smell of charred bodies wafted upward rather than through the city.

A nightmare had afflicted Morei once more tonight, one that he hadn't even recognized himself in. Eyes crimson, skin pale and damaged by blackened veins, Morei wreaked havoc on his surroundings. He drank the blood of his enemies and laughed in the face of the crying children. Fire surrounded him, bending to his will and destroying the city of Geral.

And in the black smoke, the cloaked man returned.

When Morei saw him, he started as if from a trance and dropped his prey—another dead soldier—to the ground. Then the mysterious man raised a gloved hand and pointed. Following his hand, the king looked right and beheld Syra, hair as red as fire and with the brightest green eyes he had ever seen. They made Emerald's dull. She stood there, as if captured by some unseen force, her gaze locked on something past him, before she disappeared in a trail of dust.

Then a dagger was thrust into his heart.

Morei flinched, the pain as real as the day he had died. It started in his chest, burning hot, before spreading over his limbs and down his back. In the dream, trembles racked his body, and he collapsed on his knees. When he looked down, the blackened hilt of a blade studded with rubies stared back up at him. The Demon Killer. Grappling for it, the king tore the blade free from his chest to see metal darker than midnight shimmering with the crimson of his blood under the sun.

Then he had awoken.

Morei blinked in the dark room. He wasn't sure what to make of that dream, except that it was one of the worst he'd had. Never had he felt so close to death besides the night he had been soul bonded to the demon. And never had he dreamt of the Demon Killer with such vividness. If he thought about it, he could still feel the slick rubies and the warm leather of the hilt in his hands.

The stillness of the night was stifling, deafening. It was so quiet that he could hear footsteps down the hall of his chambers.

Morei rolled over and stared up at the ceiling, although he couldn't see it. It felt like his thoughts were bombarding him all at once. Boris, Sekar, Peter, Ezra, Syra, Cu'cel, the council, city, Sorréle, everything. The king was thinking of all of it at once, and yet he couldn't process a single thread. He was grasping at everything and nothing.

It was feeding into his anxiety. The longer he lay here, the more he was certain someone else was standing in the room with him, scrutinizing and mocking him. His life was falling apart, and here he was, trying to sleep it off. That simply did not sit well with him. It made his skin crawl and his breaths short.

"Forget it," he mumbled, and sat up, yanking the sheet off with too much aggression. Exhaustion was there, reminding him of how little he had rested, but it felt like the least of his issues. With a level of agitation that felt entirely unnecessary, he pulled on some pants and a loose tunic. Satisfied, he rubbed the sleep from his eyes and stood. The floor was cold against his bare feet, just like always.

If he couldn't sleep, then he would take a walk.

Making his way out of his chamber, he eased the door shut behind him. Lanterns hung every fifteen to twenty paces along the halls of the palace so that night staff and soldiers could find their way. It gave him an excuse to go wandering instead of imprisoned in his room.

The air was dead, unmoving, confined to the halls until morning. Making his way, Morei let his eyes study his surroundings as if seeing it all for the first time. It was better than listening to the voices or acknowledging the brutal thoughts that were threatening to cripple him instead.

The shields of Geral decorated the wall in front of him—various styles of the family crest glared back, reminding him of the generations before that he had now let down. Red and black banners hung from the ceiling of the next hall, decorative but practical, complimenting the paintings of previous rulers. The queens and wives hung to the left, while the kings and husbands were on the right. Morei slowed, taking in their features, all cast in the warm orange glow of the lanterns. Centuries of rulership stared back at him, and if he looked closely enough, he was certain their eyes all possessed a disapproving gleam. Directed at him, of course.

Ahead, halfway down the hall, were his mother and father. The king came to a stop, his eyes grazing over Ivory and then Vic. They were probably the only ones who had really believed in him, despite his temperament and stubbornness.

He reeled with unmastered emotions. What would they say now?

Under their gazes, he felt like a child again—confused, uncertain, but curious. He also felt like a failure.

"I'm sorry," he whispered into the hall before he swallowed down the anguish. Geral had become unrecognizable since he had come into power, and it would only live on without him.

No matter how much he despised admitting that, he knew it was the truth. Cu'cel was happening because of him. From the moment he had become king to now, he had caused nothing but problems, no matter how much he had fought to be the best, to do the right thing. Fate seemed determined to make him the monster it expected him to be.

The people of Geral had turned on him, forgetting what he had sacrificed so that they could live. The council had betrayed him the day his world fell apart—when they had blamed him for the king and queen's murder. And now, it seemed, the Gods were going to make a fool out of him.

Perhaps he had been born a tragedy, but he would certainly not die as one.

With a final look, Morei straightened and kept walking. He would not mourn over yesterday—he simply did not have time to do so, and it would not change his present. Plus, he certainly hadn't gotten out of bed to wander the halls and have a pity party for himself.

The farther he got from that hall, the better he felt. He passed a staff member and she smiled at him, carrying a bundle of cloths and dressed in a dark maid's dress, likely preparing for the ceremonial event tomorrow afternoon to celebrate Ezra's induction into the family. Councilmembers and their family would be there, as well as anyone Ezra invited. Morei would obviously be there in support and to give a speech once the sun set. Prior to a grand feast, activities would be held—there would be jesters, musicians, epic plays, and anything the council could think of. The king often stayed out of that part of the process. While some previous rulers, like his father, had enjoyed the planning, he loathed it. And Peter had been happy to take that additional task from him.

The documents to officiate the adoption of the Geral name were already prepped and signed by the chancellor, Morei, and Ezra. The family crest had been pressed into the parchment with red wax to Ezra's delight. Peter was the royal witness, and since Morei was the only blood-born Geral family member and king, it had been his name signed to approve Ezra into the family. There was nothing else involved with the induction of an outsider into a royal family, only documentation and the king's approval. And so, when the parchment had been signed, the chancellor had gladly rolled it up to present it to the council and party members for the following day. Per royal code, an announcement would be made and posted throughout the city after the ceremonial event.

Within a few days' time, Morei would relinquish his crown and give it to Ezra. It was not a thought he wished to dwell on, because with it came the resentment for the people, the council, and the city.

A noise caught his attention just as he came upon the throne chamber. Peeking in, he saw several lanterns hung, their flames dancing with pride. Looking around, he didn't see anyone in there. Once more he heard the noise, and this time, he was able to make it out as mumbling. It was coming from ahead, rather than within the throne chamber. Morei looked forward and squinted into the hall. There, he saw the shadow of a figure paint the wall.

Curious, the king closed the gap. As he grew closer to the slow-moving figure, a familiar face revealed itself—Boris. The ex-commander was dressed in a silk purple tunic and loose-fitting pants. Warm light flooded his rich ebony features, accentuating his jawline. At the sight of Morei, the man paused and looked around before settling his gaze back on him. "Am I dreaming?"

The king slowed to a halt and smirked. "No, but what are you doing up?"

"I should ask you the same," he replied, words slurring slightly this time. He was drunk.

The idea made the king snicker. "Boris, the great commander of Geral, have you been drinking?" he asked playfully.

Boris raised an eyebrow up at him. "And what if I was, hm?"

"I'd ask why you didn't invite me," Morei answered.

Wagging his pointer finger, the man chuckled. "Next time, okay? Next time." At that, he started to trek down the hall again, and the king fell into step next to him.

"Where are your chambers?" he asked. "I'll walk you back."

"I'm not that drunk," Boris responded with a dramatic tone. Eyes glittering, he looked at the king. "I just had a few drinks. That most recent batch of Kendell's Milk is quite strong, huh?"

Morei nodded "Aye, and there will be plenty of it tomorrow night too, unless you drank it all."

Boris teetered for a moment and tilted his head to the side. "What's tomorrow?"

So the chancellor had not shared that particular fact. Swallowing, Morei answered as steadily as he could. "Ezra accepted a formal offer to be inducted into the Geral family. He'll be your new king."

Even in the man's state, the information still forced his expression into shock. With a firm hand, he gripped Morei's shoulder and narrowed his eyes. "King? You're surrendering your title?"

He nodded.

"That's outrageous," Boris blurted out, and let go. He shook his head. "Not just anyone can be king. Who's making you do this? The council?"

The king raised an eyebrow. "Were you not aware of Caster's threat to cease imports and exports if I did not step down?"

Boris tapped his chin with a pointer finger, his brow furrowed. "I was not."

That was the least of their problems, it seemed, the issue with Caster. "Hey, this should make you relieved, no?" A loaded question, given their previous disagreement, but he couldn't help it. The cold sense of humor was the only way he knew how to move past the topic.

Meeting his gaze, Boris seemed to understand the joke. He smiled, his eyes softening. They fell back into step again, with Morei's bare feet padding gently alongside Boris's boots, which echoed along the hall. For a time, that was the only noise.

Then Boris spoke. "I wish things could have been different." Morei glanced his way, acutely aware of the somber tone the man's voice had taken. "There was no training to handle what's happened to Geral, to you. Do you remember when you were little and you would sneak into the armor room and dress up like a soldier?"

That was a memory the king hadn't thought of in nearly twelve summers, but at the mere mention of it, he laughed out loud. "How could I forget? I used to hide in the barracks and then try to blend in when I was certain no one would notice me." That brought a grin to his face. Oh, how simple times once were. He'd grab a sword that was too big for him at the time and try to walk around the training area and practice with the others. It never lasted long once he got in the open. One of the lead soldiers would recognize him and take him right back to the man who now walked beside him, who would then bring him to his parents.

"I always had to present you with this all serious attitude," Boris continued with a laugh. "'Your son is sneaking into the barracks and trying to pass as one of my own,' I'd say. Your father would always have that same raised eyebrow, as if it surprised him, and then promise that you wouldn't do it again."

"And then I would," the king confessed through a chuckle. They turned down another hall, their voices carrying ahead.

"Drove me crazy too." Boris shook his head. "I was petrified you'd get yourself seriously injured and I'd have to explain to the king why his son was being tended to in the infirmary. That's why I asked your father to have a suit of armor made for you, you know. It was the only way to protect you. Now, you *had* to come to the training ring and under special instructions to be trained by me."

Morei looked at him, surprised. "You're the reason I was ordered to train with you?" When Boris nodded, he threw a hand up. "All this time, I thought I had finally convinced my father to let me train with the soldiers. Clever."

"You're welcome."

They eyed each other before both giving into a wave of laughter. It was inconceivable to think that Boris was the reason Morei had been granted special permission to train in the soldier's area, rather than in some private lesson. He had never wanted that, as he had so often argued, because as he had put it even then, "A king is as only good as his soldiers."

To know now that wish had been granted by none other than Boris felt awfully bittersweet.

"Ah," the man announced suddenly as he recovered. "This is me." He halted before a door and turned to face Morei. For the first time in a long while, Boris looked truly happy, at peace even, despite his somewhat drunken state. "You know, you should try to get some rest."

The king raised an eyebrow. "And I shall say the same for you."

Boris pointed at him, the corner of his lips still tugging upward. "You look just like your father when you do that with your eyebrow."

A ball of emotions lodged itself into the back of Morei's throat. It had been an incredibly long time since he had been compared to his father, the man he could only dare dream to be. Hearing it from Boris was the last thing he had expected. For several heartbeats, all he could do was grapple for the right words.

"Anyone can rule, but not everyone can be a king," Boris observed with a nod. "Don't ever forget that, okay?"

Slowly, he nodded. Drunk or not, the man had shown him more kindness than the people he had expected it from. If he were in Boris's shoes, he would have cursed the king, packed his bags, and left. Instead, he had chosen to stay. Perhaps it was because this was all the man knew. Or perhaps it was because he was a better person than the king could ever be.

"You get some rest," Morei finally managed to say. When Boris smiled in acknowledgment, he turned to walk back to his quarters. "Let's catch up tomorrow!" he called with a wave. Boris returned it with his own raised hand before disappearing into his room.

Once the door was shut, the king let out a large exhale. With it, the ball of emotions that had lodged in the back of his throat came loose, and he forced it back down. Boris was drunk, albeit aware enough to have a conversation, but he'd likely not remember most of what was said. Or so Morei told himself. It felt safer that way than to think after everything he had done could go ignored, even forgiven, by Boris.

He walked in silence all the way back, not stopping for the paintings or at the same maid who walked by as he had seen earlier, this time with no basket of clothes in her hands, but rather a bundle of leather pouches. What she needed them for, he did not know, and he did not stop to ask because it didn't matter.

As he strode, his hand caught the light against his paling skin. As the curse grew worse, as the demons took more of him, he was changing. Already, the memories of his childhood felt leagues away, some too far to reach while others were just barely outside his grasp. Emotions he had once felt so routinely were growing sparser, replaced with a cold bitterness that danced with a failing temperament. It felt like fate had cast him to the wolves to be devoured. The man he was becoming would be unrecognizable—and not just to the people, but to himself as well.

Perhaps that was for the better.

THE DAUGHTER
OF CHAOS

The stone underneath was like ice. The chamber was long, the ceiling vaulted, devoid of any furniture or windows. Syra glanced around until she saw a single object. Located at the end of the chamber was a large flame, suspended in the air and the richest green she had ever laid eyes on. The flame danced without noise, undisturbed by their sudden arrival.

She stood, still clutching Death's Sword and the belt to her chest. Sekar was here, his expression playful, despite the terror growing in her chest. Alone. She was alone with the Dark Lord.

The silence of the room was overwhelming after what she had just been torn from. The screams echoed, the blood stained her thoughts red, and she couldn't help but hyperfocus on Zarek's voice. He had called for her, but she hadn't been able to see him. If he died because of her—if any of them died because of her—she'd never forgive herself. Too many people had already. She couldn't afford another one.

"I liked you better red," Sekar remarked, forcing her eyes back to the man across from her. His arms were crossed, but he looked relaxed. Water still dripped from his features, as it did from her. She was soaked to the bone, a deep chill already setting in.

Before her stood the man she had spent almost an entire season with. The man who had grown to know her best, shared meals with her, and given her a safe place. Then he ripped that all away from her.

Sekar stepped forward, his boots barely audible against the stone. Syra eyed him as he stopped before her. With a gentle hand, he brushed her plastered hair away from her face. "The dye is already coming out," he acknowledged.

Without thought, she shoved his hand away. "Don't touch me," she ordered.

The God raised an eyebrow, his expression darkening. "Have you forgotten our time together?"

She took a step back, appalled. "I don't even recognize you," she hissed. Each word dripped with white fury. Her heart was racing from the hot emotion, and her hands trembled. "You didn't even have the courage to face me as you are. Instead, you manipulated and toyed with me, and all for what? So you could get the Demon Killer? Why waste your time with me, Kar?" The name slipped out, but she did not correct herself. "Why didn't you just take the blade and run? Spare me the torture of this."

Sekar took a step toward her, but she backed up. Before she could speak, she watched as his features shifted—his olive skin shimmered and changed to the pale blue color, his dark eyes transformed into the crimsons she had come to know. The Marking of all Guardians licked at the base of his neck before disappearing underneath his cloak.

Before her now stood Kar.

"Is this what you want?" he whispered.

Syra opened her mouth to speak, but the words failed to come.

He continued, ignoring her shock. "I've lived countless lifetimes. I've watched empires rise and fall and watched fate twist into something unrecognizable. *Lifetimes*, Syra," he said with disdain. "Immortality will make you patient." The God shook his head and snickered. "I never intended to tag along for as long as I did with you, Syra. If you want the truth. I came for the Demon Killer that was reported to be seen leaving Caster. I had waited decades to come across that blade. But then I saw you—" He looked at her fully now, his eyes gouging her soul wide open. "*Hair as red as the sun, eyes as green as the richest emerald ever known, and blood touched with the damned.* I knew the moment I saw you that you were the one they talked about—the heir to the throne, the Light Bringer."

Sekar's features shifted, and the Guardian traits she had grown so used to were replaced by his own once more.

"The instant I saw you, I could feel your life force. It hummed with an extraordinary sound, unlike anything I've ever felt before." The corner of his lips twitched upward. "Only the Gods possess that kind of life force." His expression softened. "I followed because I wanted to see what you would do, how you would cope, and because I enjoyed our companionship."

Syra swallowed. Her mind was full of a thousand different things, but shock kept her disorganized. She wanted to run, fight, scream, cry, all of it. But instead, she mumbled, "Where are we?"

"You know that answer already," Sekar said.

She did. Deep down, she could feel it in her bones. They were in the Soul Realm. No matter how much she wanted to disagree, to argue the point, she couldn't deny the pull her body felt to the energy of this realm. There was something familiar about it that put her spirit at ease. Syra licked her lips. "Why are we here?"

Sekar gestured behind him toward the green flame. "The Soul Realm holds a direct link to Mother, or Chaos as she is properly known as. The Eternal Flame, what you see here, is the judge of all souls that come to pass. But every so often, Chaos selects a soul that is strong enough to serve her."

The words that came out of her mouth were hardly audible. "The Gods?"

He nodded. "Our souls were selected for various reasons that only Mother understands. The abilities we were given came with duties to the people, to the Vorelians." His eyes lingered on the Eternal Flame. "We are all Her children."

Syra took a step back. A thought was growing in the back of her mind, one that was forcing her heart to quicken and panic to sink in. "Why are we here?" she repeated, quieter. Stealing a look behind her, she found a door. If she ran fast enough, maybe she could escape. She wasn't entirely sure how she was going to get out of the Soul Realm, but she could figure that out after she got away from him.

Then Sekar spoke, and she felt the blood drain from her face. "To judge your soul."

That was it. Syra didn't think twice. She turned and bolted. It was her only chance at freedom, to escape this reality. The door felt leagues away from where she was, and as she ran, she could feel him on her. She forced every bit of strength out to try and gain speed. The door was there, she was nearly upon it. A single latch, that was all she needed to move before—

Sekar's arms wrapped around her, halting her steps just at the door. Syra yelped in surprise and fumbled with the belt, trying to tear free Death's Sword, but he was faster. Sekar pinned her arms against her body, and her grip failed. The belt fell and struck the stone with a heavy thump in front of her. A whimper escaped the back of her throat. This was not how she wanted to die.

He was breathing in her ear. "It is painless, the judgment." He forced her backward, but she fought back. Trying to shake free his grip, she kicked at his leg, but instead of it startling him, he increased his hold on her. The grip was bone breaking and restricted her breathing as he started to half drag her back toward the Eternal Flame.

"You are destined for Her, Syra, I know it," Sekar told her. "I can feel it." A sob broke between her lips and she struggled against him more, only to find herself in such an awkward position that her fight was useless. Arms pinned, he held her wrists across her chest, and she couldn't get her footing underneath her. "Your place is among the dead. You belong here," he continued. "What better way to rule the dead than to be a child of Chaos? To be a part of Mother?"

"Please," she sobbed. "Please don't do this." Physically, she couldn't win against him. He was twice her size, but maybe he would show sympathy.

She didn't ask for this, any of it. The only thing Syra wanted was a chance at life. Mortal life.

Deep down, she knew there was no turning back. Regardless of what the relic told him of her, he would have her—and she wasn't sure she could escape this time.

Sekar halted and spun her around to face the green flame. "There, there," he mumbled into her ear. "All will be well, little flower. But you must trust me, okay?" He started to force her left hand forward, but she resisted. The air was cold around the flame—it emitted no heat. It danced, undisturbed, into their proximity, but Syra dug her heels into the ground, trying to force Sekar backward. He gave just the slightest, but his grip didn't loosen. Instead, he laughed.

"You will make a powerful God, Syra, but you have to believe in yourself, okay?" He was talking as if he were trying to motivate and encourage her. Tears rolled down her cheeks, blurring her vision just enough to temporarily blind her from the flame's presence.

"Stop," Syra insisted. "I don't want this. *Please—*"

A final shove from Sekar did it. Her hand sprang forward in his grip and caressed the frigid flame. Chills raced up her arm in a frenzy, consuming her entire body just as a tingling sensation raced through her. Heat followed next. It came from within, and she felt like she might overheat or perhaps explode. Perspiration sprang across her nape and down her back just as an otherworldly presence tore apart her mind like it was nothing more than a page from a book. Strength evaporated from her body, and her knees buckled. She would have collapsed onto the stone if Sekar weren't still holding her.

But none of it mattered. Before her, the flame flared blindingly bright, growing twice the size and caressing the top of the ceiling. Still, the Eternal Flame didn't make a noise as it shrank down to its normal size and evolved into a black color. It danced with more volatility than before, more life.

Syra's body lurched as Sekar forced her down on the ground. A maddened glee touched his dark eyes. "You are chosen, Syra. What happens next—" He reached into his cloak and brandished the Demon Killer. "I cannot protect you from all the pain. But I will take what I can."

The unnatural presence clung to her thoughts still, putting her in a daze. The sight of the Demon Killer forced an urgency to take over. She tried to push herself away, but her strength was nearly gone. "I don't . . ." The words came out slurred. It was as if her body were no longer hers, and a panic set in. Her mind felt leagues away from her grasp. All she could do was stare in horror at the ruby-studded blade.

Sekar raised the blade, and for a single heartbeat, a sliver of herself returned. Memories of yesterday, of last season, of six summers ago on Caster's Port—all of it flooded her in an instant. She saw the faces of her father, Dryl, her mother, and even the little girl from the Nighthunter Federation, clutching her destroyed plush. Syra hadn't wanted her life to end up like this. Mistakes had never been so vivid as they were right now. Mistakes she would never be able to correct, because they were long gone.

"It will be over soon," he promised quietly. The black steel glowed under the light of the Eternal Flame. It was breathtaking, and for an instant, it felt like time stood still, if only to capture this moment for eternity.

Then he struck.

UNFIT FOR POLITICS

Cyrus was uneasy, annoyed, and exhausted. Today had become long and miserable. Two dragon eggs, and the only response he'd gotten was unacceptable—Kyllian had intentionally kept this information from him. The *Book of Liral* was unreadable, and his mouth held a bitter taste, the remnants of his conversation with Zorya.

Now, he stood outside the king's study. Cyrus had been summoned, and Kyllian would likely make up some long excuse about family secrets. Whatever the king had to say, it wouldn't matter.

Cyrus didn't trust the man. He hadn't withheld with malicious intent, but it didn't make any of this easier. This close to the king, the only emotion he could identify with was betrayal—it boiled rich in his veins and grounded him in the justifiable argument that what Kyllian had done was wrong. Cyrus was not the enemy, but he had been treated as such.

Several maids walked by and glanced at him, their eyes holding his for too long before they murmured acknowledgments. Cyrus nodded but didn't say anything. He was more ready than ever before to leave Razan. He did not belong here.

"Ah!" The voice made him cringe.

Cyrus turned left to see Shunera walking down the hall with the most arrogant grin. "The famous Dragon Rider!" he called, his voice booming off the walls. The prince stopped before him, their eyes level. "What was that earlier?" he asked. "Seemed important."

"It was nothing."

Shunera nudged him, which about pushed Cyrus right over the edge. "Ah, come now," he pressed. When Cyrus ignored him, he added, "Do people ride your dragon?"

"No, and if you ask to, I will punch you, prince or not," Cyrus snapped. He stared at Shunera, who raised his brow in surprise. Anger overtook Cyrus, and he took a threatening step toward the prince, dropping his voice as he spoke. "Rumor has it you're arranged to Zorya. Let me give you a piece of advice, Prince." He stood so close that he could smell the man's sweat. "You're nothing special, and if you treat Zorya as poorly as I assume you treat your staff, I'll be having a word with you. Got it?"

The prince inhaled sharply and took a step back, looking Cyrus up and down. "You speak to royalty that way?"

He planted his hands on his hips. "I don't care about royalty. I care about respect."

Shunera eyed him, and a long moment passed in silence. Cyrus held him there, determined to make sure the prince knew how serious he was. Frankly, he had no idea where his temper had come from, and he didn't care. Given how Zorya thought of the man, Cyrus thought even less of him.

Shunera finally took a deep breath, but when he spoke, his voice was barely above a whisper. "You smell like dirty blood."

A yell broke the tension, and Cyrus looked toward the door. It sounded like Zorya.

Before either could react, the door swung open and there she stood, eyes wet. The princess glanced between the two before brushing past them and heading down the hall. In the study stood Kyllian, his face stuck in a pained expression. When he met Cyrus's gaze, his eyes turned to resolve.

"Cyrus," he acknowledged, then glanced at the prince. "You may want to speak to her, Shunera."

With a single nod, the prince turned and walked down the hall after her. Cyrus glanced at Shunera, wanting nothing more than to take his place. Shunera would only make matters worse.

Now was not the time to fantasize, though. Not waiting any longer, Cyrus entered the room and closed the door behind him. He did a quick check—they were alone.

It was probably best that way.

"Cyrus," the king said again, quieter this time. He had turned and was pouring himself a glass of wine. "Something to drink?"

"No."

Kyllian nodded without turning back, finishing his pour. When he was done, he set the decanter down and faced Cyrus. "You made quite the scene earlier."

He didn't step away from the door, keeping close in case he had to bolt. "Given the situation, I think it was necessary."

The king nodded and took a drink. An awkward silence washed over them, and Cyrus considered what was said between him and his daughter for her to leave so upset. Likely, it concerned Shunera once more. All that prince was good at was being a nuisance.

His thoughts returned to the book. Perhaps there was someone here who could help him translate it, someone fluent in the Old Tongue. It seemed likely in the ancient country, but he would have to find someone he could trust.

The clink of the glass hitting the table brought Cyrus back to the king's eyes. "There's something we need to discuss, Cyrus." Kyllian flicked his gaze over to the chairs. "We can either stand or sit. Up to you."

Cyrus crossed his arms. "I'll stand. Thanks."

"Very well," he acknowledged, and inhaled deeply. The king tugged at his blue sleeve, obviously uncomfortable. "How did you find the eggs?"

The question caught him off guard. This had been discussed already, and he wasn't about to divulge the truth of his dream. Not to this man. "I told you. Luck."

The look in the king's gaze said he was unconvinced. "I have reason to believe you are sneaking around my palace without my permission." While simple, the statement held enough threat to make his heart drop. "As thrilled as I am to have you here, there are certain things that must remain secret. If not for you, for the people's protection. Do you understand?"

Suddenly, Cyrus felt like a child being scolded. "Yes."

Kyllian nodded. "Wonderful. Something else has come to my attention." He stopped and scratched his cheek. "Zorya seems quite fond of you."

Panic flared in his chest, but Cyrus didn't reply.

"Perhaps you are unaware of formalities, and for that, I forgive you. If one is not raised in the politics of royalty, certain things are not taught. Again, that is alright." Kyllian smiled, but in it, Cyrus saw something sinister. "But Razan and Kalic have an agreed arrangement between my daughter and their son. In it, we hope to put to rest some disagreements."

The king leaned forward and sipped his drink.

"I didn't come here looking for anything but answers," Cyrus explained. "If you think I'm here for your daughter, you're quite wrong."

"Mm." Kyllian set the cup down. "I understand, but as you can probably guess, I am a protective father. And more importantly, a king. I am obligated to say and do certain things."

Cyrus nodded, not trusting his tongue. Now he was annoyed, and he could sense Sozar tuning in to the conversation. One wrong move and he would piss the man and the dragon off.

"Your arrival has done some damage to the work I've done to make sure Zorya understands her place and purpose. She's a tough one, I can assure you of that, and it has taken summers to get her to accept the marriage." The king raised an eyebrow. "I need your word you aren't going to intervene with this business. I'd hate to have to consider you a traitor or think you could damage the family name. Certain things require specific action. I hope you understand."

The words failed Cyrus. The king who had spoken to him earlier, yesterday, even the day before, was not the man he now faced. Before him was a power-hungry man willing to threaten a Dragon Rider to make his point clear. This arrangement between Zorya and Shunera was more than just a marriage, he realized. It was a deal for power. And if it was a deal for power, then Kyllian had intentions for Razan's future that would upset the country and perhaps the world.

Clearly, nothing would stand in the king's way.

Cyrus could sense Sozar's agitation as much as his own, but there was also weariness. They were right in the lion's den, surrounded, and if he screwed up, he could be in severe trouble. This time, he wasn't sure he could escape.

In a matter of days, they had overstayed their welcome.

Cyrus licked his lips, queasy. "I understand. I am not here to cause any trouble." It was the best he could do.

The king waved him off. "Oh, I don't think you're capable of such trouble. Like I said, just formalities that for the outsider are not taught." He snickered, but it was tense. "Politics can be complicated."

The insult was not lost to Cyrus, but he swallowed it. This was a test, and he was not about to fail, but he couldn't find the right response, so he remained quiet. They remained there, staring at each other. A conversation passed silently between the two. In it, he could sense the king's satisfaction, but also distrust. Finding the eggs and presenting the information had incriminated him, that much he knew now. Cyrus couldn't afford to go sneaking around anymore. The only thing he needed to do now was take the eggs and run.

A knock broke the silence. "Your Majesty?"

Cyrus stepped out of the way. The tension was so thick that he could have cut it out of the air with a dull knife.

"Come in, Chancellor." Kyllian's voice was steady, calm. There was no trace of the anger that had flashed behind his blue eyes.

The door opened, and a tall man with short red hair stepped in. He wore a blue robe that was embellished with silver threading and gold gems. It was the same man who had stumbled on Cyrus the day before in the hall, but he had no idea that had been the chancellor, the king's closest confidant. He nearly fainted from the surge of shock.

The chancellor's eyes flashed over to Cyrus before returning to the king's. "Is now a good time?"

"I'm leaving," Cyrus stated bluntly before Kyllian could say anything. He couldn't stay here any longer. As quickly as he could, he turned and walked out, damning formalities. Nobody called or came after him, which relieved him.

Power, war, obligations. That was all this world knew. Everywhere Cyrus turned, someone was threatening him and telling him what he could and could not do. This was not the man he had wanted to become, to be pushed around like some piece to a game. No. He was more than that—he was a Dragon Rider! Yet now he felt like he was back in the mines of Diemon, being ridiculed for some petty reason by his superiors. It enraged him—he wanted nothing to do with Razan. This was not why he had come here.

Kyllian hadn't given him the answers he had so desperately sought. Sure, he had spoken to some degree about the Rider Federation, but now Cyrus was certain that even more information was being withheld from him. And because of his curiosity, the king had threatened him. Cyrus was sick and tired of threats.

He wanted to scream, but all he could do was clamp his mouth shut and walk. So he did. He was one man against an army, and while Sozar could undoubtedly destroy a hundred men, it would do no good to spill blood. Cyrus hadn't come here for that, and he surely wouldn't leave with that kind of reputation.

He would not become a monster.

A GRAVE MISTAKE

Death was cruel. And it had spared no expense for Boris. Rage, guilt, shame, confusion—every emotion that could surface, Morei felt. He wanted to scream, cry, curse, and murder everyone in the room, anything to take away the reality of what lay before him. Lifetimes trampled his mind, teasing and mocking him, as if this were one sick joke played by none other than fate herself. For once, he had wanted to do something right. In his desperate plea to correct his wrong, he had been ignorant enough to believe that nothing bad would happen. Enough wrong was happening already, but Morei had been a fool to believe that it ended there. He had risked his failing reputation, disregarded previous royal tradition, and acted out of kindness—or perhaps it had been from guilt. The king would never know, and now, standing here, it would never matter anyway.

No good deed shall go unpunished.

It was only last night that he had walked with Boris to this very chamber. Only last night the king had shared a moment that had meant more to him than his entire season ruling this city. He had laughed it off, believing the ex-commander was drunk, but looking forward to catching up with the man today, despite the world falling apart around him. For once, Morei had believed that perhaps in all this madness, he had a friend.

Thinking back on those fleeting thoughts now, he felt like the biggest fool here.

The king swallowed down the bile rising in the back of his throat and blinked. Before him lay the man of the hour, his skin covered in tiny black tendrils, his mouth agape in what must have been a scream, his eyes solid black. The death was morbid, cursed. With arms at grotesque angles, the man's body was arched, his back likely broken by the sheer gruesome position he was in.

Next to him, a soldier coughed before turning and leaving the scene, covering his mouth and gagging. The others pinched their noses and kept a hand over their mouths, their eyes wide. The stench was of rotting meat, but that was impossible. A body could not decay this fast—this could be nothing but supernatural, evil. Never had Morei seen a killing as repulsive and unfair as this one. Everything about this was impossible.

Nobody had heard anything. By the cruel hand of the Gods, Morei had walked Boris to his chamber and bid him farewell— *to get some rest.* Now, that comment felt morbid. The rest of the night, not a soul had ventured to see him, only this morning, when a soldier—Cade—had wished to pay the man a visit before reporting to duty. He had knocked, and when Boris hadn't responded, the soldier had found it unusual and checked the door, only to find it unlocked. Without hesitation, he had opened it and found Boris in the middle of the chamber, still dressed in the same outfit Morei had seen him in last night.

That meant he had died shortly, if not directly, after the king had wished him farewell.

"I just saw him last night," the man to his left whispered, blond hair tied back in a loose bun. "We shared a drink and were supposed to see each other today." He looked at Morei, eyes glassy. "What happened?"

"I saw him too," he mumbled, drowning in his own thoughts. The images flashed behind the king's eyes—the plague, Sekar's tactics of tormenting his victims, the dreams, and then the final act where the victim's life is taken. Boris's words to the king just yesterday had been a warning, a message, and now the man was dead.

"For the sake of Eazon, what happened?" Ebin whispered, as if speaking too loud might anger the Gods. A hand covered his mouth and nose, and his ebony skin shimmered with a fine layer of sweat.

"I don't know," the king breathed. But he knew. He had known the moment he walked in and saw Boris's body that this had been the work of a God—a God that was determined to send a message. "We need to burn the body."

The soldiers looked between one another. "What if it's . . . contagious?" one asked.

"It's not," Morei stated firmly. The image of the Diemon soldier crossed his mind—the one who had been possessed by a demon and sent to for the king. What a horrific night that had been, but reflecting on it now, he realized it had been a part of something so much bigger. All along, his life had been at the mercy of Gods and fate. Whatever horrendous method Sekar had used to rip Boris's soul from his body had involved demonic possession. "He has no indication of the illness ravaging the city, men."

Cade nodded. "Should we look for a perpetrator, Your Majesty?"

The king almost laughed—a manhunt for a God would surely turn heads. "No." He turned to see the chancellor step into the doorway and immediately yank the tunic up around his nose. "Peter," Morei acknowledged, the name bitter on his tongue. "I was almost scared you'd miss the party."

The chancellor's blue eyes dropped to Boris's body and then back to him. He froze.

"Happened overnight," the king explained, voice strained. After all the blame that the city had put on him for Cu'cel, Morei was scared to mention that he had been the last to see Boris alive. They would blame him for it, even if they couldn't prove it. "Cade stumbled on him."

When Peter looked back down, Morei added, "This is not Cu'cel." He motioned the chancellor over, stepping away from the soldiers. None of them paid much attention. Once they were separate, the king asked quietly, "Are the preparations for Ezra's induction on schedule?"

He knew how it sounded, but he made no attempt to apologize—the show must go on, as his father had once observed.

Peter eyed him. "Do you really want to proceed with the celebration?" His tone wasn't accusatory, but the king still felt that poison-laced blade twist in his chest.

"Yes," the king answered, and then stole a look at the soldiers behind them. One was wiping at his eyes while several others began grabbing the top sheet off the bed. When he turned back to the chancellor, he continued, "We cannot risk lowering morale. If we cancel, and this"—he motioned at Boris—"reaches ears, we might as well as set the city on fire. Do you understand?"

He knew Peter would. That was what he liked about the man—the chancellor was always thinking about the people, the grand scheme. Somehow, they always managed to come to an understanding. It was why they worked so well, but that did not excuse what had transpired yesterday or the gap that was now shoved between them. "I hate it," the chancellor sighed, and dropped his tunic, revealing the rest of his face. "But you are right. If not for Ezra, then for the public's view."

Morei wrapped a hand around Peter's shoulder and squeezed. "In the meantime, this does not make it to the council or anyone else. We wait until the ceremony is over." Morei needed some time to collect his thoughts "Do you understand?"

"That's against—" The chancellor pursed his lips, obviously struggling. Rule breaking was not his strongest trait. "I guess it doesn't matter."

It didn't. In a few days' time, he would no longer be king—his sole purpose would be torn from him not by choice, but because the city feared him. The council would not waste their time chasing him down for this because to them, to the city, he would be gladly out of sight. The less he interacted with them all, the safer they would be.

"Excuse me, Your Majesty?"

The words broke the sanctuary of his and Peter's conversation. The king turned to face the young soldier, who had to be no older than nineteen, one of the additional helpers who had arrived to move the body. All of them had already pledged secrecy about the abnormal murder, understanding the consequences if they chose to speak about it to anyone, even family or loved ones or amongst themselves. At Morei's hand, it would be certain death, and they all knew that. "Yes?"

Carefully, the soldier lifted his hand and unfurled his fingers. "I found this underneath Boris, Your Majesty. I don't know what I should do with it." As he spoke, the other soldiers filed out of the room, the body between them. The hall had already been cleared by another soldier. They could take no risks. Boris would be burned in a private space underneath the palace, not with the victims of Cu'cel.

Morei lowered his gaze to the ring in the man's hand. It was silver with a large emerald in the center that was wrapped in silver vines. To the ordinary eye, it might've looked like it belonged on the hand of a king, but to Morei, it reeked of evil. That grabbed his attention.

"It was underneath Boris, you say?" Morei asked as he reached for it, sweeping it up from the soldier's grip almost too quickly. The metal was warm from being held.

"Yes."

"Thank you," the king told the young man. "You may go."

The soldier looked between him and the chancellor before he lowered his eyes and walked out of the room. When Peter did not speak up right away, the tension from yesterday's conversation became palpable, despite the current circumstances. Clearing his throat, the king said, "It must be a family ring."

"I can take it back to the family," the chancellor offered.

"No, no." Morei closed his hand around the ring and dropped it to his side. He met the chancellor's quizzical gaze. "I should do it. It is only fair, after what I did to the poor man."

At that, the chancellor's curiosity was satiated. "Understood."

"Would you give me some time, Peter?" He wanted to be alone. The ring was teasing the edge of his mind, almost playfully, as if it were an old lover come to greet Morei, only to prefer that the king come to it. He would gladly do so. There was immense power locked inside the jewelry, that much he could sense, but he did not understand why or for what. Even though a small part of him warned against it—that this might very well be the reason Boris was dead—the king could not ignore the deepening thrill at having the hunk of cursed metal to himself. Whatever it was, he wanted to know, and he needed to know now.

"Of course." The chancellor cleared his throat then and turned to the door. "I will prepare the documents for Boris's passing," he added somberly as he left.

When Morei was certain everyone had vacated the hall outside the chamber, he walked over and closed the door. With Boris gone, the stench of rotting meat had dissipated to a far more manageable level, but mainly closed the door for privacy. Once it was locked, the king scanned the room. Nothing out of the ordinary. The room had hardly been touched, the bed barely amiss besides the top sheet that had been pulled. There was nothing here that indicated Boris had been getting comfortable, which validated his theory that the murder had happened almost immediately after they had spoken.

Now, thinking back from finding Boris wandering the halls, he couldn't help but wonder if this ring had been in the man's pocket all along—an execution just waiting to happen. Perhaps the king had delayed it, intervened, only to abandon him. Maybe, just maybe, he could have stopped this from happening. It felt unlikely, as Boris hadn't offered information about the ring or how he had even come to have it, but still, the thought lingered with a sour stench.

He rolled the item between his fingers, acutely aware that the metal was humming to him. It was faint enough that a common Energy Harvester would probably have overlooked it, but to him, it was loud and clear. This was not a family ring, it was something more.

A message.

Every part of Morei knew that. He was meant to find this ring, and looking at it now as the light danced off the emerald, the king felt an urge to put it on. The metal beckoned him as if he had worn it a thousand times before today and it was good to be back. Hesitant, the king eyed the shimmering metal, aware that something horribly wrong could happen if he tried it on. But it wasn't like the city needed him—rather, it wasn't like the city wanted him around. The king had nothing left to lose, nobody to mourn him, and if he died putting this ring on, then it might be for the best. At least he would know what the energy was hiding.

With a deep breath, Morei slipped it over his index finger.

The room dissolved almost instantly and was replaced by confusion. The king inhaled just as the darkness erupted in flames before him. Carnage passed in a blink of an eye, accompanied by high-pitched screams that made him flinch. A warm sensation ran from his face, and Morei wiped at his cheek, finding it coated with blood. Horrified, he blinked. Then, as quickly as the vision had appeared, it shattered.

Peace was the first sensation he felt after such a scene. He was surrounded by quiet blue skies on the top of a mountain that hugged a wide river, a fjord. But when he looked ahead again, he found himself staring at Cyrus.

The silver-eyed man was looking right at him, unblinking. Morei's breath caught, and he swallowed, unsure of what to say. He had been searching for the Dragon Rider for what felt like an eternity, even though it had hardly been a moon cycle since he had escaped the dungeon. So much had happened since then that the king almost felt guilty standing here now—locking Cyrus up had not been the smartest move, given the immense power stored within him. This was not an enemy he wanted or could afford. Seeing the Rider now, it unnerved him. On Cyrus's hip, a sword was sheathed—one of majestic build based on the handguard, and his hands were gloved. The once-uncertain Rider looked stoic, cold, and determined.

Cyrus blinked as a gust of wind rushed by them, but Morei didn't feel it. He couldn't feel the ground or even smell the river or grass. It was all vacant to him.

The Rider stepped forward, but his eyes stayed stuck ahead. It was only then that the king realized that Cyrus had no idea he was there. Both relief and frustration washed over him; he'd pay anything to speak to him, to explain that his intentions had been unclear and unfair, but he couldn't. Whatever the Dragon Rider was focused on outweighed any foolish apology, so he turned around and—

A cold hand wrapped around his throat and smashed the vision, enveloping him in darkness. The king was staring at a woman with shredded skin and black hair. Blood oozed freely from the wounds along her arms and face. The whites of her eyes stared back at him, and she lifted her other hand—it was clawlike, inhuman.

Morei gasped as he felt the hand begin to squeeze harder. Panic gripped him with an iron hold as he grasped for the ring. It was the only thing he could think of, and as he wrapped his fingers around the metal, the lady's brow furrowed in rage.

Morei yanked the metal off, feeling it resist at first before submitting over to his demand. The image dissolved instantly, and he fell forward, catching himself in the last moment on the cold marble. Heaving for air, he felt for his neck and looked around.

He was back in Boris's quarters. Back in Geral, in the palace.

The ring mocked him with the beauty of its craft. Morei steadied himself, realizing the reality unfolding around him. Boris had died in the grips of this ring, but how had he even come to possess it?

The dead waited for their victims in these visions, and Boris had become one, likely caught up in whatever the man had been shown. The images . . . they were pieces of the future. This was a power that had only belonged to one person, a part of history that had been loss centuries ago. The making of this ring was known by one person, and at the fall of the Lirallian Empire, it and the two other relics had been lost.

One had been discovered already and was wanted by half the world, that much he knew, its design so unique that a blind man could identify it—the Demon Killer. And now the second relic mocked him, the very item once worn by Henry Junok. Old stories claimed this was the ring the false god had used to erect his empire.

The Lirallian Ring.

DESTINY WILL
HAVE HER WAY

The otherworldly power took every part of Syra's consciousness apart. Chaos tore it down to its bones, exploited the fabric of her reality and infiltrating her body. Strength had evaporated altogether, making her victim to the reality unraveling before her. All she could do was watch, dazed and completely separated from herself, a bystander.

Sekar was over her, the Demon Killer bloodied. He was chanting something in the Old Tongue, but it was so quick that she couldn't focus enough to listen. Behind him, the Eternal Flame danced madly, as if it had gained the very strength she had lost. The air was freezing to her skin, sending constant waves of chills through her. It felt like she had been caught in a snowstorm, unprepared.

The God glanced her way. "Ah, you're awake. Perfect timing." His dark eyes were warm, affectionate, despite the gruesome ritual happening.

Syra couldn't react, only watch, as he lowered the blade to his wrist and sliced it clean open. Sekar hardly flinched from the deep cut, and blood immediately began to pour from his wrist and over her torso. The blood was hot against her freezing form. He learned forward, presenting her his bloodied wrist. "Drink," he ordered.

She might have been compromised, but that request awakened a deep terror in her. As she tried to fight, to move, she found she couldn't. Her body was numb, and she could hardly summon it to lift a hand.

"I am helping you," he continued. Blood dripped onto the base of her neck. "I can't save you from it all, but I am absorbing as much as I can without interfering with the process."

Syra vaguely remembered his promise to take the pain away, but if it cost her the ability to fight, she didn't want it. The words wouldn't come, though. Her tongue wouldn't cooperate, and before she could blink, his wrist was pressed against her lips. The thick stench of metal overwhelmed her senses as blood coated her mouth. Her body wanted to reject it, to spit and gag, but it wouldn't. She couldn't.

The blood dripped down her throat without permission, and she swallowed on instinct. Somewhere in the depths of her mind, where she could still process her surroundings, she was screaming. This was a true black ritual—evil and irreversible. She didn't know what it was that he was doing, but it was wrong.

Sekar smiled. "Good." He withdrew his wrist then and reached for hers. She watched as he brought down the blade and sliced her wrist clean open with a swift motion.

She didn't feel a thing.

He set the blade down and brought her wrist to his lips and drank. Every piece of her wanted to rip her arm away, but she couldn't. Her body was not hers to control. It was his.

This was exactly what he had wanted.

When he pulled away, he wiped his lips clean and met her eyes. The glee that filled that gaze of his made her heart drop. "We will be bonded for eternity, Syra."

He jumped back into chanting again, eyes closed, the Eternal Flame reacting to his every word. Syra stared at it, stunned and captivated. When it danced, so too did the force in her mind. Everything was syncing up, like a heartbeat. As Sekar spoke, Chaos responded.

The sliver of her that had returned was slipping away again. She grappled for it, begged it to stay, but it would not listen. As Chaos sank its teeth into the last piece of her, Syra felt a darkness steal her away.

The last thing she saw was Sekar's eyes snapping open.

THE SWEET TASTE
OF REVENGE

Cyrus rolled over on the ground to reach an itch on the back of his leg. He was lying with his eyes facing the intricate and detailed ceiling. Flowers, symbols, soldiers—all of it was captured in paint in the finest detail. The day clung to him like mold, and no matter how hard he had tried to shake himself of it, the details and conversations remained on the forefront of his mind.

We need allies, Sozar advised, his voice rumbling through Cyrus's mind. The dragon had been talking about this since Cyrus had left the king's study. As much as he wanted to jump up and tackle the world, he couldn't. The fury from earlier had come late, and he had damn well nearly barged in on the king's dinner and spoken his mind. But like always, he kept his mouth shut. For once, he was starting to get annoyed with himself.

And for what? Cyrus rolled onto his back again. The marble underneath was warm from his touch already. He had been lying here since Kyllian's threat. The night was here, and he had been summoned for dinner by a maid a bit ago, but he had refused, instead requesting that a meal be brought to him. The less he showed his face, the better.

His family was long gone, as far as he knew. Nobody knew who they were, and there was nothing he could do about that, which angered him more than anything else. The journey Cyrus had started well over two moon cycles ago had started with one innocent goal—to find answers about his heritage, an explanation for why him. But it was becoming extremely clear that the man who had set out for those answers was not the same man he was now.

In a full day, Cyrus had learned that the Rider Federation was overwhelmed with strange creatures, two dragon eggs had been discovered, and the *Book of Liral* was more bizarre than he had originally thought. Oh, and there was another Dragon Rider flying around, eager to start a war for the sake of peace.

Coming here to Razan had done more harm than good, he realized. Acknowledging that was so devastating that he had been able to do nothing but mope in his own mess. Deep down, he knew there was only one solution: fight. Embrace himself and become the face of the new era.

He couldn't bring himself to do that yet.

There will come a day that we won't be able to run anymore, Sozar answered, knocking Cyrus back into reality. He grimaced at the dragon's response, choosing not to reply.

One thing was for certain. If these dragon eggs hatched, war *would* happen. There was no doubt about that. Even the most diplomatic person would go to war to get their hands on a dragon or two. Kyllian's volatile behavior was proof.

Thunder bellowed, echoing through the chamber from outside. The storm was still raging outside with no end in sight. It had been the sole reason he hadn't jumped on the dragon and left the moment he walked out of the king's chambers. After the disastrous flight in the Releuthian Mountains, he had a respect for storms and wouldn't take risk flying in one if he didn't have to. With the night upon him, Cyrus could no longer see the mountains or the clouds, left only with the bright flashes of lightning and rain.

He felt like cornered prey.

We should talk about Kyllian. The dragon was quieter now, obviously testing Cyrus's temper. Somehow, that only annoyed him more.

We shouldn't and say we did, Cyrus retorted.

But—

There is nothing to discuss. It was true, there was nothing more to say. Sozar always tried to talk everything out, but sometimes, like now, there was simply nothing to say. What was done was done. If he could have turned back time, Cyrus would have, making sure he never came here. It had done nothing but make a mess. By the hand of Greve, he couldn't even fight with a sword or harvest energy. At the end of the day, he felt completely useless. There was one thing he was fantastic at, though, and it was getting himself neck deep in business that wasn't his to care for.

Sozar grumbled, clearly unsatisfied and annoyed, but Cyrus didn't care. He kept his eyes focused on a painted soldier above him, noting the cracked paint that indicated its age.

If you mope anymore, I'm going to fly off without you, Sozar remarked.

A knock echoed through the chamber, so quiet that Cyrus barely heard it over the thunder. "Sure you will," he mused, and rolled over to stand. He stretched his arms up, popping his back, before walking to the door. He had no idea who was coming to see him this hour, but it was likely a staff member. Cyrus was really starting to loathe the sound of knocking. It wasn't something he was accustomed to, and he would have been alright never hearing it again.

Cyrus took a deep breath and laid his hand on the cold handle. A shiver raced up his back from the touch, and he stole a quick glance over at the patio doors. He should have closed them but hadn't, letting the cool air in, which was chillier than he anticipated. Without further ado, he turned the handle.

Zorya stood there in a red silk robe with a decanter of wine and two goblets in her hands. Her hair fell over her shoulders, and she blinked up at him with those beautiful dark eyes. "I thought we could start over," she said softly.

Cyrus raised an eyebrow at her. "I thought we were trying to stay away from each other." The words tasted bitter on his tongue, but he couldn't help himself. Given how earlier had gone, she was the last person he had anticipated seeing. Yet the only thing he wanted to do was yank her into his room and taste every inch of her. His guard was down, the king's threat had soured his attitude, and the idea of having her to himself pleased him in more than one way.

She shrugged. "If you want, I can leave." As she turned to go, Cyrus reached out and grabbed her by the arm, halting her. Zorya raised an eyebrow at him.

"Don't," he insisted. "I'm sorry about earlier." When she didn't pull away, he motioned for her to enter. "I'd love some company."

He had no idea why she was here, what she had to prove, or what had gotten into her, but it didn't matter. Truthfully, Cyrus was thrilled to have her here with him. He had been foolish earlier. That was not a mistake he would repeat, and given how the day had gone, Cyrus decided nothing would hold him back anymore. If he wanted to spend time with her, then he would. Damn the politics, the marriage arrangements, all of it. He was done being polite.

Sozar's presence stirred. *Ah, the lady has returned*, the dragon teased. He sounded as relieved as Cyrus felt at her appearance. *I'll leave you alone.*

Cyrus rolled his eyes as he closed the door and locked it.

"What have you been doing?" Zorya asked. The sound of glass hitting the table met his ears as he turned around. She was pouring the red wine into the goblets. "Staring at the ceiling?"

"Yes," he confessed, and walked across the chamber. His feet slid against the marble, the stone cold, as he approached the spot on the floor where he had lain. "Listening to the storm, thinking"

"I see. Here." Cyrus turned to see her next to him, holding a drink out. He took it, and she spun on her heels, walking over to his bed. The sword and sack were stuffed away, unseen. "I hope you don't mind." Zorya sighed and sat down, drawing her legs up. "I've had a long day."

"You and me both." Cyrus crossed over and sat on the bed, leaning his back against the large pillows and headboard like her. Thunder rolled outside, this time closer than the last. He watched as she took a long drink, eyes ahead. When she didn't speak right away, he took the chance. "Earlier—"

"When you and Shunera saw me storm out?" Zorya interjected, meeting his gaze. "Yeah. Another fight." She shrugged, but it was weak. "My father is traditional. It's extremely difficult for him to see that this isn't what I want."

He nodded, but he wasn't entirely sure what to say. After his conversation with Kyllian, he wouldn't necessarily use the word "traditional" to describe her father. More like selfish and power hungry, but that was not his place to speak of. If he had known Zorya for a summer or two, perhaps, but not now. "What did he say?"

"The first time we spoke today, he told me that I need to learn to accept what cannot be changed," the princess explained. Her fingers danced around on the goblet's silver as she spoke. "The second time—what you saw—was him telling me that he already spoke to Shunera and that the marriage would happen in less than a week. He had granted permission for it already."

"I'm sorry," Cyrus whispered.

She scoffed. "You probably wonder why I showed up at your door after everything with wine." Zorya stretched a leg out. Bare skin hinted underneath the robe, taunting for him to look. "Shunera wanted to stay with me tonight, obviously, but I don't—" She inhaled deeply. "I don't like the way he touches me. He's inconsiderate and rough." The princess flicked her eyes up at him, her gaze unsure. "And tonight, he was drunk. If I hadn't left when I did, he would have probably forced himself on me."

Cyrus took a deep breath. He wanted nothing more than to beat the prince into the Afterlife. Tightening his grip on the goblet, he kept his voice soft. "Has he done it before?"

"Of course," she answered with a half laugh. "The culture here, it might be beautiful in its own ancient right, but that's all it is, ancient. Certain things haven't ever changed, especially in Kalic. They are brutes."

All Cyrus could do was think of what Kyllian had said about the long-standing deal to marry his daughter off, and for nothing more than to smooth over some disagreements and gain more power. If this wasn't considered cruel, then he didn't know what was. "To do this to you—" He shook his head and looked at her. "It is wrong."

"It's to keep the peace," she replied. "As simple as that."

Zorya took a drink then, and Cyrus followed. The wine tasted heavily of cherry, and it was delicious. Back in Diemon, it had been rare in his childhood to come across fruit. Only when he was mining and recognized for his work by the royal family did he ever receive treats, such as fruits and specialty-made pies. When he lowered the goblet, the princess laughed. He raised his brow. "What's so funny?"

"The whole situation." She shook her head, still chuckling. "All of it. It feels like today was a lifetime ago already. It's so strange."

Cyrus smirked. Her laugh was music to his ears. "It's not strange to me, you know." He nudged her with his goblet of wine.

"Let's just act like earlier didn't happen, hm?" There was no doubt he felt terrible for what he had said earlier, but it seemed she was willing to move on, and he was more than happy to do that. They had both had a long day, and sharing this moment felt like a fresh start.

"Just think," she remarked playfully. "We started off threatening each other, and now we're sharing wine. What's next?"

That was a loaded question. Cyrus wasn't ignorant to how he felt for her or what he wanted to do. He took another drink instead of answering, hoping she didn't see the way he had dragged his eyes over every curve.

As the night progressed, they spoke of various things, from where they'd travel to if they could, to what their fears were, and whether they preferred winters over summers. Cyrus learned that Zorya hated the taste of black coffee, preferring to load it with a large amount of honey and milk. She loved winter, for little snow was seen on this side of Eiyrǎl, and she wanted to visit the Mourale Mountains one day in Diyrǎ. "I hear they have peaks that are snowcapped all through all the seasons," she told him. "We're lucky if we get a flurry of snow, if at all, in the winter."

The wine was long gone by the time they stretched themselves on the bed, listening to the ongoing storm. The rain had lightened up, but the thunder had intensified, shattering the sky.

"Just wait," Zorya told him in a fit of laughter. Her cheeks were flush from the wine. "One, two—there it is!" A crack of thunder broke her count, echoing across the chamber's walls.

Cyrus propped himself up on an elbow to look down at her. The red robe hugged her body, accentuating her curves and the shape of her breasts. Skin peeked out here and there, taunting, beckoning him closer. Logic was gone, and all Cyrus was aware of was how delectable she looked right then and there.

Her hand brushed itself against his cheek, the touch warm. The contact grabbed at his senses, suffocating out the last bit of reasoning and dragging him under the control of lust. Cyrus reached out and wrapped his hand around her wrist, bringing her hand to his lips. Without taking his eyes off her, he kissed the skin softly. The desire that burned within his body was enough to challenge the Gods.

Zorya's hand wrapped around the back of his neck. Leaning forward, he brushed his lips against hers, tasting the remnants of the wine as he parted them. Cyrus explored her body, roaming over her breasts, down to her hips, and over her legs. Every part of her aroused him.

Pulling himself over her, Cyrus deepened the kiss. Their tongues danced, and she nipped the bottom of his lip, making him moan. She tugged at his shirt and he broke the kiss, allowing her to remove the fabric. Once it was off, her hands grabbed at him, tracing over his back. He dropped down and met her lips again.

Sliding his fingers down to the knot of the robe, he undid it. The fabric was soft to the touch but nothing in comparison to the way her skin felt against his fingers. Subtle, hot, *his*.

Cyrus pulled his lips away from hers, wanting to explore. He drew the robe aside, revealing her to him. As slowly as he could, Cyrus kissed her breasts, letting his lips roam over her. She inhaled sharply, so he kissed even slower, hoping to drive her a little crazy.

Every part of her was as soft and delicate as the last. As he moved his way farther down, Zorya moaned, and he pressed his lips against her inner thigh. Drawing his hands over her, he moved his mouth closer to the one place he had been dying to taste since he started.

Cyrus had *her*. He teased her at first, making her moan before he let his lips and tongue explore. Zorya tasted as good as she looked. Caressing his fingers over her, he made sure to satisfy, only stopping when she quivered underneath him. He smiled, nipping at her inner thigh, making her cry out.

Zorya pulled him to her, forcing her lips onto his. Cyrus trembled as a hand teased him through the fabric and her other hand pulled the belt loose. He couldn't wait any longer.

"Hold on." He broke the kiss, and as quickly as he could, he discarded the fabric, watching as Zorya's eyes danced over him. She reached forward, beckoning for him to come closer, and he obeyed, more than happy to have her.

As Cyrus parted her lips, he wrapped a hand around her back, her skin coated in a fine layer of sweat, and pressed himself into her. Euphoria rushed him, and he thrust. Her body was made for him.

Zorya's nails dug into his back as he took her. Cyrus broke the kiss, pulling her head aside with his other hand so that he could nip her ear. She cried out in response, driving him mad. As much as he could, he showered her in kisses as he continued to have her. Every part of her tasted divine. The sensations rushing through him were incredible, enslaving him to her touch. Cyrus didn't want it any other way. He would have this moment for as long as he could.

The night took them.

BITTERSWEET

"Oh my, just hold still, Your Majesty," Debra insisted. The seamstress was doing a quick alteration on his sleeves, having not liked the length when Morei had walked in to show her the new design. It had been made a half moon cycle ago, but given the events with Diemon and then the king's ten-day endeavor, the last thing he'd wanted to do was try on new clothes. The seamstress had insisted on it for tonight, though, hunting him down in the halls and dragging him back here.

She had no idea that he had come from washing himself clean of the horrors that had perpetrated his morning. Nobody had any idea what had happened, save for the chancellor and select soldiers who had pledged their oath to not speak about it.

The Lirallian Ring sat comfortably in the pocket of his pants, a source of energy humming constantly in the back of his head. Between that and the voices that were always there to remind him of his connection to Dark Energy, the king felt distracted—not even to mention the visions that he had been shown, snippets of the future that he did not know when or how would come to be.

"Is that alright?" The seamstress motioned to his sleeve on his right arm. The gold cuff looked fine, pristine—he couldn't identify a difference between when he had walked in and now, but he wouldn't tell her that.

"It's wonderful," the king complimented, and drew his hand back. He toyed with the lion-shaped cufflinks—three of them, all small and roaring. "You and your ladies are incredibly talented."

Debra beamed, creating deep smile lines. "I would not let a king such as yourself be dressed in anything less than extraordinary, Your Majesty. Ah, especially for such an event!"

He smiled, but it was lifeless. Already, the day felt decades long, but he could not speak on the matter. The idea of sitting for the afternoon and well into the evening for this induction ceremony made every part of him cringe. All of it was for such show—a public display of power and celebration meant to increase morale and remind the people that Geral was still thriving, despite Cu'cel. He understood the purpose, but he could not ignore the true meaning of today. It was the end of an era—his era—and the beginning of a new one. Ezra Geral.

The ladies had worked overtime to ensure that the new Geral would have a proper outfit for the event, and they had not failed. Lying on the table in front of him was the shirt Ezra would wear, a true show of the family colors, with a black base and red stitching along the sleeves and collar. The same roaring lion cufflinks were attached, but his were red, while Morei's were black. The silk reflected light, even from here. It was a fine shirt, and next to it lay a pair of black pants that had been custom fitted for the Energy Harvester. Red stitching ran all the way down the sides. They would be the nicest pair Ezra had ever worn, of that the king had no doubt.

It was bittersweet. Sweet because Morei was giving Ezra a purpose, a family, a newfound life. There was so much he had gone through—damn Greve, Ezra should have been thrown into the dungeons for killing his father—but he hadn't by some bizarre chance of luck. That dirty secret stayed between the king and him and would forever be so. Sometimes, people had to make sacrifices for the greater good—sacrifices that broke laws, bent morals, and changed a man. Sacrifices that Morei could sympathize with.

But it was bitter because of what it all symbolized. In different circumstances, the king would have brought Ezra into the Geral family out of pure compassion and because he would want a brother in all but blood. He would be a prince and could carry the name forward, but it would never be that way. Morei would forfeit his title and never be an equal in the eyes of the city. A city, he reminded himself, that only existed because of his bloodline.

The people had taken advantage of him, of the Geral name. They had forgotten what the Geral family had done to erect this city centuries ago. Greedy, that was what they were.

"Your Majesty?"

Morei directed his eyes down to Debra. "Yes?"

"You're all set." The seamstress smiled and dipped her head in respect before stepping aside. His glanced over the black button-up. The gold stitching was molded into a massive lion's head on the back, mane and all. How the ladies had pulled that off was outside of his imagination. His pants were embroidered with gold down the sides, much in the same fashion as Ezra's. On any other occasion, he would have felt proud to walk into that hall and show off his royal attire, but tonight, he felt like a fraud.

"Thank you," he acknowledged, and stepped away from the mirror, grateful to remove himself from his own reflection. All that stared back at him was a man in a mask, one with paling skin and sketched with veins that were darker than the night sky. In the mirror stood the man he was destined to become, and Morei wasn't sure he was okay with it yet. He could not fully accept this destiny, even with it barreling at him at full speed.

Sooner or later, he would have to face that man.

For now, though, he would ignore him as he has so many times before. The king glanced up as he heard the door open. Ezra stepped through, dressed in a dingy tunic that was stained with sweat along the collar and arms. His amber eyes found Morei's almost immediately, and he grinned. "You look fantastic!"

The compliment made him grimace, and instead of acknowledging it, he gestured to the outfit on the table. "The ladies did an amazing job, Ezra. You will look like royalty."

The Energy Harvester nearly ran to the table, but in all that excitement, he touched the fabric as if it might fall apart. Debra waited, hands clasped in front of her, while the king observed. Once more, the thought crossed his mind that Ezra would make a fine king.

"Is this really for me?" he asked, and turned around to look at Morei. In all the madness the city and council had caused, this precious moment would stay with the king for the rest of his life. "I don't think . . . I mean—"

"You will," Morei cut in. "As a Geral, you will be expected to be the best dressed in the finest fabrics." Motioning at the table with a nod, he added, "This will be one of many outfits you will be wearing."

Nobody knew he would be the future king yet. Nobody but Peter, him, Morei, and the council, as well as Ezra's mother. For them all, this induction meant far more. Today, Cu'cel felt leagues away.

"Go ahead," the king insisted. "Debra will help you and ensure the fabrics fit you fantastically."

Taking his leave, Morei slipped past Ezra and the seamstress, relieved to be done with his fitting. That was grueling. In his pocket, the Lirallian Ring bounced, reminding him of his own secret.

As he stepped out into the hall, Emerald was right there, and he just about ran into her. The queen jumped in surprise and yelped. "You scared me!"

"Sorry." The king checked around to find they were alone, save for the occasional staff member rushing by. "Come to see Debra?"

Emerald nodded. "Just wanted her to snip a thread off." Her eyes raked over him before returning to his own. "She did a marvelous job with you."

And she had done a breathtaking job with the queen of Junok. The seamstress had spared no expense with a fitted gown for Emerald, choosing a crimson red that was encrusted with gold jewels along the shoulders and deep neckline, leaving almost nothing to the imagination. Emerald wore her hair down, having styled it so the waves were accentuated in bold curls. A glossy red painted her lips, likely made with crushed berries—Morei knew it must taste delicious.

"You are stunning," he said in return, and smiled. "Are you happy with it?" Despite their previous conversation, she was still a guest in his home, and he expected only the finest treatment for her. It was what she deserved.

A smile broke across her face, her green eyes glittering. "I am taken away by the level of quality your seamstress possesses. Debra has a gift unlike any other seamstress I've ever met."

He nodded. "Good."

For a moment, he recalled the first day they had met, when she stood proud in the throne chambers with a gorgeous white cape and ivory clasp. So certain, quick, and clever. Those had been the first things he saw in her, outside of her beauty. That same beauty still existed, albeit tarnished by her actions, but Morei was still willing to believe her heart was large.

But it ended there. Before she could reply, he asked, "Are you prepared to leave tomorrow?"

The queen nodded curtly. "Everything is ready. Kiren extends his gratitude, but I am sure he will tell you himself when we depart."

"I'm sure he does," Morei observed dryly. He was fully aware that her commander's jealousy issue would be satiated by leaving—Kiren would have Emerald to himself again. Above all, the king was beyond relieved. This lessened the liability that something could happen to her while she was under his care. If she died here, the council of Junok would never forgive him, and he would be forever haunted by it. The worst thing that could happen among the royal families outside of outright betrayal was having one die in the hands of another. It might as well as be treason, and was punishable by death.

"Thank you." The queen's eyes held him in place, once more sifting through his soul and its belongings as she had so many times before. "Above all, your hospitality has meant more to me than I could ever explain."

"There is no need." Morei took a deep breath and smiled at Kaleb, the young scribe for the council meetings. The boy was dressed in a blue button-up, his hair neatly trimmed around his ears. He would be chancellor one day, the king was certain of it. "It is my duty to care for you."

Pursing her lips, Emerald took a half step forward and crossed her arms, keeping her voice low. "I did some thinking, and I think there might be a cure for what's happened to you." The statement was so sudden and outrageous that Morei froze.

She must have taken that as a sign to continue. "My family was required to read quite a bit of work on demons, ancient energy rituals, and such. I won't know for certain until I'm back home and can go through my library, but I came across something once that involved a Death Seeker. It involved their blood, that's all I remember."

That forced the life back into the king, and he raised an eyebrow. "We often avoid those people, no?" When she didn't find the humor in his comment, he sighed. "Emerald, I appreciate you taking some time to think about this, but it is not your problem. Remember, this is not the path you are supposed to walk."

She stared at him, and by the look in her eyes, he was certain her feelings were hurt. Perhaps she thought by presenting a possible solution to his failing sanity, he would get on his knees and beg for her to stay, maybe even take her hand in marriage. "There's no cure," he whispered. "If the demons don't consume me first, the Dark Energy will. Now, please, I must go and attend to several things before the induction begins."

Stepping away from her, he was relieved to be out of her line of sight. Morei did not look back to see whether she still stood there, shocked by his refusal to hear her out, or if she had gathered herself and stepped inside. Looking about, Morei let his eyes wander across open windows and desert landscape that stretched beyond. For the first time in a long while, he saw just how beautiful it all was. The sand sparkled in the sun, like thousands of gems tossed together. The sky was a rich blue, clear and crisp. He couldn't remember the last time it had been as vivid as it was today.

Forcing a deep breath, the king inhaled the wafting smells of roasts, pastries, oil perfumes, and he could hear laughter from a nearby hall. A child shrieked in joy from somewhere.

It had been a long time since the palace had felt this alive.

THE GODS SPARE
NO ONE

eat caressed Syra's skin, and the familiar sound of waves lapping against a beach met her ears. The air smelled of salt, just like home. She lay there, feeling like old times, when she used to come to the beach to escape the noise of the city. She'd travel north, to a spot that she'd called her own, and sit in silence, watching the Merrél Sea dance. The thought made her smile.

She had done that a lot when she was younger, but as she had grown up, she'd found solace on the port, watching the thunderstorms late at night with Kaeyle. Those were the memories she held on to, even after all these summers. Those were simpler times.

The sound of sand shifting caught her attention, and she opened her eyes. She was on her back, and when she looked around, she was speechless. This was it. This was her spot. Syra looked right, and as expected, the city of Caster rested a league away. The stone walls were washed out from the sea salt, and ships were docked, but Caster's flag flew proud. The gold wolf sat in a sea of blue, howling at the sky.

"I thought you'd appreciate a taste of home," Sekar stated softly. Syra whirled her head around and found herself next to the God, who was seated on the sand. He had a blade of grass in his hands and was messing with it, but his eyes were on her. "You haven't had the best of luck."

A breeze ruffled the air. She tried to back up, but her head swam violently and her vision threatened to black out. The sudden disorientation made her stop in her tracks, and she focused on her breathing, keeping her eyes locked on the sand beneath her. It was all she could do to stay conscious.

A hand kept her from toppling over and she was vaguely aware that it was him, the God, the traitor, but she couldn't react on it. Not until her vision began to return to normal and the dizzy spell ceased. A headache followed, angry and without mercy.

"Sit," Sekar ordered, and pushed her down. "You will thank me later."

She couldn't argue, even though she wanted to. Her muscles protested, her energy was drained, and she didn't have the strength to run. But as she sat down, she made sure to put obvious space between her and Sekar.

One thing she could do was get answers. Any fight was long gone. Syra was outside the city she had called home all her life, sitting next to the man that she couldn't get rid of. At this point, she was completely isolated from any outside help. He was persistent, and far more powerful than her. It would be useless to start a fight that she couldn't win. She couldn't afford to lose the little bit of strength she had.

Syra couldn't say she was surprised. In the time she had come to know Kar, she had learned that he was not only persistent, but also cruel, and spared no mercy when he wanted something. The man beside her was that same man, even if he looked different. The familiarity of his presence tugged at her heart. It felt like she was sitting with an old friend, even though every other part of her knew this was the Dark Lord. The God she had been told horrific stories of all her life, the God who did not receive praise, but judgment.

"Is this real?" Syra asked, and rubbed her face. The headache quieted without sudden movements, so she would be careful.

Sekar chuckled and crossed his arms over his legs. "Yes, this is real. No tricks."

Lowering her hands into the sand, she found it hot to the touch. "What happened in Raveer. Was that real?"

He hesitated. "Yes."

The emotions of the disaster that had unraveled shook her to her core. The screams, the pleas for help, the beast, it all consumed her, and she fought back a rogue tear. "Why?" she whispered. "What was the point of it all?"

"I am not responsible for the consequences of Yalana's decision," Sekar answered without missing a beat. "That is what she wished for, and I simply gave her the opportunity. What happens afterward to her or the city is not my problem."

"But the people—"

"The people will learn to survive," he interrupted, and raised an eyebrow at her. "They've survived for centuries. I firmly believe they will continue to do so. The Vorelians are resilient creatures."

"You say it like it's no big deal," she replied. "As if slaughtering innocent lives is nothing more than what you want for dinner."

"And how should I respond, Syra?" The question came out as a challenge, and she swallowed. "You've seen only part of a single lifetime, while I've seen countless. It is a matter of perspective, and with time, you will come to understand that." Syra bit her tongue. This was not a philosophical debate she wanted to get into, so she changed the subject. "The others. Are they okay?"

Another breeze tousled her hair, and she looked down to realize she was in her cloak once more. She touched her torso but felt no pain. The memory of the Demon Killer being thrust into her chest buried in an instant. The ritual, the blood, the Eternal Flame—all of it came crashing down on her. Syra grabbed at her cloak, pulling it aside to yank up her tunic. She needed to see for herself.

"Syra—"

"Don't," she snapped, suddenly invigorated. Her head pounded, but she shoved the discomfort aside as she beheld a mark on her ribcage. Letting her fingers graze over the raised skin, she stared at the symbol. It was three interlocking circles, perfectly round, small enough to be missed. As she let her fingers wander over it, another mark caught her eye, this one on her wrist. It looked like a scar. It was raised and gray, stretching around to where she couldn't see it.

Sekar's words broke her shocked silence. "Every child of Chaos is marked during the Krisár ritual. But do not let others see. Ancient practices still recognize the mark, such as the Lirallians. They will take advantage of you and try to exploit your abilities."

Instead of replying, she touched the scar on her wrist. He continued. "That—" Sekar hesitated, and she looked at him. His expression was final, and his next words were full with resolve. "That is your mark for our energy bondage. It is the Zyulë Bond, used to bind two souls equally." The God pulled his sleeve back of his right wrist and exposed the same scar. "This will protect us both."

She let the tunic fall back down. "I don't understand," Syra confessed. Energy bonds were ancient—she didn't even believe them to exist anymore. They were told in old stories for shocking appeal. She only knew them to be used for enslavement, not by choice.

Not that she had been given a choice on the matter.

A cold smile touched his lips. "I didn't live this long by trusting people." He pulled the sleeve back down. "The more people learn of you, the more danger you will be in. If there ever comes a time that you are in a life-threatening situation, I will know. The same will apply to me for you. Our life forces are eternally linked now. We cannot live without the other."

Those words shook her. "You did this on purpose." Tying himself to her like this protected him.

He leaned in and narrowed his eyes on her. "I did this to protect you."

"You're lying," she seethed, overcome with rage. "You gave me no choice." Syra made to stand, to get away from him, but an iron grip on her arm shoved her back down.

Sekar was in her face, his words hot. "The Gods want you dead. Helyna, Eazon, Greve, and Hyle, they all want to sabotage you. They are fearful of you and have been for a long time." He let her go. "But not me. You are the future, Syra—but you won't be if they get their hands on you."

Her jaw was slack. The shock of his words shattered all her previous emotions. "Then why am I still alive?" Syra motioned at him as she spoke. "You can go anywhere at any time. How have I lived this long if they wanted me dead?"

The very Gods she had prayed to all of her life wanted her dead. It was a morbid twist of events.

Shaking his head, Sekar scoffed. "Because they hoped you'd never face the Eternal Flame. If you never knew your destiny, your heritage, then you would never be a threat." He dug a boot into the sand. "It was a deal made centuries ago, when word of your existence came to pass—"

"The Soothsayer," Syra interjected. Sekar nodded.

"Things worked out on their own, as they always do, when Nala left the Soul Realm. But because nobody knew where she went, we lost track of her and her life. She did a good job at removing herself completely from everyone's eyes." He glanced at her. "Never did we realize she was the one who would bear you. If we had ..." Sekar trailed off and shook his head.

He didn't need to finish. "The others would have killed me then," she said. It was not a question.

"The legend of you and the Soul Realm did not go ignored by the Gods. There was fear among the others that if you came to be, you would not only save the Soul Realm, but be more powerful than the others if Chaos chose you. That your connection to Mother would be greater than the rest." He looked out toward the lapping waves, and his next words came out barely above a whisper. "It was why I was banished. I was a threat. My link to Mother was greater than theirs, and Eazon grew jealous, so he turned the others against me. Made up lies, false accusations, anything to see to it that the trust in me was gone."

Syra's mind was racing. The information he was throwing at her was overwhelming. "Then why didn't you stand up for yourself? Couldn't they have just found you?"

He gave her a mischievous look. "Why do you think I was a Guardian for over four centuries? I could only run for so long until they would find me, so I went with the last option available—I impersonated a Guardian. The real Kar died during the Commitment Ceremony. I merely took his place."

Syra shook her head, agitated. "I don't understand you. What is it? You were entertained by me and my life falling apart, or you're trying to protect me? You surely didn't protect me in the Nighthunter Federation, so thanks for that."

The muscle in his jaw ticked. "I have obligations, Syra. Obligations that outweigh even you. Besides, I knew you would be fine. You somehow manage to always survive, no matter how bad your luck may be."

"But Dryl didn't," she snapped, and stood. Her head swam, but she ignored it. She felt like she had just betrayed the entire world by sitting here with Sekar himself. After everything he had done to her, it felt like a sick game that he had the nerve to tell her he was protecting her. Damn the Gods. "You're a monster."

He followed and grabbed her wrist. Syra yanked it back, but he was one step ahead of her and hooked his other arm around her, pinning her in place. Her body was smashed up against his, her eyes locked on Caster ahead. Hot breath blew in her ear as he spoke his next words.

"You don't think I'd burn this city down for you? You think so little of me after all the time we've shared?" Sekar inhaled deeply. "I've just risked everything to give you the fighting chance you deserve, and instead, you want to blame me for your regrets?" His grip tightened. "You don't know me," he said as he let go.

Syra was confused, exhausted, and agitated. She was torn between wanting to scream for an apology or hug him, but she did neither. Instead, she covered her face with her hands to fight off the raging headache.

"The next four to six days will prove to be extremely difficult," Sekar told her, his tone cold. "Your body must acclimate to your newfound connection with Mother, and it will reject it at first. It always does. Do not be surprised if you grow sick."

She snorted and was about to reply with a sarcastic remark when he spoke over her.

"They are fine." Sekar's dark eyes drilled into her. "Do not take me for a fool, Syra. I know better than to harm your friends, regardless of their importance."

A wave of relief washed over her. In the heat of the conversation, she had failed to follow up on that, and guilt welled up inside her for it. They could have been dead all this time, and she had not a moment to even consider them.

Licking her lips, she could taste the salt from the sea. "What now?" she asked quietly.

"Whatever you decide." His voice sounded strained. "You may return to your friends or stay."

The answer was easy. "I want to return." She already felt guilty for putting them in this mess. Abandoning them was out of the question.

Sekar raised an eyebrow. "Every choice has a consequence. Are you certain this is what you want?"

If he was trying to steer her direction, she wouldn't have it. "Take me back, Sekar. You've messed my life up enough. At least give me this."

A muscle in his jaw twitched at her reply, but he didn't argue. Syra watched him take a deep breath and pull back his cloak. He unhooked a belt that was sitting on top of his own—her belt, with Death's Sword. Careful not to let either touch the ground, he handed them back to her. "Then you will need this."

Syra grabbed the belt without hesitation. The familiar weight felt far heavier with her waning strength, but it was comforting to hold the item again. She hooked the belt around her hips, relieved. "Thank you," she replied, and she hoped he heard every bit of gratitude in those two words. If she had lost this belt and its belongings, she would have been crushed, but more importantly, he was respecting her wishes to return. Regardless of the risks involved, he was not going to hold her prisoner. Whatever title he held, he was still the same man she had come to know and care for.

Sekar stepped toward her until they were close enough to kiss. The look in his eyes was one of resolve. He knew she would want this, Syra realized. "Protect yourself above all else," he told her. "I bonded our energies together because I believe in you, Syra, and I want to help, even if my obligations forbid me."

Those final words echoed through her head as the world around them dissolved into darkness.

OVERSTAYED WELCOME

A pounding noise breeched Cyrus's consciousness, dragging him out of slumber. He blinked and rolled over, annoyed at the disturbance. It had to be just past sunrise based on how groggy he felt.

Hot skin brushed over his fingers as he readjusted, and Cyrus opened his eyes. Zorya's back was facing him, her body rising and falling slowly. He let his hand graze over her skin, relishing in the touch. Last night had been divine. It had been so long since he had slept with a woman, let alone the woman he wanted. Zorya was magical, angelic even. And he wanted to give her the world.

The pounding came back, stronger than before. Cyrus stretched and lifted his head toward the door across the chamber.

"Cyrus!"

His body tensed. It was Shunera.

Zorya stirred then, and Cyrus turned back to her. As gently as he could, he laid a hand on her shoulder and gave it a soft squeeze. "Zorya," he whispered. "We've got a problem."

She let a low groan out and tugged at the sheet over her. "Go back to bed," she mumbled.

"Cyrus!" Shunera yelled. "Piece of maggot shit, I swear if she's in there, I will break your damn neck."

That got Zorya awake, and she bolted up, holding the sheet over her, eyes wide. "Sekar's grave," she cursed.

"Yeah," Cyrus sighed. "Got an idea?"

"I could hide."

He weighed it. It could be their only chance. "Closet. *Now.*" Cyrus jumped out of bed just as she did and started throwing on his clothes. It took a minute to find his shirt, and he finally did underneath another blanket that had been kicked off at one point over the night. Zorya looked around and grabbed at anything that might have been hers before she bolted for the closet, the silk robe billowing behind her.

"Cyrus—"

"Yeah," he called back, cutting him off. "Do you want me to answer the door naked or clothed? Give me a moment."

"I want you to open this door *now*," Shunera retorted.

Cyrus rolled his eyes. In all honesty, this prince felt minuscule compared to his life's problems. What should have made him nervous didn't. He wasn't sure if the situation with Evander or Kyllian or even last night had altered his priorities, but it didn't matter. What mattered was dealing with this selfish and ungrateful bastard.

He approached the door and took a deep breath. Cyrus tousled his hair with his fingers, hoping to make it look okay before he opened the door.

Shunera barged in, his face contorted in a scowl. "Where is she?" The thick scent of spices followed him in. It was overwhelming, and Cyrus wrinkled his nose in response, but instead of closing the door, he left it open. If Shunera was going to make a fool out of himself, Cyrus had the full intention of making sure anyone in the vicinity could hear.

"She?" Cyrus raised an eyebrow. "As in Zorya?"

"Don't play with me," Shunera spat. "I can see the way she looks at you, like you're something special." He scanned the room, hands planted firmly on his hip. "So I'll ask again, where is she?"

"Not here." Cyrus shrugged and crossed his arms. "She got any friends? Why are you asking, anyway?"

The prince's jaw was so tense, he saw a muscle twinge. "None of your business, snake tongue. Do I have to tear this whole place up to find her?"

Agitation flooded Cyrus, and his heart skipped a beat. "I'm pretty sure if she didn't want to see you, finding her won't solve the problem."

Shunera scoffed and started walking toward the bed. "Messy sleeper?" He gestured at the shambled sheets, his tone full of malice. "For a single man—"

"If you came here to pick a fight, then have it," Cyrus interjected. Sozar's presence brushed up against his mind.

Do not do something unforgivable, the dragon warned. To make his point clear, the image of Kyllian and his threat danced across his thoughts.

Ignoring the warning, Cyrus stepped forward. While he was certainly no warrior, he could throw a good punch, and he was more than happy to draw blood with this prince. "You've obviously got a problem with me, so let's have it." He gestured at their surroundings before adding, "Just think what reputation you're making if you come after the only Dragon Rider."

The prince exhaled, the breath sounding strained. Then he shook his hands out and looked up. "Greve, give me strength," he mumbled.

Cyrus scoffed. "The Gods haven't helped you with Zorya, why would they help now?" The question was harsh, challenging, and he immediately regretted it. Shunera turned toward him, face contorted, and lunged.

He jumped out of the way, but he was too slow, and Shunera's meaty hands latched on to his shirt. The force of the prince's attack dragged them both back, and Cyrus lost his footing.

They dropped, his shoulder taking the brunt of the fall. Shunera grabbed at his throat and shirt, but he was so enraged, he was sloppy, and Cyrus shoved the prince off. Just as the bastard turned to stand, he swung and connected his fist into the man's jaw.

"What in the world—"

Cyrus startled. Charles, the chancellor, and Kyllian were standing there. Staff members peeked over their shoulders and bolted down the hall. The chancellor looked like he was hiding a smirk, his lips twitching up before falling again. The king, however, looked like he might stab Cyrus. Cheeks flush with rage, Kyllian stepped into the room.

Well, he had gotten the scene he wanted, but it was backward. Cyrus stood over the prince, and on first impressions, it did not look good.

To make matters worse, he could sense Sozar's disappointment flood their link. It was enough to make him cringe.

The prince shoved himself back, away from him, and slowly stood. Shunera raked his fingers over his head. "Your Majesty," he quickly acknowledged. "I am embarrassed that you have to see this." As he finished, he moved his jaw around and shot a glare at Cyrus.

But instead of speaking, he only faced the king. There was nothing to say, and he surely wasn't going to beg for this man's forgiveness when Kyllian was not only not his king, but had gladly withheld information and threatened him.

Kyllian could have cut glass with the look he gave the two. Cyrus only hoped that the princess wouldn't be foolish enough to bolt out of the closest and take responsibility, but he didn't look back—that would be too risky. And stuffed behind the bed, in the mess of pillows, was the ancient Rider Federation sword and book. It suddenly felt like he'd made the worst decision in his life by allowing Shunera in and keeping the door open for all to see.

"I should say I'm surprised," the king announced before settling his glare onto Cyrus. "But I'm not."

"I was looking for Zorya," Shunera piped in. He took a step forward, as if that would somehow prove his innocence. "I was looking for her and stopped here, and all I did was ask a few questions—"

"Enough!" the king snapped, face flush with anger, hands clenched into fists. "I am ashamed of you, most of all." He dropped his voice into a hiss. "Have you forgotten our agreement?"

Shunera's face became expressionless in a single heartbeat, as if all the emotions he had felt were drained from him. Cyrus watched, impressed at Shunera's quick shift of emotions. "No, Your Majesty."

"Then I will see you in the council meeting. Charles, take him."

"As you wish." The chancellor made a slight turn and gestured for the prince to follow. The man's eyes danced over the prince's head, looking straight at Cyrus. It was not a fleeting look or one of judgment, but one of a thousand words. Words he could not decipher and did not have time to understand. "Come, the meeting is set to start soon. We will see you there."

The prince stole one final look in Cyrus's direction. He swallowed at Shunera's hateful stare. He had believed yesterday was bad, but this outdid the previous events. All Cyrus had ever told himself was how bad he was at confrontation, but in a matter of days, he had proven to himself that he wasn't bad at it, but in fact spectacular at creating such a mess that not even he could see himself out of it.

All it did was prove to himself that he did not belong in this world—this world of royalty and politics. He was far too volatile and untrained. More importantly, he couldn't stand the obligations and expectations. King or not, prince or whoever, Cyrus gave respect where respect was due, not because of someone's title.

Sozar's growl echoed across their link. *We have overstayed our welcome.*

You think? Cyrus replied, amused. Deep down, though, he was ashamed. This was not the man he knew himself to be.

Or maybe it was, and he had never known.

"Where is she?" Kyllian asked, voice low. It was now just the two of them in his doorway, and Cyrus found himself wishing for the company of others. In the presence of this king, he felt like he was on trial with Death herself.

"I don't know." The lie came cleanly.

With a nod, Kyllian took a step forward, dropping his eyes to meet Cyrus's. He was tall, the king, and that was impressive given the Rider's own height. Under the scrutinizing gaze of the man before him, he squared his shoulders and held his chin high. There was no way he would cower to him, king or not.

"Have you forgotten our discussion?" Kyllian hissed.

"No."

"Then why have you caused such a mess?"

Cyrus was annoyed. The emotion flooded his senses, overtaking whatever nerves had gripped him before. To think that Kyllian believed himself powerful, like he had some sway over what Cyrus decided or did—it was enough to cast aside the last bit of doubt he had. It was time to leave.

"Your precious prince caused the mess, king," Cyrus bit back. "Perhaps the forced arrangement is not the best decision."

A muscle in Kyllian's jaw twitched. "If I were you, I'd stay out of business you don't fully understand. It makes you look like a fool."

For a moment, neither spoke. The tension was thick enough to create what felt like an impenetrable shield, as if neither could strike the other, only stare. Then Cyrus spoke. "One day, your little plan will crumble, and when it does, remember this conversation."

Those words had come from someone who was cold, ruthless, unrecognizable. Yet they had come from his own tongue, and he felt good.

The king remained expressionless as he dipped his head lower. In a whisper that was barely audible, he said, "If I were you two, I'd leave separately. You may be a Dragon Rider, but that does not protect you from me or any king."

Then he raised his head and turned. Without looking back, he walked down the hall, his silver cape flapping behind him as he went. The farther he got, the less brave Cyrus felt. His actions were hitting him like he had just gotten smacked in the face with a sack of flour. Bruised, that was how he felt. And he was more than eager to leave.

I will be waiting. The dragon's voice penetrated the shock. *The weather is clear. Warm, but clear.*

I need the eggs. Cyrus turned back inside just as Zorya stepped out from the closet, dressed in her robe, her hair billowing around her delicate features. For Eazon's sake, she was gorgeous. And outrageously dangerous.

"I heard everything," she mumbled.

Cyrus closed the door this time. "Did you?" He laughed. "Did you hear the last part? Your father wanted me to give you his regards." When the princess tensed, he added, "How long are you going to let this go on for, Zorya? Are you really going to marry Shunera, all for politics and peace?"

For the life of him, he could not grasp why people did things like this for others. This was her life, and that meant she had the choice to do whatever she so damned pleased. He was growing tired of walking around on eggshells for everybody else.

Zorya fumbled with her fingers. "I was ready to, but when you arrived . . ." She trailed off and looked back at the bed. "I realized I wanted more for myself. I don't want any of this."

"Then don't take it." The statement came out firm.

She scoffed. "And do what? 'Father, I don't want to marry Shunera.'" The princess crossed her arms, looking smaller. "Guess what he'll say? 'The marriage is arranged, and there is nothing you can do about it. Be the queen I raised you to be.'"

Cyrus swallowed. "And what is that?"

"To marry the future king of Kalic, bear his children, and create a new generation of rulers. I am the key to Razan's future. Eiyrăl will be a country ruled by one empire, not by two king-doms." As the final word left her lips, she looked at him fully now, eyes hard. "And in time, we will rule the world."

Madness. That was the only word that came to mind for Cyrus as he gaped at her. "Is that what you want?"

"No."

"Then leave," he insisted. "Do *something*, Zorya."

"I tried," she snapped back. "I tried to do something, but you wouldn't have me."

Cyrus held his tongue. The princess had a point, but it was incomplete, and he took this chance to collect his thoughts. Zorya walked by him and toward the door, obviously done with the conversation.

"The life I have and will have is not the life I would wish on my worst enemy," he said, turning to face her back. Her hand was on the handle, but she did not turn her head to look at him. "You want to talk about choices, you have plenty. You can be whoever you want, do whatever you want, and go wherever you want. You are not chained by the Gods to do their bidding like I am, Zorya, so be thankful for that."

Heartbeats passed between them, but her eyes never met his. This was not how he wished to leave things. Most of all, the princess did not deserve it. Her life was already destroyed by the politics of her family. The least he could have done was give her a good time, but he couldn't even do that. No matter where he went, he was bound to make enemies.

Because nobody would ever understand what it was like to be a Dragon Rider.

The handle twisted downward. "Goodbye, Cyrus." A part of him wanted to yell for her to stay here, to acknowledge what he had said, but he didn't. He just watched her go for the last time.

As the door closed behind her, Cyrus was overcome with rage. He was better off alone with his dragon, where people didn't expect things from him. All he had done was screw everything up. Before his arrival, the Razan family had secrets, but they were their secrets, and no one expected answers. There were obligations, expectations, and so much more, but at least there was acceptance of all of those. With his arrival, he had taken a hand and smashed all of that in a matter of days.

The morning was still young, but he was ready. There was no home for him, no place where he could lay his head down at night. Evander had been his first warning, but as the palace walls loomed around him, it became obvious that this was the Gods' way of letting him know that the next time he tried to make a friend, it would end worse than this.

He didn't need a third reminder.

Grabbing his stuff, Cyrus quickly belted on the Rider's Sword and tied the sack to the belt. The book banged against his leg, heavy, but it would have to do. Then he put on his boots and cloak. With one final sweep, he decided to also take additional socks and a white tunic, stuffing them into the sack with the book.

Food would come later.

Facing the door, he took a deep breath, hoping to breathe in the courage he would need for the next part.

He did.

A CRIMSON KISS

The roasted pig was divine, the wine the finest Geral had to offer. And the side dishes of mashed potatoes, fresh rolls, jams, butter cake, all of it, circled by, handed out by staff members who served modest portions on the plates of councilmembers, family, and royalty.

Those were just the few options Morei had elected to be served, but there were a half dozen other types of meats and countless other side dishes as well. At one point, he was certain that an entire decanter of Kendell's Milk had been served to a pair at the end of the table—Lord Jire and his brother. Kaleb sat next to them, and at one point, Morei saw the lord offer the boy a taste of the creamy liquor, which Kaleb was repulsed by. The men laughed and poured more for themselves.

Dinner was underway, but the first half of the induction had been spent with entertainment from all sorts of artists, all the way from jesters to epic plays of old Vorelian tales. People the king had never seen acted out scenes from stories he had grown up listening to, like the tale about the knight who claimed to have been taken by Hyle to see what lay beyond the Unchartered Lands to the west. The belief was that it was a tropical paradise, untouched and ready to be conquered. A story told time and time again, but tonight, it felt as if he were hearing it for the first time.

Ezra was sitting next to Morei to the right, dressed in his black shirt with red embroidery. The attire fit him like he had been born into the family. The Geral stamp of the lion reared proudly in red on the back of his shirt—an outfit meant only for royal blood. The young man beamed proud, his amber eyes twinkling and his face stuck in a permanent grin. No longer would he ever dress in sweat-stained, low-quality clothes. To see Ezra so thrilled brought a smile to the king's face. This was all for him.

Just next to the Energy Harvester sat Daneka, his mother, whom Morei had adored immediately. She had thick, dark hair that fell halfway down her back, and her eyes were the color of hazelnuts. Her honey skin contrasted beautifully against a rich, royal-blue dress that had likely been loaned and fitted by one of Morei's maids. It was pristine silk—a fabric that he knew she and Ezra couldn't afford. But she wore it with the dignity of someone who belonged.

To his left sat Emerald. She was holding her head high, as if nothing had transpired earlier, and had leaned over on several occasions and shared a joke with the king. It was nice to put the previous events behind him, and he knew she thought the same. This night was not about them, but Ezra—and having a good time. Tomorrow, she and the commander, who sat next to her along with his men, would leave and be on their way back to Junok. Tonight, there was no point in arguing over what couldn't change. What was important was to have fun and forget the cruel circumstances they were all in.

But as much as Morei wanted to forget about Boris's death, he couldn't. The images of his grotesque body randomly flashed behind his eyes, sometimes catching him by surprise. It was a reminder that no matter how hard he tried to enjoy himself, he couldn't. Not when the Gods themselves were playing with his life like he was their toy.

Peter leaned over to Ezra and whispered something. The young man laughed nervously, and his cheeks flushed. Morei knew the cue and cleared his throat. Emerald touched his hand quickly and raised an eyebrow. For a fleeting moment, he saw the woman he had seen the first time they'd eaten a grand feast like this—playful, teasing with those green eyes, and innocent. But then it vanished, and he stood. Eyes turned upward to meet his, and Morei found Ezra's mother instinctively. Daneka had the kind of smile only a mother could wear—pure.

"Everyone," Morei announced, letting his voice carry through the large hall. Peter dug into his coat and pulled out the rolled parchment that had Ezra's new official name and leaned over to hand it to the Energy Harvester, who then shakily handed it to Morei. As the king took the scroll into his hand and began to untie the leather strings, a smile broke his lips, even as his thoughts raced. This was the first time he was dining in this room since the dreaded night the Diemon soldier had been dragged in by his men. Between that night and now, it felt like an entire lifetime had been lived—one full of anguish, sorrow, and fear.

Tonight was different. Tonight was a celebration.

When the music had ceased and the room was quiet, the king unrolled the parchment and turned it around so that the ink faced the table. The next words were bittersweet—the start to the end. There was no turning back now. "Tonight marks a new beginning for the city of Geral. Tonight marks the start of new blood." Morei motioned to the man next to him. "Ezra, please stand." He waited as the young man fumbled before standing tall. He fidgeted with his hands, then clasped them in front.

Morei smiled. Ezra might act tough, and rightfully so, but he kept a vulnerable piece of him locked away. He would be a good king. "As you are all aware, we aren't here simply for a grand meal—we are here to celebrate the induction of Ezra into the Geral family!" Immediately, the people roared, and for the faintest moment, he thought the Energy Harvester would crawl underneath the table, but the man remained where he was.

When everyone had settled down, the king continued. "When I decided Ezra was more than capable of supporting the family name, I pulled the records of our family. Do you know how long it has been since we've done something like this?" Morei looked at everyone, catching Lady Ferrel batting eyelashes at the new Geral. "It has been nearly three centuries— since Prince Garrisyn. Can you believe that?" With a shake of his head, he rolled the parchment back up and handed it back to Peter, who tied the strings and tucked it away.

"We should not be judged by our name, but by our hearts. We are lions, after all. We are a proud and courageous people, are we not?" The guests stared at him, and some lifted their goblets in response, yelling their agreement. "Strength is a choice. And tonight, tomorrow, and moving forward, we will be strong!"

The entire hall exploded. Yells, cheers, clapping, and drinks clanking against one another deafened everything out. The energy was contagious, filling Morei with jitters as he sat back down and repositioned himself. Emerald leaned over and motioned him close, so he obliged, letting her hot breath tease his skin.

"That was fantastic," she told him.

Ezra shoved himself into Morei's line of sight. "Is this *really* happening? Like really?" He sounded like a child who had just been given their first horse.

Laughing, the king turned to face Ezra fully. "As real as you want it to be."

And just like that, the night flooded them with music, food, and laughter. Morei called upon Daneka, happy to listen to her stories about Ezra when he was a boy. Daneka had the same coy smirk his mother would when she went off on him about something in his younger summers. He let her go on and on about stories that would have been boring to many, but not to the king.

Morei was so engrossed that he nearly punched the man who latched an iron grip on his arm. When he looked over, he saw the future king drunk.

"I can't even thank you *enough* for this."

The rest of the world came back—the conversations, music, all of it. It was deafeningly loud, and Morei spied Emerald's seat empty, Kiren deep into conversation with his men. Everyone looked happy for once, even Lord Polis with his flashy ring. He looked at the newest member of the Geral family. "Do you still have that sapphire I gave you?"

Ezra's eyes lit up. "Of course!" He dug into his pocket then and pulled out the small blue gemstone. "I always take it with me. A reminder, just like you said."

That made Morei smile. "Good. Your responsibilities and reputation just got a lot more important, Ezra. How's your practice coming along?"

The young man waved him off. "Practice, practice. I know. Look—"

Morei closed his hand around the Energy Harvester's and laughed. "Whoa, let's not, okay?" At Ezra's drunken expression, he added, "Remember, some things shouldn't be so openly publicized. Got it?"

The Energy Harvester sighed, disappointed, and stuffed the gemstone back into his pocket. "When I'm king, I'll make it a law that we don't judge people for their gifts." While the statement was innocuous, Morei still felt his heart drop at the mere thought that their plan might had been revealed to the whole world. But nobody had heard, all caught up in their own festivities. Even Daneka remained placid about the comment, choosing instead to take a drink of her wine and pat her son on the shoulder.

The king finished his wine and quickly switched seats, so that he could sit next to the lady of the night. "Your son is admirable for what he did."

Her face fell immediately, eyes hard.

Morei reached out and gently touched her hand to reassure her he was not going to drag her or anyone away for the murder of Ezra's father. "I've done things I'm not proud of either, Daneka," he quietly told her. At that, her expression softened. "We've all done things, but that doesn't make us bad people. It's all a matter of perspective, isn't it?"

The woman pursed her lips and lowered her eyes to his hand, where the black veins stretched across his skin in a ghastly fashion. The king didn't move his hand—there was no point in trying to hide the truth anymore. That had become obvious when he visited the city and saw the horrors of what the people thought. Surprisingly, she clasped his hand in both of her own. The hands of a mother—gentle but firm.

"Ezra speaks highly of you, Your Majes—"

"Call me Morei," he interjected. "Please."

Daneka smiled. "Morei," she breathed, and gave his hand a squeeze. "What you've given us is unrepayable. Ezra is all I have, and to see him so proud gives me purpose. So thank you. You will always have a place at my table."

The king was at a loss for words, so overwhelmed by her genuine kindness that all he could do was stare. Even after everything, she didn't care about who had said what or what had happened. Daneka saw him for who he was, a man trying to do the right thing. It was more than he could ever want.

Laying his other hand across hers, the king gave a firm squeeze and nodded. "Your words mean more to me than any amount of gold ever could. Thank you."

As the conversation returned to normal things, Morei took it as his sign to step away for a few. Most of the afternoon and evening had slipped by, and the king was feeling antsy for some silence. The noise was louder, it seemed, and the people more and more drunk as the night grew older. While he was thrilled that everyone was enjoying themselves and had temporarily forgotten about him, he was more than happy to slip away.

When the king had excused himself, he found not a single pair of eyes traced after him, and that was a relief.

Two soldiers stood on guard at the entrance of the dining hall. They greeted him as he passed, and Morei returned it. Out here, as his steps echoed across the marble, he smiled to himself. The noise inside was already growing distant, the music fainter. This was peace.

He only passed a handful of staff members as he wandered. They were either switching shifts or doing something for the festivities. Even the soldiers seemed at ease tonight. Those who had been a part of this morning's treacherous discovery had kept their word, and Morei was incredibly thankful for that. The last thing he wished to do was punish them.

Coming around the corner, Morei found himself at his quarters. The door stood there, inviting him in, and he happily obliged. The celebration could wait a little while longer for his return. Perhaps he would step out onto the patio with a drink. Enjoy the desert night before the fires were lit and the smells of the burning dead saturated the air. It would not be much time until he was no longer in that room anyways—he might as well as enjoy it while it was his.

Laying a hand on the cool handle, the king opened the door. And froze.

There, on the ground before him, lay Emerald. But it was not her horrified expression or wide eyes or even the supine position in which she lay that tore the air from his lungs. It was the blood.

There was so much blood.

The once-crimson dress was decorated in splotches of deep red where handprints had smeared, likely hers as she fumbled at what could have only been a stab wound to the chest. Blood still seeped freely from the wound, turning gold gems into bloodstained rubies, splattering the floor where she had fallen.

"It is so good to finally meet you," a voice acknowledged warmly from his right. The king spun to see a tall man standing next to his bed, using the top sheet to wipe clean the blade with which he had murdered Emerald. The blackened metal glimmered savagely from the lantern lights. He had already seen it in his dreams and heard of it in stories. It was the blade of Henry Junok.

The Demon Killer.

"Apologies for the mess," the man continued, flashing a smile. "I am usually quite clean about my kills, but she was a special one." The tan skin, eyes as dark as the night, and nearly black hair were unrecognizable to Morei. The man was dressed simply, as if he had come from the villages, in a loose-fitting black tunic and pants, but the belt on his hip was of high quality, and he carried himself like he had waited lifetimes for this moment.

The king found his tongue. "You've killed a queen. That's punishable by execution."

"And so is killing a commander, but here we are."

Now, he no longer felt like a king, hardly even sure of himself. This morning's images ravaged his mind at the mere mention of Boris and his gruesome death. Morei had been certain that it was only Sekar who was capable of such acts, but before him stood a man no older than thirty summers. A man, he realized, who had a well-thought-out plan.

Licking his lips, he became acutely aware of the voices whispering to him. The fire was within reach, but he would have to act fast. "You killed Boris?" he asked, hoping to buy some time. If he was going to execute a plan, he needed to know every single backup plan following that if things went wrong.

The man smirked and sheathed the Demon Killer. "There have been so many . . ." He tapped his finger almost playfully against his chin. "Was he—ah yes, your friend from this morning." It was meant as an insult, but Morei did not fall for it. "Such a curious man, but I'm sure you knew that, didn't you?"

He refused to play these games. "Who are you?" The door was open, he could yell, but he was certain this man was more powerful than he was letting on. It wasn't by luck he had come to possess the most wanted blade in Vorelian history. That weapon alone was powerful enough to crumble cities if the wielder knew how to use it.

With a tilt of his head, the man smiled. "Oh, come on now, don't be so dull." He stepped forward and peered at Emerald's body. "Such a pretty thing, you know, but I do like my ladies with a bit more—what's the word? *Fire.*"

"You've got my attention," Morei said. "But I'd suggest next time just setting up an appointment."

"That's the king I know," he complimented with a nod. "But I don't like that look in your eye."

Morei dropped to his knees without warning. Control evaporated from his body, and he felt his entire mind seized, like an army had just laid waste to his own home. Panic flared through him. The king had spent the last five summers training against this very thing, to recognize the signs and to be on the defense, but in an instant, he had become the very victim he was terrified to be.

"How . . ." Morei whispered. Even his tongue fought against him. The voices were hushed, shoved aside like they had been scolded. He was completely defenseless.

The man stood before him, relaxed. Not even a bead of sweat had sprouted on him, and his breathing was even, as if he were enjoying a leisurely conversation. Perhaps, from his perspective, he was.

"How can I summon energy without alerting anyone, you ask?" He laughed, but his eyes were cold. "I've spent lifetimes mastering that tactic, Morei."

If he could have spoken, he would have screamed. If he could have run, he would have. Panic molded into an icy terror that consumed him. Before him was no ordinary man. It felt like his entire life had come to this exact moment, as if he had been destined to be on his knees before the very thing he had once renounced so freely.

"Is it coming to you now?" Sekar inclined with a head tilt. "Are you putting it all together?" The God stepped closer until he knelt beside Emerald and brushed a strand from her face, almost delicately. "She was a thorn. I merely plucked her from your side."

"No," Morei hissed. Speaking that one word took an immense amount of strength, but he sensed it was exactly what the God wanted.

Sekar met him at eye level. "Do not spare me your feelings for her. She was a nobody, and in five summers, she will be nothing more than a dwindling thought." Standing, he closed the gap between them and latched a hand onto Morei's throat, forcing his eyes upward. "You were in love with the idea of her, but not her. You were so desperate to find acceptance that you were willing to put aside your morals for her. What does that say about you, hm?"

The king's neck strained at this angle, but it was not in his control to fight. He couldn't do anything but behold the Dark Lord for exactly what he was—evil.

"A king of no one," Sekar continued with a sneer. "That is what this city has made you, and deep down, you know that. The people have rejected you, your own council can't stand the sight of you, and your precious new heir will abandon you once he is sure of himself." Tightening his grip around Morei's throat, he squeezed the last bit of air he had in his lungs out. "So why do you keep denying your path, Demon King?"

Morei couldn't spare the strength to speak, choosing instead to try and save what little air he could manage. Already, his lungs were burning. Before this God, he felt helpless. Before Sekar, he was a nobody.

"You know exactly what you want to do, and all the while, you've been fighting so hard to deny it. But you and I both know you can't keep fighting it. And you know why?" Sekar leaned in closer, keeping his eyes locked on the king. "Because Destiny always has her way."

At that, the God shoved Morei aside like he weighed nothing. He landed hard on his shoulder, his head knocking against the marble with a sharp pain. The sight in front of him was no longer of Sekar, but of the queen's ghastly expression. She had died in absolute terror, and no matter how hard he tried to move, to stand up, he couldn't. His body would not obey.

A fog teased the edges of mind, slowly at first but then faster, stronger. The force was unnatural and suffocated all his thoughts, even his emotions. Numbness overpowered him, and with a blank stare, the king watched Emerald as she fell from his vision.

The last thing he saw was Sekar's boots, polished with a sickly gleam.

FEVERED AND HUNTED

Syra was spotted by Roman first. His yell alerted the others. Sekar had been telling the truth—they were okay. Scratched up, but alive. The storm above rumbled with a threatening tune, not done yet, but for now, the rain had ceased. Her boots sank into mud as she stumbled into their line of sight. The stench of rain was thick. Her skin was on fire, her head pounding.

It was already starting.

The conversation with the God, the man she had come to know, captured her thoughts. Words repeated over and over in her head. *The Gods want you dead.* She couldn't shake it, and the more time that passed, the more she regretted turning away Sekar's protection. If the Gods truly wanted her dead, a God by her side felt like the most appropriate response. The energy bond would alert him if she was in grave danger, but it might not be enough.

She couldn't leave them, though. As they ran toward her, Zarek shouted something that was lost in the wind. Behind her, the city of Raveer was under attack. Yalana was having her way, and nobody could stop her. Smoke rose in the air, and screams echoed. The distant crash of breaking stone traveled across the rolling hill and met her ears, but she couldn't look back.

As they neared, she could see everyone was nearly dried from the earlier rain, but most importantly, they were alright. Syra's knees buckled, and she collapsed into the mud and grass, bracing her fall with her hands. A sob broke from her lips.

They were alive. She was alive.

A strong hand pulled her up. It was Zarek. His other hand pinched her chin and forced her eyes up to his. "What did he do to you?" It was the first question out of his mouth, but he asked it as if he already knew the answer. The finality in his words beckoned more tears.

"Let's get her on the horse," Roman insisted. "She can't stand on her own."

"Hey, fierce warrior," Zane acknowledged gently. He touched her cheek, but his touch was frigid to her, and she shied away. "You okay?"

"No, she's not," Zarek snapped. "Let's hold off on questions." The Guardian nudged her forward, keeping an arm wrapped around her to keep her up. Syra's legs wobbled weakly as she walked, but she was grateful for the support. All she wanted was to close her eyes. If she could only rest, then she would feel better.

The steeds were staked to the ground to prevent them from running. Roman's sword had been shoved into the soil, the reins tied around the handguard. If the horses spooked, they'd surely take the sword with them, but for the time, it had worked, as they remained stationary. All except for Uyul, who stood next to the three tied steeds and flicked her midnight-black tail.

Syra was led over to Uyul, but before she could protest, Zarek spoke up quietly. "She's offered to carry you. It's easier this way. You are in no shape to steer a horse." As he said so, Uyul knelt down, so that it was easier to get on the creature's back. Zane untied the reins of the other steeds while Roman sheathed his sword. It was time to move.

Zarek helped her up, practically hoisting her by the waist. The dark leather saddle protected her legs and bottom from the bony structure. She started to shake from the chill that clung to her bones as she reached for the knob on the front of Uyul's saddle. "Okay," she mumbled, and looked over at Zarek.

He was staring at her.

Slowly, he reached forward and grabbed her left wrist, sliding the cloak back. Nothing, but he was not satisfied, and reached for her right hand. Syra let him have it, knowing she couldn't hide it. He slid the cloak back, and the breath caught in the back of his throat. He ran a thumb over the raised, dark gray scar, the skin tender to his touch.

But as quick as he revealed the Zyulë Bond, he let the cloak down and gave her hand back. Zarek met her eyes once more but did not speak a word. He didn't have to. Syra could understand everything he was conveying. The Eternal Flame, the ritual, the Gods—he wanted to know if it had happened. If she had been judged and deemed to serve Chaos, or Mother, as Sekar had so warmly referred to the force. Slowly, she gave the slightest of nods, not trusting her tongue.

His eyes flashed over to Uyul in what she could only imagine was a conversation between the two. If she'd felt wittier, she would have given him a hard time for not telling her what he was thinking, but she couldn't.

Zarek took off his cloak and rested it over Syra, revealing his black leather armor underneath. The cloak was twice her size and engulfed her like a blanket, already hot from the Guardian's wear. Grateful, she hunkered down in it and smiled at Zarek.

He patted her leg. "If anything feels out of the ordinary, tell me." He didn't need to explain himself.

Before more could be said, Zarek turned around and clapped. "Alright, let's get this going, shall we? I want several leagues between me and this place by the time the moon shows her face, got it?"

Uyul made to stand, and Syra reached for the knob on the saddle again to keep her balance. There was so much conversation to be had, but she was relieved that Zarek had not requested information from her. Even talking sounded like a strenuous activity, so she remained silent. Once Uyul was standing, the beast started her trek over to Zarek, who had jumped on Hazel. The horse took well to him, and without further hesitation, they were all trekking forward.

"Roman, what's our timeline?" the Guardian asked. He gestured Hazel closer, so that he and Syra could walk side by side.

The man cleared his throat. "Given the progress we've made, we should be on the outskirts of the Mourale Mountains in five days. The Infernol would be about a three day's trek in."

"We need to travel harder," Zarek stated. "Eight days is too long."

"Agreed." There was no further discussion. If anyone was wanting to argue the point, they didn't speak up. They were already risking a lot by traveling in the daylight, but they didn't have a choice in the matter.

Syra let her body sway to Uyul's movements. She kept her eyes locked ahead on the horizon, here a faint outline of mountainous structures was visible. Five days. That was all. Once they were in the trees and out of public eye, she would feel better. They just had to get there.

Her eyes drifted closed several times, but she fought it. She was extremely comfortable riding horses, but Uyul was a different beast, and that made her nervous. Even as she tried to keep herself awake, though, slumber teased her, and eventually she gave in.

* * *

"Syra!" The jolt to her body startled her awake, and she blinked. Her body was slouched over Uyul, and she straightened immediately. Her muscles ached, and her hand tingled from having fallen asleep at an angle against the saddle. Wiping her eyes, she glanced around, but she didn't need an explanation for the firmness in Zarek's voice.

Riders were coming toward them from behind. Riders who were dressed in bones and skull heads, with swords strapped to their hips and braids. Their steeds' nostrils flared, and they shouted a triumphant call. Her jaw went slack, and her heart sank.

Tribal hunters.

They had come after all.

"Don't run," Zarek warned everyone. He halted Hazel, and Uyul followed immediately.

Zane spun around on his horse and motioned at the oncoming tribe. "We can't just do nothing—"

"Don't run," the guardian hissed, his voice hot with agitation. He glared at Zane. "Tribal hunters have a philosophy—if their target runs, they die. If we don't put up a fight, they'll simply take us back to their tribe and we will be sold."

Zane snorted and glanced between them and the dozen hunters. "*Simply?* Is this a pastime for you?"

Zarek smirked. "I've had my fair share of experience, Commander."

The pounding of the hooves against the ground was growing in strength as the tribal hunters neared. Syra was weak, her heart racing, and not just in panic at their situation. It felt like her heart might burst from her chest and run off. Forcing a deep breath in, she wiped at her brow. Her hand came away with a fine layer of perspiration, but she was freezing, even with two cloaks.

The clanking of bones met her ears as the tribal hunters came upon them. Roman backed his horse up until the steed's back end brushed against Uyul. He looked over at Syra, and she nodded. There was no way out of this one. Four against twelve meant Syra would have to put up a fight against three of these hunters, and in her current state, that wouldn't last more than an instant, which meant the remaining three would be up against four each. That would only be successful if they could put a fight up like a Guardian.

No. They couldn't do it. It would be a direct way to meet Death herself if they tried fighting their way out of this one.

One tribal hunter, whom she assumed to be the leader, raised his hand, and the rest of the members stopped in their tracks. Their leader had long, dark, braided hair that was decorated with gold rings, and he donned a large skull as a helmet. Two horns jutted from the sides and curled around, while the man's face was encompassed in the mouth of the skull. A pair of incisors pointed upward from the lower jaw. He wore tattered tan pants that to Syra looked intentionally destroyed. A bow and arrow was strapped around his torso, followed by five different strands that held various-sized bones in place of a proper shirt. Two swords were strapped to his hip, along with a dagger.

The others bore similar items, but none wore a horned skull like he did.

Roman dropped a hand to his sword, and their leader saw. Syra watched as the man gestured his horse closer, also decorated with bones. "You," he acknowledged, his accent thick. "Do you have a death wish?"

Slowly, Roman lowered his hand, but Syra saw a muscle in his jaw tick. "Just didn't expect company," he replied.

Their leader smiled, smug. "We've been tracking you for the last day. Where are you heading?"

"We're bypassing Raveer," Zarek interjected. "I'm assuming you saw the attack on the city." It was not a question, but the Guardian did not offer more information. Syra bit her tongue. The tribe leader looked dissatisfied.

"A Guardian, two men, and"—his eyes flashed to Syra—"a woman. Care to explain?"

"No." Zarek's answer came out so quick that their leader had hardly finished the question.

"Hm." The man sat in silence, and nobody else in the group moved a muscle. The only noise was that of the steeds' breath. Syra could taste the tension in the air—it was bitter on her tongue. She was growing anxious, and she saw Zane fidget. But Zarek remained as still as a statue, his expression placid. Uyul's ears flicked.

"There's a bounty," their leader finally said, letting the words draw out slow. "For a woman"—he settled his eyes directly on Syra, and her breath caught—"who escaped Caster for her crime of theft and disobeying royal order. Treason. You wouldn't happen to know anything about that, would you?"

Syra swallowed, her answer barely above a whisper. "No."

The tribal leader nodded. "Tie them up!" The order was followed by half the hunters descending from their steeds and removing ropes from the saddles. Syra followed Zarek, who remained motionless on Hazel, even as two men approached. It was bizarre watching them restrain a Guardian—they treated him like he was nothing special, as if they had come across countless Guardians in their hunts. They undid his belt and took his weapon, draping it over one of their horses.

Then they grabbed her. Syra turned her hands downward and clutched the cloak's sleeves to protect the scar from being seen. She didn't know their level of knowledge, but she couldn't take any risk. If they were this comfortable around a Guardian with his beast-like steed, then they may very well recognize the unique mark on her skin.

The hunter glared at her with brown eyes and then tied the rope around her wrists. He spared no mercy when tightening it, and she was relieved for the fabric that separated the rope from her skin. Without it, she had no doubt her skin would have been rubbed raw. When he was done, he reached around and unsnapped her belt. "A Guardian's belt and sword," he remarked, and looked at her again. "Did you steal it?"

Syra gaped at him. "Do you take me as a thief?"

He shrugged and threw the belt over his shoulder, but it was the kind of shrug that made Syra cringe. "Are you not well?" The question was cold, even as he motioned at the additional cloak.

The last thing she wanted to do was confess her poor health. "I'm fine, just chilled from the rains."

The hunter eyed her but didn't question more as he walked back toward his horse. Roman and Zane had been tied and their weapons removed. The only thing they could be dreaming of doing was jumping their steeds and run, but that would be an outrageous attempt. Even if they happened to land on their feet and get a head start, they would be sourly outmatched against galloping horses.

Once everyone was restrained, two hunters took rope and tied the group's steeds to their own to keep them from running. Uyul didn't protest as a rope went around her black bridal and was secured to a steed that was smaller than her.

"Ready?" the leader asked as the hunters ascended their horses. When everyone nodded, the man grinned. "Good. We're four days from home. Let's make it three, got it?"

In unison, the tribe nodded and shouted in agreement. Syra took a deep breath as the group steered to the left and off their path toward the Mourale Mountains. Now rolling hills lay ahead. The storm roared, and a raindrop struck Syra's cheek, cold. She was certainly in no place to pray, but she still did silently. Although she was certain now that prayers meant nothing.

When she was done, she looked over to see Zarek watching. He raised an eyebrow and dropped his gaze to her wrists, acknowledging her sleeve trick. Then he turned his face ahead and didn't engage anymore.

Taking a look around her, Syra noted the four horses guiding theirs were ahead with four behind, one on each side, and their leader taking the lead with the remaining members. That had to be the Energy Harvester, she noted. He had the white horse and blond, braided hair. There was no way to confirm without asking, but she was going to make the assumption. It would only be appropriate for the Energy Harvester to pair up with the leader, much like how a chancellor and king worked together.

The headache had yet to cease, but all she could do was think about their situation. If they arrived wherever this tribe was located, they might be separated, which would put them at risk of being killed, sold off for Krye, or tortured and killed. She was certain the ruler knew who she was, based on his tone, but Syra wasn't about to ask. If they could stay together, they had a better shot at getting out of this alive.

Despite her pestering exhaustion and fever, Syra could not rest. All she could do was think of every possible scenario and how wrong it could all go. It felt impossible that they would get everyone out alive, but she scolded herself for thinking such a thing. She, Roman, Zane and others had made it off the Raveerian ship with an Onye on board. Sure, circumstances were a bit different, but they had nonetheless made it out alive.

They would again. They had to. Syra saw no other option.

DEALS WITH
THE UNDEAD

Cyrus didn't wait to see if anyone followed him as he traversed through the halls to the door that led into the tunnels. By the time he reached it, he was certain not a soul was following, and it was better that way. Rosarie's small frame was nowhere to be seen, not even when he passed the statues of the Gods. Yet as he passed the deities, he couldn't help but feel their scrutinizing gaze follow him, judging his actions with disappointment. This was not what a man should be doing, sneaking around and preparing to steal valuable items right underneath a king's nose, no less a Dragon Rider.

At this point, Cyrus was getting really good at running. It felt natural, easy, and he no longer felt the same remorse as he had bolting from Diemon, Geral, or even Evander's. Then again, nobody was dead this time either. That surely made a difference.

Until otherwise noted, Sozar would not move from his spot in the courtyard. The dragon would wait, patiently and quietly, so as not to draw any unwanted attention. To the unknowing, he was simply sunbathing, but the dragon had tucked underneath his chest the basic leather that they'd used to fly across the Ashen Sea. Once they were out of Razan's reach, Cyrus would strap it on so that he could fly more comfortably.

He did a double take behind him to ensure no one was following before he slipped through the door and shut it with a soft thud. Cyrus took a deep breath, inhaling the thick scent of mold and moisture. He reached over and grabbed a lantern off its hook. It was already lit. Odd. The tunnels were in terrible shape and as far as he knew, no one else came down here. A lit lantern indicated he wasn't the only one exploring underneath the city.

It was just like last time: dark, damp, and isolated. He took two steps at a time, and the air cooled immensely as he descended farther. This time, he thought, he was alone, without Zorya for company.

Desperation nagged him like a fly. He nearly tripped down the stairs and face planted on the wet stone beneath him three times, only saving himself by the slimmest chance of luck, for he did not believe the Gods were with him now. Once he reached the bottom, he bolted. It was risky, running with a light that was being choked out by the overbearing darkness around him. But his patience was fried, and his need to get to these eggs and get as far away from Razan as possible had a stronger hold over him. The Rider's Sword and sack bounced off his legs as he ran, the cloak billowing behind him.

He came upon the chamber and stopped. Cyrus heaved for breath, only halting long enough to force air into his lungs to stop them from screaming. After a moment, he turned right and ran.

Between the slamming of his boots against stone, the water grew louder, until he was certain it was just to his left. Cyrus didn't risk looking. One wrong step and he might trip and shatter the only light he had.

Cyrus saw a door out of the corner of his eye, and he skidded to a stop. Swinging around, he blinked and approached. It was the door from his dream. On the stone floor, like last time, the Old Vore sigil of death glared.

His breaths came out ragged as he grabbed the door handle and opened it. Had he closed this door when he and Zorya had bolted out of here? He couldn't recall, and it didn't matter.

As the door swung open smoothly, he stopped. There they were. The eggs. Just as he had left them last time, nestled quietly in their chest, the lid closed. *That* he remembered. He had shut the lid as he marched out, determined to get answers with the princess following closely behind.

Cyrus let a pent-up breath out and took several steps forward before he stopped again. Someone was breathing behind him.

Without thinking, Cyrus swung around to face the intruder. Nobody there.

Heart slamming against his chest, he stared. His legs felt heavy, his hands clammy. The lantern was slick from his own nerves, so he tightened his grip.

Sozar's presence breached his frenzied thoughts. *Are you alright?*

I'm fine. Cyrus swallowed down his fear. *I just thought I heard someone behind me.*

The mental link they shared fluctuated with concern so thick, it made his own heart skip a beat. *Are you sure you weren't followed?*

Yeah—I mean, no one was there when I entered the tunnels.

Hm. The dragon's simple response didn't ease the tension building in his shoulders. *Keep me near, hatchling. Are the eggs okay?*

Yes. At that, Cyrus turned around to face the chest once more, and closed the gap. At the podium, he lifted the lid to reveal the two silver eggs, humming with life. The energy emanating from them was stronger than last time, as if his very presence was awakening them.

Cautiously, he reached forward with his free hand to touch one. He needed to *feel* they were safe. Seeing was one thing, but maybe this was all an illusion, and they weren't here at all.

The entire room went still as he laid a hand on the first egg. It was warm to the touch, alive. Cyrus let out a shaky laugh, relieved. Caught up in his own thoughts, he had felt like it was a race to get down here first. He had been racing the Gods, Dameon, the king, and Destiny herself. Feeling the life pulse underneath his hand put his thoughts at ease. The pandemonium he had created with his presence here suddenly melted away. None of it mattered anymore.

The echo of boots caught his attention, and he whirled around. A man raised his hands and smiled. He was dressed in a red cloak that was etched with black sigils Cyrus couldn't decipher. The man was hairless, his pale skin glistening with a ghostly glow in the dim light, but upon his skin were countless red tattoos—all which looked to be copies of the sigils stitched into the fabric. Ice-blue eyes stared back at him, and for a brief moment, a familiarity tugged at the back of Cyrus's mind, but he shoved it off. Before him stood a stranger.

Sozar's growl just about took Cyrus to his knees with its intensity, even through their mental link. The dragon felt ready to explode and destroy the entire palace.

No. Cyrus spoke up quickly before Sozar could move or give away their position. *Don't do anything. I can handle myself against one man.*

You are in danger, the dragon snapped. *And you don't know who he is.*

Cyrus stared at the stranger. He appeared to have no weapon, but that didn't mean one couldn't be hidden beneath the robe's fabric. He might even be an Energy Harvester. *I want to hear what he has to say.*

Besides, this was his chance. For once, he felt in control, even standing before this threat.

The man took a step forward, but Cyrus put up a hand, and he stopped. "Who are you?" Cyrus asked, his voice firm, which surprised even himself.

Hands still up, the man spoke gently. "I am an observer of history, that is all. And you"—he gestured at Cyrus—"must be the Dragon Rider."

I don't like him, Sozar commented.

Give me a moment. At his request, the dragon subsided, but he could still feel Sozar's presence like an itch behind his ear.

"How did you get down here without me hearing?" Cyrus pressed.

"You were running pretty hard," the man answered. "It was easy to follow." Before Cyrus could reply, he added, "I am not here as your enemy. Quite the opposite actually."

"That's what they all say," he replied coldly.

The man took another step forward, and this time, Cyrus dropped a hand on the Rider's Sword. "Easy," the man assured. "I've already seen the eggs. If I had wanted to take them before you came back, I would have."

Cyrus narrowed his eyes but didn't take his hand off the pommel. It was already unclipped, the sword ready at the slightest threat. He needed to protect these eggs at all costs, but he was curious to what the stranger had to say. "What do you want?"

"Please, call me Leonzo." With a nod, the corner of his lip tugged upward. "As I said," he began, and side-stepped away from the doorway. It gave Cyrus an out if he needed. "If I had wanted to take the eggs, I could have done it before you arrived here in Razan, but I didn't."

"Why?" Cyrus interjected. This stranger had been here before he arrived. Perhaps he was the one who had lit the lanterns.

Leonzo gave him a sympathetic look. "I can't talk to you if you don't let me, no?" He took another step toward the eggs. "I knew the eggs were here about ten summers ago, but knew they were safer down here than in the open," he explained. "And besides, I don't have the blood of a Dragon Rider. I would merely be putting them at risk by taking them from here." The man sighed and slowly dropped his hands. "I've waited for you,

Cyrus. That is the truth—isn't that what you want to hear? Hm." A small smile crossed his face. "You aren't the first of your kind, but you are the first nonetheless."

"I don't understand," Cyrus whispered. His heart had slowed to almost a stop. Somehow, this man also knew Dameon and Ashtir existed.

"Apologies," Leonzo told him, now close enough to reach out and touch. He stood at Cyrus's height. "It's been a long time since I was in the presence of someone as extraordinary as yourself." His blue eyes dropped to the eggs and then rose again. "Your lineage is what makes you unique."

Cyrus scoffed, unable to help himself. "I was orphaned, abandoned—I'm sorry, who are you? And don't give me a drawn-out explanation about waiting or history. I get it, you're thrilled to be here."

The man didn't flinch at his tone, instead resting a hand on the podium. "Your animosity is understandable, given how the world has treated you thus far." He looked around, as if he were taking in the chamber for the first time. "Vorelians aren't the same as they used to be. They've grown fearful of the very ground they walk on. A shame, really." Leonzo took a deep breath then. "I used to be a king, but not in the sense of Kyllian. I was more than that, but the world wasn't ready for me then. Patience is a virtue, no?" he finished with a chuckle.

Cyrus nodded, although he wasn't entirely sure what he meant and didn't care enough to ask. "Wonderful. Now let's take a step back. What do you know about me or my family?"

"Ah, where to begin." Leonzo drummed his fingers against the stone, filling the silence between them. "Your mother was kind, gentle even, but her spirit was fierce. She got herself in trouble quite often, but she knew how to talk her way out of it." Leonzo's eyes twinkled. "To some, she was considered a witch, but properly, she was an Energy Harvester. Your father . . ."

He trailed off, letting his eyes wander back to the eggs. "I don't know who your father was, but I know that it destroyed your mother to abandon you."

A lump rose in the back of his throat, but Cyrus refused to let it show. He was overcome with a dozen different emotions that he hadn't been ready to deal with. "How do you know about her?"

Leonzo smiled. "She was the only one who showed me kindness when others abandoned me." He closed the gap between them. It felt as if he were in the presence of a friend rather than a stranger. "I know what it feels like to be abandoned, Cyrus. I know how lonely it can feel. For the longest time, I didn't have anyone to lean on, like you have with your dragon. But when I showed up on her doorstep, near death, she took me in and gave me a place to heal. I owe my life to her."

Cyrus forced a swallow down, finding his voice. "Why now? Why tell me this?"

"To show I am not your enemy, but your ally."

All he wanted was to hear more about his family, his mother—this had been the one thing he begged for all his life. Now, the opportunity was before him, but it was overshadowed by the obvious. "What do you want?" Wariness itched at his skin. It had been so long since he could trust anyone that he wasn't sure he knew how anymore.

The man smiled warmly. "To give you a path." Leonzo lifted his hand from the podium and rested it on the silver egg. "I know you can't harvest energy. I've known since the day you were conceived that your life would be extremely difficult. I can help you unravel the secrets that bind you—that keep you from your true potential."

Cyrus stared, unsure of what to say. His heart was beating so loud in his chest, he was certain Leonzo could hear. Sozar had gone intensely quiet through their mental link, as if he too was afraid to move. Even the water from the tunnel sounded leagues away.

"Before you were conceived, there were things that would happen during your mother's pregnancy—I was still around at the time. She didn't share it with anyone except me, because I am an Energy Harvester, with knowledge on ancient practices. These things that were happening were because of you." Leonzo sighed before pulling his hand away from the egg. Cyrus held his breath, afraid the sound might shatter this moment. The entire world had ceased.

"We knew that you were a risky pregnancy, but she was committed to carrying you through—mothers are extraordinary creatures, aren't they? Even when faced with death, they will do anything for their children." He laughed, but it sounded heavy. "When you were conceived, your mother wanted nothing more than to protect you. Your blood was rich with power—so much that it nearly killed her—and she knew that if she didn't do something, that power would consume you. It would ruin the purity of your childhood and distort your view on the world. Are you following, Cyrus?"

Numbly, he nodded.

"In order to keep you safe, we had to conduct a ritual that would bind the energy that burned in your blood. But your mother refused any energy bond—she wanted to give you a fresh chance at life, and a bond would mean you still had that power, but it would be constantly controlled. More importantly, you would be chained to her. We couldn't risk that, not when we didn't know our future. So we had to bind your power to a curse that would limit your chance of harvesting and, in so many words, extinguish the fire altogether."

Leonzo inhaled deeply. "But the least expected thing happened—you became a Dragon Rider." A noise escaped the back of his throat. "And you have become far more important than anyone was prepared for. It seems destiny always knows how to get her way."

Cyrus licked his lips, confused and angry. The truth wasn't what he wanted to hear, and as he spoke, his mouth was incredibly dry. "You damned me to be this victim," he whispered. "Damned me to be some pathetic Dragon Rider—"

"Your damnation became your salvation," Leonzo cut in, tone cold. "I am here to tell you that the curse can be undone, but only if you want what I have to offer. What your mother wanted was to protect you—that was the only goal she had, but as hard as she fought to keep you from all the madness, you still managed to get right in the middle of it all."

Sozar's presence stirred, and Cyrus felt a strong wave of sympathy wash over him from the dragon. He was finally getting the answers he wanted, but everything came at a cost, it seemed. "So," he exhaled, and rubbed a hand over his face. "What now?"

"These eggs . . ." Leonzo motioned at the two. "I can hatch them, but I cannot raise them alone. They need a mentor, a safe place, and that is you and your dragon." Meeting his gaze, he smiled, almost playful. "Don't you want to give them a chance?"

Cyrus stared. He wanted nothing more than to give these dragons a chance at life. They had been locked away in their shells for too many summers, and it was no longer an option of when they would hatch, but how. He felt possessive of them in ways he could not describe, and it manifested into an obligation to see them thrive under his watchful gaze. "I want nothing more than that," he confessed. "But they will not be weapons to the war ahead."

"Of course not," Leonzo agreed. "You will have the final say on their upbringing, but they are intelligent creatures, as you know. They will make their own decisions when the time comes, and that may not be what you want. Are you prepared for that?"

They will have me, Sozar chimed in before Cyrus could reply. *I will show them everything I know.*

He tore his eyes from the man to look upon the two eggs. *Sozar, what do you want?*

The dragon was silent, his emotions withdrawn from their bond. Heartbeats passed, and Cyrus was increasingly aware that Leonzo was still watching them, but he wanted the dragon's opinion, so he waited patiently.

We have an obligation, Sozar finally said. *And that is to ensure the future of our kind have a chance. You have an obligation to yourself, hatchling, and this is your chance to get the answers to everything you wanted. Don't you owe it to yourself to learn who you really are?*

I'll be able to protect them, Cyrus added. *But what of Dameon and Ashtir?*

Destiny showed us them for a reason, the dragon answered, *but I do not think it was because we were meant to accept their offer.*

Affirmed, Cyrus looked back to Leonzo. The man still stood there, but he no longer felt like a stranger. There was warmth to his eyes, and while they still had that familiarity, they no longer scared him. Everything about this moment suddenly felt intentional, as if he had always been always meant to come here, no matter what he had done previously. This was true purpose. This was his decision. And he knew what he wanted.

"If we lift this curse—"

"When," Leonzo corrected.

"When we lift this curse," Cyrus softly replied. "Will you help me"—he licked his lips—"harvest energy?"

Gently, Leonzo placed a hand on Cyrus's shoulder, just like a father would a son, and smiled. "I'll teach you everything I know."

That was what he wanted to hear. More than anything. Not only did he have a purpose—a chance to protect these dragons—but he would be given a true chance to become the Dragon Rider he deserved to be. Everything his life had been this last

456

season—the run, the fight, the desperation—it had all come down to this. Things happened for a reason, and perhaps this was the reason all along.

Squaring his shoulders, Cyrus looked Leonzo straight in the eyes. "Then I'm prepared."

THE DEATH OF PEACE

Something nudged the king's shoulder, cautiously at first, before it turned into an aggressive shake. Morei stirred, his head aching from the impact of his fall, followed by his sore shoulder. As he came around and blinked, he saw that he was no longer staring at Emerald or the blood on her dress, but Peter.

The chancellor was as white as a ghost. If his wide expression didn't tear the king out of the fog, it was the ten soldiers, Lord Jire, and Kiren. Their faces were stuck in an appalled expression, and when Morei sat up, he felt his left hand wrapped around something sturdy. When he dropped his eyes to see what it was, horror filled him, and he released the bloodied dagger as quickly as he could. It clanged against the marble with a deafening noise.

Everything came down around him. The walk, Sekar, the Demon Killer, the debilitation as the God had seized his mind and body as if he were no more powerful than a commoner. It all hit him like he had been the one stabbed, and he began to hyperventilate, dragging himself away from the queen's dead body. The sensation of loss of control overwhelmed him, and he grabbed at his neck, certain he would still feel the God's claws around his throat. But there was nothing there, and as his back struck the wall, his eyes searched the surrounding people in desperation.

The faces all glared at him.

"It was . . ." Morei cleared his throat, finding his voice dry. "It was Sekar. He was here. I found him standing over there." He motioned with his chin toward the bed. "He had the Demon Killer, and he—"

Emotions unlike anything he had ever felt bombarded him. The king had swallowed everything in his terror when facing the God, but now that it was all coming back to him, he felt like he was reliving the moment in full clarity. Memories consumed one another, and he saw his murdered parents before him once more. It was the blood he would never forget—the true horror that had engulfed him at the scene when his entire life had shattered. Right here, he felt like a little child, weak, defenseless, as if he were nothing more than a bystander in his own life.

And just like before, everyone looked at him as if he were the culprit, as if he had taken the knife and thrust it into the heart of the queen himself. "Sekar put the knife in my hand," he quickly explained. "I don't own that blade." When they didn't react, not even the chancellor, panic flared. "Look at it! It is a commoner's blade. Why would I own—"

"Enough!" The intensity of Peter's voice shut the king up. It was not normal for the chancellor to yell, let alone raise his voice, but when Morei looked upon the large man, he did not see compassion or understanding. Only anger.

The chancellor took a massive breath. Kiren looked like he might explode, his cheeks flush with rage, his jaw working like he was preparing a long speech. But it was again Peter who spoke, his voice so low that the king hardly recognized the man before him. "I have put my neck out for you for so long. Over and over, I protected you, but this"—he pointed at Emerald—"I cannot and will not protect you from. You are sick, but you are far worse than I ever anticipated."

"A monster!" Kiren screeched. The commander lunged forward, only caught by the surrounding Geral soldiers, who held him back with struggle. "She trusted you, and you killed her like some monster."

Betrayal bubbled up in the back of the king's throat. "This was Sekar. I promise! I swear upon my life I would never raise a hand against her—she, you, you all were leaving tomorrow." Morei slowly stood, keeping his back pressed against the wall. Next to him, the table that held his sheathed sword lay, as if to mock him. "The Gods are real, okay? I looked Sekar right in the eye, and he did something to my head, took control over me—"

"Do not blame the Dark Lord for your actions," Kiren snapped, still restrained. "Have some courage and be a man. You did this."

Morei fumbled for his words, trying to figure out a way for them all to understand this was not him. This was divine intervention, a God screwing with the king's life like it was some game and he was now sitting back, waiting for the show to start. As he tried to put some thoughts together, the chancellor spoke.

"You can either come willingly, or I will have to order these men to detain you. The choice is yours, but do not let me regret giving it to you when it is so clear to me now that you deserve nothing less than rotting in a dungeon cell."

Those words knocked him out of his shock. Everything he had come to know, every feeling he had ever felt, all shushed as cold resolve washed over him. He finally saw these people for exactly who they were.

"No."

The answer made every man in that room tense, and it was exactly what he wanted. Peter licked his lips. "Morei, don't do this."

He reached over and grabbed his belt with the sword—a sword with a family name he would never rightfully belong to again—and hooked it around his hips. "And why is that, Chancellor? Afraid I might do something terrible?" A smile teased at his lips. Never had he felt so certain, so resolved, as he did now. "I've fought tooth and nail to be the king you all wanted me to be. It was my purpose to protect you all, but you never wanted that. From the moment I took that throne, you all wanted me to fail. Congratulations—you will get the monster you so desperately needed me to be."

Before any of them could react, Morei summoned the Dark Energy that had been begging to play since he had awoken. The flames in the lanterns that hung through his chamber flared with life, shattering the glass that encased them. Soldiers flinched and reached for their weapons, letting Kiren go. The commander bolted for the king, a maddened expression contorting his face. But just as Kiren reached for his sword, Morei let the fire have him. It started in his stomach, forcing the commander to twist from the pain and stumble to a halt. Taking two steps forward, Morei grabbed the man around his throat and yanked him closer. Face red, the king smiled as Kiren's organs began to be consumed by a starved force.

"I never liked you," Morei spat, and dropped him to the ground. A scream erupted from his lips, music to the king's ears.

The voices were chanting, thrilled, and he was pleased to give them another soul. Glancing at the frozen Geral soldiers, he regarded them with their swords half drawn, and then he looked upon the chancellor. They were afraid of him, as they should be. If they were smart enough, they would know that no metal could protect them. With Dark Energy, Morei could burn them all alive with a flick of his wrist.

"If I were you," Morei said, keeping is eyes locked on the chancellor. "I would choose your next words very carefully, Chancellor."

Peter stood there, as if frozen by some force, eyes wide. His mouth hung open, dumbfounded, before snapping shut.

Morei nodded. "Good." Stepping forward, he passed the soldiers, acutely aware that they could lash out at the faintest opportunity, but they didn't. They wouldn't. Some of these men had been on the battlefield the day the king called upon Dark Energy for the first time. And all of them knew the stories of the charred bodies and scorched land where the fire had touched.

He would do it again if they dared to lift a hand against him.

"Take care of Ezra," Morei called as he exited the chamber. "He's going to need it after tonight."

Because he was far from done. If Geral wanted a show, a reason to hate him, he would give it. He was done ignoring the signs, swallowing the rumors and turning a blind eye in hopes that the citizens would one day forgive him for being . . . him. Tonight made it clear that that would never happen. The people had taken advantage of him, betrayed his trust, and stolen his purpose. They had done so the moment he had taken the throne, but it had taken a season for him to finally come to terms with it all. And with himself.

Morei was tired of being someone he wasn't.

NO GOOD DEED SHALL GO UNPUNISHED

The tribal leader was Rül, as Syra had come to find out on their travels. The Energy Harvester was known as Grim, although she was certain that wasn't his real name. They had stayed close, even when the tribe had stopped for the evening and set up a makeshift camp. Several fires were lit using wood that the tribesmen carried on their horses, and they even caught a few rabbits with Grim's help. It wasn't enough to feed sixteen people, but they had passed the rabbits around and offered the meat as more of a dessert to their dried foods. When it came to the four of them, the tribesmen tore off several pieces and fed the meat to them before passing the rabbits along. It had been dry and chewy, unsatisfying.

Roman, Zane, Syra, and Zarek were sitting next to one of the fires, their hands bound and their legs crossed. They had been allowed to go to the bathroom only once, and that was not a situation Syra wished to repeat. Her mouth was dry, her muscles ached, and her fever raged. The flames danced with animated moves, and she was half certain she was hallucinating at one point, but she could not take her eyes off the fire.

The tribesmen talked to each other. Some laughed, and others were making bets, but Rül and Grim kept their heads down, discussing something apart from the rest of the group. Syra could see them between the dancing flames—they had hardly moved since sitting down.

Moisture still clung to the air, the humidity thick, but the clouds had cleared for the evening, sparing the group from any more rain.

Syra was baffled at the length of her day. Even in her compromised state, she couldn't help but relive everything in as much detail as she could. This morning, she had awoken in some sort of dream state and wandered out of Joshua's barn. Frankly, she didn't know when fiction became reality or if it all had been real from the moment she opened her eyes. What she did know was that she had befriended a God, and not just any God, but the Dark Lord himself. Sekar may want to claim ancient titles, but to her and to Drügalism, he has always been the God of Darkness, and she wasn't entirely sure how to cope with that.

Syra had finally met a God, but at a significant cost.

He had toyed with her emotions, allowed a Firóle to slaughter countless, and then proceeded to drag her into the Soul Realm to face judgment by Chaos through the Eternal Flame. A piece of Syra had died today, and she still wasn't sure how to digest that. So, instead, she'd packed up the events of today and stuffed them aside to deal with her current situation.

Still, occasionally, a string of thought escaped, reminding her of the life she now lived, and what she was.

Something was happening to her body, to her soul, to her life force, and there was nothing she could do to stop it. Who would she become? To be truthful, Syra wasn't sure who she was even now.

That was a humiliating revelation. It seemed Sekar knew her better than she knew herself. At the very least, he had more belief in her abilities than she did.

"The Gods want you dead." That made Syra shiver. She was walking around with a target on her back, no matter which way

she went. If the dead didn't want her, the Gods did. And that didn't even count her bounty from the living.

"You alright?" Zarek asked, and nudged her. Syra blinked and looked over at him, startled out of her thoughts. The orange hue of the fire decorated his skin and made his crimson eyes twinkle. "How are you?"

She offered a small smile. "Well, I'm tied up, I haven't bathed in days, and my meal was gross. I'd say I'm doing great." With the tribal hunters there, she withheld sharing the events in her sarcastic remark. Too many prying ears for that conversation.

The Guardian cracked a smile and dipped his head. "Fair enough."

Zane leaned over into Syra's space, so that he was closer to Zarek. "Can't you get us out of here?" He kept his voice low.

The Guardian raised an eyebrow at him. "And do what precisely?"

"I don't know. Like magic or something," Zane answered.

Zarek narrowed his eyes. "Remember what I said about sounding like an idiot?"

Syra couldn't help but chuckle, and Zane shot a glare at her. "So, we're just going to sit here and do nothing. Got it." The words were cynical, and he straightened. His face was hard, his eyes dead set on the fire. He was clearly annoyed, but there was nothing she could say or do about it. Nobody could.

Unless there was a miracle, they were cornered. There was no way she was going to test the tribal hunters' philosophy about running. She had a sneaking suspicion that it didn't matter who anyone was—if they ran, they were dead.

"You done talking?" It was one of the tribesmen, and his voice had come from behind. Syra stiffened in response. Zarek looked like he hadn't expected anything else, and Zane looked on the verge of screaming.

And Roman—

Syra took a double take. Roman's ropes were loose in his lap. She could tell based on the way the rope bent that it wasn't securely wrapped around his wrists. Something silver flashed between his fingers—a small knife perhaps. Almost immediately, she met Roman's eyes. They were devious, determined.

As subtly as she could, she shook her head. This couldn't happen. It would be certain death to make such a move. Surely Roman had to know that. There was no way he had made it this far in life doing what he did otherwise. They were facing an Energy Harvester and eleven other tribesmen who looked like they could break a man's neck with their bare hands.

"Hey, I asked a question." The man behind them nudged Syra's back with his boot, and she twisted in her seat to look up at him. His brow was raised with a judgmental glare.

Syra bit her tongue, almost saying something sarcastic that would have surely landed her a kick. It wasn't worth it, though, no matter how much she wanted to piss the hunter off. "Yes," she muttered, and turned back around. Taking a deep breath, she spied Rül staring their way.

Cautiously, she peeked in Roman's direction. Zane had dipped his head in the older man's direction and was whispering to him so quietly that she couldn't hear a word said. She was certain it was a warning. Yes, they all wanted to get out of here, but it wasn't worth the risk. More than anything, Syra had made a promise to herself that she wouldn't let anyone else die because of her. All they needed to do was play by the rules long enough for the tribesmen to grow lazy and then make their run for freedom.

Zane stopped and leaned back, but his eyes did not leave Roman's. She felt like a bystander, and frankly, she was. Already, a plea was building in the back of her throat as she met the man's eyes for one last time.

He was going to do it.

"Ro—" Syra's word was cut off as the man stood and, in one smooth motion, let the ropes drop. He produced a short knife and immediately shoved it into a tribesman's shoulder.

Everything that happened next was so fast that Syra barely had time to move, just watch as the tribesman grabbed Roman's face with his beefy hands and twisted his neck until a loud snap radiated across the camp. Dead immediately, the man she had come to lean on and trust in such an unexpected fashion slumped to the ground. His eyes were wide but dull, vacant of life.

Unbelievably, the hunters didn't even move. They all stared, surprised, and watched as the tribesman grabbed the hilt of the short knife and pulled it out of his shoulder. He dabbed at the bloody wound and grunted before tucking the dirty weapon into his belt. Then he nudged Roman's body with his boot and raised an eyebrow at the remaining three.

"Any of you plan on trying something foolish?"

Between his accent and nonchalant attitude and the lack of response from everyone else, Syra was in complete shock. Zane and Zarek didn't reply either, only stared. If this tribe had any shred of emotion, it was not spared for the life that had been taken.

"Good," the tribesman remarked, scratching his chin and then kneeling. He picked up Roman and flung him over his shoulder like he weighed nothing more than a small sack of flour.

Seeing the body of what was supposed to be her friend get tossed around like he was worthless forced air into Syra's lungs. "What are you doing with him?" She saw Zane shoot her a questioning glance, as if he thought she had lost her mind.

Perhaps she had.

Without turning around, the man trudged away, letting Roman's arms bounce off his back. "I ain't sleeping with the dead, woman." He continued until he was well out of sight from the camp, but she continued to watch, as if she might see her friend come back, fine.

Instead, it was Rül's voice that met her ear, forcing her to look up at the leader. His dark hair was braided down his back, and he was no longer wearing his grisly skull. "You want to tell me what that was all about?"

The Guardian next to her answered in the same calm voice used by Rül. "Courage. Perhaps a little foolishness too, but you can be satisfied to know we will not try such an act." Then he smiled wide. "When we do try something, it'll be better planned."

That didn't please the leader. His expression faltered just the slightest before recovering into that permanent smugness. "I look forward to it," he replied. Then he walked away, returning to his seat next to Grim. She watched, and as he settled back down, Rül looked her way, meeting her eyes before she averted her gaze to the ground.

There was not a doubt in her mind that he knew who she was. The look had said it all.

As quickly as that had all happened, normalcy settled back over the camp. The tribesman returned and sat back down, and conversation continued. They treated the loss of life like another meal.

Syra could not shake the final look Roman had given her before he'd gotten himself killed. There was so much life in those eyes of his, despite his outrageous act. Whatever that was, it had been intentional. Maybe she was crazy for thinking it—perhaps the man had a death wish, or maybe he was wild enough to believe the knife would have created enough commotion to get the upper hand. Whatever it was, it didn't matter, and it never would.

Hot rage burned her blood. This was not how things were supposed to go. Nobody was supposed to die for her anymore.

It didn't matter who told her this was Roman's own foolish mistake, she would forever see it as more blood on her hands.

Zarek brushed his shoulder up against her own and offered her a reassuring smile when she looked at him. But at the sight of the Guardian, tears ravaged her vision, and she began to cry—for Roman and the lives that had been tarnished because of her. Raveer, a whole city, had fallen victim. The thought of the immense number of lives lost because of the Firóle, because of her, made her shiver.

This was not the life she wanted.

A SEA OF STARS

Leaving the palace of Razan had been easier than anticipated, and it was because Cyrus didn't leave with a chest full of dragon eggs, but rather gloves, the sack with several goods, and the sword strapped to his hip under his cloak. To the untrained eye, he didn't look to be going anywhere.

If someone had known what they were looking for, it would've been clear that Cyrus was not just leisurely walking around the palace, but no one stopped him. Not until he was clambering onto Sozar did the soldiers passing through the courtyard ask what he was doing. He simply raised his hand, waved, and let the dragon unfold his beautiful leathery wings and launch himself into the sky with his back legs. The cracked stone echoed across the courtyard where Sozar's talons gouged the ground, briefly deafening the soldiers' yells. Cyrus had no ill will toward the staff of Razan—they were simply following orders, without knowledge of Kyllian's intentions or goals.

But he did have ill will toward the king himself. Kyllian had been reluctant to share and be honest with him. It was betrayal in its most docile form. Yet to Cyrus, it had hurt more than anything. It was one thing to act out in anger or fear, to bluntly be cruel like Morei Geral; it was another to lure one in and feed them lies in hopes they will be foolish enough to turn a blind eye.

The wind forced his thoughts to clear, sweeping them to the side and replacing them with the view of the city. The Ashen Sea lay ahead, just as Sozar turned, and to his left, the untouched landscape of Eiyrǎl. Wide-leafed trees stood proud, decorating the ground along with long, wispy grass. Hills sprinkled an area farther north, shielding the northern city of Kalic. But from here, in this daylight, Cyrus could see it. Distant, but there, and looming with a menacing scowl.

It was not a city he ever wished to visit. If Shunera was their future king, then that was all he needed to know about the culture and environment. It didn't matter if the city was beautiful and old, not to him. Geral had been a stunning city too, with unique architecture that complemented the desert landscape wonderfully. Then the king had soured such a place for him, and Cyrus would be satisfied with the knowledge that he would never step foot on that side of Sorréle again.

Such thoughts pestered him as Sozar steered toward the untouched land. One thing they had agreed upon was to speak with Dameon one last time. It was not because he had an agreement or because he had unanswered questions, but because he didn't want to leave the only other Dragon Rider without closure. They were on two separate paths, perhaps only destined to cross when war was imminent, but he hoped that would never come, because then they would be on opposite sides. It would be a true fight, and Cyrus had never been in one before.

He would learn, though. Slowly, surely, and with patience. He might not be an Energy Harvester yet or even a proper swordsman, but he was cunning, clever, and quick to act. Those traits would keep him alive on the journey ahead.

It pained him to leave Zorya behind without a proper good-bye, but the more he thought about it, the more he realized that she had already known he was leaving. It had been in the words she spoke and the final glance his way as she left the room. Her path and purpose was not one for him to worry about.

He couldn't afford to. The life before him, its demands, would challenge what he thought he knew.

No, he decided. It was better this way. It always had been—to be alone—but it had taken him longer to realize, and cost him a good friend in the process too.

One day, when the world was right, he would pay the princess a visit. Perhaps by then, things would be settled, she would be queen, and he would be surer of himself.

Perhaps.

These thoughts gripped him even as the day slipped by. Sozar had landed far from the city, about where they had first met Ashtir and Dameon. They waited quietly, and only spoke when they thought they heard something or to check in with each other. Cyrus took the time to strap the leather onto the dragon, ensuring it was fitted comfortably for what would be a long flight ahead. He kept the sack and sword strapped to his hips. The leather canteen of water was fitted snuggly around a horn, and the sack of food that he had ransacked from one of the galleys hung on the other side of the dragon.

What he had managed to take would get him started for the journey, and he intended on stopping in either Ferguson or Gamer's Village in Sorréle to resupply himself. Geral was out of the question, Diemon would be too dangerous, and Caster was a brutal and violent city. Ferguson was quiet, but the village along the Sorréleian River was even quieter. It would give him the chance to get in, grab some supplies, and continue his journey south.

When he arrived in the pirate country, Creitón, he would go to Delion, the city snuggled up between Saveen and Barnǎl. There, he would find that his mother, as Leonzo promised, was still alive and living in a small home just outside the main city, along the shore. It was there he would break the curse cast upon him. Somehow, his mother was the key to this.

None of that mattered. What mattered most to Cyrus was that he would finally meet his heritage. It was that which kept him going. All his life, all his dreams, had been about that. To know he was not alone. It was what every orphan dreamed of—that they had a home somewhere that was meant for them, not some stranger's bed.

As Cyrus had told Sozar already, to the dragon's agreement, Leonzo was being honest with them. They could both feel it. This was what they were meant to do, and when the curse was broken, he would be shown his next steps, the ones that Leonzo had promised them. He was not abandoning them, he was helping. And for that, Cyrus was in his debt.

The wind shifted, drawing him out of his thoughts. The dark sky was decorated with bright stars. Constellations that he had never seen before watched him carefully, but that was not where his eyes were drawn to. It was the large figure approaching with the low thump of beating wings.

Dameon and Ashtir had arrived.

The nerves that had settled now stirred with a nasty vengeance. Cyrus swallowed it down, or tried to, and felt the comforting presence of Sozar wash over him. The dragon could sense his anxiety.

All is well, hatchling.

With a nod, Cyrus stood from his spot on the ground and cleared his throat. He watched as the pearl-white dragon slowed and Dameon rose from the straps of his saddle, waving at them. The Rider wasn't wearing his mask this time, likely because he had removed it before the oncoming landing. Regardless, the smile was there—the smile that believed Cyrus had taken him up on his offer.

It made his stomach drop, but he knew the conversation needed to happen.

Ashtir landed gently against the ground, barely tucking his silvery wings in before Dameon was jumping off. His eyes danced over Sozar and then back to Cyrus. "You're coming?" His accent was thick, making the words sound like a royal speech rather than a simple question.

Cyrus took a deep breath as the man slowed to a stop before him. "No, Dameon," he confessed. "I'm not. I can't. I am needed elsewhere."

The smile slipped. "Have you decided to be the king's pet?"

"No!" The idea startled and repulsed him. "I am leaving Eiyrặl altogether." He and Sozar had agreed that they wouldn't speak about where they were going to the Dragon Rider. It was safer that way. He wanted to trust the man before him, especially since he was the only other person who would ever truly understand the hardships that had unraveled. But he knew better.

Dameon eyed him. If he was trying to hide his anger, he was doing a poor job at it. Finally, he licked his lips and looked back at Ashtir before speaking. "The world is not an easy place for our kind," he whispered. "And it is an even crueler world when we are forced to take different paths." The statement made Cyrus shiver. Dameon looked at him now, silver eyes twinkling under the night sky. "The eggs. Did you find them?"

"No," he lied. "The tunnels are heavily guarded." Leonzo would take care of the eggs, but hopefully Dameon did not disrupt the peace of Razan with his demands. Cyrus had already done enough damage.

For a moment, nobody spoke. Sozar waited behind him, while Ashtir tilted his large head and huffed. Dameon lashed out suddenly, his fist connecting with Cyrus's jaw and sending him to the ground. The pain was immediate, hot, racing over his face. His footing gave out, and his shoulder took the brunt of the impact. Almost immediately, the other Rider was on top of him and gripping his shirt, yanking his head up.

"Do you take me as a fool?" Dameon sneered. The look on his face would have made the Dark Lord proud. "I was raised to recognize liars like you. So I'll ask again. Did you find the eggs?"

Sozar's head came into view, lip curling upward while a growl emanated from the depths of his chest. Ashtir was immediately next to his Rider, returning the same growl, eyes locked on Cyrus's companion.

Don't, he pressed. *We can't afford to fight.*

The dragon's mind was coated in fury, nearly unreachable—he wasn't even sure Sozar had heard him. Taking a deep inhale, he ignored the intense throb that radiated throughout his face from the hit. "The eggs were gone. The chest was there, but the eggs weren't. Someone must have moved them or already taken them."

As he spoke, he saw Dameon's face soften by the smallest degree. It was enough to give him the upper hand.

"When I confronted their king about it, he told me the deal had been made with his family centuries ago, right about the time it's stated in that record you recovered. But he said about three centuries ago, the eggs were reported missing. They haven't seen them since."

The lie came so easily that for a moment, Cyrus believed it himself momentarily. Ashtir and Sozar had stopped growling, and Dameon's grip laxed. He kept his mouth shut, watching, waiting for the Rider to speak.

But instead, he got up and turned around to face the white dragon. Cyrus scrambled, backing up against Sozar, only stopping when he felt the scales dig into his back. He watched as Dameon took several deep breaths, eyes down.

The Rider looked up without turning around. "Did he say anything about how they were taken?"

Cyrus swallowed. "No, he would not say."

Dameon nodded and approached Ashtir. "Then I supposed a visit will do him good."

That startled him. "Wait, what? Why?"

As Dameon ascended onto the white dragon, a cold smile painted his features in a ghastly fashion under the moonlight.

"For two reasons, Mountain Flyer. To see if you're lying, and to get information about the eggs."

Cyrus's heart stopped, but he couldn't speak up and risk giving away their position. Sozar's presence intruded so loudly into his thoughts that he couldn't think for himself. *Leave them. Speak and you risk him doing something neither of you will be able to be forgiven for. If he goes, there is a chance he will do this peacefully.*

That was not the answer he wanted to hear, but he couldn't argue with the dragon. Deep down, he knew Sozar was right. Cyrus could feel it in his bones. So instead, he held his tongue, not trusting himself to speak.

Goodbyes were becoming horrid endings for him.

Wind tickled his skin, and the area where Dameon had struck him stung. Raising a hand, he carefully touched the spot and found it wet with blood. Just a little, enough to startle him back into reality. Dameon had struck with enough force to hurt, and it reminded Cyrus how volatile this Rider was.

"Your sword," Dameon said, now sitting on top of Ashtir. "Where did you get it?"

Cyrus pursed his lips, realizing the fall had forced the Rider's Sword into the open. Glancing down, he saw the hilt peeking out, majestic and stunning just like when he had found it. "I found it on my travels back in Sorréle," he replied, and pushed the cloak back over. "Why?"

"It is a Rider's Sword," Dameon told him, not catching on to the next lie Cyrus had told. "And it looks original."

Forcing air into his lungs, Cyrus asked, "What do you mean by that?"

"It means that you have one of the exiled Rider's Swords. The rest were destroyed or buried so deeply under rubble from the Fall that they are unreachable or severely damaged." Dameon raised an eyebrow at him. "But I'm sure you knew that, Mountain Flyer."

Before Cyrus could say a word, Dameon spoke again. "One day, we will cross paths again, and when the time comes, I will not show you the same patience as I have tonight. I pity you, Cyrus. I truly do. You've run for as long as you can, but it has cost you your morals—and time you will never reclaim." Ashtir unfolded his wings in preparation for flight. One crimson eye glared at Cyrus, as if the dragon could see right through his façade. "In the end, there will always be a stronger Dragon Rider, and I sense that will not be you."

The white dragon launched himself into the sky with a twirl. The wings caught the air and drove Ashtir upward. Dameon did not look back, but even if he had, Cyrus would not have seen, for his eyes were still locked on the spot where they had taken off from. The gouged ground and upturned grass mocked him, even as the Dragon Rider faded into the night toward Razan.

Sozar's hot breaths ruffled his hair, and Cyrus inhaled deeply, meeting one of the dragon's fiery yellow eyes. *I've done nothing but fail, over and over again.* The words came out barely above a whisper, even between their bond.

Nonsense, the dragon replied, just as soft. *You are on a different path than he. That makes nobody right or wrong. Have you forgotten Creitón? Your mother?*

Cyrus looked toward the ancient city. "We should go and intervene."

And do what? Sozar challenged, but gently. *That is not your battle, hatchling. The battle that lies ahead is bigger, and it will require all of you. If you turn back now, you risk entangling yourself in a situation you may not come out of.* The dragon nudged his arm. *You do not owe Razan your life. They have done nothing but fail you.*

Failing him or not, Cyrus had never openly turned his back from someone who needed help. All he could think of was innocent people getting hurt at Dameon's hands. As much as he wanted to believe the man would land and peacefully demand an answer, he couldn't. The Rider was volatile, mean—Cyrus had gotten a glimpse of that side of him tonight, a side that was cold and ruthless, and gave evil a name.

There was nothing he could do but hope that Dameon kept that side locked away for the sake of the people, the king, queen, and most importantly, Zorya.

She will be fine, Sozar offered. *She is tough and smart.*

Cyrus swallowed the growing dread bubbling up in the back of his throat. There was only one path forward, and it did not involve anyone from Razan. Slowly, almost methodically, he turned and climbed the dragon, settling himself in the gap between his shoulders and placing a hand around the horn in front of him. He did not need to tell Sozar to go.

The dragon unfurled and jumped into the sky. The beat of his wings was a soothing melody most of the time, but right now, it only reminded Cyrus that they were leaving Razan to Dameon and Ashtir. He had failed Evander, Diemon, even Geral, and now he had failed Razan as well.

The idea that he would one day be a true Dragon Rider felt further and further away.

But Sozar continued to flood him with warmth and affection, no matter how hard he fought to relive his mistakes. It felt like the dragon was smothering him in a hug, reminding him over and over again of their purpose, his mother who waited for him, the eggs that would soon hatch and be theirs to protect, and of the future. Tomorrow was a new day, and when the moon submitted itself to slumber for the sun to take its place, Razan would be behind him.

And Cyrus would be there to watch the sun rise.

INTO THE HANDS
OF FATE

"Almost ready?" Rül asked. His tone made it clear that something was annoying him. He had awoken the group just before dawn and ordered the tribe to pack and prepare for travel. The three had watched from their place next to the long-gone fire.

Shoulder aching, Syra had spent the majority of the night on one side, unable to get comfortable because of the ropes. When the heat of the fire had died, she found herself at the mercy of her chills. The headache was still angry, loud, even deafening at times. Sometime in the night, Zane had pushed himself up against her to share some of his body heat, but it hadn't worked for long.

At one point, Zarek had asked how she was holding up, only to have a tribesman snap at them for speaking when everyone was supposed to sleep. So for the longest time, she had stared at the stars, eyes dry from the tears, mind sluggish. Her stomach growled, and even that felt grotesquely loud against the silence of the night. When the tribe awoke, she had never been so relieved for the commotion. She could drown out the thoughts that were threatening to surface and devour her.

Thoughts about how she had failed Roman, Dryl, her father, the world. Even thoughts about Sekar and what had happened to her, no matter how hard she had tried to avoid confronting that reality.

Zane was hauled up next to her then, and Syra blinked and looked over at the man. Syra blinked and looked over at the man. The rope binding was so tight, she could see the skin pulling where it hadn't broken yet from all the wear. Zane grunted, obviously uncomfortable.

Unable to hold her tongue, Syra commented, "You think these ropes are tight enough?"

"I'll break your fucking wrists if I want to," Rül retorted as he passed by, speaking before the tribesman could. She raised an eyebrow at him. The leader returned her gaze with his own ruthless expression. If he was hoping to win the battle of stares, Syra was going to give him a run for his coin. Patience fried, she was on the verge of screaming. The lack of sleep and proper food, plus yesterday's events, were the perfect storm to leave her on edge, regardless of how sick she felt.

After only a few moments, though, Rül tore his eyes from her and kept walking toward his steed.

"He's interested in you," Zarek observed from behind, where he was tied on Uyul. "Try not to piss him off."

She scoffed. "I sense a marriage in our future." At that, she heard the Guardian snicker, and a wry smile tugged at Zane's lips.

"Let's move!" The order came from Rül, who was now on his steed with the bold skull helmet. The bones reflected the light that had now breached the horizon, painting the sky in bright oranges and soft pinks. Dawn was upon them.

The wind tousled her fading dyed hair, which now looked more and more like a botched job than anything. The air was crisp for the morning and kissed her skin with a chill, even through the cloak. As of this morning, they had taken the additional cloak from her and shoved Zarek's arms through it before binding him. She was freezing but refused to complain.

The rhythmic beat of the hooves from their travel serenaded Syra as they rode. But as the sun rose higher and clouds begun to sprout from various parts in the sky, she couldn't help but relive Roman's final action over and over. Her thoughts reeled, and it felt like everything was crashing in around her. All the emotions and memories she had so methodically stored away for a later time were bombarding her at once. She was reliving everything she had ever done in her life, down to the instant she had run into the burning home to find her father in his dying breaths.

The emotions came and went with each passing memory—she felt angry, scared, humiliated, sad, even happy. By the hand of Greve, the night she had sat outside on Jared's porch with the man she had believed to be Kar was precious to her. The world had shushed for that singular moment. But ever since then, it had only grown louder and crueler.

As the day became older, the air stiffened with humidity. No longer did the morning chill hug her, but the heat did little to chase away her feverish shudders.

Already, the clouds were growing taller, darker, snuffing out the blue sky. It would be a nasty storm, and based on the speed of the cloud development, it would be raining very soon. The wind already carried the stench of moisture.

As she watched the sky, she thought over how they could escape. It would be risky—any option they tried—but she refused to waste this time when she could be planning an escape. Last night, it had become clear that someone from the tribe remained awake to watch them, and perhaps there were even shift changes. But that meant only one tribesman was awake during that time, and three against one was worth the risk to Syra.

They would have to manage to loosen their ropes, but she had no doubt that was the least of their worries. If they were placed next to a fire, they could pull one of the rogue pieces of wood and try to shred the rope that way, so long as the tribesmen were as sloppy with their fire as they had been last night. Or if there was a jagged rock, which felt unlikely given the state of these hills, they could try to cut the rope that way too.

More than anything, she wanted to twist around on Hazel and look at Zarek, try to signal she had some formation of a plan, but the bindings would not give her that freedom. Syra could shift from side to side, but if she tried to spin on the saddle, she'd fall off without the aid of her hands. She tried to look anyway, but only made it halfway, unable to see the Guardian.

"Eyes ahead," the tribesman to her right ordered. Syra groaned and straightened. Ahead, she saw Zane turn his head slightly to acknowledge her, but he too was limited by the lack of use of his hands.

She would have to wait until they stopped to share her idea.

The time passed painfully slowly. And as the thunder started, Syra started counting the time to mark each bellow. It did little to ease her fluttering heart, but it helped keep her thoughts at bay. The sky darkened, the heat was sucked dry, and shadows painted the land. The wind picked up speed, now tossing the bones the tribesmen wore in a sporadic tune and sending Syra's cloak in every direction. Rain permeated the air, and Syra wiggled her nose in response.

All around, the grass flattened and tossed as the wind grew stronger. The air was buzzing with life, and Syra stole a glance up to see the black bottom of the storm over them. Just then, a bright flash erupted as lightning streaked across the sky.

A thunderous roar followed almost immediately, startling several of the horses. Hazel took a quick step forward, her ears flattening, but she didn't spook as bad as several of the others. Syra thanked the Gods for Hazel's composure, briefly forgetting her strike against them. She was in no shape to settle the horse with her bindings.

Zane's steed was one of the few that did not startle, but even Grim's spooked so bad that the Energy Harvester had to jump off. It made her laugh, and she saw Zane's shoulders bounce in his own humor, watching the man.

Rül shouted something that was lost in the wind, but Syra still strained her ears to try to catch what he was saying. The leader gestured hotly at another hunter, who seemed to be just as upset. The wind's ferocious behavior made it damn near impossible to hear anything, but after a moment, they stopped arguing.

Another crack of thunder erupted, this one startling Syra so bad, she ducked as the light painted her surroundings in white. Her heart just about ruptured from her chest, and she found her hands trembling from the surprise.

This was bad. A storm like this meant they needed to find cover.

As the thunder died out, Syra heard shuffling behind her. The steeds were restless, and she couldn't blame them. Hazel side-stepped just then with a sudden jolt, and Syra didn't act fast enough. Her body lurched and she slid off, landing on her shoulder with a gross impact. The pain was immediate, and after the last two days, the tears soon followed.

Groaning, she pushed herself away from Hazel's hooves to avoid being struck by accident. The grass tickled her cheek but right now, it did nothing but make her more annoyed. "Can someone—"

Her voice was cut off by a yell. Syra glanced up. A tribesman was standing five paces away, pointing behind her. Rül's expression contorted into rage, eyes lit, and he shouted. The wind shifted, and Syra heard him yelling to prepare for a fight. She tried to look behind, but her position didn't allow it—and she didn't have time.

It was pounding hooves that she felt first, the vibration jarring her senses. Syra sucked in a breath and tried to shift herself away from whatever was happening, but as she did so, one of the tribesman's steeds bumped into Hazel, sending one of the horse's hooves into her calf. Hazel hit it with just enough force to create a siege of agony that raced up her leg, but not to break the bone. Syra yanked her limb up, cursing the Gods.

Mass confusion exploded above her. Syra blinked, disoriented, as thunder ripped through the sky. The sound of metal rang, and there had to be a dozen more horses than she remembered. Someone jumped over her, swinging a sword. The weapon landed true on a tribesman, catching him off guard as he defended himself against another attacker. His body slumped onto the ground, too close for her comfort.

She was going to be trampled to death if she didn't get her footing. Whatever was happening was beyond her understanding, and she didn't care enough to go ask the dying man to her left, who appeared to be choking on his own blood. Shoving herself backward, she flipped over and began dragging herself away with the use of her knees and forearms.

Rain pelted her back, the sky opening up with a vengeance. It was pouring.

A body fell on top of her, startling a yell from her lips. She was pinned and—

"It's me," Zarek told her, his voice hot after the cold touch of the rain. "You're going to get yourself killed, and I will not live with the knowledge you were trampled to death by one of the rogue horses."

In the disaster unraveling, Syra laughed, even though the Guardian's weight was crushing. "What's happening?" she asked, just as a horse cut close enough to make her shrink further underneath Zarek's mass. The steed was riderless, running from the scene.

"Ambush," he answered. "But it's not another tribe. I don't know who it is, but I'm sure we will soon enough. Hold your hands out." A flash of metal caught her eye, held between his bound hands.

Elation was an understatement. How he had come across that, she had no idea, and she didn't care to ask. She pushed them out until he could hold the blade against the rope and begin to saw at it fiercely. At the rate he was going, she was certain he would slice right into skin, but right now, she couldn't have cared less. A small cut was the smallest of her worries.

Above them, two men stumbled. One tripped over Zarek, driving the blade into her wrist. She inhaled sharply, but the Guardian got right back at it. Her arms were almost free. The tribesman was trying to regain his footing when the second fighter struck Zarek's leg and tripped. Just as he did, the rope finally gave, and her wrists separated.

The attacker, dressed in brown-fitted leather, laughed and sank his short blade deep into the tribesman's chest. As the man fell, he yanked his blade free and turned back to the fight.

Without a word, the Guardian dropped the knife, and Syra picked it up. He put his bound wrists in front of her, and she started cutting, noting the blood that stained the hem of her cloak now.

But as the thunder died, she heard the sword fighting cease. Panic arose in the back of her throat. Sawing faster, she felt the knife slip from her wet hands and into Zarek's palm. "I'm sorry," she whispered, and picked the knife back up. If the injury hurt him, he did not tell her, nor even shift an inch. Heart pounding, she focused—the rope was nearly sawed through. Just a little bit more, that was all. This was it. They needed to get out of this alive, and get Zane too. Syra couldn't see it any other way.

"Hurry," he told her. A single pair of boots was approaching. The sound of them deafened Syra, and she nearly choked on the terror bubbling up in the back of her throat.

The last of the rope was tearing, and she could nearly taste the freedom. If they could run fast enough, maybe they could create enough space between themselves and these attackers to lose them. It was desperate, but it was all they had. The horses would come later. Raveer couldn't be more than a two-day walk from here.

The rope broke. But even as the binding fell to the ground, Zarek didn't move. Instead, in a silent whisper, he said, "Follow my lead."

Another set of boots was approaching, this one farther behind, but nonetheless, she obeyed. If they had any chance of surviving, they needed to work together.

A pair of boots stopped near her head, the black leather visibly worn, even with the wash of the rain. Syra swallowed, not daring to look the man in the eye. Unless instructed, she would wait for Zarek's lead and then act. They had a slim window of opportunity to do this right, but she would rather take the risk and die trying than be imprisoned again. And she was fairly certain Zarek was ready to fight with her. They had played by the rules to save themselves a torturous death from the tribesmen, but this was different.

The next words made every thought dissolve and her heart skip a beat. If she hadn't already been prone, she would have collapsed.

"They're alive."

DAMNATION

orei let the sound of his boots against the gravel speak for him as he approached the city center. Countless people knelt around their shrines to the Gods. Their voices rose and fell in perfect harmony as they all prayed to the deities who had abandoned them.

Gods who had let Morei's life become their entertainment.

The night was clear; not a cloud splattered the sky. Stars twinkled above but were muted by the surrounding torches. Just outside the city, the fires had already begun, burning more victims of Cu'cel. The smell drifted through the street, rotten and bitter like his attitude. Wails met his ears from those suffering, their only chance at peace being given by none other than Death herself. Children cried, their sobs muffled by the skirts of their mothers or the shouts of their fathers.

By now, the palace was no doubt searching for him. Peter may have let him disappear out of fear for his own life, but Morei wasn't ignorant enough to believe that he would be allowed to completely slip away unnoticed. It was only a matter of time before soldiers would swarm the streets, courageous, as if they hadn't quivered at the sight of him in his chamber.

But Morei would be long gone by then. He only needed a little bit of time to do what he needed to do—what he wanted to do. The thought made his mouth water and his heart race in anticipation. It had been so long since he had heard proper screams.

A cloak hid his features, pulled well over his head. He had snatched it in the barracks on his way to the barn, where he had tossed a simple saddle on Sunny. The Shire had whinnied in excitement, oblivious to the destruction that lay ahead or the shattered dreams behind. Still dressed in his attire from earlier, he would buy new clothes out of the city with the Krye stuffed into the coin pouch on his belt, but he had been lucky enough to find gloves that would conceal his hands for the travels ahead.

Sunny remained on a side street, waiting for his return. The steed was the only living soul that had never seen him as anything else than what he was, but the rest of them? They had put on a façade and lied right to his face. Perhaps even Skye had tricked him, dragging him in with a dying husband, so that she could tell the rest how she saw the ill king for herself. The thought fueled his disdain.

They were all fucking liars. And he hated liars.

The voices of the citizens rose at the height of their prayer as he came upon the city center. Wooden stakes for Greve cast shadows that danced in response to the light of the two bonfires. A woman hushed a child quickly as they walked by, keeping their heads low. Her shoulder brushed his arm, but she did not apologize, only moving as briskly as she could away from the prayers.

Halting, Morei watched the citizens as they repositioned and lowered their heads once more, ignorant of his presence. A quick wave of murmurs swept the crowd before they fell into a prayer to Greve.

He recalled the conversation with Boris just the night before. Perhaps if the man was standing here now, he would advise the king to turn away before he did something he would regret for the rest of his life. Or maybe Boris would encourage him. All it took was a simple beckon, an invite, and the fire would come to life and bend to his will. And just like his dreams, the Dark Energy would devour the souls of the helpless and satiate his growing compulsion. It could not go ignored any longer.

There was nothing left of him here. Nothing that could be said or done that would prove otherwise what he had always meant to these people. If they begged, it was only because they were afraid. If they cried, it was because they knew their judgment day had come sooner rather than later.

If they wanted a monster, they would have it.

He let the barriers of his mind down, allowing the Dark Energy to consume him. The power burned along his fingers, and the voices in his head came to a near shout before ceasing at Morei's command, obeying. Like a trained beast, it waited until he summoned the power.

The flames of the bonfires clawed at the sky, flaring bright enough to interrupt the prayer. With a quick wave of his hand, Morei willed the fires to turn onto the shrines. The flames leapt with hunger, consuming the wood, letters, food, Hyle's Beads, all of it instantaneously. Screams erupted from the closest citizens as the heat kissed their skin. People shoved themselves backward, away from the burning shrines and into the heart of the scrambling crowd.

But it was too late.

Just to his left, a man burned alive at the hands of Dark Energy, his scream short-lived, as the flames crawled into his mouth and raced down his throat. As the citizen's life was taken, euphoria rushed through the king. His heart fluttered in excitement, and a maddened smile brushed over his lips.

Others bolted, but Morei gave no hesitation. He unsheathed his sword and plunged it into the nearest man, killing him instantly. As a woman passed in a hurry, Morei reached out with his other hand and grabbed her by the fabric of her dress, hauling her back to the center. She fell on her ass and scampered back as quickly as she could, screaming. Tears shimmered across her cheeks in the light of the flames.

The king pulled his blade from the body, sending blood splattering to the ground beneath him. As the flames licked the closest citizens, he willed energy to halt several who tried to run. Their bodies froze midstride, their mouths agape in terror, screams cut off as he ceased their ability to continue. In a single gesture, he allowed the fire to encircle them all, giving the citizens nowhere to run. The heat was intense, but he could hardly feel it.

Approaching, he passed the two who had attempted to flee and looked them right in the eyes. He wanted them to see who their killer was. With a flick of his wrist, he willed blood to fill their lungs, erupting the veins that webbed through. Their bodies twitched in protest, but they couldn't move. All they could do was slowly suffocate to death. He watched until he saw blood drip from the mouth of the man to his left before releasing his hold. The two collapsed to the ground in a mess, dying and unable to run. With them taken care of, he turned his attention to the remaining citizens, who clutched one another as the flames crept closer.

Crimson dripped from his blade as he beheld the terrified crowd. Eyes were wide, and some had wet themselves in terror, while others mumbled their pleas with tears. Pathetic. That was what it all was. Now that they were forced to face him, they begged he spare their lives, all the while praying behind his back that the Gods deal with him.

Raising his sword to his lips, he ran his tongue right across the metal. The blood tasted as good as he remembered, and he smiled. The citizens were captive for him, the fire soaring high. It was so hot that sweat glittered across his brow and those of the people. The stench of iron and charred wood filled his nose, hushing the burning stench of the dead.

To these people before him, Morei was a monster, but they would never understand him or what he had done for them. And it would never matter, because as of tonight, he would no longer be the king of Geral—he would be the Demon King. And a king of that power did not belong in a city that did not accept him for what he was.

A monster was not born but made. The citizens of Geral had made their very own.

Letting a smile sneak across his lips, Morei regarded the people one last time. He would enjoy this next part.

"Death sends her regards."

THE RESURRECTION

Eight Days Later

The parchment was old, yellowed and marked by tears and faded ink, but it would do. A map of the Vore world stared up at Ku'sar. That was what they called him, what they had called him for centuries. And despite his return, they still insisted on calling him such things—Death Dancer. But he was more than that. He had beaten the Gods and perhaps even Destiny herself.

He cleared his throat and reached for the goblet of wine waiting for him, bold and strong enough to take a man off his knees. Precisely how he liked his wine. It had been a long time since he had enjoyed this luxury without looking behind his back. Even after all this time, the halls still felt like home. The smells of sweets roamed the rooms. The furniture was freshly dusted, the shields and swords polished along the chamber's walls, and the fabrics he wore clean. It was almost like he had never left.

He set the silver goblet down and settled a finger over Geral. The City of Blacksmiths was its nickname, although given the recent events, he was sure it would find a new name, one that made observers shiver. Cu'cel's City. The Home of the Demon King. The Dead's Empire.

Names that would undoubtedly take over the world once the cities caught wind of the new rumors, the new stories. The thought made him smile.

A knock brushed the door ahead, tearing the man's attention from the city of Geral. "Yes?" Despite the distance, his voice carried. It was the voice of authority that had taken lifetimes to master.

With just the faintest gestures, the beast of a door cracked open. "Ku'sar, she is here to see you."

"Already?" He glanced outward, the window to his right filled with the endless waters of the Gulf of Beritisian. A familiar tug pulled at his insides, but he refused to let the expression show. The follower, dressed in red, in rebirth, could not afford to see the emotion that he felt.

"Send her in," Ku'sar whispered, blue eyes hovering over the waters.

"With honor." The door shut, and Ku'sar wrangled in his emotions until nothing but the dull rage he had grown accustomed to settled coldly over him. He must not feel, he reminded himself—the heart was cruel and would betray him. Emotions would not raise his empire. Only a strong hand would.

A moment such as this was beautiful. Not a sound intruded on him. During many summers, he had been left with nothing but the dark. Even the sight of water had become sparse, and regardless of what he told himself, it had not come close to the moment when he had seen the sun for the first time, or when he stepped onto the sands to witness the majestic nature of the sea. Such power.

Power that he was nearly able to harvest.

"Silence, my dears," Ku'sar whispered, hushing the voices that had grown louder and tempted his hand. On command, they fell faint, but they were always there, and it had been a long time since he had given them reign. The energy beneath his skin shifted, aware of his thoughts. "Soon," he promised.

The door opened, and he tore his gaze from the waters and onto the woman who entered. But she was no ordinary woman, even though she had the curves of one who had lured count-less men—a siren to some, a monster to others, but above all, a Goddess. Well-polished horns breached from either side of her head, curving backward into a blackened tip that acted as a crown. However, she did not need one, given her air of authority and certainty. Gold irises glittered in the light as she entered, her skin the color of honey and her silky hair blond. She bore a tapered maroon dress that dipped too low for any man to ignore, and on her wrists, gold bangles danced to her motions.

Every movement was deliberate, and every act was for atten-tion, but not because she needed it, no. It was a test.

The Goddess of Love, so many had endearingly labeled Helyna. She was far more than that, though. She was a Goddess, yes, but she was cruel, calculating, and devoid of empathy.

The stories were that in her mortal life, she had been so desperate for love that she had scoured the countries for a man willing to accept her and her poor fortune, for she had been born disfigured and rejected by even her family. But on a night of bad luck, Helyna had found herself cornered by brutes who had believed her disfigurement a sin, and in a drunken rage, they had beaten her in a barn. Death had been the only one to accept her, but upon judgment, Chaos had found her soul worthy and chosen her to serve.

Helyna had died a mortal and been reborn a merciless deity, with the power to give love to others but forever unable to receive it. Perhaps in mockery, Chaos had bestowed her horns, for even immortality did not erase the scars of the past.

That was a story, though, and nothing more. Ku'sar couldn't ask her such details of her centuries ago, well before his birth and long before Diyrǎ or Sorréle had been settled.

"Even Death grew tired of you," Helyna acknowledged, stopping across from him. The map lay between them, silent and unmoving. A thick scent of berries washed over him.

The corners of his lips rose in a smirk. "You have been well?"

"Small talk after all this time? Have you grown dull?"

Ku'sar took a deep breath, satisfied. "Wine?"

Helyna took him in, her eyes scrutinizing his features. He knew how she saw him, how they all saw him. The mop of midnight hair and his rich olive skin that once glistened under a moonlight's stare was gone. His skin was now pale and covered in red markings that kept him alive, but his ice-blue eyes remained the same as they had been all those summers ago—ruthless, all-knowing. They had watched millions fall, now they would erect an empire once more.

For some, he likely looked like the embodiment of evil, but for others, he was a new beginning—a new era.

"Those markings—"

"Gifts from your brother," he interjected.

Her gold eyes hardened at once. "He is not my brother. You know such things."

"You are bounded together by Mother herself," Ku'sar observed. "In all but blood, you are siblings, separated by decades, even centuries, but still . . . siblings."

The Goddess crossed her arms, the gold bangles striking one another. She raised her chin at him. "Have I come here for you to teach me the lessons of my own servitude? Or do you wish to anger me, like you always did"—Helyna's eyes raked over him with iron spikes—"before death took your humanity."

Ku'sar felt the insult burn a hole inside him, but he kept his expression stoic. "The king," he announced, and tapped the city of Geral, choosing to move forward from the antics. "Have you watched him while I've been away?"

Helyna raised an eyebrow. "I have not been able to get close, not even to the city." Before Ku'sar could ask, she continued,

"Guardians. They've been there for nearly two decades without letting up. There can be no other reason than that they know of his prophecy."

He took a deep breath and let the words sink in. Helyna waited without a word, and a tense air took shape between them. When he finally spoke, he let his anger slip in. "Then how did Sekar enter without issue?"

Helyna's body tensed. "Not all of us were gifted with his abilities, and you know that. If I were to make guesses, I'd assume he bypassed your orders for his own game. Always his game," she finished with a hiss. "Not even you can control him, and that irritates you."

Refusing to take the bait, he withdrew his hand from the map and reached for the goblet. It was true. Sekar had walked between realms and tricked even the Death Seekers about his whereabouts, only to slaughter the queen of Junok in some sick twist of events. But they had already spoken, and Ku'sar could reason with the God's motives. He trusted the Dream Walker, even if he was untamable.

"The queen is dead," he stated calmly, moving on. "We are to take Junok before the first snow. My men are already infiltrating the city, integrating with the people and taking jobs in the palace." Ku'sar took a drink, pleased with himself. As he swallowed the liquid, he glanced at the waters, sensing their call. "I want you to ensure Emerald's brother, Nerius, returns to take the throne by any means you see fit." There was no need for him to explain himself. Helyna understood well enough what he meant.

Once Junok was taken, the city would merge its resources with his own, and the start to the end would begin. Diyrä would be his soon enough, and the world would be next. Ku'sar would not make the same mistake as last time.

"Ah," the Goddess sighed darkly, pulling his thoughts back to her. "You wish me to be a dog at your service. Has hiding all

496

these summers made you ignorant, oh great Ku'sar, the Death Dancer?" She snorted. "It is you who should be serving m—"

"And yet you come when I call," he cut in, keeping his voice low. When she did not continue, he looked at her fully, noting how she composed herself. Her lips scowled downward, and her eyes were sharp enough to cut steel. "Deals are deals, no matter the time that passes. You of all people should know that, and when the time comes and our services are fulfilled, I shall satisfy my promise to you, Daughter of Chaos. Do not take me as a fool."

Heartbeats slipped by, and he took the opportunity to sip his wine, but the cherry tasted lifeless against his tongue. Helyna huffed and looked out of the window toward the gulf. For the moment, he admired her and her beauty. A jawline cut out of stone, skin as soft as a lover's touch, but her eyes were frigid as they swept back over to meet his.

"You seek to put the Junok bloodline back in power not because you want to, but because you need to." The words echoed with finality, and she nodded as if to reassure herself. "I have not forgotten our deal, Death Dancer, and I never will."

The intensity of her words was palpable, but he hoped she did not see how they impacted him. He had escaped the merciless clutch of death, but not even a fool could outsmart a God forever.

"The Rider," Helyna quickly added. "Does he follow your path?"

The memory of the young man made him smile—so much purpose and power. The Rider was dangerous, but he didn't know it yet. "He does."

"And the eggs?"

"Here."

"Wonderful." Helyna turned and traced a finger over the map as she before crossing her arms. She walked, her sandals padding softly against the polished stone, and stopped at the window. "You are walking into uncharted grounds. Not even Mother knows what lies ahead."

He leaned against the table, letting his left hand support him. "I know."

"And you trust Sekar? Despite his meddling with the girl?"

The question struck him as odd, and persistent, but not surprising. "You know I do. It was he who helped me accomplish the impossible." Ku'sar did not find the Dream Walker's fascination with the redhead a problem. Sekar had promised himself it was all for the greater plan, and he trusted that. But he was never one to turn a blind eye either—he had continued to keep a close watch on the God's motives. The fall of the Lirallian Empire was due to betrayal. It would not happen again, no matter how much he owed Sekar his life.

"And it will be him who strikes you when your back is turned," the Goddess stated, then turned to face him. Those eyes glittered once more. "I know what he is capable of, and I know he does not know of our deal, but do not take him as a fool. Sekar tricked the Guardians into believing he was one of their own for four centuries. He hid from my brothers and me, and he can persuade even the deaf into believing in him. You think you're not just another piece in his game?"

Ku'sar felt the muscle in his jaw twitch. Gods were grudge holders—he had learned that the hard way. Their ability to hold on to a lifetime of resentment made mortals look petty. "Your bitterness will not deter me, Helyna. I trust him."

"And I don't." The Goddess turned and walked back to the door, her dress billowing behind her as she strode. There was no point in arguing with one like her, so he didn't.

He would have let her go if she wanted, but instead, she stopped and peeked back at him. "Your interest with the king of Geral is peculiar. Why?"

Even after all the time that had passed, Helyna still had a way of catching him off guard. "He is destined to be at my side, the key to it all." Ku'sar licked his lips and added, more to himself, "The Demon King."

They held each other's gaze for what felt like an eternity. There was so much she did not know, that not even Sekar knew, but it was safer that way. Gods were volatile creatures, and he could not afford to appear vulnerable to them. In times of war, friends didn't exist, only acquaintances—acquaintances who would stab him in the back if he let them. Quietly, he repeated the mantra that had defined him for nearly three centuries: he must not feel.

Finally, she broke eye contact and opened the door, but a closing statement rang between them just as she slipped out. "Not even Gods can share that kind of power."

Then she was gone, the door closing behind her. All that was left was the map before him, the goblet, and the silence. The room felt larger than before she had entered, and the sun suddenly felt too bright. Ku'sar took several deep breaths, shaken by his encounter with the Goddess. Helyna was clever, but she was vicious, and she was only working with him because of a deal he had made at the height of his power, now centuries past. Their obligation to one another would have ended long ago if not for the betrayal and fall of his empire.

If he failed her, she would destroy him.

"Demon King," he mouthed, the words barely audible. His thoughts returned to the young man. Morei Geral was the cornerstone of everything. Every action he took followed a path that Ku'sar had already seen once, long ago. A cause and effect that only the mother of energy, Chaos, understood. It was the way of the Ghrynál—the path forward—and so long as Morei followed it, everything would work. But if he stumbled from the path, there would be severe consequences. The bitch from Junok had nearly caused such a mess.

Morei had already become more than Ku'sar could ever have imagined, and he was only growing stronger, colder. He could relate to the king in more ways than one. The man was sick, just like him, but Ku'sar had spent lifetimes mastering the ailment and forcing the voices into submission. He glanced at the red marking along his hand and remembered the black veins that had once decorated his skin. It was Mother who'd kept him alive, and Sekar who helped him achieve the connection to that vast power.

He could help Morei to achieve such mastery, but he couldn't intervene. Not yet. Ghrynál forbid it, and Ku'sar understood the philosophy well enough to know that his entire future lay in the hands of patience.

Destiny would have her way with the king of Geral, but when the time came, Ku'sar would be here, ready.

In time, the empire would reign again as it had those many summers ago.

VORE TERMINOLOGY

Assane (Ah-sane) – Northeastern city of Diyră. One of the only major cities to still allow for smaller territories to be ruled by tribes, the tribal territories make up the vast landscape of Assane. The primary income varies between tribes, but eccentric and unique gods are well known to come from this region.

Barnăl (Bar-nahl) – Eastern city of Creitón. A brutal past with strong armed forces. Historically remembered as the city that enslaved its princess. Supplies cities with ships, gathering supplies through a deal with the ancient Venkar City.

- Tyrik Village – Small and quaint, but best known as the village massacred during the White Horn pirate raid approximately 434 summers ago.

Caster – Eastern city of Sorréle. Known for its high crime rates and violent culture, the city's economic income weighs heavily on the production of wines and trading. All goods, exported or imported, must pass through Caster's Port, giving the city a significant advantage over all others.

Chaos – Often referred to as 'the mother of energy' or 'Mother.' Without Chaos, there would be no Vore World. Dark Energy and Light Energy are both sub-energies to Chaos. Every being, object, realm, and even death are linked to the mother of all energies.

Creitón (Cre-ton) – Nicknamed 'pirate country.' There is no clear record of whether Creitón or Eiyrǎl came first, and the answers will vary by individual. This country is well-known for its ports, ships, and the cultural significance of the sea. It is true that most of the pirates Vorelians meet consider Creitón their home, but it is certainly a well-established country with strong values. Main cities: Barnǎl, Saveen, and Delion. Lesser cities: Venkar City, Ruby Village, and Tyrik Village.

Crystónity (Cris-ton-ity) – Branch of Drügalism. This monotheistic religion only celebrates Sekar and does not consider the other deities significant. Crystóns are secluded worldwide, but the City of Liral is the only location to practice openly.

Cu'cel (Su-sel) – Sinister illness responsible for the deaths in Geral. Old Tongue translates to 'evil' or 'ungodly.' Refer to Grënyl for a description.

Dark Energy – A more prominent form of energy, sometimes referred to as 'the sister of Chaos' or 'the dead's power.' This energy is raw, untampered, and pure, derived from the souls of the damned locked in the living realm and unable to pass into the Afterlife. Dark Energy is nearly impossible to master by an Energy Harvester, given the incredible power of the force. This power is often known to consume and kill the harvester and is considered a bad omen by most Vorelians. Dark Energy is embodied in the purest elements: water, wind, metal, and fire. Historically, only two have mastered the energy: Selena Delcate (wind) and Henry Junok (metal). Morei Geral (fire) is now the third Vorelian to master it.

Delion (Dee-le-on) – Northern city of Creitón. A quiet city that keeps to itself. It is commonly referred to as the heart of Creitón because of its central location, although the city remains compact and smaller in stature, unlike Saveen and Barnǎl. Do not be fooled by the city's quiet demeanor, as the toughest citizens live here, with many working the sea as their source of income.

Diemon (Di-mon) – Northwest city of Sorréle. The city of gems, or as some refer as 'the gem city.' Stationed up against the Releuthian Mountains, its primary income is from mining and jewelry.

Diyrằ (Di-rah) – Founded over 1,500 summers ago and well-known for its gruesome history. At the height of the Lirallian Empire over four centuries ago, Henry Junok led a bloody domination that slaughtered millions, now known as the Diyrằllian Massacre. Main cities: Assane, Raveer, and Junok. Lesser cities: Nighthunter Federation, Jasper Village, and Whale Village.

Diyrằllian Massacre (Di-ral-lian) – The largest massacre in Vorelian history that occurred over four centuries ago. The Lirallian Empire carried it out under the guidance of Henry Junok. Millions of lives were lost across Diyrằ, and the summer has become known as the 'Blood Summer.'

Drügalism (Druug-al-ism) – The primary religion of Vorelians, embodying all five Gods: Helyna, Greve, Hyle, Eazon, and Sekar.

Eazon (E-zon) – God of Luck. Ritual of Contact: a bundle of Krye placed on a cloth and surrounded by candles.

Eiyrằl (Eye-ral) – An ancient country with conflicting settlement records, although many agree it was well over 2,000 summers, with some estimations as high as 3,000. With no clear indication, it is well-known as the Dragon Riders' home. The ancient country holds traditional Vorelian values that are entirely lost to many outsiders. More interestingly, Eiyrằl is withdrawn from many political movements and is independent of a lot of activity with other countries. Main cities: Kalic, East Razan, West Razan, and Rider Federation (destroyed in the Great Fall).

Ferguson – Northeast city of Sorréle, more commonly referred to as 'the silk family.' Ferguson's economic income is primarily from clothing, specializing in silks. An eccentric group of people that remain withdrawn.

Firóle (Fur-ole) – Giant serpents that once ruled the lands of Diyră and traveled openly. The Firóle were hunted for their scales and fangs during the height of the Dragon Riders, driving them to extinction. Very few remain and stay in hiding. They are ancient beasts and possess many characteristics like a dragon, such as telepathic communication and intelligence.

Geral (Geh-ral) – Western city of Sorréle and nicknamed 'the blacksmith's city.' Geral's economic income weighs heavily on the trade of metals, including armor and weapons. A city that takes pride in its strength and independence.

Ghrynál (Ghrin-all) – A philosophical belief quite literally translating to 'the path forward.' Everything has a cause and effect; every action dictates a different path. The mother of energy, Chaos, knows all paths forward. It was once revered in traditional Vorelian culture but has since become less known, specifically in Sorréle and many parts of Diyră. Guardians of Death adhere to this philosophical approach.

Gray Realm – The space between the living and Soul Realm. Often believed to be the realm closest to Chaos. Given its vast and uncontrollable environment, no one goes here, and it is acknowledged by Energy Harvesters or Vore students. Very few cultures address the Gray Realm. Sekar is believed to be the only God who freely travels to and from the Gray Realm, using its volatile and secretive nature to his advantage. With so little knowledge of this realm, no one truly understands what or if anything lives there.

Grënyl (Greh-nal) – Ailment associated with Sekar. Old literature discusses Grënyl to be the mark of the Dark Lord and how he identifies his next victims. Symptoms include black rotting pieces of flesh, fever, and mental deterioration. Sekar utilizes this tactic to weaken the life force and bring them to the Gray Realm, a space between the living and dead realms. Ancient texts theorized Grënyl only came to those with fractured loyalty to the Gods, such as Greve, Hyle, Eazon, and Helyna.

Greve (Greeve) – God of Strength. Ritual of Contact: wooden posts with letters nailed to them, followed by a hand gesture over the heart.

Guardian of Death – Warriors that belong to the Soul Realm. They are responsible for the guidance of souls from the living to the Afterlife. Guardians are also responsible for the protection of the Soul Realm against all forms of threats. They are mortal boys taken before ten after a tragedy and raised in the realm of the dead. Countless summers of training and mastery of their skills and emotions make them savage competition in a swordfight. Upon training completion, they undergo the Commitment Ceremony, which involves the bondage of a lesser demon to their soul. The ultimate test is surviving this ritual, and those who do are honorably gifted Death's Sword and become a Guardian of Death. Details of the Commitment Ceremony are not shared; Guardians do not speak highly of the seven-day ceremony and a few that have emphasized that it is unbearable. The iconic characteristics—pale blue skin, red eyes, black hair, and Marking—all result from the ceremony. In cultures where they are less accepted and perceived as bad omens, they are called 'Death Seekers.'

- Shevana ceased all further training of Guardians, and the numbers are now the lowest they've ever been.

Helyna (Hel-e-na) – Goddess of Love. Ritual of Contact: a glass of wine with use of the phrases 'Love is endless' and 'Helyna bless you.'

Honuyál (Hon-u-al) – A grotesque and ruthless species of beasts. They are power-hungry and feed off souls. They follow traditional values and place a high emphasis on female rulers. Noted traits include leathery skin, large and strong bodies, dagger-like teeth, slitted noses, and tusks. They have amassed numbers in the Soul Realm.

Hyle (Hi-le) – God of Courage. Ritual of Contact: silver beads with a small wooden sun, widely named 'Hyle's Beads.'

Junok (June-oke) – Northwest city of Diyră. The largest territory of all Vore cities and best known for its gory history and rich Energy Harvesting bloodline. The Junok family is most notably known for Henry Junok, despite the family's expulsion of the prince and his title from the family lineage. Junok's Port is the major port of all trades for Diyră, making up a significant amount of city income.

Kalic (Kal-ic) – Eastern city of Eiyrăl. One of the smallest cities in the world. Well known as one of the only cities to enslave people still. Its brutal punishment system and predefined roles make the city ancient in its practices. Primary income is weapon and armor production.

Krisár (Kris-har) – One of the dark rituals of old Vorelian practices. Involves the consumption of the participant's blood and the recital of an ancient text spoken in Old Tongue. A blade of power must be used in the ritual for it to be successful. It is forbidden in most cities across the Vore World, given its highly dark association with the dead and curses. The ritual was outlawed after the fall of the Lirallian Empire and all books associated with Krisár and equally dangerous rituals were said to be burned.

Ku'sar (Kuh-sar) – Old Tongue for 'Death Dancer.'

Light Energy – The weakest but most malleable form of energy, as it is impure and tampered with. All life is made of Light Energy. All Energy Harvesters lean heavily on this form, as its ease and stability make it reliable. Commoners often refer to this form as 'magic,' which indicates a lack of education in energy.

Móermism (More-mism) – Spiritual religion. Followers place their value and respect in energies and are considered extremely spiritual, often praising Mother, or Chaos, as the ultimate deity. This old practice is seen rarely but is scattered throughout the world, and followers are known best as Móers.

Nighthunter – The best assassins in the world. Trained for up to eight or more summers under the guidance of skilled assassins and must earn their sword in training. They hold tremendous value in the Old Laws and will hunt anyone.

- Upon the formation of the Nighthunters, a deal was made with Junok. In return for land, the Nighthunters would never take a bid against the Junok family.

Nighthunter Federation – A southwest city located on the panhandle of Diyră. The city is well known for its zero-crime tolerance and is the only city in the world to offer asylum to all refugees. However, the Nighthunters are more than just soldiers, but the best assassins in the world. An underground market allows travelers from around the world to come and bid for a Nighthunter. The federation is a hotspot for illegal trade.

Old Laws – Old text written over 200 summers ago. These laws were the original promises of the Nighthunters and define the guild. To break one of the Old Laws is to break the oath of a Nighthunter.

Raveer (Rah-veer) – Eastern city known for its brutality and ancient values in Diyră. The city has become revered for its armed forces; they are trained for twice the number of summers than the standard soldier observed in other Vorelian cities. The primary city income is metalwork.

Rider Federation – North city of Eiyrăl, or the remains. The city was destroyed over 800 summers ago during The Great Fall. The city's remnants offer sanctuary to strange beasts, volatile energy, and secrets. Often, citizens of Kalic and Razan come to offer gifts and say prayers.

- When it stood, the Rider Federation was glorious and home to some of the most influential people in the world. The federation kept peace among the cities worldwide and led massive explorations.

Saveen (Sa-veen) – Western city of Creitón. Saveen drives global trades of jewels and unique goods. The city is known for its exquisite architecture and attitudes, but they are masters of the seas and should not be misunderstood.

- The prince of Saveen, Dameon, is the second Dragon Rider to soar the skies in over 800 summers.

Sekar (Seh-kar) – In traditional culture, known as the Dream Walker or God of Dreams. More recently, heavily regarded as the Dark Lord, God of Darkness, and unacknowledged by some cultures altogether for the belief that such action brings bad luck.

- Ritual of contact as Dark Lord: blood sacrifice and recital of cursed text. Punishable by death if caught performing this ritual in most cities.

- Ritual of contact as Dream Walker: Prayer before bed. The method of contact is through dreams, so many would pray to Sekar for him to visit and guide them while they dream.

Sorréle (Sor-rel) – The youngest country of the Vore World, founded over eight centuries ago. The establishment of this country originates in a political dispute between families in Diyră. Main cities: Geral, Ferguson, Diemon, and Caster. Lesser cities: Gamer's Village.

Soul Realm – The realm of the dead. Commoners refer to this location as the 'underworld,' but this is inappropriate, as the Soul Realm lives parallel with the living—not above or below. Souls pass into the Soul Realm and exist until they are ready to be guided to the Afterlife. It is ruled by a select family who the Gods chose to uphold the responsibility of caring for the dead. The Soul Realm is critical to the living—it brings order and balance to the energy system. If the Soul Realm fails, the living will follow, and vice versa.

- The Soul Realm was notably once beautiful, with flowing rivers and vivid colors. It has since become the embodiment of ghastly and horrible imagery. The malevolent forces entered with permission under the guise of promised power and have slowly devoured the land.

Soul Speaker – People who have a connection to the dead. They see, hear, and speak for the deceased. Some cultures regard Soul Speakers as bad omens, while others revere their gift.

The Great Fall – The fall of the Rider Federation. Upon the death of her Rider, Vikter, Aythen went mad with rage and destroyed the city. It is said only a handful escaped the carnage, but what happened to the survivors remains unknown.

- Prior to The Great Fall, two Dragon Riders fled in the middle of the night with their weapons and gear. What became of them remains undetermined—no further dragon sightings were reported, and no one by the iconic silver eyes was documented following the destructive events. Cyrus is believed to possess one of the Rider's Swords that was saved before The Great Fall.

Ve'hem (Veh-hem) – Old Tongue for 'the burdened one.'

Vor'gal (Vore–gal) – Old Tongue for 'the pit' or 'underworld.'

West and East Razan (Rah-zan) – Western city of Eiyräl and second largest in the Vore World. Rich in ancient culture and values and is considered one of the oldest cities. One of the only cities in the world where people will walk without a weapon in the streets. Energy

Harvesters are welcomed and highly regarded. The Razan family occasionally opens their gates and allows citizens to explore the vast palace. An extensive underground tunnel system accommodates the palace. Income varies, given the city's adaptability to economic changes.

- West Razan was once known as Suniyr (Sun-ear), a city of occult followers. Approximately 1,100 summers ago, Suniyr was dissolved by Razan after a political war. The Suniyr family was executed publicly.

Zimbórism (Zim-bor-ism) – Branch of Drügalism. This religion identifies Greve as the primary God and is heavily recognized in Diyră, although there are a small number of Zimbór followers across the Vore World.

Zyulë Bond (Zule) – A type of energy bond that doesn't identify a master. The equal relationship that results is often referred to as a God's Bond. Both individuals must remain alive; the death of one will result in the partner's death. This peculiar characteristic makes it both dangerous and extremely useful. Both participants must adhere to the rules of Krisár. Individuals of Zyulë Bonds possess a silver raised scar on their wrist and are extremely valuable in some traditional cultures.

ACKNOWLEDGMENT

If you had told me five years ago that I would finally be pursuing my dream and sharing stories with the world, I'd have crawled under the table. But here I am. It would be irresponsible for me as a writer to tell the world the second book was any easier than the first. Storytelling takes a whole lot of heart and leaps of faith, and most importantly, a lot of support and words of encouragement. My word of advice to the budding storytellers out there: find your voice and then find your people.

Once again, my greatest appreciation to my editor, Dylan. I give the story heart, but you give it legs to walk with and air to breathe. You know when to challenge me and aren't afraid to tell me what's not working. Simply put, you're a ruthless tyrant with a soft spot and that's how I like it.

The story would not be complete without all the remarkable work done by my interior designer and formatter. Dragan, you are a beast and have made me laugh on countless occasions. Your candid support has meant an incredible amount to me. You've made the process easy, entertaining, and memorable. If I had to guess, you may be a king in another life, or a saga.

The relationship I've built with my cover designer has been so much fun. Cherie, I found you on accident, completely virgin to the world of covers and unsure of how to capture the vision I had in mind. But you took an idea and have brought to life my world not once, but twice. A book is nothing without a proper cover and you've exceeded in every aspect of design work imaginable. You are a warrior in my eyes.

Eve, you are one of the most meticulous and kindest people I've stumbled across. You are a sorcerer with your tools and have brought the Vore World to life with outstanding precision. It has been such an honor to work with you. In another world, I sense you are an Energy Harvester, capable of manipulating any force to your commands.

Dylan, Dragan, Cherie, and Eve: we may be countries apart, but we are an unstoppable force. Thank you.

To my epic *(supernatural)* support group, Charles and Danielle. Can you believe it's been nearly two years since we first met? You've given me a place to call home for my thoughts and more inspiration than I could ever have room for. Danielle, keep charging forward. You are a force to be reckoned with and I fear anyone who would challenge you. Charles, stay poetically humble of the world. You have lifetimes of wisdom to offer and are an old soul. Both of you are incredible storytellers in your own realms. We are an unruly bunch, but I'd not have it any other way.

Ivy, it wouldn't be proper for me to write an acknowledgement page without mentioning you. You are not only an outstanding storyteller, but an amazing friend. You've taught me what it means to have a friend in many ways that I will never be able to accurately put into words. I may be a terrible texter but know this: I would burn the world down for you.

To all the Vorelians who have joined this Empire. It would take a novel to list you all, but I want to make sure you all know just how extraordinary it's been to connect with each and every one of you. You took the first book and embraced it and gave me confidence—it was you all who made me believe in myself when I failed to do so. Your constant support, check-ins, excitement, and patience has made the process so rewarding. You all hold an enormous place in my heart for without you, this saga would be nothing.

So, Vorelians, as I've said before and will say here: Keep your swords sharp and let the Empire reign.

Made in the USA
Middletown, DE
06 March 2023

26219941R00305